PENGUIN BOOKS

Over Sharing

Jane Fallon is the multi-award-winning television producer behind shows such as *This Life*, *Teachers* and *20 Things to Do Before You're 30*. Her *Sunday Times* bestselling books – *Getting Rid of Matthew*, *Got You Back*, *Foursome*, *The Ugly Sister*, *Skeletons*, *Strictly Between Us*, *My Sweet Revenge*, *Faking Friends*, *Tell Me a Secret*, *Queen Bee*, *Worst Idea Ever* and *Just Got Real* – have sold nearly 2 million copies in the UK.

D1102515

Over Sharing

JANE FALLON

PENGUIN BOOKS

PENGUIN BOOKS

UK | USA | Canada | Ireland | Australia
India | New Zealand | South Africa

Penguin Books is part of the Penguin Random House group of companies
whose addresses can be found at global.penguinrandomhouse.com.

First published by Penguin Michael Joseph 2023
Published in Penguin Books 2024
002

Copyright © Jane Fallon, 2023

The moral right of the author has been asserted

Typeset by Jouve (UK), Milton Keynes
Printed and bound in Great Britain by Clays Ltd, Elcograf S.p.A.

The authorized representative in the EEA is Penguin Random House Ireland,
Morrison Chambers, 32 Nassau Street, Dublin D02 YH68

A CIP catalogue record for this book is available from the British Library

ISBN: 978-1-405-95113-5

Dedicated to the wonderful dogsonthestreet.org
for their work with the homeless and
their pets in London

PART ONE

I.

Iris

I'm happy.

I am.

I know it's possibly not very convincing if I have to announce that fact rather than it be apparent in my smile, my laugh, my sunny demeanour, but I've always had a bit of a resting bitch face, so you'll just have to trust me on it.

I have it all, on paper. Almost. Friends (who I increasingly see less frequently as their lives are consumed by mumhood. That's not me being sneery by the way, that's me being envious), a good (but not exactly challenging) job, my own flat (well, owned by me and HSBC but mainly full of my lodger, Carol). All my own teeth. That last one's a joke. I mean, I do have all my own teeth but it's something my dad always used to say when he was teasing my mum about what a good catch he was. I never really got it, but I used to laugh. My dad told terrible jokes, but he told them so hopefully it was impossible not to give him the response he was looking for.

It's just that I thought there would be more. Four years ago I also had a husband, a house. We were trying for a baby. Really trying, like it was going out of fashion. With an app and a thermometer in place of lust and lingerie. With phone calls in the middle of the day that said

'We need to do it now. Can you meet me at work, we can nip into the loos for a quickie.' It hadn't totally taken over our lives, though. At least, I didn't think so then. It felt as if we still had time, we just wanted to complete our little family. Although I was starting to get more nervous with every month that passed. I'd even brought up IVF. Casually, as if it was just a conversation topic and not an actual possibility in our lives. I threw it in in between asking what he fancied for dinner and what he felt like watching on TV that night. *Oh, I was talking to my mum and her friend's daughter had IVF and it worked second time. Maybe we should think about it?* And Tom hadn't baulked. He hadn't rushed straight in saying *Over my dead body* or *Are you out of your fucking mind?* which I'd taken as a positive sign. We were in it together. That's how I saw it, anyway. Maybe Tom thought differently. Maybe he thought all the spontaneity had gone and he just wanted sex to be sex again, not an appointment in the calendar whether you felt like it or not. He never said. It turned out there was a lot he didn't say.

Sometimes, these days, I feel as if I'm going backwards. Losing accomplishments rather than gaining them. So I try to count my blessings. Write them in the ridiculous 'Gratitude Journal' Daisy gave me, every night. They're always the same: Health, Mum, friends, job, flat, teeth. Imagine if that had been all Samuel Pepys had to say, I don't think we'd still be poring over his diaries four hundred years later. It's not that I'm complaining. I just sometimes think there should be more to show for forty-four years on this planet, that's all.

4

Daisy also gave me some healing crystals, some cleansing sage and a copy of *Owning Your Own Pain* by some wiry old yogic guru, when Tom left. Daisy is – to be brutally honest – batshit crazy, but she's my only sister and I love her. In increasingly small doses.

I snuggle back under the covers, trying for a Saturday morning lie-in. My weekends are always a masterclass in avoidance. Not of doing anything, but of bumping into Carol the lodger. One of the other downsides of finding myself suddenly single at forty was the need to share my home with a stranger to make ends meet. Tom and I sold our little two-up two-down terrace for way more than we paid for it, due to the area we lived in surprising us all by gentrifying around us. Where there had been an old key and shoe repair shop was now a GAIL's. Itsu had moved into the run-down greasy spoon. The life and soul had gone out of the place and in its stead the prices had gone up. We still had a sizeable mortgage to pay off, but I ploughed my share of the profit into buying the most expensive property I could afford, in an OK part of Kingston that had still not quite up-and-come, but was threatening to, in the hope that it would be an investment for the future. An area randomly chosen because there was an opening in a branch of Marlborough Kitchens there that I could apply for a transfer to. And because I wanted to get as far away from Tom and our history as I possibly could. Don't get me wrong, it's still only a bog standard two-bedroom. Tiny. But it's in a smart new build with an easy walk into the centre of the town. It should earn me some kind of decent return when I decide where I really want to put down roots. I don't want to end up living out my days in a place chosen only by circumstances. I have no ties here beyond the financial. But then I don't really have any ties anywhere. Not any more.

I knew the mortgage would be a stretch on my own, but I resisted the idea of a lodger for as long as I could, hoping my life would suddenly take a turn for the better. After a year or so I knew I was defeated. I'd spent any savings I had left just on getting by. I had two alternatives: sell my flat and buy something smaller in a much worse neighbourhood, or rent out my spare room. I was too old for any of my friends to be unsettled enough to need to share a flat. They all had lives, families, mortgages of their own. So I advertised. I lucked out first time. Quiet, unassuming, only-in-London-from-Sunday-to-Thursday Joanne, who scarcely left her room and then, when the pandemic started, worked from her family home in Manchester and still paid the rent, until she realised she never needed to return to the office and could save herself a fortune. Carol is her replacement. From the sublime to the ridiculous.

So now I fill up my social calendar just to get out of the house – brunch with Cally, a long walk with Fay, drinks in the evening with whichever thinks they can stay awake later than nine that night. They both have babies, Fay's Kieran is almost one and Cally's Frankie just eight months. Spur-of-the-moment plans have long gone. Now their lives are one long negotiation with their partners about whose turn it is to do childcare while the other goes out and pretends they wouldn't rather be at home. Our thirties were all about partying. So far, our forties seem to be mainly scheduling-based. Sometimes I feel like the oldest teenager in town next to my friends, but it's not through choice. My life just hasn't quite turned out like I planned, like it was supposed to. They have moved on, checking off the grown-up milestones, while I've stagnated. I'm stuck in quicksand. But most of the time that's fine. I'm luckier than many. My problems are firmly first world. No one has ever died because their friend cancelled their plans to see *The Book of Mormon* three times when their baby wasn't sleeping. Like I said, I'm not pissed off, I'm jealous. I would love to have a baby who kept me awake all night. I wouldn't care if I never slept again.

I give up trying to go back to sleep and get my phone and a coffee from the kitchen instead, checking first that the flat is quiet. I turn up the thermostat on the way back to bed. Fay always tells me that one way in which she envies my life is that I am mistress of my own heating system. No passive aggressive battle over the controls for me. They are firmly my domain. Fay is always cold. Always. It started as a running joke that she would turn up the radiators whenever her husband Steve left the room, and he would turn them back down whenever he came back in, but now it seems to be a metaphor for everything that is wrong in their relationship. Fay and Steve have been struggling since little Kieran was born eleven months ago. Steve is – and I don't say this lightly – a complete and utter cock. I didn't like him much before they got married, to be fair. He's one of those eternal lads. Responsibility averse, Cally calls it. *Her* partner, Jim, on the other hand, is pretty much perfect. Kind, funny, a fabulous dad. He can't stand Steve, literally can't bear to be in the same room as him, so nights out with the five of us are out of the question. Quite often, though, me, Fay and Kieran will go round to Cally and Jim's for the evening and Jim will cook for us all and entertain the kids, and Cally has to listen to me and Fay ramble on about how we'd trample over her cold dead body in a heartbeat to snap him up if she keeled over prematurely. I don't think either of us mean it, by the way. At least I don't, Fay is anybody's guess. But I do adore him.

I scroll through Twitter reading odd bits of news, check out Instagram where I never post anything, I just like to lurk judgementally. I love this time of the morning. No phone calls, no texts, the world slowly waking up. I can hear birds outside where usually there's only traffic. The day feels full of potential. Hopeful. Before life steamrollers in and crushes all our dreams. I check my emails, something I usually avoid at the weekends in case I see an overlooked message concerning work and that ends up hijacking my attention. I like my job, but I like the two days a week when I don't have to think about it more. I deliberately chose a clock-on/clock-off career, one with no homework or extra-curricular reading, for that very reason. I wanted to make sure I had time to have a life.

I spot an email message from Fay. It's unusual for her to email. We have a WhatsApp group – she, Cally and me – and that tends to be our preferred means of inter-action. If two of us are conspiring against the other

8

one – to decide a birthday present, say, or express a secret concern about Steve's latest behaviour – we'll text or, more likely, phone. Emails are for work or things that are never good news like gas bills. This one though is just titled *OK, there's no good way to show you this, but isn't this HER?*

There's no message, just a link. I hesitate for a second, wondering if Fay has been hacked and I'm about to unleash a fatal virus on my computer. Not for the first time. I have a complete inability to ignore even the most potentially threatening-looking attachments 'just in case'. The message could be headed 'This is a virus' and I'd still feel compelled to look. Even so I force myself to text her – '*did you just email me?*' She replies immediately: *Yes! Open it! I'm here if you need to chat.* I know she'll be giving Kieran his breakfast, choo-choo training spoonfuls of cereal into his open mouth while Steve has a lie-in. The link is to a YouTube video entitled 'PJ Day'. It's a family: mother, father and two identical little girls all dressed in matching leopard print pyjamas performing a choreographed dance to 'Tiger Feet' in a verdant child-friendly garden. It's slickly edited, with wacky shots of swinging backsides and OTT expressions – all wide eyes, raised brows and open mouths. There's a thick veil of smugness, of 'aren't we cute?' slathered over the whole thing.

It's nauseating.

And yes. It's her.

It's Maddy.

The woman who ruined my life.

2.

I watch it eighty-seven more times. A mere blip in the apparent five hundred thousand views it's already had. It's definitely Maddy, but I don't recognise the man. He's tall, dark and not particularly handsome in my humble opinion. What he isn't is my ex-husband.

I've spent the past four years imagining Tom and Maddy in their new, perfect, post-me world, but it seems that maybe I've got it all wrong. We cut ties fairly dramatically once he told me about her, communicating only about the sale of our house – our home – and the division of the spoils. I had been tempted to refuse to move out, or to go out of my way to spook any potential buyers, but after a while I thought, *what's the point?* Once I realised my marriage was definitely over, I needed to move on. Or try to, at least. So it all happened very quickly, very smoothly. Ten years of my life swept away in a couple of months and a handful of solicitors' letters.

I scroll through the comments underneath the video. Over six hundred of them.

Your family are so adorable!!!
I just love you all!!!
You brighten my day!!!!!

And on. And on and on. It's like exclamation marks were going cheap and they all decided to bulk-buy.

WTF??? I send Fay.

I examine the page again. The channel is called 'Fun with the Fulfords' and has over a hundred thousand subscribers. There's a link to a TikTok account and another to Instagram with the same name, which boasts a staggering six hundred and eighty-three thousand followers. There are reams of videos. Scores of them. The YouTube channel has been open since 2020 and Insta the same. TikTok seems to have been added later. I start to watch them, jumping back and forth in time with no apparent logic. Singing, dancing, Maddy addressing the camera teary-eyed about a Mother's Day card, painting, baking, family life ad nauseam. In the early days Maddy and The Man wave the two babies in the air like a pair of foam hands at a football match. These are definitely Maddy's children. This is definitely her family.

There is definitely no sign of Tom.

My phone pings and I see that Fay has sent me a vomiting emoji. It makes me laugh, but nothing can distract me from my viewing for long. I decide to take a more systematic approach and trawl back until I find the very first video. The babies are wearing matching sunflower hats. They're tiny, a couple of months old maybe. Maddy introduces herself and her husband, Lee, both dressed in bright yellow sweatshirts and bright white smiles. Their twins, Ruby and Rose. It's amateurish, none of the polish of the more recent efforts, but they sing an idiotic song swaying the babies back and forth like they're blowing in the wind. There's a lot of self-conscious laughing and Lee looks as if he wants to murder someone, his grin pasted to his face like clown make-up. This is definitely Maddy's rodeo. 'Follow our journey with these two little munchkins,' she trills. 'Subscribe today or join us on Instagram!' She points downwards and the account name pops up on the screen. But all I can fixate on is the date.

Tom told me it was over between us on 5th February 2019. I remember the date without trying because it was my fortieth birthday. The middle of my birthday dinner, to be precise. Between the hamachi starter and the black cod main. I had organised it. We never really did birthdays. I mean, we bought each other nice presents and made a fuss, but we didn't tend to go out specially. Not for years, anyway, preferring the sofa and Netflix and maybe cake if we were pushing the boat out. But everyone kept asking me what I was doing for my 'big one' and I'd got fed up of making excuses. Fay and Cally were threatening to kidnap me and make me go clubbing if I didn't mark it in some special way. And besides, I felt as if something was wrong between Tom and me. Something was slipping away. A night out with no talk of babies and ovulation and which position might give us the best chance of success would do us the world of good. Help us to reconnect as people, partners, lovers, rather than two would-be parents who had made trying to get pregnant their full-time occupation. So, I'd booked a table and surprised him with it, first checking his schedule that he'd pinned to the fridge with a magnet. He was working away four or five nights a week at that point, installing a new computer system in an office block in

Birmingham. Or, at least, I'd thought he was. *I can't do this any more* he'd said, his hand on top of mine, pinning it to the table. *I love you, but I can't.* My first reaction had been to hope the people at the next table couldn't hear, that there wasn't going to be a scene. And then the full force of what he'd said had crashed down on me, leaving me gasping for breath. *Is there someone else?* I'd asked. It was such a cliché but I had to know. *No. Of course not. It's us. It's me. I just . . . I don't want this any more.* And a couple of days later, while I cried and begged him not to give up on us, I'd got him to admit it. He'd met a woman through work. Nothing had happened but he wanted to be free to pursue it. I knew he was lying. People need an impetus to break up even the most basically functioning marriage, a cast-iron guarantee of something else on the horizon. Something free of baggage and disappointment and resentments. A blank slate they can project a new, improved version of themselves on to. They don't leave to pursue something; they leave because that pursuit has already been successful.

By – I check the date on this, the first clip, again – May 2020 Maddy was married to someone else with twin baby girls. The babies look to be at least two months old. Still tiny, but definitely not newborn. So she must have been pregnant by August of the year before. September at the latest.

She broke up my marriage, ruined my life, for a relationship that was over six months later? Less?

I push my laptop away. I feel sick.

I know, of course, that the blame doesn't all lie with

Maddy. Less than fifty per cent, if I'm being honest, because she wasn't the one who had promised to love and to cherish me, to forsake all others and stick with me no matter what. She wasn't the one who lied to me for months. Who listened to me cry when yet another treacherous period started, and told me it would all be OK. That we would try again. That we had years to make it happen. But she's still the woman who decided hooking up with a married man was acceptable. She didn't know me, but she knew what she was doing to me.

If it hadn't been for her, me and Tom would have worked things out. Got over the issues that I didn't even know we were having until it was too late. If it hadn't been for her, he would have stayed.

I have to resist the urge to call Tom. *It wasn't even serious? You didn't even have the decency to make a go of it?* There's no point. No good could come from it. He's almost certainly changed his number anyway. In fact, I know he has. In the early days I used to phone him sometimes – usually when I'd had a couple of drinks – and ask him why, when, how. I wanted details. Hard facts. I'd moved out to stay with Cally and Jim while I tried to accept what was happening, to plan what I would do next. The house was already on the market – Tom must have called an estate agent the minute he'd broken the news to me, before, even, it occurred to me. To be fair to him, he had offered to be the one to leave, but I couldn't bear to watch a stream of wide-eyed young couples planning their futures in the living room I'd painted myself. At first he used to indulge me, although without ever really answering any of my questions. After a while I think he just got bored. He wanted to immerse himself in his shiny new life without the inconvenience of a tearful ex-wife reminding him it was built on ruins. No one wants to think they're living on landfill. I rang him one night and the number was dead. Just like that. His office told me he'd moved on and, no, they couldn't divulge where. I haven't spoken to him since. I tried his old family home too. I'd always got on with my in-laws. They were good people but, like all devoted parents, they were protective of their son. 'He doesn't want to speak to you,' his mum said, sadly. 'After everything . . .'

'He cheated on me,' I shouted. I blush thinking about it now. 'He's shagging some other woman.'

His mum had cleared her throat. 'I'm sorry, Iris, but I think it's better if you don't call again.'

And so I had turned my sights to Maddy.

Now I call Fay, knowing I won't be able to get her full attention but needing someone to just acknowledge that what I've just watched is real.

'I thought I should show you before you saw it some-where else. Just . . . you know. It definitely is her, isn't it?' she says without even bothering with hello.

'Definitely. I don't get it.'

'She's an influencer. Kieran, don't . . .' I can almost see her flap her fingers in quote marks as she says the word influencer. We are not fans of the species.

'I know. I mean, I guess so. But where's Tom?'

'No idea. It obviously didn't work out.' I can hear

banging. Kieran thumping his spoon on his plate like a chubby little emperor. Feed me now.

'But . . . I mean, I thought at least he'd dumped me for the love of his life . . .'

'Maybe it was her,' Fay interrupts. 'She grew tired of the wonders of Tom.' Fay has never really liked Tom. She thinks he's too full of himself, which he is, although that's a criticism I would definitely also level at Steve, not that I'd say so out loud. And actually, it's not true that she's never liked him. Both Fay and Cally loved him in the beginning. Back when he was chilled and funny and he so clearly made me happy. I don't remember when that changed. They were my joint maids of honour at our wedding, both weeping noisily and laughing at the same time as they walked behind me down the aisle. I was the first of us to get married. Cally was already seeing Jim, but Steve was yet to appear on the scene and bulldozer over Fay's life. At first we would all have nights out together – Tom and Jim got on fine, although they were too different to ever become close mates – but Steve's arrival put paid to that. Steve doesn't have a chip on his shoulder, he has a whole bag. And probably a piece of fish, too. And extra mushy peas. He decided early on that Tom and Jim looked down their noses at him. (Not true. Neither of them is exactly royalty. But Steve brandishes his working-class roots like a weapon. No one can have had a harsher upbringing than him, no one can have experienced any greater hardships than him, no one can have had it as bad as his poor old mum, et cetera, et cetera.) Everyone that isn't him is basically an overprivileged fucker even if they grew up on a rough estate too, like Tom, or had a drunk for a father like Jim. And some of his attitude rubbed off on Fay, I think. And then, by osmosis, Cally.

'So, she fucked up my life and then got bored of him?' I say now, angrily.

'It takes two to tangle,' she says. Fay loves mangling a cliché. She started off doing it deliberately to make us smile, but now I sometimes wonder if she can even remember what the correct sayings are. 'He's like a duck out of water,' she'd apparently said to her health visitor the other day, when asked how Kieran was getting on with crawling. 'I'm not actually sure what that means,' the woman had said, pen poised in the air. 'Is that good or bad?'

'Either way you're better off without him,' she says now. For someone with such a messed up relationship herself, Fay has a lot of opinions on other people's.

'That's not the point. I wasn't given the choice. Are we still walking at ten?'

'Shit, can't,' she says. 'Steve's told his mum we'll take Kieran over for a visit.'

I sigh. I hate last-minute cancellations. I hate suddenly finding myself staring at a day with nothing scheduled in it. 'Can't he go without you?'

'She'll think I'm avoiding her. You know what she's like.'

'OK,' I say. There's no point arguing.

An hour and a half later I'm still not dressed, but I know all the words to 'Let It Go' and my brain is scrambled with

Maddy's megawatt grin and perky nuggets of happy family wisdom. 'Make time for each other!' she opines while sitting wistfully on a sunny bench. 'Remember who you were before you were mummy and daddy.' This one from her big farmhouse kitchen, the two little girls in highchairs behind her. 'Not that I would ever want to be anything else,' she chirps. 'But me time is important too.' She, Lee and the toddlers do 'The Locomotion' and 'Oops Upside Your Head' and the Chicken Dance, always in matching outfits in lurid colours. By the time I finally force myself to stop watching I feel as if I've overdosed on sickly sugary syrup. I need to get out and clear my head. Carol has been pottering around singing to herself for the last forty minutes or so. She loves to sing. The louder and more tunelessly, the better. Even though it drives me insane it's quite useful in that I always know where she is. Like a dog with a bell on its collar. I wait in the hope that she'll have plans and, thankfully, after about a quarter of an hour I finally hear the front door slam.

In many ways, Carol is the ideal flatmate. She's fairly clean and tidy. She doesn't want to have parties or play loud music. She doesn't eat my food. She's just . . . well, annoying. What she failed to mention when she came for the interview and to have a look round was that she was looking for a ready-made social life. I would have gone with sullen Sian who made it clear she much preferred animals to people if I'd realised. The day Carol moved in, I made her a cup of tea. That was my first mistake. I realised as soon as she sat down at the table and told me how much she was looking forward to us having a girls' night out that I'd made the wrong decision. She lies in wait in the kitchen hoping that I'll venture out to put the kettle on and she can tell me about her day. She spends her evenings in the living room – Fay warned me I should make the living room off limits or I would eventually lose control of it, but I thought she was being alarmist. It seemed unreasonable to charge someone to live in my flat and then deny them access to the main heart of it – remote in hand, ready to pause *Strictly* or *BGT* or *Coronation Street* if I come in so we can watch together and chat about it. Consequently, I now spend my evenings in my room, watching Netflix on my computer. She's always trying to get me to go out on the town with her. 'Two single saddos on the pull together' as she laughingly put it once. She's a divorcee, same as me, a similar age, something I thought would be a positive. But I hadn't reckoned on her having a mission in life to 'show her ex what he's missing' by texting him photos of her wild nights out. Except that she doesn't have any wild nights out. She doesn't seem to have any friends, anyone else to socialise with – I have no idea why, I've been too scared to ask – so she's set her sights firmly on me. I feel sorry for her, of course I do. I know what it's like to be suddenly, shockingly alone. I just don't want to be her wing woman.

I decide to walk along the river from Richmond to Teddington like Fay and I had planned to do before she blew me out. I wonder about ringing Cally but I already know she has something on this morning that meant she couldn't join us in the first place. She hasn't responded to my email yet, so I know she hasn't seen it. Cally keeps on top of life by never procrastinating. No long to-do lists for her. She treats a request for a routine reading of her gas meter with exactly the same urgency as she would an email saying her supply was going to be cut off if she didn't pay her bill in the next three minutes. It's a skill I envy, but I sometimes wonder what would happen if she let one tiny thing slip. If her life would collapse like a game of Jenga.

Somewhere in the fallout after Tom's announcement at that fateful lunch and his subsequent confession, I had found out Maddy's full name. He'd told me they'd met through work and that Mads – as he called her – had been speaking at a conference he'd attended in Brighton some four months before. *Have you seen her since?* I'd asked, and he'd said no, he hadn't, but he couldn't stop thinking about her, wondering if the connection he'd felt was real. *For four months?* I'd asked, incredulous. *She's probably forgotten you exist.* The idea that someone could meet the love of their life and start a passionate affair at a conference about big data and advances in quantum computing has always baffled me. I remembered him coming home full of what I thought was inspiration. Fired up.

'It was fantastic,' he'd said when I'd asked how he'd found it. 'Best one I've ever been to.' And now I finally knew why. Mads was some kind of life coach, a job I've always thought was made up, and she'd been brought in to lecture about work-life balance and burnout. Tom's work colleagues were the driest, least sexy bunch of humans I'd ever encountered. No wonder he'd noticed her.

'Did she advise you all to shag around?' I'd said, petulantly. In truth, I was shattered. Broken. I had never imagined that Tom would meet someone else. I had never rehearsed how I would react if he ever told me he had. He was a little bit full of himself, Fay was right, but not in the way that made him think he was god's gift to women. Not in a way that made him think he could do better than me. At least so I thought.

I googled the conference, certain that knowledge would help me. I needed to find out more about this Mads. I wanted to see what I was up against. And there she was listed on the programme: Maddy Cartwright, Life Advisor, with a list of topics she was covering: *Perform at your highest level. Reach your confidence peak. Overcome fear of failure. Learn skills like Active Listening and Visualisation.* As if no one had ever managed to get through life without being told how to do it correctly. Fay, Cally and I spent a weekend hunting out every fact we could about her. Which turned out to be precious little. She had no social media presence at that time. At least none we could find. There was a website, but it was a dry list of achievements and services offered, along with a phone number to book an appointment. But she was on LinkedIn. And there was a photo. She was my worst nightmare. Flaming red curls, big green eyes, luminescent skin. The vibrant opposite to my mid brown hair, my sludgy grey eyes, my tired-looking complexion. I have never forgotten that picture.

It turned out I was wrong. Knowledge did not help me. It made her real.

Halfway between Petersham and Twickenham, I realise I could just google her again. Maybe now she's some kind of internet sensation there'll be salacious details of her life for me to pore over. I wander away from the towpath and find a bench, type in her name. There's nothing much of interest. It's almost a relief. But then I remember she's no longer Maddy Cartwright. She's Maddy Fulford now. At least I assume she is, going by the name of her channel. Lee's surname, I'm guessing. I try again. This time it's different. There are pages of results. She's definitely a big deal. My stomach turns over. Of all the potential fates I imagined her meeting, becoming a household name was not one of them. She isn't – not yet – but she's getting there. She has adoring fans who hang on her every word. Six hundred and eighty-three thousand of them on Instagram for starters. Six hundred and eighty-three thousand people think she's a celebrity. OK, so no one outside that bubble knows who she is yet, but that's a huge base to grow from. To put it into context, I have seventy-six. Not seventy-six thousand. Seventy-six followers.

Most of the information seems to be gleaned from her videos and one small article by a mummy blogger. Former life coach, married to Lee, with whom she has twin daughters. No mention of any previous relationships. Either she's very private or it's all carefully curated. My guess is the latter. She's building herself as a brand. She doesn't want random stories about broken marriages and infidelities floating around, waiting to come back and bite her. She's Mrs Nice. Mrs Family Friendly. Me and Tom don't fit into her narrative.

I don't even know why I care. *If* I do. I wouldn't take Tom back now if he crawled in on his hands and knees and begged. But would I still be with him if he hadn't strayed? Almost certainly. We had history and it's hard to overestimate how much that counts for.

We'd met at a party, Tom and I. I could never remember whose. And neither could Tom. We both must have been there as some random friends' plus ones. 'We don't even know who to thank,' I said to him once, laughing. 'I can't even remember who I went with.'

'Fate,' he'd said with a raised eyebrow and a smirk. He was a complete non-believer in fate, as was I. I still am. Daisy has enough belief in it for the both of us. She uses it to excuse every bit of bad behaviour, every fuck-up, every hook-up that peppers her life. I wonder what he made of all Maddy's Goop-inspired hokum. Was that a bone of contention between them, or did he come round to her way of seeing things in the end? Start burning vagina-smelling candles and consulting the universe before he made any decisions?

What I do remember about the party is talking to almost no one else all evening. I remember noticing that his piercing pale blue eyes gave him a kind of vulpine look. Taking in his broad shoulders and the fine hair on his tanned arms. I remember us exclaiming as we found we had more and more in common. Not so much the facts as the likes and dislikes. We watched the same things, listened to the same things, liked the same food.

'Are you just copying me now?' he'd said with a twinkle when I gasped that Atkinson Grimshaw was my absolute favourite artist too.

'This is insane,' I remember saying. 'It's like the plot of a bad romcom.'

'I love romcoms,' he'd said and I'd slapped him on the arm. 'Shut the fuck up! Me too! What's your favourite?'

'*My Best Friend's Wedding*,' he'd answered without hesitation.

'No fricking way! That's mine.' I'd swiped his arm again.

'Are you always this violent?' he'd laughed.

'Only about things I like.'

'Good to know,' he'd said. 'I'll make a note of that.'

Somehow even on that first night we'd talked about how much we both wanted a family one day. Both of our upbringings had been stable, happy. He'd never even realised he was poor, he said, until he went to uni. He had no siblings and he doted on his mum and dad. 'They're just good people,' he said. 'I want to give them lots of gorgeous little grandkids.'

'Same,' I'd said. 'Three, at least.'

He'd held out a hand for me to shake. 'Three.'

When the evening had ended it was just assumed by both of us that we'd see each other again. 'Is tomorrow night too soon?' he'd said, and I'd shaken my head. 'I think we're supposed to play it cool and not talk to each other for three days or something but, yes, tomorrow night.'

We'd been through so much together since. The deaths of both our dads. Moving in together. Getting married. The failed attempts at getting pregnant. We were bonded for life, or so I'd thought. Yes, we'd been going through a bit of a rough patch. Yes, conceiving had become a bit of an obsession. But soon I would have been expecting and all that would be in the past. We would be back to being Us. The new improved Us, with a baby in tow.

And the truth is we probably *would* have a family now if we were together, that's the real kicker. Eventually I know it would have happened. Somehow. We'd be the ones with two little girls in sunflower hats. Of course, if it hadn't been Maddy it probably would have been someone else, I know that now. But that doesn't really help. The whole point is that it *was* her. That she was the one who said yes.

The timing is what kills me. If it had happened a couple of years before, it would still have been devastating but I might have met someone else I liked enough to have children with while I was still young enough to have them. Don't get me wrong, it's not that I wanted kids at any cost. Fay once suggested I just sleep around a bit in the hope of getting pregnant.

'I don't mean pick someone up in the street,' she'd said, when I'd pulled a face. 'I mean go on the odd date here and there and just be a bit careless.'

'I want to be a family,' I'd said. 'I'm not setting out to be a single mum. It's hard. Really hard.'

'It would have been no different if you and Tom had got pregnant and then he'd left once the baby was born. That definitely wouldn't have been out of the question.'

I'd shaken my head. 'No. Because he would have been there in the background somewhere helping out. We still would have co-parented, supported each other.'

'What if you had kids with someone and then they dropped dead?'

'Jesus, you're cheerful today,' I'd said, trying to laugh it off. There was no point talking about it. It didn't help. It was what it was. And maybe what it was was pretty shit, but there you go. I hadn't been given any choice in the matter. Maddy had seen to that.

3.

Cally and I are meeting at a pub called the Whippet Inn, near to her and Jim's home in Queen's Park, at half six, for a quick drink and, hopefully, something to eat. You never know with Cally. I'll ask a passing waiter for a menu and she'll sheepishly tell me she ate half of Frankie's pureed broccoli and spinach while she fed him his. So, we've given up going to anywhere but the least formal places where they won't mind if we don't order any food. I could get something for myself, obviously, but since the night we went to The Wolseley for a special treat and she sat and watched me chew my way through three courses while the waiter glared at her (I know I didn't have to order dessert, but I'd never been there before, and it looked incredible. When was I ever going to have the opportunity again?) I've decided it's usually better to wait until I get home and shove in some toast in private if I have to.

Tonight she arrives at five to seven announcing she's going to 'get wasted'. She looks exhausted, bags under her hazel eyes the size of suitcases, pale blonde locks scraped back into a thin ponytail. I almost can't see the eighteen-year-old girl I met on my first day at uni – she was moving into the room next to mine in halls, Blur blaring from her CD player – in there. Fay came later

27

when she transferred on to my design course, halfway through the second term, having given up on Fine Art, and breezed confidently into the room lighting it up with her hot pink hair and megawatt smile.

'I'm free,' Cally says, laughing as she hugs me. By which she means she's expressed enough milk to keep baby Frankie happy till Monday and that Jim is on overnight childcare duty and all day tomorrow if needs be. I also know from experience that a glass and a half of wine in she'll feel guilty and switch to lime and soda, and then she'll be falling asleep by nine and we'll call it a night. None of this bothers me in the slightest. I go along with her delusion because it makes her happy.

'Yay!' I say, hugging her back. Cally is my rock. The sensible, kind heart at the centre of our three-way friendship. Fay is honest and fearless. I like to think I bring the fun. Or at least, I used to. Now I mainly bring the complaining.

'So, you watched it?' I say after we've ordered drinks. She'd replied to my email earlier with a shocked face emoji.

'Cringiest thing ever,' she says.

'She's not been with Tom for years, though, by the look of it.' I pour sparkling water into both our glasses just as the waitress arrives with our wine. 'Those kids are at least three.'

Cally looks at me wide-eyed. 'I hadn't even thought of that. I was too busy being sick. God. Unless . . . no.'

'What? They're his?' This had occurred to me too, in a painful middle-of-the-night thunderbolt last night, and I'd got up and rewatched as many videos as I could bear, looking for clues. 'She talks about finding out they were pregnant in one of the early ones, her and Lee. And, besides, they look exactly like him, don't you think?'

'You're right. The eyes. Absolutely.'

'I don't know why it's bothering me so much.' I pick up a menu. 'Are you eating?'

'Sure. Well, nibbling.'

'I'll get something we can share,' I say.

'Great. I'm happy with whatever.' She says this as if I've forgotten she is the world's pickiest eater. I run through her list of no-nos in my head as I check out the options: mushrooms (slimy – see also aubergines), leeks (chewy), asparagus (the whole weird-smelling wee thing), cabbage (just no). And that's just the vegetable section. In the end I wave a waiter over and order fries.

'It bothers you because it makes it meaningless. If Tom and Maddy had ended up having the Greatest Love Story Ever Told you would have at least understood what was going on eventually. That they were powerless to ignore it.'

'I think you're right. Do you think she's earning loads of money from it?'

Cally nods vigorously. 'Did you see how many subscribers she's got? And billions of followers on Insta.'

'Fuck. For prancing about dressed like an idiot.'

'It's embarrassing, right?' She gazes out across the street watching two ancient Lycra-clad cyclists riding slowly past. I see her mouth twitch into a smirk.

'What?'

'I was just thinking. Imagine if it *was* Tom in the

29

videos. You'd be having to say to people "I used to be married to that prat in the pyjamas."'

I laugh out loud. 'Street cred gone.'

'Yes, because you have loads of that.'

It feels good to be able to laugh about it. That, I realise, is the way to deal with this. Take the piss with my dearest friend. 'Did you see "The Locomotion"?'

Cally snorts into her sparkling water. As suspected, her wine is almost untouched. 'Oh yes. I've watched about a hundred of them this afternoon. Jesus Christ. To be fair I quite enjoyed that one.'

'Traitor,' I say, picking at a chip as soon as the waiter places the bowl between us on the table.

'Ignore it though, Rissa,' Cally says, a note of warning in her voice. Fay and Cally have always called me Rissa ever since I complained to them that Iris was a name that didn't lend itself to diminutives. (*Neither does mine,* Fay had said. *And thank fuck. Don't either of you even start thinking about calling me Fifi.*) 'She's nothing to do with you now.'

'Of course. You're right. I need to forget about it,' I say, waving a hand to order myself another glass of wine. I hold up a finger with a smile to confirm just one. 'I didn't even know about it yesterday. It doesn't change anything.'

'I'll drink to that,' Cally says, clinking her glass against mine and taking the tiniest sip. 'Christ, I feel as if I've drunk too much already. I'll order a soft drink.'

Back home and tucked up in bed by half past nine my resolve weakens. I'll just have a quick check of Maddy's channels to see if she's posted anything new. Is this how the slippery slope starts? One final farewell puff on the crack pipe and suddenly all your teeth have fallen out and your mugshot is on *Crimewatch* on a list of Britain's Most Wanted?

There's nothing new on either YouTube or Insta and I feel strangely disappointed. Without thinking why, I sign up to receive a notification next time she posts a video. Might as well keep on poking that wound.

I'm with a customer on a grey, chilly Tuesday morning when my phone beeps. I work as a senior kitchen designer for one of the mid to higher range companies, which basically means I sit in a shop surrounded by sample cupboards and hope someone wanders in who is looking to spend forty thousand plus on a refit. Much of my day is spent lurking while couples browse, ready to dive in with the lowdown on marble versus composite worktops or the benefits of a butler's pantry if they give me the slightest hint of encouragement. My favourite part of the job is the quiet hours once I've managed to snare someone, spent drawing up plans, rearranging footprints, coming up with solutions. The pleasure you receive from the joy on their face when you tell them you've managed to squeeze in a rolling spice cupboard shouldn't be underestimated. Today I'm at that tipping point with Mrs Dolan of Hampton Wick. She's tempted to commit. She's on the verge, except that Harvey Jones have a sale on and what I'm suggesting to her is a little out of her price range. Same old same old. I'll find a couple of solutions to bring the cost down, a discount if she signs on the dotted line by close of play today.

Nothing galvanizes a customer like a deadline with a hefty price drop. She'll prevaricate until she realises there's no more to be squeezed out of me. We'll either come to a deal or not. It's a dance I have little patience for but it's a necessary evil. If I can leave Mrs Dolan congratulating herself that she's got a bargain while not bankrupting the company, I've won.

Usually I turn my mobile off while I'm in a consultation, but Mrs Dolan's visit was unscheduled. My job is very much of the feast or famine variety. Hanging round the empty showroom for hours on end waiting for a customer, or full-on back and forth with ideas and price negotiations in an attempt to seal a deal. I was having a leisurely morning playing around with sizes for an island unit in Richmond when Mrs Dolan and her Harvey Jones quote breezed in. This is her third visit and I know she wants to make it work with us. I just need to do whatever I have to do to get her to hand over a deposit. So, I ignore my phone. Reach out a hand and turn it over so the screen doesn't distract me. It's only once Mrs Dolan has said her goodbyes and promised to get back to me by the cut-off point at the end of the day, that I turn it back to see what I've missed. *Fun with the Fulfords has posted a new video*, the notification says. For a second I'm confused, but then I remember that I signed up for just this purpose. The shop is empty – Zak, my co-worker, is in the office at the back doing admin. Or Wordle. One or the other – so I click play. This time it's Maddy on her own, bright-eyed and bushy-tailed, in a green cap-sleeved T-shirt, her copper hair falling in waves around her face.

'Guess what!' she squeaks. She has a high-pitched voice, breathy and childlike. In the past few days I've found myself wondering what Tom thought of that voice. If he found it sexy. Or if it started to grate on his nerves after a while. Too mannered, too affected. Marilyn Monroe with a helium balloon. The camera must be set up on a tripod because it's perfectly still. Fixed. I find myself wondering where Lee and the girls are.

'No idea,' I say drily, as if she might be able to hear me.

'I . . .' she says, leaving a dramatic pause, '. . . have got a book coming out!' She holds up a hardback. *Making Family Fun* by Maddy Fulford. My stomach lurches. Maddy grins maniacally, drunk on her own success. 'It's going to be published in June, just in time for the school holidays when you might be spending more time with your loved ones than usual, with all the stresses that can bring. We love 'em but sometimes they drive us mad, right? Well, my book is full to the brim of ideas to help you all get the best out of one another, to make sure those precious years really do bring the joy and fulfilment we all want from our families . . .'

'Is that the Fun with the Fulfords woman?' I jump as Zak appears behind me, looking over my shoulder. Press pause. 'I love them,' he says, not waiting for an answer.

'I think she's quite annoying,' I say defensively.

'Coffee?' he says, heading for the front door. I nod. I don't need to spell out exactly what I want. Zak knows my preference for skimmed milk, no foam, extra hot.

'Thanks.' I wait for him to leave and then I restart the video. Maddy burbles on a bit more about how you have to work at your relationships, how there will be both good and bad times, but with her (almost certainly unqualified) help you can 'bulletproof your family' and 'keep each other at the centre of your universe'. 'And you know that thing they say on airplanes?' she squeaks. 'That you need to put on your own oxygen mask before helping anyone else? Well, that applies here too. If you want to be the best parent, you have to take care of yourself first.' It's a bunch of clichéd drivel. She's not actually saying anything, she's just parroting out soundbites. What if someone comes along and makes a play for your husband, I want to say. Someone who couldn't give a fuck about how bulletproof you think your marriage is? I don't care that Tom is more to blame than she is, Tom is not – to my knowledge, anyway – prancing about all over the internet banging on about how perfect his life is. The perfect life that she built on the bombsite of mine.

I have to rewind a bit because I've missed her last few pronouncements. It's more of the same: let me help you be as fabulous and happy as me. 'So, apologies that you'll be seeing a lot of me over the next few months,' she chirps. 'My publishers are just juggling all the TV chat show offers, so watch this space.'

Bullshit, I think. But what if it's not? Stranger things have happened. People have become millionaires lecturing us all about how to clean the toilet with lemon juice or the best way to arrange our sock drawers. What if she becomes some kind of Nation's Sweetheart? I couldn't bear it. Couldn't stomach the hypocrisy.

I can't let it happen.

4.

Before I know what I'm doing, I've posted a negative comment.

> *This woman is a complete fraud. She doesn't value family life at all, at least not other people's.*

I add in all the hashtags Maddy uses: *MumsOfInstagram, InstaMums, FamilyLife, FamilyFun, LoveMyFamily.* I wonder whether I should be more specific, spell out her crimes, but I don't want to give myself away. I press send and then immediately feel grubby. I don't want to think I'm that person. A troll. I've always imagined them sat in a shabby bedsit that smells of takeaway pizza, sweat and shame. Saddos with greasy hair and no friends. But this is different, isn't it? I'm not throwing shade at the way a celebrity who doesn't even know I exist looks. Maddy has wronged me. I'm owed.

I panic that there might be something on my profile that gives away who I am, but there's nothing. My username is an anonymous FlowerGirl with some random numbers attached. Like I said, I'm there to watch other people, not join in. I check Maddy's post again, seek out my comment. There are already twelve replies: *What are you talking about? Maddy is an angel! You don't know anything about her! Maddy and Lee are GOALS!!!* All of them have the hashtag #MaddysArmy. I try to resist the urge to argue my case. I'm saved from myself by the return of Zak and the coffees. I put my phone in a drawer and busy myself with checking the installation schedules.

In the end, Mrs Dolan doesn't even have the decency to return to tell me it's all over between us. They often don't. You're still planning their perfect layout and spending a whole afternoon trying to fit in a wine fridge while they're off signing a contract with your arch rivals. It's a cutthroat business, the world of kitchens. Anyone can be lured away with the promise of a free boiling water tap. The awkward thing is deciding when it's definitely the end. Was she on her way here to give me the good news when she got knocked down by a bus? In which case the decent thing to do would be to keep the offer of the discounted price open for a few more days, at least until she's out of intensive care and can hold a pen. Do I keep working on her plans for another morning? A whole day? But, as I lock up for the night, I know in my heart that's the last I'll see of her. Sometimes the hours wasted in this job schmoozing lost causes are just exhausting.

By the time I get home, after a quick glass of wine with Zak in the pub on the corner (his girlfriend has moved in and they're both finding the increased hours spent together are grating on their nerves, so he's always up for an after-work drink. I try to tell him this doesn't bode well for their upcoming wedding and their future life together, but he insists they just need a bit of time to adjust) and allow myself to check Maddy's Instagram again, she's blocked me. Is she really that sensitive? One critical comment and I'm out? I almost laugh. I knew I wasn't cut out to be a troll. I'm obviously doing something wrong. I should have gone to troll school. Seriously though, a part of me is glad it doesn't come naturally.

I force myself to go and make something to eat, tiptoeing down the corridor past the open door to the living room. The TV is on and I can see the back of Carol's head, a wine glass on the arm of the sofa, a magazine folded open beside it. Her feet are up on the coffee table. Bare toes waggling in time to the *Emmerdale* theme tune. Carol is one of those people who takes up space in the world. She unpacks herself wherever she goes. She's a small woman, but she spreads herself wide. And not with anything I can pull her up on. I find myself wishing that her biggest fault was watching TV too loudly. I could ask her to turn it down. Or leaving the bathroom dirty. I could tell her to clean up. But her looming presence is nothing so tangible. It's *her* that fills up the space and disturbs my peace. She talks, she sings, she bangs pots and pans around, she stomps, she sprawls, she even snores loudly enough for me to hear it through the wall. Basically, she has a presence that's too large for my little flat. I feel edged out. Squeezed into a corner.

The kitchen smells faintly of the pizzas she likes to order in, but it's clean at least. I would love to spend a leisurely hour or so preparing a meal from scratch, listening to the radio, winding down. It used to be one of my favourite things to do. But I know I have to be in and out like an SAS operative on special manoeuvres. I dig a frozen butternut squash curry out of my side of the freezer – I'm forty-four and I only have use of one half of my freezer. The centre line is formed from boxes of Carol's staple garlic bread. She never encroaches on my side and I know that's something I should be grateful for. I just can't find it in me sometimes. I shove the curry in the microwave and hotfoot it back to my room, shutting the kitchen door behind me as I go to, hopefully, minimise the aroma. When I emerge to claim my meal she's hovering by the fridge, wine bottle in hand, sniffing like a bloodhound. I curse myself for not cooking something less pungent.

'I didn't hear you come in,' she says.

'Oh. I said hello. I'm just . . .' I wave a hand towards the now beeping microwave. Carol opens a cupboard and gets out another wine glass. I tip my curry into a bowl and find myself a fork, wondering what excuse I can now give for wanting to eat alone in my room. She fills both glasses and plonks herself down at the kitchen table.

'I had the worst day . . .' she says, and I realise I'm going nowhere.

Still, at least I manage not to think about Maddy and her gilded life for an hour. I bet not many trolls can say that.

After a couple of days, though, I have withdrawal. I find myself trying to sneak a peek and having to face rejection all over again. I'm still blocked, of course I am. I borrow Zak's phone and look her up on there (Zak follows her, which is annoying in itself). There's a new video with them all dressed in dungarees, paintbrushes in hand. A half-painted wall behind them in what looks like the living room. They all wiggle about to 'Walking on Sunshine' while occasionally slapping up a bit of buttercup yellow. Inevitably they start to flick it at each other. Oh, the originality. The hilarity. The comments are orgasmic: *You are the absolute best!!! These videos make my day!! I'm ROTFLOL!!!!* There are a couple not so gushing: *I hope that's child friendly paint!* and *Cringorama!* My people, I think. My soulmates. Hashtag Maddy's Army have pretty much eviscerated them, though. I'm trying to work my way through all eight hundred and twelve comments when Zak demands his phone back.

'Why can't you do that on your own mobile?' he says, when he sees I'm on Instagram. 'Also, I thought you couldn't stand her.'

'She's blocked me,' I say without thinking.

Zak pulls a face that can only mean he thinks I'm a monster. 'What did you do?'

'Nothing. Jesus.' At thirty-one, Zak is still starry-eyed about the world. Nothing too terrible has happened to him yet. He still has both parents, a devoted fiancée, the promise of a life.

'Well, I made a snide comment,' I say. 'Which I know I shouldn't have . . .'

Zak's face screws up as if I've just told him I kicked his puppy. 'Why?'

'She's the woman my ex-husband went off with . . .' Maybe this is the way to go. Track down Maddy's fans

39

one by one and tell them the story. It would take the rest of my life but hey, it's a hobby.

By the time we leave to go home a couple of hours later Zak has quizzed me like he's Maddy's defence lawyer. He looks as if he's aged five years. His innocence shattered.

'What do you think their sex life's like?' I ask Fay when I've insisted we watch 'Walking on Sunshine' four times in succession. We're in the garden of the White Swan trying to pretend it's not too cold to be drinking outside. The couple at the next table glare at us every time I restart the video, the tinny music shattering the peace. Evenings with Fay are the opposite of evenings with Cally. She's on a mission. Kieran is with Steve's mum for the night – Steve is on a bender with his mates. The idea that he might stay in looking after their child while his wife goes on a rare night out is risible. An affront to his manhood. Steve is one of those blokes for whom Friday night drinks with the lads is a sacred ritual never to be missed, regardless of what Fay's plans are – so she fully intends to make the most of it. I'm trying to drink slowly. I don't enjoy getting wasted these days. I hate that feeling of being out of control, of knowing you're going to suffer the next day. Luckily Fay is not one of those people who expects you to match her drink for drink. Just don't try and slow her down. It's not pretty.

Now she grimaces. 'There's no way you can sleep with someone after you've watched them do that.'

'So maybe her life isn't as perfect as she makes it look?'

Fay snorts. 'Of course it isn't. It's literally her job to make you think that it is. I bet her house is filthy or Lee's shagging the hot neighbour.'

'I hope so. I don't see why she deserves the happy ending.'

'Happy endings only exist in massage parlours,' Fay says, draining the last of the bottle of Pinot Grigio into our glasses. I laugh, but at the same time I feel sad for her that she's stuck in a marriage that makes her feel she has to get competitively drunk just so she can show her husband she's having as good a time as he apparently is.

Something fizzes in my brain as if a light bulb has spluttered into life in my head. Fay is right, Maddy's life can't be as idyllic as she claims. No one's is. There must be a skeleton lurking somewhere. Well, there is. I know there is. She's a husband stealer. My single, childless self is living proof of that. Shit, I must be drunker than I thought. I pour myself a glass of water. I need to put out that spark.

'I guess so. I should go home,' I say. I suddenly just want to go to bed. I love Fay but I'm tired and I'm too old to be getting wasted in a pub because my friend is on a mission. Fay's problems with Steve are not going to be solved by raucous nights out. Their issues are much more fundamental. I book an Uber before she can protest. As always, I'll get them to drop her off first, even though it's miles out of my way, and wait while I check she gets through the front door in one piece.

The flat is quiet when I let myself in. There's no light under the door of the spare room. Hopefully Carol is in bed already. She tends to use her room only for sleeping. If she's awake she's in the living room or the kitchen. Still, I creep around, brushing my teeth, fetching a glass of water, scared of waking the beast.

I sleep fitfully. I turn over what Fay said in my head. She's right. Maddy's life can't be as perfect as she insists it is. I bet even Marie Kondo has one cupboard that's a bit messy. That if you looked behind Mrs Hinch's toilet you'd find a stray ball of indeterminate fluff. She's asking her followers to buy into her Hallmark Movie dream (literally buy into it – as well as her upcoming book, she's always trying to talk them into purchasing some new educational toy or child-friendly yoghurt or serotonin-enhancing bath oil, which she's clearly being paid to do. Her posts are littered with #Ad or #Gifted) but I know she's a fraud. A charlatan. I know things about her that no one else knows. And that's eating me up.

I find myself wondering where Tom is. What happened next for him. I've googled him from time to time. Idle curiosity more than anything else. But with a name like Tom Smith he's not exactly easy to find. 'Tom Smith IT' doesn't help much either. He never did social media or LinkedIn or any of those things that might leave a footprint. For someone who worked in IT, he had zero interest in anything extra-curricular that had to do with computers. I always liked that about him. He didn't feel the need to try and make friends outside of our little circle. He didn't need approbation from strangers. We and our small social life were enough. I flush a deep red now thinking about how deluded I was.

When he first left I was fuelled by a rage that quickly gave way to a deep grieving for the family I knew I was never going to have. For a – very short – while I put myself out there on an online dating site. Trying to find, not a sperm donor as Fay suggested, but a new life partner. I thought if I could throw myself into a relationship there might be time for it all to happen organically. You hear stories all the time about people who find their soulmate, move in together and start trying for a baby within the space of a few months. I mean, not really all the time, but it happens. It's possible. But after a couple of first dates I knew it was a mistake. Desperation poured from me like sweat. I clutched at any positives I could find. Maybe I could ignore his bad dental hygiene or his habit of referring to his ex as 'The See You Next Tuesday' and fall in love quickly enough to find my happy ever after. It was a disaster. I couldn't stop talking about how much I wanted to have a baby. 'Two at least. I need to make sure there's time for a second,' I'd said to one of their horrified faces. At the other I'd cried. Actually blubbed about how broody I was. In the end Cally had gently told me it was too soon. I needed to mourn my marriage, sort my own life out, before I could move on.

Tom and Maddy meanwhile had moved away. Out to Rickmansworth. Not that he told me that himself. Like I said, he communicated only through solicitors once he'd dropped the big bombshell on me. I'd found out because Maddy's practice had moved there, her treacherous website giving her away.

I have a confession to make. I went there. I booked an appointment at the Holistic Centre in Watford where Maddy gave consultations between ten and two on Tuesdays. She also saw clients at home on other days, but I obviously wasn't going to risk that. I had no idea if Tom was working, or where. He's always had the kind of job that could be done virtually. I gave the name Kate Marshall – I have no idea where that came from, it just popped into my head – and clicked confirm once I realised there was (rather naïvely, I thought) no request for a deposit upfront. I could pay in cash, who cared if she thought that was odd. I just wanted to see her, to get a feel for her. To – Daisy would probably claim – get a look at her aura. By which I mean see if she seemed like the entitled bitch I assumed her to be. See what it was she had that would make Tom give up our dreams. I booked a forty-five-minute introductory session where, her website told me, Maddy would listen to my concerns and lay out the ways in which she might be able to help me if I decided to proceed with a course.

I took a day's holiday. Caught the train via Clapham Junction, trying to pretend to myself that it was just a day out, no big deal. I had dressed as anonymously as I could, as if I were on my way to commit a murder and didn't want anyone to remember seeing me. To be fair it probably crossed my mind. Charcoal trousers, a pale grey blouse and a black pin-striped jacket. Low heels. I parted my hair on the side, unusually for me, as if I thought Maddy might go home from work and say to

Tom *Guess what! I had a session with a woman with a centre parting today.* I wore the glasses that I keep in my bedside drawer for emergencies. Very few people have ever seen me in them. I'm strictly a contacts woman. I remember getting lost on the way, panicking when I couldn't find the street. I remember sitting in a pleasant-smelling waiting room alongside people waiting for acupuncture and reiki, looking at the handwritten sign on the door on the left that said 'Maddy Cartwright. Life Advisor'. I remember feeling sick and wanting to back out.

I remember the moment she put a warm hand in mine to shake it.

I can't really recall what I said. I had come up with some story about hitting a glass ceiling and a frustration that I had an artistic pursuit that I had always wanted to follow but lacked the courage. Maddy listened, nodding occasionally, and then softly told me how she could teach me techniques that would help me achieve my goals. I didn't take in the details, I didn't need to. But I studied her as she talked. The big eyes, the full lips. I imagined Tom kissing her, his hand working its way up the creamy skin of her thighs. There was something about her that made you feel as if you could climb on to her lap and she'd make it all better. Maybe that was what attracted Tom, the maternal thing. That and the undeniable beauty. I wished I hadn't gone. I wanted to hate her – I still did hate her – but she'd made it harder. I'd wanted a pantomime villain to focus my vitriol on, but what I'd got was a real-life woman who, if I didn't know what I knew, would have seemed quite nice.

I handed over my fifty pounds in cash to the receptionist and told her I'd be back in touch about booking a course once I knew my schedule. I couldn't get out of there quickly enough. I'd thought it might be quite a funny story to share with Fay and Cally, but in the end I'd shared it with no one. Truth be told, I was a bit ashamed of myself.

I wonder if that's still where she lives with Lee. Rickmansworth. If Lee was their neighbour or a work colleague. If he too has a devastated ex-wife somewhere watching the videos with the same horrified fascination as me. I google his name – I assume he's Lee Fulford – and find him almost exclusively in tandem with Maddy. No mention of what he does or who he is as an individual. He exists solely as Maddy's partner. It's all about her. I remember Maddy being much more open on her early posts. Naïve, maybe. Unaware of how many strangers would one day be poring over the details of her life. I'm sure there was one where she talked about her home town, something about the river and taking the girls to see the boats. Is there a river in Rickmansworth? I click on to YouTube and work my way back. You can literally see the gloss strip away as the years go past. Back to the days when her vlogging was a hopeful hobby, not a money-spinning occupation. I land on a couple of nonstarters before I finally hit gold. She and the girls are standing in a park, a kiddies' playground behind them, the river in the deep background. It's a sunny day and the three of them wear matching sunhats and sunglasses. The twins are about a year old, wobbling on the spot as if they've been planted out on a windy day. Maddy reaches down a hand to steady one of them.

'Aren't we lucky to have a place like this on our door-step,' she exclaims. 'Fresh air and the space to run around is so vital for our little munchkins. Even if you don't have a garden you can always escape to a beautiful public park like this one,' she adds, completely oblivious to her thousands of fans living in urban sprawls with no access to nature beyond picking their way round dog turds on the pavement. I get the impression Maddy has always had a charmed life. Always got exactly what she wanted. Told she was the prettiest princess in the world so often she believed it. She waves an expansive hand around and the camera – manned by Lee, I assume – follows, taking in an imposing church spire in one direction and sweep-ing back past the tantalising glimpse of boats to a small café with tables outside. Its name on a sign. I pause, skip back, and watch again. The Resolute. Before I know what I'm doing, I google that too.

It's not Rickmansworth. It's Marlow in Buckingham-shire, a pretty, aspirational Thames-side town about an hour outside London. I could just get in my car and drive down there tomorrow. Tell myself I'm having a day out. Daisy will understand if I cancel lunch. My sister is the queen of unreliability. Not because she doesn't value other people's time but because she's flaky. *Time is elastic*, she said to me once, and I'd said, *It really isn't, is it? It's all done by atomic clocks now, so it's really precise.* She probably doesn't even remember our arrangement anyway. And if I happened to find out the actual address of where

47

Maddy lives before that, then what would be the harm in strolling past her house? It's an itch I feel I need to scratch. I don't know why. I won't mention it to Fay or Cally, I decide. They'd think I've gone crazy and maybe I have. I know they worry about me sometimes, all on my own, going quietly insane. But I just feel as if I can't sit back and let Maddy take the world by storm while my own life stagnates. I have to do something, however pointless.

I decide to sleep on it. If it's a nice day I'll do it, I tell myself. I'll let the weather gods decide. Daisy would approve.

The sun is streaming through the gap in the curtains when I wake up. I can hear water running in the flat and for a moment I'm disorientated. I still can't get used to Carol's presence, even after almost six months. I make a dash for the kitchen, make a cup of tea and take it back to bed. I have research to do.

I google Maddy's name and 'Marlow, Bucks'. Click on to news. There are reams of stories about her success, her local philanthropy, her attendance at various events. I'd bet my life she called them all in herself. Local papers are always grateful for anything to fill the pages. There's nothing fruitful so, remembering her early lack of guile, I work my way back through the years. The mentions get more sparse. And then, there it is, the mother lode. In a brief piece detailing a sponsored Baby Fun Run she organised for mums with their little ones, Maddy is described as Maddy Fulford of

Hanwood Lane. I'm pretty sure she hasn't moved in the interim; she would have made fifteen videos detailing packing every box, singing a song about deciding what to throw away, and dancing with the removal men if she had. That's the thing about influencers. They never waste good material. So that's it. I'm decided. I'll have a day out by the beautiful Buckinghamshire riverside, swing down Hanwood Lane to get it out of my system, have lunch in a nice pub, come home and get on with my life.

What could possibly go wrong?

5

I hate driving. What kind of person enjoys getting into a tin can full of petrol and lighting a spark? Playing cat and mouse with other equally volatile machines that seem dead set on ramming into you? Bring on the driverless cars, I say. At least then you know if you end up in a collision it would be down to a malfunction, or some kind of AI plot to wipe out the humans and take over. Not just wilful idiocy. But getting the train seems to involve multiple changes as well as walks in between stations. So, I give myself a talking to and get into my trusty Mini. I always prepare for a journey like I'm off to conquer the Eiger: water: check, snacks: check, map: check, distress flare: check. If I get a flat tyre I'm stuffed, but if I get lost for days in a remote wasteland off the M4 I'll be laughing.

My phone beeps twice while I'm on the road and I steadfastly ignore it. The headline 'Multiple pile-up caused by idiot reading text' flashes through my head and I grip the steering wheel tighter.

Fifty minutes later I'm there, cruising over the majestic suspension bridge. I pass the park on my left and find myself in the centre of things, with cafés both sides spilling out on to the pavement and shops whose names I don't recognise, which is always the sign of a thriving local economy, it seems to me. It's bustling with shoppers. I find a parking spot only after cruising the High Street twice. The first thing I do is check my messages. The first is a YouTube notification. Maddy's YouTube Channel has steadily languished as her Insta presence grew, but she still occasionally puts content up, it appears. I check the other message first and see it's a voicemail from Zak. He always works Saturdays and has Mondays off but he rarely, if ever, needs to call me.

'Iris,' he says in a loud whisper. 'Mrs Dolan is here. She wants to go ahead. I'm just checking if you're nearby and want to pop in, otherwise, you know, she'll be my customer . . . she's insistent she wants to do it today . . .'

Fuck. We get paid a decent salary but there are bonuses for snagging buyers. Zak could, if he wanted, put my initials on the contract, enter my details into the system as the salesperson responsible – technically that's not allowed, but I would do it for him and there's no doubt that Mrs Dolan is my catch – but implied in his message is that he's not prepared to do that. He knows I don't live close enough to get there in time even if I was at home, dressed and ready to walk out of the door. He's covering himself. I dial his number.

'Hi,' he says, somehow making it sound apologetic, and I know I'm too late.

'Did you put it through already?' I know I sound annoyed, but I don't care.

'I had to. We would have lost her otherwise. I did try . . .'

'And you put her down as yours?'

'I had no choice, Iris,' he says defensively. 'They know you don't work Saturdays.'

I wonder if I've taught him too well. I should have hinted at the grey areas more. There's nothing I can do. If I make a fuss about it he might complain to the boss and I'd be the one who got in trouble. 'Fine,' I say, not meaning it. Three weeks of wooing Mrs Dolan down the drain. Of micro-managing her neuroses, tiptoeing round her paranoia that we were somehow trying to rip her off, finding solutions to her worries, complimenting everything from her hair to her choice of our horrendous brown and salmon-pink swirly marble for the countertop.'

'Did you give her the discount?' I ask, sulkily.

'I did. I thought because . . .'

I cut him off. 'You shouldn't have. The deadline had run out.' I end the call before he can respond.

Mood ruined, I sit in the car and wonder what I'm doing here. I don't really have the heart for my ridiculous quest any more. But, apart from anything else, I need time to recover from the drive down before I attempt to do it in reverse, so I may as well at least have a look around. I remember Maddy's new video, so I click on to YouTube and savour the delights of the twins splashing in a paddling pool in the garden, dressed as mermaids while Maddy caterwauls 'Under the Sea'. Halfway through, Lee fake-swims his way past with a shark fin on his back. The comments are flying up. *LOL! Hilarious! You guys! So cute!* I keep my fingers firmly away from the keyboard.

I get out and head for the park, stroll past the café and down to the river. It's picture-postcard pretty. I try to kid myself I'm just here for a holiday. Taking in the scenery. But I keep a hawk-like eye out, just in case. You never know your luck. There are families everywhere. Dogs chasing balls. The lucky few lounge on moored boats, the envy of all. Gleaming white cruisers, slim barges, roomy houseboats. It takes aspirational to a new level. I shrug my faded jean jacket off and soak up the sun.

After about ten minutes I wander back up to the café and buy an avocado and mozzarella sandwich and a coffee and then reclaim my bench by the waterside. I could spend all morning here, but I know I'm just stalling for time. The focus of my day – an almost certainly anti-climactic stroll down Hanwood Lane – will take up twenty minutes at most. Less, probably. I don't want to peak too soon.

Eventually I can't put it off any longer. I check the map on my phone and meander in the general direction, past playing fields and tennis courts. My heart starts beating faster as I see the turning. I have no idea what I'm doing, what I'm hoping to achieve. I remind myself that Maddy has absolutely no idea what I look like, unless she and Tom spent a cosy evening going through his old family photos, which seems unlikely. She certainly didn't recognise me when I was sitting opposite her, waffling on about my mid-life crisis. I'm just a woman walking down a street and it's my absolute right to do so. Still, I'm a bit shocked when I see that Hanwood Lane only has seven or eight houses in total. Neat, well-kept detached boxes, slightly bigger than average, with compact front gardens. It looks like the kind of place where the residents might phone the police if they saw someone loitering. Not a wheelie bin is out of place. Or even dirty. Who cleans their wheelie bins? Do they get together to employ a wheelie bin cleaner? Some poor local lad who gets two pounds fifty for scrubbing away all their unsightly grime. The 2020s equivalent of sending a small boy up your chimney.

I try to walk purposefully but not too fast at the same time, taking it all in. I know from forensically examining the videos that Maddy's house is painted cream. Or, at least, the back of it is. Her back garden is one of her favourite filming locations. I'm able to discount two of the candidates. Probably. Possibly. But I still reach the end of the road none the wiser. I turn right into the next street and then decide to walk back the way I came. I can kid myself I'm just ensuring I don't get lost. I retrace my steps. But on the opposite side. Number 5 has a sporty-looking red car on the drive. Definitely impractical with small children. But maybe Lee is having a mid-life crisis and has blown their newfound wealth on the status symbol of his dreams. Or Maddy has. I decide to eliminate number 5 from my enquiries for now. Next door gives nothing away. Slatted wooden shutters in the windows, all perfectly spaced. Tom and I had some in our old house and they always looked uneven, as if someone had run a drunken hand down them. I was forever trying to rearrange them, twiddling the pole at the side and forcibly shoving some up or down. In the end I just gave up and tried not to look at them. Maybe the bin children have a second business on the side perfectly positioning the slats each morning. Surely little three-year-olds would find them irresistible, wouldn't they? Shoving their sticky fingers through the gaps and disrupting them. Number 6 might be off the list of suspects, too.

The next house along, the second from last – number 7 – is the biggest in the street, thanks to a large loft conversion. The home of a family who moved in and then suddenly found themselves raking in more cash than they'd expected? There's a four-by-four parked outside. A tank for transporting a family. I slow down to a snail's pace. There's a pink sticker in the rear window of the car. *Twin Babies On Board!!!!* it proclaims. Bingo. She might as well have stuck a photo of them all in there.

I almost stop dead in my tracks. This is it. This is what I'm here for. Now what?

I keep walking. Quicken my pace, in case either Maddy or Lee look out of the window. I don't slow down till I reach the High Street and my heart is threatening to explode out of my ears. I have an overwhelming urge to laugh. Loudly. Madly. Like when I was a teenager and me and my friends did something bad and got away with it. By bad, I only mean stealing a plaster gnome from someone's front garden or shoplifting a magazine. Those were the outer limits of my rebellion.

To calm myself down I nip into Starbucks, order a takeaway latte and use the loo. I sit in the car trying to slow my breathing while passing motorists eye me up hungrily, watching to see if I'm going to vacate my precious parking space. On impulse I start the engine and drive down to the park and round the corner, turning right into Hanwood Lane. I cruise past Maddy's house, the four-by-four gleaming in the drive. Then I turn round and park up at the junction of the adjacent street, far enough away – hopefully – not to be noticed. I have nothing better to do, so I may as well sit here until I feel brave enough to face the M4. To kill time I set up a new anonymous Instagram account, follow Maddy and trawl through the comments on all her old posts. I follow anyone who has said anything even halfway negative. There are a surprising number of others who find her irritating and seemingly want to tell her so. It's weirdly comforting. She hasn't yet brainwashed the whole world into thinking she's a sweetheart. That's the price of fame, I suppose. There will be haters.

For the lack of anything better to do I call Daisy.

'Where are you?' I ask as soon as she answers. I can hear what sounds like a duck quacking.

'Wild swimming,' she says. 'Hackney reservoir.'

'Is that safe?' I have visions of dark undertows and deep, freezing cold water. My sister's pale skinny legs flailing.

'Of course. There's a café and everything.'

'Oh, well, if there's a café I'm sure no one's ever drowned.'

She laughs. 'You know what I mean.'

'They could throw you a doughnut if you start to struggle.' A movement catches the corner of my eye. A flash of red hair. Daisy starts to tell me about a mime class she went to yesterday, but I tune it out. To be honest, I'd tune it out anyway even if I hadn't just spotted Maddy and the twins walking towards their house from the opposite end of the road. Daisy's life is one long struggle for meaning through ever wackier pursuits – tantrum yoga (not tantric, nothing so tame. In this one, the participants scream and shout angrily as they do their sun salutations to release their inner anger. For someone with zero stress in her life, Daisy has a lot of inner anger bursting to get out), sexual energetic cleansing to remove the traces of past lovers from her womb, cord cutting rituals to expunge toxic relationships – and she likes to describe them to me in great detail hoping, I think, that I will sanction her choices. Usually I laugh. I can't help myself. It's either that or get irritated that she hands over money to any old charlatan who can convince her they'll change her life. Beyond the odd night working behind the bar at a festival or a gig she earns almost nothing; she just sponges off our mum. Who most definitely can't afford to be sponged off, but is too soft to say no. Anyway, in contrast, wild swimming seems like a sensible and almost mundane thing to be doing.

Maddy holds hands with the girls, one on each side. I can see them both talking away, skipping along. My heart clenches. What I would give for that. The little things. The inane chatter. The tiny hand in mine. Tom and I always talked about having three children – two girls and a boy or two boys and a girl, we didn't care so long as it was a mix. 'What if we have three boys in a row?' I'd said, so secure in the fact that the babies would come. 'Then we'll just keep going till we have a girl,' Tom had smiled, looping his arms around me from behind. 'Practice makes perfect.' In the end we only practised for a year. Two maybe. I've often wondered what would have happened if I'd conceived quickly. Where we'd all be now.

Maddy's kids each carry tiny backpacks, one hot pink and one orange. The one with the pink backpack wears bright orange dungarees and vice versa. They look unbearably cute. Mini Maddies. As always when I see Maddy, the song 'Jolene' fires up in my head. Flaming locks of auburn hair, ivory skin, eyes of emerald green. She's a head-turner, but today she looks a little drawn. Worn out, actually. I imagine an afternoon of looking after twin three-year-olds will do that to you. It can't all be singing and dancing.

'Hold on a second, Dais,' I say, when I realise she's stopped talking. I watch as Maddy leads the girls up to the front door of number 7 and closes it behind them. I'm too far away to see if there's any activity inside so I just stare blankly at the house. That's it. I travelled all this way on safari and caught a fleeting glimpse of three of the big four making their way home from the watering hole. Barely worth the effort.

'I'll talk to you in the week . . .' I jump as Daisy's voice cuts through my thoughts.

'Shit, sorry . . .'

'Where are you anyway?'

Stalking someone. Watching their house without their knowledge. 'In the Waitrose car park. Speak to you soon.'

Considering all I've just witnessed is a mother walking

up the road with her two children, my heart is overreacting a little. I breathe in slowly through my nose, out through my mouth. But she's not just any mother. I've thought about her every day for the past four years. Actually, that's an exaggeration; I was getting on with my life quite happily for a while there recently, until Fay sent me that video. I was over her. Over him. Over what it meant for me, more importantly. Yes, my life felt empty, but I'd stopped obsessing about it. But now it feels as if it's all come crashing back. She stole my life and then threw it away. Created her own better, more fabulous one. I've imagined confronting her many times over the years, but truthfully that's not my style. I've never found it easy saying what I think to people's faces. If you can't say anything nice then don't say anything, my mum used to say to Daisy and me when we were little, so most of the time I just keep my mouth shut.

I try to examine whether anything has changed, whether I feel any better for my excursion. But what I actually feel is numb. A bit grubby. A bit like I imagine it must feel to wake from a long coma and think, what the hell am I doing here? Still, I've hopefully got it out of my system at least. I've been to Loch Ness, seen the monster, and can vouch for the fact that it's real. Now I should just leave it to get on with its life and try to move on with mine. I feel a bit ashamed of myself, if I'm being honest. I know that the reason I lied to Daisy, that I didn't tell Fay or Cally my plans, is that coming down here was not a socially acceptable thing to do. That they'd worry about my motives, my state of mind. It wouldn't be the first time. Well, that's it, I tell myself. It's done. I can go home and get on with my weekend. I have tickets tonight for *Relatively Speaking* at Richmond Theatre, a semi-regular Saturday night date with my friend and former colleague Verity, who was Zak's predecessor. Truthfully, we don't have much in common except that we love theatre and we don't want to spend our Saturday nights home alone – or in my case, home under siege from Carol – but I enjoy our trips. We always have a quick drink after to dissect the performance. Make plans for the next one. Living close to a rep theatre definitely has its benefits.

I go through my little pre-driving ritual: check my seatbelt and the position of the seat (which I never move, but I have an overwhelming fear of feeling my feet can't touch the pedals halfway up the motorway), adjust the rear-view mirror and readjust it back to where it was before. Sit up straight, hands a perfect ten to two. I'm about to start the engine when a silver car pulls in from the other end of the street and stops outside number 7. I slump back down. A man – Lee – gets out. He looks around and I feel myself shrink down even further. It strikes me as an odd place to park, blocking the drive and his wife's car when there's space to nip in beside her. I watch as he walks up the drive, waiting for him to disappear inside before I start the engine and drive past.

But then he does a strange thing. He looks up and down the street again, almost furtively.

And then he rings the doorbell.

6.

He's forgotten his keys, I think. He was on his way somewhere in a hurry and realised he'd forgotten his keys, so he's rushed back to get them. Left the car on the street so he can make a quick getaway. Still, I don't move. I tell myself I'll leave as soon as he goes inside. Except that he doesn't. He stands looking at his feet, casting occasional furtive glances up and down the road. After a couple of minutes the two little girls spill out of the front door, backpacks on. They wave back at whoever's inside – Maddy, I assume – and head towards the car. Lee ruffles each of their heads and smiles down at them. They pile into the back seat and there's a bit of faffing around as – I assume – he fixes them into car seats.

My curiosity is piqued. Why did he wait on the doorstep? If he'd been out and just got back in time to take the twins to a playdate or wherever, wouldn't he have gone into the house? Maybe Maddy was angry with him for cutting it so fine and so he thought he'd keep his distance, give her time to cool down. Before I know what I'm doing, I'm following as he drives away. He crosses the High Street and weaves through residential streets, thankfully at a snail's pace. In a matter of moments we're on the road out of town. I mentally try to calculate how long I'll keep going for. If he gets on the motorway? If

61

he speeds up towards Birmingham? Scotland? I decide I'll stick with it so long as it's local streets. Nothing too scary. A couple of miles further along, we come to another, sadder looking High Street and he turns left into what looks like a small industrial estate and pulls up in front of an unfriendly-looking red-brick building with a sign declaring it to be 'Tumble Tots', a kids' soft play area and café. I'm almost on top of him before I realise he's stopping, so I have to overtake and keep going, watching in the mirror as he gets out and starts to unload the girls. So he's just taking them for an afternoon out. Nothing strange there. There is though, I know it. Why did he not go into the house? Why did he need to ring the bell?

I pull in and wait to see that they do indeed go inside. They'll be at least an hour, I imagine. Half an hour, anyway. I feel compelled to wait, see where they go next. Just to satisfy my curiosity. Because it looked to me as if everything was not rosy in paradise.

I can't just sit here, though, so I drive back out to the road, park up and wander to the main street. I don't even know what town I'm in. I buy yet another coffee in Costa and potter up and down the row of shops aimlessly. This is definitely it. I'll see where Lee goes once he leaves Tumble Tots and then I'll make my way home. I check my phone – it's nearly three o'clock. I can't hang around too much longer if I'm going to be on time for Verity.

I have to wait another twenty minutes for them to emerge once I'm back in my spot. I try to distract myself by reading a book on my phone, but it's impossible to concentrate. At one point Fay calls, but I can't face lying to her about where I am, so I let it ring out. And I definitely can't tell her the truth. She would worry herself sick if she thought I was down here sneaking around. I play Wordle and Quordle. Fuck them both up because I'm so distracted. I'm struggling through a Spanish lesson on my long-abandoned Duolingo app when I see the doors to Tumble Tots open and Lee and the twins barrel out, all laughing at something. They've obviously had a good time. It's sweet, I'm not going to lie. But sweet in that way that we all go a bit gooey about a man spending quality time with his kids but give the mothers no credit at all when they do it day in day out. I wonder if he's one of those Saturday dads who makes a huge deal about the one afternoon a week they spend doing solo childcare. To be fair, he looks as if he's genuinely enjoying himself and not because he thinks he has an audience.

I get a proper look at him while he's distracted. He's all arms and legs, ungainly, just like he looks on the videos. His features are sharp – long nose, pointy chin – and his face falls into a natural frown. But when he looks down and smiles at one of the twins who is gabbing away at him animatedly, everything softens. He pulls a face at her and she squeals with laughter.

He hasn't noticed me parked up along the way, and there's no one else around so I stay low in my seat. He packs the girls in the back of the car, pulling more faces to make them laugh. And then we're off again.

I try to stay back, like they do in police thrillers, a couple of cars behind. But then I get into a panic that I can't

63

see him indicate and I'm going to lose him, and this whole shambolic, shameful afternoon will have been a waste, so when I get a chance I catch up. I'm pretty sure he won't be checking his rear-view mirror to see if he's being followed unless he has a whole criminal life I have no idea about, interspersing singing along to Kylie with blowing people's heads off with a sawn-off shotgun. To be fair, all the prancing about on camera might well drive you to that.

We seem to be heading back towards Hanwood Lane so I relax and drop back a bit. This would be a nice place to bring up kids, I think, allowing myself to look around. Green space and fresh air and shops selling hand-crafted toys and tiny trainers that cost more than my own size sixes. I pull into the street just as he parks up across the drive again, so I cruise on by and round the corner, then manoeuvre into my spot at the top again, only this time slightly closer to number 7. If nothing else, my three point turns have had a lot of practice today. I'm tired. I want to be at home eating toast and drinking tea in my room. I can't face the theatre.

I watch as Lee helps the twins out. Walks them up the drive. Once again, he rings the doorbell. This is most definitely strange. I catch a flash of red hair as the door is opened. The girls jump up and down, babbling away. Then Lee leans down and hugs them both in turn and they go inside. The front door shuts abruptly, leaving him standing there.

He stands on the step for a moment. His shoulders droop. I sit up, energised by the sight of whatever it is that's happening. Something is rotten in the state of Maddy and Lee.

Lee turns and shuffles back to the car. He looks deflated. Miserable. It's probably the first time I've seen the real man, not someone putting on a show – for his kids, for the camera. It's impossible not to feel a bit sad for him. Once again, I follow as he drives off, this time up the High Street, past the shops, to the top where we turn right. A couple of hundred metres along, we turn right again into a small close with a row of small, scruffy seventies houses. At least, I start to turn and then realise that there's no escaping Lee seeing me in this dead end if I follow him. Even though he has no idea who I am, I have no desire to bump right into him. So I swerve out again and pull up on the pavement which, I'm sure, is highly illegal but I'm going to take my chance. When will I get another opportunity like this? I get out of the car and double back, enter the turning in time to see Lee disappear round the end of the little terrace of houses. I try to saunter along casually, although there is literally no excuse I can come up with as to why I'm here if asked. The last house has Flat 1 written on the front door. At the end, obscured from the road, where Lee turned, is a flight of metal steps leading up to the first floor, and an arrow on the wall pointing up to Flat 2. Is he living here? Have he and Maddy split up? But she posted a video this morning. Lee swimming by with his shark fin.

I feel suddenly nauseous. Excitement or anticipation. Maddy, my nemesis, the woman who is about to cash in on her superior knowledge of how to have the perfect marriage and the happiest family, is, it seems, living a lie. I can't believe my luck.

7.

Before I know quite what I'm doing, I'm ringing his doorbell. I need to establish whether what I think I've found out is true. If I don't, I might never get another chance. First, I nipped back to the car and scrabbled around in the glove compartment, coming up with a leaflet for the Cats Protection League that someone handed me in the street the other day. Now I clutch it in my hand, trying to look confident. I hear footsteps inside. A cough. The door opens and there is Lee. Tall. Gangly. Irritated-looking.

'Hi?' he says. A question.

'Oh.' I cough. 'I'm collecting for Cats Protection . . .' I wave the leaflet as if it were an ID badge, hoping he doesn't see how much my hand is shaking. I try to peer behind him. Is there anyone else there? Is he just visiting? Is this some kind of office he's set up where he can work in peace? (Does he even work? I have no idea.) I can see through an open door at the end of the short corridor that there's a double bed, unmade. There's a stack of what look like moving boxes in the corner. A pile of clothes on the bed. There's a faint smell of paint with an undertone of dirty laundry and takeaways. As if to prove a point, there are four Domino's pizza boxes stacked up beside the front door, and next to them a paint tray with a roller and crusty flakes of magnolia.

He hesitates. Trying to suss out, maybe, if I'm a con artist. 'Um . . . I'm not sure if I have anything . . .'

I wait.

'I actually don't think I have any cash. Sorry.'

'No problem,' I say. I try to make a joke of it. 'No one really does, these days. They need to give us card readers.' There's not much else I can do. I've seen enough to be pretty certain that he's living here. That he's recently moved in. That he's intending to stay a while. 'Thank you anyway.' I start to move off down the steps when he calls after me.

'Is there a website where I can make a donation? I feel bad . . .'

'Oh,' I say. That's nice of him. 'Yes. It's on here, I think.' I scan the unfamiliar leaflet. 'Yes. There, look . . .' I hand it to him. 'Thank you so much.'

Once I hear him shut the door behind me, I turn and snap a picture of the metal stairs, the scruffy front door. As if I'm going to need to look at it later to remind myself that what I've just seen is real.

And that's it.

Back at the car I'm shaking so much I can't stop, but I'm still parked blocking the pavement, so I need to at least move out of the way. I manage to pull round the corner, park up in a quiet street and lean back in my seat. Maddy and Lee are separated. She's about to do the rounds promoting her book, promoting herself, trying to take her happy families brand stratospheric, while her husband is living in a run-down one-bedroom on his own eating Pot Noodles and omitting to wash his socks. I have no idea what to do with this knowledge, but I feel as if I've found a golden ticket. I'm desperate to talk it over with someone but I don't know who. No one would understand, not really. I know that because I don't really understand it myself.

By the time I get home I'm exhausted. I texted Verity before I left to tell her I was unwell and wouldn't make the theatre. I know she'll go on her own, and she'll be fine, so I don't feel too guilty. I've ordered a Thai curry to arrive between seven and half past and I'm going to luxuriate in a steaming hot bath till then, a glass of wine in one hand and a book in the other. I can almost feel myself relaxing in anticipation as I unlock the front door. And then I hear the sound of Sam Smith coming from the bathroom. A splash of water. There's a hint of White Company Winter candle in the air. *My* White Company Winter candle. Carol has beaten me to it. I fight back tears of irritation. I could wait until after she gets out, but it'll take ages for the water to heat up enough again afterwards and besides, there's something about a damp bathroom, still steamy from someone else's ablutions, that creeps me out. It reminds me of being a kid and standing on the soaking bathmat after Daisy had finished. Her calling first dibs because she was older. Me having to wipe the opaque mirror clear. The window foggy with mist. A faint rim of scum round the water line. I pour myself an oversized glass of wine and retreat to my bedroom to wait for my food.

My mood is ruined. Why am I living like this? Hiding in my bedroom while an interloper splashes around in my bath like a captive walrus? I think about Maddy's beautiful home in the pretty little town by the river. OK, so her marriage might be on the rocks, but she has the twins, the house. Before I can stop myself, I'm writing an Instagram post. I put up the photo I took of the outside of Lee's flat.

Is everything not happy in the world of Maddy and Lee Fulford, of Fun with the Fulfords fame? It seems that Lee has moved out of the family home and into this bachelor pad!

I don't have any followers yet on this new account, but I tag all the people I can find who made disparaging comments on Maddy's last post. I add the various negative hashtags some of them have attached. There's no reason Maddy herself will ever see my post – I haven't drawn her attention to it – so she won't block me again, but there's a chance I might start a small ripple of gossip. That one of these people might investigate further. It's a horrible thing to admit, but it makes me feel better. Powerful. As if I have a say in my own destiny finally. I change the bot-like random configuration of numbers that I had chosen for my new account name for something more eye-catching – Truth Teller, with a bit of nonsensical punctuation between the two words to differentiate it from all the other Truth Teller accounts out there – and swap the grey head in the profile picture for a shot of the sea that I have on my phone, and then I put up the post.

I eat my Thai meal in my room. It suddenly strikes me that I'm not so different from Lee. I was so busy thinking that his life was sad, alone in his tiny flat, eating out of a carton and crying into his pillow for his lost relationship, that it didn't occur to me that we're not so dissimilar. At least he's not having to share a bathroom with a stranger. At least his freezer is his own. At least he has kids he can take to Tumble Tots on a Saturday afternoon.

So, who's the really sad one in this scenario?

8.

By the time I wake up on Sunday morning, my comment has elicited a few excited responses. All seemingly via the hashtags. *No!!!* says one. *Is this actually for real? How do you know?*

Wow!!! I have so many questions!!!! Imagine if this is true! #Mindblown says a second.

Another just says: *Proof??*

As they say: I feel seen. But there's nothing much more I can add. And a photo of a scruffy-looking flight of steps up to Flat 2 would not stand up in court as evidence that Maddy and Lee are over. I have nothing to back up my claims. I should have got more. Something concrete. Although I have no idea what that could be.

I turn on the bath taps as soon as I get up to make a coffee, staking my claim. I know that Carol loves to wallow on a Sunday morning. Well, she can be the one to wait for the water to heat up again today. When I get out nearly an hour later, after steadfastly ignoring the sounds of her huffing and puffing up and down the hall, I take my White Company candle into my room with me.

By Tuesday evening I'm feeling anxious. The small spark I ignited has fizzled out. My Instagram feed resounds with silence. Maddy posted a solo post again yesterday bigging up her new book. She talked about grabbing moments of solitude when you can, of not being ashamed to relish the times when you get a few moments alone. 'Luckily Lee is more than happy to take the girls to the park,' she said with a wistful smile. 'I know it's much harder for you ladies who are on your own, but maybe try and set up a circle with a friend or two. Schedule shared childcare to give one of you a break. Babies need their mummies to be as healthy as they can, and that means taking care of your mental as well as your physical health, ladies. And remember, visualisation. Imagine yourself to be calm and unruffled and it will happen! And breathe!' She takes a long slow breath in through her nose, opens her mouth and breathes out noisily. I scour the comments to see if any of her detractors who reacted to my post about Lee have responded. Just one so far. Lara K, who has a bunch of bright red tulips as a profile picture. 'Haven't seen much of Lee lately,' she writes, followed by a smiley winking face. I like her post.

Fay, Cally and I sit outside a Queen's Park wine bar while Jim babysits the two kids. Cally fondly tells us she left him covered in streaks of avocado, which Kieran was throwing at him as if to say how dare you insult me with this unmanly green shit? Where's my steak? Kieran is built like a little 1930s circus strongman. Alpha Baby. I'm finding that without being able to admit to them what I just did, I have precious little to say. My brain is so preoccupied with Maddy and Lee. Which is fine, because Fay is on one. I know that a lot – most, I always thought – of her tales of her irritation with Steve are for comedy value. Exaggerated to make Cally and me laugh. Or groan. Or both. Lately, though, there's been more of an edge to them. An underlying hint of bitterness. Fay, for all her front, can be endearingly old-fashioned. She always wanted to play out a relationship in the 'right order' – meet a man, fall in love, get married, have a baby – but I often wonder if she rushed into it all because of that. If she married Steve because he happened to ask her at the time she started getting broody. I wonder, too, if she's starting to regret that now. Not Kieran. She adores Kieran. Everyone does. He's impossible not to adore. Although the very things that make him so cute now: his heart-stoppingly beaming smile, his demand for everyone's attention, his utter conviction that he should get whatever he wants, will probably make him a monster in later life. I'm sure his father was a sweetheart at a year old. She'll stick with it though, Fay. Mother, father, baby all living together because that's how it should be. Even if it's toxic. I can't even fathom my own fucked-upness, let alone anyone else's, but I'm pretty sure her dad leaving when she was nine, and her mum falling apart, has something to do with this.

So Cally and I catch each other's gaze behind her back, an acknowledgement that we'll talk about this later, just the two of us, and we let her vent. It's the same old same old: nights out with the lads, his utter failure to act like a responsible father. I don't doubt that Steve loves Kieran, but he loves him like an irresponsible uncle. He comes home from work, hypes Kieran up with a bit of rough and tumble and then leaves Fay to deal with the fallout. I don't think he's ever read him a story or put him to bed. Stayed up all night with him when he had colic. The real stuff.

Because Fay never really wants to hear what we think (leave him, get away, start a new life with just you and Kieran) we just let her get it out of her system, tutting occasionally. By nine the evening is over. Cally is falling asleep in her lime and soda. Fay has opted to stay at Cally and Jim's so she can be with Kieran. It's miles away from where she lives in Wimbledon, so it's not worth her going there, uprooting him and trailing all the way home. I watch them climb into their Uber as mine pulls away.

On Wednesday, Maddy is back with a full-on production number. She wears a pink T-shirt with 'Mummy Bear' emblazoned on it, as she prances about in the kitchen to 'Pour Some Sugar on Me' by Def Leppard. I'm transfixed. The song choice is utterly bizarre. Meaningless to anyone under forty, surely. But she's gone for literal. She's making a cake, chucking ingredients into a bowl along to the chorus. The air is full of clouds of flour. Suddenly the twins appear at either side of her as if they've stepped up on stools behind the counter. Their tops – matching lilac – both have Baby Bear written on them. Maddy gives them a bowl each, and a wooden spoon, and they stir along. And then, just as I'm about to pause the video because I can see a woman mooching about in the showroom, looking at taps, Lee shimmies in behind them all. He's – of course – wearing a Daddy Bear T-shirt, and he wraps his arms round the three of them, kissing Maddy on the top of her head. Is this an old video? Has she got stockpiles of them just in case of emergencies like her marriage breaking down? Or . . . is it possible he's still going along with the illusion that they're a happy couple so as not to ruin her big chance? Maybe that's not as outlandish as it seems. This is their income after all – I still don't know if he works or not. Big money is apparently on the horizon. They're not going to let a little thing like a separation get in the way at this crucial stage.

'Excuse me . . .' I jump as a face appears round the door. I hit pause.

'Oh, sorry,' I say, blushing as if I've been caught out looking at porn. 'I was just . . . what can I help you with?'

Fifteen minutes and a very in-depth chat about swivel ranges and flow rates later, the customer has found the tap of her dreams and I can go back to the video. I scour it for clues as to when it was filmed although, apart from the fact that the sun is shining through the window and the weather is lovely at the moment, there's nothing. Lee looks manic, but then as he always looks like a man held hostage and made to dance or his wife and children get it, that's not evidence of anything. Either way, Maddy is presenting it as yet more proof of their enviable happy home. There's no coda across the bottom of the screen: Filmed last month before it all went to shit, or Mummy Bear and Daddy Bear are no longer together. At the end, as she closes the oven door on the tray of brownies and then, as if by magic, opens it again to find them cooked, she plugs her book again. So it's recent. She only mentioned the book for the first time a couple of weeks ago. So either Lee's departure is a very new development, or my hypothesis that they're selling us a pretty big deception is correct.

I click through the comments, ignoring the usual sycophantic suspects. There's no one, so far, questioning why Lee is there. Nothing from Lara K. My gossip probably now looks like just that: malicious rumour-mongering. An unfounded assertion to garner attention and followers for myself.

Before I know what I'm doing, I've booked two nights at the Premier Inn I spotted near the park in Marlow. I tell myself it's a weekend break, a way to get out of Carol's orbit, a bit of R&R. But I know what my agenda really is. I just don't want to admit it to myself out loud.

I make the mistake of mentioning that I'm going on a little trip to Fay and Cally when I meet up with them at the playground near Cally and Jim's in the afternoon, using up a half-day I'm owed because I let Zak have a morning off to look at wedding suits. It's a long way to come just to see my friends for forty-five minutes before they go off to the local library for Reading Circle – it took longer to get here – but it's worth it. I watch as Kieran is repeatedly helped down the baby slide while Frankie sleeps in his papoose. Fay's first reaction is that she could come too. Disaster, obviously. I'm going for a purpose. And not one I want to tell her about. Ordinarily, I would love the chance to spend time with her, to give her a break from Steve. I'd relish the hours spent with Kieran, the intense cuddles he gives when he's full of food and tired, climbing on to my lap like a hefty kitten. But this time, I make up a lie about going with Verity. I tell her Verity is going through a hard time and I'm trying to take her mind off things. They've never met. There's no reason they ever will. Fay's all sympathy and wants to know the details, so then I have to make up an existential crisis caused by her turning fifty and the first murmurings of the menopause.

'Has she grown a moustache?' Fay asks. Fay is obsessed by the menopause, the inevitable dark sweaty cloud in all our futures. She pores over articles about the symptoms – the more unlikely, the better – and regales us with the gory details. Burning mouth syndrome is her current favourite. 'It tastes as if you're eating metal all the time,' she said, wide-eyed with relish, when she first read about it. 'Hot, melting metal.'

'If she has, she shaves it off.' Thankfully she seems to believe my story. Why wouldn't she? What I'm doing makes no sense to me let alone anyone else, I imagine.

I find myself looking forward to my weekend away as if I really am just going for a holiday and not on a fact-finding mission. London suddenly seems to be stuffy and hot. Too crowded. Too angry. I'm still pissed off with Zak for stealing my customer and finding it hard not to let it show. It's not even about the money – it's not as if it's that much, a tiny percentage of a sale – it's the principle. I can't trust him any more. He seems oblivious, wittering away about his fiancée Darcy and their wedding plans any chance he gets. Usually I tease him, call him Bridezilla, quiz him about why he's settled on a particular choice of cutlery or napkins for the big day just to watch him go into a tailspin. Now I can't be bothered. I grunt acknowledgements when he speaks, but no more. At one point he asks me if everything's OK and I try to raise a single sardonic eyebrow, but I've never been able to pull that off, so I imagine I just look surprised.

On Friday I leave at two, telling him I have a headache. I don't care if he doesn't believe me. 'I hope you feel better,' he says as I grab my bag. He digs around in his desk drawer and hands me a pack of Migraleve. 'Just in case you don't have anything at home.' I instantly feel horrible. He's not a bad person. All he's really guilty of is doing his job by the book, something I should probably admire. He'll learn to loosen up.

'Thanks,' I say. 'Sorry if I've been a bit off all week. I just have stuff going on . . .'

He reaches out a hand and rubs my arm. 'That's OK. Take it easy this weekend.'

I'm tempted to enjoy my empty flat for a while before I leave. It's such a rarity. Carol's job in the accounts department of a car showroom is just around the corner, meaning she always leaves after me in the mornings and gets home before me at night. I could sprawl in the living room undisturbed. Rustle up a complicated curry. Luxuriate in the bath.

But I know I should get going before the weekend crowds build up on the M4. And, if I'm being honest with myself, I need to leave before I chicken out. Or come to my senses and realise what I'm about to do is ludicrous at best and inappropriate at worst. Actually, it might be criminal at worst. I'm pretty sure hanging around watching people, following and sneakily photographing them must be illegal. But all I want is some proof that Maddy is a fraud. It's only a month till the book comes out. I just need a photo or a bit of footage. Something I can post that might get a bit of attention from the other people who have a grudge to bear with her. That maybe a random blogger might see somewhere. Even if it has no more impact than Maddy seeing it eventually and knowing people are on to her, that will be enough. I might not be able to prevent her becoming successful, but I can at least take the shine off it.

Is it odd to be fuelled by revenge like this? Probably. It's an instinct we all understand, I think, the desire to punish those who have hurt us. To regain the upper hand. But few of us act on it. It's regarded as unseemly. Unhinged, even. Definitely unattractive. All the Uns. The negatives. But this is different. I'm only doing what a reporter might do, if they had a hint that a new about-to-be-the-next-big-thing influencer was a fraud. Yes, I'm doing it because I hate her. But all I'm after is the truth. I'm doing the world a favour.

I check in at the Premier Inn at about half past four. The room is neat and clean, with a view over the park. It feels weirdly liberating being in a hotel, as if I've stepped out of my real life for a moment. I could be anyone I wanted here. I could reinvent myself as a happy, fulfilled and functioning human being. Kids? God, no! They'd get in the way of my fabulous adventures! I'm a free spirit! I mean, look at this weekend. I just booked it on a whim. I couldn't do that if I had kids weighing me down!

I have no plan beyond mooching about in the town and maybe wandering past both Maddy's and Lee's homes. I'm not expecting to see anything this evening. Tomorrow I'm going to arm myself with coffee and sandwiches and stake out the family house. I have no doubt that unless they've all gone away for the weekend – which it strikes me now is entirely possible – Lee will visit his daughters at some point. And I intend to capture it all on video.

This evening though, I'm going to relax. Walk by the river. Maybe eat outside at one of the restaurants on the High Street. People-watch. I can feel myself beginning to unwind. It's such an unusual sensation that I realise how tense I must actually be most of the time. Braced against the world, even in my own home. Rigid with anticipated irritation. I stroll across the road and through the park. It's quiet, except for the families with little kids at the playground and a few school-age teenagers hanging out. It's too early for the post-work dog walkers. There's already a full flotilla of boats moored along the riverbank. I peer into them all, smiling at the couples sitting on the decks in the sunshine, almost all sharing a bottle of wine. It looks like bliss, I'm not going to lie. My chest aches. Maybe I could still have this, at least. Not all couples have children. Not all healthy, happy relationships are based on being a family rather than a duo. Isn't there supposed to be a crisis looming in the future because of the amount of people choosing a child-free life? There's going to be no one to look after the ageing population. I can contribute to the problem rather than trying to help solve it for once. Sod being responsible.

I stroll along the towpath, taking deep breaths of the fragrant fresh air. A couple of joggers trot past, a woman on a bike. An overexcited spaniel races up to me and jumps at my hand. The owner smiles an apology and I find it easy to smile back. 'Sorry, she's a bit muddy,' she says, and I ruffle the dog's bony auburn head. 'She's lovely.' Maybe I should get a pet, but it doesn't seem fair inviting a needy animal into my cramped space with its toxic atmosphere. They would probably pick up on the tension between me and Carol and take sides. I'm not sure I could take being rejected by my beloved labradoodle because my lodger was more liberal with the treats.

It's a textbook perfect day. The sky is blue (cerulean B14 in our Shaker cupboard paint option range) and it's warm enough not to need a jacket but with a fresh breeze coming off the river. There are ducks and swans and birds I can't identify quacking about on the water. Tiny ducklings follow along in a line. They look so vulnerable out there in the elements. It's a mystery to me how any wild animal ever makes it to adulthood, the odds seem so stacked against them. But still, they have that over-whelming instinct to reproduce. That it's worth the risks. I can relate to that.

I sit on a bench, my face tipped up to the sun. Close my eyes. I could almost let myself forget what I've come here for.

9.

I don't, of course. By half past eight on Saturday morning, I'm in my car loaded up with cheese and pickle sandwiches from Sainsbury's, a bottle of water, and a huge coffee from Starbucks. I've located the toilets by the café for emergencies. Last night, after my walk in the park, I ate in the Botanist, sitting in an armchair beside the floor-to-ceiling windows that open on to the street. It was full of after-work crowds celebrating the start of the weekend, but I took my time, sipping a cold beer and watching the world relax around me. When I left I took a long detour and walked up and down Hanwood Lane, but there was nothing to see. Back in my room I opened the bottle of Merlot I'd picked up in the supermarket with my supplies and nestled back on the duvet with my book. I woke up at midnight, still lying there in my clothes, and crawled under the covers, falling into a blissful deep sleep, barely stopping to take off my T-shirt and jeans. All that stuff they tell you about fresh air must be true.

I'm sure the way you feel about a strange town is completely coloured by the weather while you're there. Even the ugliest objects glisten in the sunshine. In the sparkling morning light, this already shiny place seems to glow. People smile hello at each other and no one says

'What are you looking at?' in a tone that suggests that a smile might be grounds to start a fight. Don't get me wrong, the area of London I live in is nicer than most. At least, I'm bordering on the nice bit. In walking distance. Nice adjacent. But this place takes things to a whole other level.

This time I park nearer to Maddy's house, with the front door firmly in view. If she spots me and thinks anything of it, she still won't know who I am or why I'm there. What's she going to do? Come out and confront me about why I'm eating a sandwich in my car? But I'm still going to try to remain anonymous. I don't want her or Lee to behave in any way differently because she thinks a devoted fan has somehow tracked her down. I also don't want to be arrested.

The first half-hour or so is fun. I watch as various neighbours take out their dogs or their rubbish. I listen to music. Eat one of the sandwiches that's supposed to be my lunch. After that, I start to get a bit fidgety. I need the loo but I don't want to abandon my post this early. I try to distract myself with Sudoku but it just makes me feel inadequate, so I read a book on my phone for a while, but concentrating is impossible.

I call my mum and tell her I'm having a lovely weekend away. I never really give her anything other than positive news. She's lonely. She worries about both me and Daisy and our life choices – or lack of choice in my case. She just wants us to be happy and I always feel a wash of guilt that I can't give her that. So I pretend. Daisy, on the other hand, likes to regale her with every trauma, big or small, in her overly dramatic life. It's always been a bone of contention between us that she's never outgrown the teenage habit of phoning home in a flood of tears when the slightest thing has gone wrong in her life, and then ending the call having more or less forgotten what it was that so upset her, leaving Mum fretting for days and reaching for the chequebook.

'Poor Daisy,' is a frequent conversation starter, and I always sigh and say, *What now?* This time I tell her that Daisy really doesn't need five hundred quid to go and learn circus skills in Bulgaria. What she needs is a job.

'This might help, though,' Mum says.

'With what? There's not a lot of call for unicyclists in Hackney.' Actually, now I say it I'm not sure that's true.

'She said she might be able to busk more. You know she can't cope with a nine to five.'

None of us can, I want to say. We're all exhausted and fed up and wishing we would win the lottery, even if we have jobs we quite like. Instead I just say, 'Make sure she pays you back this time.' Mum grunts in a non-committal way.

I describe the town to her. The river. The boats. Mum loves the countryside and refuses to leave her tiny village in Dorset to move nearer to either of us. But her social life has dwindled as old friends relocated and the one and only local pub shut down due to lack of custom. There's still a village shop but if – when, undoubtedly – that closes, she'll be cut off from everything. It's something we're all going to have to address in the future but she's still only seventy-six and fighting fit, so I've filed that worry away for now. She hates London. She can't understand why either Daisy or I would choose to live there.

'And how is Verity?' she says when I tell her the same lie I told Fay and Cally, although leaving out the part about Verity having a peri-menopausal crisis. Mum would want details and she'd see through my lie immediately.

'Good, fine. She's just popped back to her room and then we're going for a long walk along the towpath.' I think about how much I would love to be doing that right now, rather than sitting in the hot, stuffy atmosphere of my car. I could. I could just forget my ridiculous quest. The world's your lobster, I hear Fay say in my head.

Mum tells me about the plans for the village tricentennial celebrations. There's a WhatsApp group that has taken passive aggressive posturing to new heights. 'Listen to this. Hold on . . .'

I wait while she looks for something on her phone. All is quiet at the Fulford home.

'"As agreed, the celebrations must not extend over the boundary of number seventeen." That's Linda. You remember her,' she adds. '"This does not just mean tables and chairs, it means the bunting too."'

I laugh. 'Why doesn't she want bunting outside her house?'

'She's obsessed with bunting. She's already made them order some from John Lewis when everyone else was up for the children from the local primary school making it.

She thinks it brings the tone down. "Also, as agreed, the street party will end at eight p.m. sharp."'

'She loves the phrase "as agreed",' I say. Linda is my mum's nemesis. The pisser on all local bonfires.

'That's her trump card,' Mum says with a chuckle. 'She thinks if she says that we'll all think it's been signed off somewhere. Which it hasn't. I'm going to be out there till midnight, I don't care.'

'Good for you,' I say, smiling. 'Drape yourself in cheap bunting and stand in her driveway.'

I start as I see Maddy's front door open. I roll up my window. Prepare for action.

'And they're arguing about the vegetarian option in the sandwiches.'

Maddy emerges, the two little girls behind her. The three of them have matching ponytails and the twins are dressed in frilly pink ballet gear, again with their backpacks on their backs. Maddy is wearing a dress that looks as if it came from Stevie Nicks' dress-up box, but she somehow carries it off. None of them turn to look at me as they turn left out of the drive and walk off, holding hands. I wait a few moments and then slip out of the car following behind. 'At the moment they've decided on coronation chicken and roast beef, but someone suggested that the vegetarian option should also cover any vegans and it all kicked off.'

'A vegan in Little Hadham?' I say. 'It'll be communists next.'

Mum laughs her throaty laugh. I slow down. I'm in danger of catching my prey too soon. 'Anyway,' she continues, 'they're having a meeting about it on Tuesday. I'm going to go just for fun.'

'Bring up gluten-free.' Maddy and the girls turn on to the road that runs alongside the park. 'That'll probably finish them off.'

'I'll make notes,' Mum says. 'Report back.'

We say goodbye and I remember I'm supposed to be filming the evidence, so I take a quick video but it feels a bit weird and besides, what does it prove? That Maddy has taken the girls out on her own? So what? I need to be patient. Something will emerge. I follow as Maddy and her enviable gym-toned body leads the twins across the road towards my hotel. There's a tiny church hall a few doors along with a cluster of other mini ballerina girls in pastel leotards and tutus waiting to go in. I assume the class will be an hour or so long, and that Maddy is not the kind of mum to leave the girls to it, so I decide to wander up to Lee's place after a quick visit to the park loos. I double-check the time. It's five to ten, so the class must start on the hour.

The little close where Lee lives is quiet. At least, it's not quiet because it's right beside the main road, but there are no people about. I wander aimlessly around the back of the building, looking up at the windows. The one I assume is Lee's bedroom has dingy net curtains that sag slightly from a broken pole. I assume there's a limit to how much he wants to do to a place that is, presumably, temporary. A lick of paint but nothing that's a big outlay. That's understandable. I walk round the side, past wheelie bins labelled Flat 1 and Flat 2. I whip open the lid of the Flat 2 recycling bin and find it full of takeaway boxes – more Domino's, a white cardboard carton caked in flecks of rice, plastic trays with orange streaks of curry. I find myself wondering if you're allowed to put those in with your recyclables. I've never really understood the rules and I defy anyone else to tell me they do, either. There are beer bottles and wine bottles. The detritus of a miserable single person. I turn on video and film the contents and the number 2 on a white sticker on the side. This is good stuff, I tell myself, while trying to ignore a wash of shame creeping up around my ears. I'm about to walk on round to the front of the building and the metal staircase up to the top flat when I hear a voice and leap backwards squeaking.

'Can I help you?' Thankfully it's a woman. Not Lee, wondering why the Cats Protection League lady is going through his bins.

I turn round to see the ground-floor window is open and – I assume – the occupant looking at me. She's in her sixties, I'd guess. Face lined from smoking and sunbeds rather than age.

'Oh,' I say, playing for time, 'I was just . . . I went to put my coffee cup in the bin and I dropped my keys. I was just trying to fish them out.'

She frowns at me. 'It looked like you were taking a picture.'

I laugh nervously. 'I was using the torch on my phone. I found them,' I add, pulling my car keys out of my pocket and waving them at her.

She's having none of it. 'Why are you even round the back here anyway?'

'Um.' I feel myself gulp. 'I was dropping something off for Lee.' I flap a hand up the stairs and say a silent prayer that he won't decide on this moment to leave home.

Thankfully, Mrs Flat 1 breaks into a smile. 'Well, why didn't you say so? I thought you were up to no good.'

I decide to chance my luck. 'I haven't seen him since he moved in and I wanted to check he'd settled in OK. I mean, it's been, what . . .' I wait for her to fill in the blank and god love her, she does.

'Six weeks probably. It's nice to have him up there, not that he's said much more than hello. But it'd been empty for too long. Are you his girlfriend?' She scrutinises me.

'God. No. Just a friend. Ex colleague . . .' I need to get out of here before she starts asking too many questions.

'Something with the internet, isn't it?'

'Exactly,' I say, none the wiser as to whether she means Lee has a job in tech or if she's referring to his and Maddy's Insta career. I wonder again how much they must be earning to be supporting a family of four. A family that now has to run two homes. But if he had a good job he'd be living somewhere a bit nicer, wouldn't he? And he wouldn't need to fake his life with Maddy. Unless he's feeling guilty. For some reason I'd assumed that Maddy got bored of his sourpuss face and lacklustre dancing and threw him out, but maybe he's the one who left. 'Anyway, I'd better . . .'

I indicate towards the road.

'See you again, love,' she says, closing the window. I wave as I walk purposefully away. Ideally I need to get some footage connecting Lee to this property, but now is not the time to hang around.

I have a bit of time to kill, so I mooch around the shops on my way back down the High Street and end up buying a pretty flowery notebook in a smart stationery shop. I'm a sucker for notebooks. I can't resist them and I have literally nothing I need to use them for. It'll end up in a drawer with the others, but for today it makes me happy. I buy a huge cinnamon pastry in the café next to the church hall and another coffee and I wait at a discreet distance for Maddy to emerge.

It's almost ten past by the time they do, the twins now dressed in baggy sweatpants and hoodies like a couple of mini rappers. One pink on top and orange on the bottom and the other the opposite. I wonder if they argue about who wears which combination, or if one of them wants to go head to toe in one colour. Their tutus, I assume, are stuffed into their backpacks. I walk behind them to the park where they run on ahead and into the kiddies' playground. Maddy pushes them on the swings and waits at the bottom of the slide, and generally keeps herself to herself. There's nothing I can really do except watch from a nearby bench.

After twenty minutes, every part of me is screaming with boredom. I stroke every dog that walks past. When I look up from tickling a Jack Russell under the chin and chatting to its owner about the upcoming concert in the park, there's no sign of either Maddy or the girls. I panic. Look left towards the river, right towards the main road, but they're nowhere to be seen. I mutter a hasty goodbye to my new friend's owner and make a quick decision. I run towards the side road that leads to Hanwood Lane. If I've chosen wrong then my whole day will be out of sync. I'll be two steps behind Maddy and Lee and miss everything.

Thankfully I see them up ahead. Maddy's red hair. A twin each side holding her hands. This is where I came in last week, I think, looking at the time on my phone. Only then I was at the other end of her road in my car. If things play out in a similar way, then Lee will collect the kids for a daddy/daughter outing soon after they all get home and I need to be able to record the handover. And I need to be careful to wait where Lee won't see me. I don't think I'm that memorable, but he might have some kind of superpower for remembering faces. Tom was like that. We'd be walking down the street and he'd see a man at a bus stop and say 'Remember him?' to which my answer was pretty much always 'no'. 'He was at that pub we went to in Hammersmith. About five or six years ago. Sitting at the fruit machine all night.' I'd wait for an anecdote that would make the man stand out in my memory – he fell off his stool, or won the jackpot – but there never was one. His very existence was memorable enough for Tom. I can't believe he never found a career that could make use of this – apparently pointless – skill.

I have to be close enough to record the whole

handover, but as I'll need to get out of the car anyway, I don't need to sit within sight of the door – thus, hopefully, making myself less noticeable and, therefore, less suspicious – so once Maddy and the twins are safely inside I jump in the car and drive back along the road. I've dressed all in black today: black baggy sweats, black T-shirt, black trainers. I was going for inconspicuous, but I actually look as if I'm going to hold up a bank. I pull up outside Maddy's neighbour's, number 8, facing away from the direction I assume Lee will arrive from, assuming this really is like Groundhog Day. I might not be able to turn round and follow him without making it obvious, but I know he'll be back here later and his interactions with Maddy are more important than following him to Tumble Tots or wherever today's equivalent is.

At a couple of minutes before midday, Lee pulls up. I slide down in my seat, bury my head in my phone, but he doesn't notice me. He slams the door and stomps up the path. I climb out, make sure I'm recording video, and sneak up behind next door's hedge. I haven't yet seen any sign of life at that address, so I'm hoping they've gone away, but I have absolutely no excuse if I get caught. I stay as still as I can, just in case they have some kind of motion-sensitive doorbell camera and they're even now getting a notification that a strange woman is creeping round their front garden while they sun themselves in Barbados.

Lee waits, looking up and down the road as he did last time. I try to hold my phone steady. Maddy takes so long to answer that I start to wonder if she's out, but I realise she's been rounding up the twins so that she doesn't have to invite Lee in to wait. The girls throw themselves at their dad. Maddy and Lee scowl at each other over their heads.

'Make sure they're home in time for their nap,' Maddy says, her usually breathy voice devoid of any warmth.

'Obviously,' Lee says. 'Come on, girls.'

He turns and leads them towards the car. They trot behind, waving goodbye to their mum. I step back out on to the pavement, checking first that Lee is occupied settling the girls in their car seats, and I hotfoot it towards the main road. I can come back for my car later.

My heart is pounding, and not just from the exertion. No way do a happy couple communicate like that about their beloved children. This is gold.

10.

This is not my first time skulking about spying on an unsuspecting subject. I'm not proud of that fact. A couple of months before Tom left me for Maddy, I had suddenly started to worry about him and a female co-worker – Lola – and whether something might be going on between them. I can't even remember now what those suspicions were based on. In all honesty, it might just have been her name. It's hardly forgettable. So, when he'd begun to drop it into conversations here and there my ears had pricked up. I was feeling insecure. Unwomanly because I didn't seem able to conceive, unsexy because Tom and I spent way too much time discussing the rights and wrongs of the ways and times of day we slept together to ever feel spontaneous or even slightly horny. I was a seething mass of baby-making hormones that had nowhere legitimate to go. I cried at everything: an advert where an old man found a teddy in a puddle and tracked down the distraught child who had lost it, Tom making a joke that the kid threw it away as soon as the old man left because he'd chucked it in the puddle deliberately in the first place, a 'Cat Found' poster on a lamppost, a woman in a shop telling me I had nice hair. You name it, I would cry at it. I didn't feel like myself, and I didn't recognise the person I felt like.

I tried to talk to Tom about it, to explain that I knew I was being irrational, but could he, maybe, possibly, reassure me that there was nothing awry? Just this once. To be fair to me, my default had never been to be jealous. I had always trusted Tom. I tended to trust people instinctively until they gave me a reason not to. I had never seen every woman as a threat. That thought was, frankly, insulting to me. I would hate for a colleague's partner to assume I must be lusting after their husband just because I was a female in close proximity. But, like I said, I was not entirely in control of my emotions.

You would think that Tom would have taken all that into consideration, my mitigating circumstances. I thought he would hug me and tell me that he understood. That he was happy to put my mind at rest. Instead, he'd growled like a dog caught with his face in someone else's dinner. How dare I accuse him? How could I think that of him? Could I not even trust him to go to work and do his job without straying?

And that was when my suspicions really ratcheted up a notch. I had no idea why he was being so defensive. Suddenly in my fragile mind he didn't just have a crush on Lola, they were having a full-blown affair. I had no idea what to do about it. I couldn't confront him without any evidence. So I called the company and found out Lola's surname. She was easy to track down on Facebook, posting plenty of pictures of herself with her inoffensive-looking husband and two kids aged about eight and six. She was nice looking, but nowhere near as glamorous and exotic as her name had made her sound.

I couldn't imagine her having an affair with anyone, to be honest. I had to be sure though. So, I followed her home from work one night, when I knew Tom was at his mum's. It's harder than you think, stalking someone across London on public transport in the rush hour, but eventually the bus dropped us off in Ealing, and I walked behind her to a small but cosy-looking terraced house. I waited till she let herself in, just to be sure I hadn't just trailed her on a random visit to a friend's, and then I trudged back to Camden. After that, for a couple of weeks, whenever Tom worked late or had a night out I would find myself drawn to her street looking for evidence. But after a while I had to concede that she was always home and so was her husband. In fact, they seemed to have no social life at all. I felt a bit sad for them after that.

I felt stupid, of course I did. Lola was just a work colleague, and one who looked like she'd be a nice one at that. When had I ever resented Tom having friends? I stopped my evening expeditions and tried to make it up to Tom by being as much like old Iris, the one he loved, as I could manage.

Later, of course, I realised that I hadn't got it as wrong as I'd thought I had. This would have been around the time that Tom met Maddy. I had obviously picked up on some subconscious tell. Maybe he wasn't having an affair, but he was thinking about it. He was considering it. He was feeling pre-emptively guilty, as if I'd seen into his thoughts and caught him cheating there.

I I.

After a quick refresher trip back to the hotel room, I'm back at my post. I've turned the car round so that I can follow Lee after he drops the kids off, but I'm still close enough to be able to jump out and start recording when I need to without missing anything crucial. To change things up, I sit in the back seat. Less obviously notice-able when he pulls up. I'm only just in time. Lee's silver car swoops in just as I'm settling down. I start my phone's video, poised like a coiled spring.

One of the twins is a bit grizzly when Lee lifts her out of the car. He chucks her under the chin and ruffles her hair. She fights a smile and my heart melts. As soon as he leads them to the path I reach for the door. I rattle the han-dle twice. Nothing happens. The child lock has come on.

'Jesus. Fuck.' I clamber over the centre console and into the front, all pretence of looking legit forgotten. Thankfully I can hear Maddy and Lee still hissing at each other in loud whispers as I ease my phone round the neighbour's rose bush.

'. . . just tired,' he is saying angrily. 'It's too much for them all this running around.'

'Maybe if you just took them for lunch instead of Tumble Tots . . .' she snaps.

'Maybe if you didn't let them wear themselves out at

the playground after ballet. I just want to have fun with them. I can hardly take them to my flat, can I?'

I hear myself gulp. Lee has just admitted on camera – my camera – that he now has his own place. This is better than anything I ever imagined I'd get. Honestly, I've missed my calling. I should have been a detective, or one of those investigative reporters who used to try to catch drug-abusing celebrities out in the nineties by pretending to be a rich sheikh. I can see that my hand is shaking so hard that what I'm filming must look like earthquake footage. I reach out my other hand to steady it and accidentally knock the phone to the ground. I freeze, waiting for Lee or Maddy to notice the noise.

'We need to film two tomorrow,' Maddy is saying, oblivious. Shit. I need to get this. I reach a hand down into the flower bed, try to ignore the thorns scratching at my fingers. 'So, let's say eleven.'

Lee sighs as I raise the camera back up. 'Sure. Anything I need to bring?'

'It's all under control,' she says, sounding a little softer.

'OK . . .' Lee says, and I realise they're winding up, so I race back to my car and throw myself into the driver's seat. I start the engine and back further along the street so I'm not right in his face when he gets into his own. I'm awash with adrenaline. I can barely control my limbs. Lee sticks to the script and turns the car around, driving up the High Street in the direction of his flat. I prop my phone up on the dashboard to record the journey and follow. I'm ready for him to turn right into the small dead end where he lives, and I pull up on the pavement again then hang back, recording him trudging towards the stairs to his flat. I tiptoe along behind, angling the screen round the corner, capturing the whole thing for posterity. His slumped back going up the stairs. The defeated sag of his shoulders.

I'm out of there before he can turn round.

I walk round the nearest corner and sit on a wall. I feel triumphant. I can't believe what I've managed to record. At least I hope I have. I fumble with my phone to check but my hands are shaking so much I almost drop it again. Finally I manage to accurately stab the camera icon and there it is – a little line of videos. I ignore the one of Maddy on her way to dance class and start the next one – Lee picking up the girls – and turn the volume right up. The sound is terrible and you can hear me breathing heavily, but all the words are audible if you concentrate. There's no doubt I have the weapon here that could damage Maddy's shiny armour.

I shove my phone deep into the drawstring waistband of my trousers. Tie my soft (black, obviously) cardigan tightly around me to anchor it there. I'm not risking it going astray. I know I need to move but I'm struggling to calm my breathing. I'm desperate to get back to my hotel room, to really see what I've got and decide what to do with it.

Evidence. That's what I have. Irrefutable evidence that Maddy and Lee's marriage is over, or as good as. That she's unable to practise what she preaches. An hour or so later, I have three shaky but neatly trimmed down videos: Lee collecting the twins, dropping them off again and discussing filming a new dance routine tomorrow, and his lonely return to his shabby bachelor pad.

I decide to sleep on it tonight. I want to make sure that I can live with whatever decision I make. Although it's tempting, I'm not out to completely ruin her life, I just want to take the gloss off it, to have her feel what it's like for someone to swoop in and pull the rug out from under her. She'll get over it. She just might have to reinvent herself a bit. Rethink her ambitions.

Same as I did.

To distract myself, I go for a walk – the formerly fictional walk I told my mum was about to happen earlier – through the park and along the towpath. Once the line of moored boats runs out there are just fields and water, and people walking their dogs. Teams of rowers practise on the river. I wish I had someone with me to share it with, in that way that sharing an experience makes it feel real. There are witnesses. I should come down again, I think, for a holiday with Fay or Cally. No hidden agenda. Just walks and meals out and relaxing. My life in London is so frantic. It's how I like it, don't get me wrong. I've always packed my diary full of fun distractions – even more so since Carol arrived, obviously, and hanging out at home became more of a stress than something to be enjoyed. But I should get away more. It occurs to me that I could go home now. I booked myself in to the Premier Inn for two nights in case I couldn't get what I needed in one day. I suppose I could spend tomorrow morning filming Lee arriving and leaving, maybe trying to find a way round the back in the hope that one of the videos they're making is an outdoor one, but there's no point. I'm not trying to compile evidence for a court case. I have enough to start some rumours. I have no reason to be here any longer. Except to actually have the relaxing weekend break that I claimed I was having.

Despite finding most of Daisy's attempts at self-help pointless at best, and exploitative at worst, there is one coping mechanism she showed me after Tom left and I found myself incapable of moving on or making any decisions, that I find quite effective and I decide to use it now. When presented with two options that you can't decide between, consider both 'without judgement' and see how your body reacts. Basically it means picture each scenario and see how you feel. It's hardly rocket science. I walk till I find a bench, sit and close my eyes. I imagine myself back home in my flat, hiding from Carol in my tiny bedroom that gets no sunlight after eleven in the morning, and I feel my stress levels rise immediately. I know I'll spend the whole drive home with my shoulders round my ears planning how to get from the front door to my room via a quick trip to the kitchen without bumping into her. Consequently, if I do run into her I'll probably snap at her for no real reason except that she exists and she's in my space, and then spend the rest of the day feeling guilty. I don't even need to do the second half of the exercise to know what the obvious decision is. I'm staying here.

I ask myself what I would be doing now if I really had

chosen to come for a holiday. Walking the towpath, obviously, exploring the town, looking at the houses, pottering round the shops. Just existing in the moment and taking it all in. I stand up and turn back the way I came, determined to make the most of the afternoon.

Hours later, after I've dropped off bags of random purchases at my hotel – a canvas bag, a hand-thrown pottery vase, a box of homemade truffles – and had a shower, I sit outside a restaurant in a little cobbled fore-court, headphones in, and watch all of the videos on my phone. I trim them all down a bit more and then open them one by one in an app that allows me to add shocked face emojis at salient moments and lines of text. 'Did you hear what he just said???' one of them screams just after Lee has mentioned his flat. I have no idea what I'm doing really, but Fay, who loves a pouting Insta video as much as a *Love Island* hopeful, gave me a crash course the other day although with no idea of the real reason why I needed it. She didn't even ask. She just assumed I finally wanted to join the fish-lipped masses.

I eat little bowls of harissa hummus and spicy prawns with warm flatbreads and sip an ice-cold glass of Pinot Grigio. I take a photo of the food and the fairy lights against the darkening sky, but I don't know who to send them to. In the end I text them to Daisy and she sends back a smiley face. My phone beeps and I see she's sent me a picture of her own dinner – a greasy cheese toastie – on the tiny café table on the little section of flat roof she's commandeered by climbing through the land-ing window of the house where she lives. For all her obsession with herself and her own wellbeing, Daisy eats like an eighteen-year-old student away from home for the first time. I text her a laughing face.

Videos finished, I try to concentrate on people-watching but I'm too distracted to lose myself in it like I usually do. I'm itching to post them, but I have to stick to my promise to myself to wait until morning. To strike my blow with a clear head, not two glasses of white wine down. There's a family at a nearby table, the little girl in a highchair, her parents taking turns to make sure some of what's on her plate makes it to her mouth. She laughs with delight every time she succeeds in hitting the spot. I look away, feeling tears form in my eyes.

I don't know if I can do it. I don't know if I can ever be that person who knowingly shatters someone else's life whatever they might have done to me. I've always thought I was fundamentally a good person. Kind. I'm not sure who I am if I give that up.

On my walk back to the hotel, Daisy calls. 'Please stop eating that shit,' I say, laughing when I answer. 'I need to teach you how to cook.'

'I have something to tell you,' she says, and my heart sinks. She's finally joining a cult. For some reason, this has always been my biggest fear with Daisy. She's so suggestible, so desperate to create meaning where there isn't any. I feel as if anyone could persuade her to do anything if they promised her it would realign her chakras. That one day she'll call me and tell me I'll never see her again and that, by the way, her name is now Sister Moonbeam.

'God,' I say. 'What now?' I can't help myself.

'No, it's good. You're the first person I'm telling.'

'OK.' I detour down through the park towards the river.

'I'm pregnant,' she says, triumphantly. I stop in my tracks.

'How? I mean . . .'

'Christ knows. I wasn't trying.'

Honestly, if I believed in God I would think he had a warped sense of humour.

'Wow,' is all I can come up with.

'Aren't you going to congratulate me?' That's another thing about Daisy. For all her woo woo about love and light she has skin as thick as a rhino when it comes to other people's feelings.

'I guess. Are you happy?'

'I don't know. I haven't digested it yet. I literally found out this morning.'

'How long, do you know?' The question I really want to ask is who the father is. Daisy hasn't had a relationship for a while, so far as I know. But that feels as if it would seem judgemental.

'Eleven weeks. I know for definite because . . . you know . . . that's the only time in living memory.'

'And you only just found out? Didn't you wonder where your periods had gone?'

'Not really.'

I force myself to sound positive. 'OK. Dais, this is amazing. Congratulations.' I want to cry. I want to say why you and not me? 'Is he . . . I mean, have you told him?'

'I wouldn't know how. I think his name was Leaf. It was at that reiki retreat I went to, do you remember?'

I remember that it cost Mum three hundred and eighty-five pounds. 'You're not still in touch?'

'No. I mean, I wasn't expecting this, obviously. I should have it, right?' she says as if she's thinking about buying a new yoga mat.

'What? I mean . . . do you want to? It's a big responsibility . . .' Daisy has never expressed any interest in having kids. I mean, never. The opposite, in fact. Why tie yourself down like that? she used to say. Plus there are too many people in the world already.

'Search me,' she laughs. 'What do you think?'

She's infuriating. No, more than that, she's insensitive and self-centred and flat-out unfeeling. 'How can you be so fucking blasé? You know I was trying with Tom. You know how much I wanted kids.' Mortifyingly, I burst into tears.

'Shit, Iris, I didn't even think . . .'

'Of course you didn't,' I interrupt. 'You never do.'

'I'm a year older than you. You still have time.'

'With who?' I shout. A young mum steers her toddler away from me. 'Should I just go out and pick up some random bloke who doesn't even have a real name? Maybe I should start sponging money off Mum to learn some completely useless life skills and get someone to knock me up at the same time?' I'm overreacting, I know I am. I shouldn't have said that. But I can't help myself.

'Uncalled for,' she says.

I hang up and turn my phone off so she can't call me back. It's not fair. It's not fucking fair. Everyone else seems to find it so easy. Even if they don't even want to.

Even if they have one-off sex with a man called fucking Leaf who they've known for five minutes and whose surname they haven't even bothered to ask. I'm not judging my sister's actions, by the way. All power to her. I don't care if she shags Leaf, Tree and Bush all in one afternoon. She's a single grown woman, her body is hers to do what she wants with. Except get pregnant with a baby she doesn't even know if she wants, whose fate she'll probably decide based on its potential star sign or the alignment of the planets the night it was conceived. A baby she'll never be able to provide for with her car-crash itinerant life. I could have given a child a beautiful home. I would have.

If Maddy hadn't got in the way.

I know what I need to do. I line up the first little film – Lee collecting the girls. He rings the doorbell. Waits. The twins throw themselves on him. 'Make sure they're home in time for their nap,' Maddy says. 'Obviously,' he snaps back.

Is it odd that Lee Fulford has to ring his own doorbell? I write. Then I add in all the anti-Maddy hashtags, checking the list I've made in my new notebook. Tag my little band of haters. I check the time. Twenty past five. That seems to me like a perfect time on a Saturday afternoon when people might be lounging around, checking their social media. I hit Share and wait for the post to appear on my page. I know it might be hours till anyone sees it – I only have three followers at this point but I've planted my bomb. I've lit the fuse. Now I just need to wait for it to go off.

12.

There's been a diplomatic incident. I opened the freezer when I got home tonight and a pack of Carol's 'restaurant quality' fish fingers was sitting on my side. I tried to move it across, but her designated area was crammed full and even if I squashed everything down it wouldn't fit. Before I could stop myself, I was stomping into the living room with the offending box in my hand. Carol was sitting on what I had always thought of as my side of the sofa, feet up, plate of pasta on her lap, TV on.

'Oh, hi,' she said when she saw me. She hit pause. 'You OK?'

'Could you not put stuff on my side of the freezer?' I waved the box at her. I knew I was being unreasonable but I was powerless to tone it down, it seemed.

'It's only temporary.' She pulled a quizzical face. *What's your problem?* 'I didn't realise how full it was in there and I could hardly leave them out to go off.'

'You don't need ten boxes of garlic bread. No one needs ten boxes of garlic bread. And why aren't you at least eating some of it now?' I indicated her spaghetti. 'If you know you have too much stuff in the freezer, why wouldn't you prioritise eating that?'

'I didn't realise it was such a big deal,' she said, and I had no option but to say, 'Well it is,' and stomp out, stopping only to stuff the offending item back in the freezer. Back in my room, I felt ridiculous. I knew I was acting like a child and that I should probably go and apologise, but the truth was, however petty it seemed, I thought I was in the right. Sharing a flat with someone is all about boundaries. It's a delicate ecosystem. One packet of rogue fish fingers could bring the whole thing to the brink of collapse.

Now I can hear Carol in the kitchen shoving stuff around. There are thuds and loud sighs. I resist the urge to go and see what she's doing but, once it all goes quiet, I venture out there and see a half squashed, unopened carton of garlic bread poking out of the bin. In the freezer drawer the fish fingers now sit on Carol's side. It's like being a teenager again, sharing a bedroom with Daisy and fighting over dressing table space. Me, once, drawing a line in lip gloss down the middle and lining up all her toiletries on the other side of it. Balancing the can of hairspray we shared precisely in the middle. I push Daisy out of my mind. I don't want to think about her now.

There's a sudden flurry of activity on my Instagram. Lara K has reposted my video (how do you do that? I didn't even know you could. I make a note to ask Fay) and several comments have appeared. All incredulous. All excited. I feel a rush of adrenaline. It's working. Now I have their attention I post the second video – Lee dropping the girls off again and making arrangements to go round the next day. This is the one where he mentions his flat, and where I've added on some text to make sure no one misses it. The quality is terrible, both picture and sound, but maybe that adds an authenticity.

Listen carefully and you'll hear Lee mention that he now lives in his own flat! More of that later! Is that the end for #Madlee ???

I've made up 'Madlee' and I'm quite proud of it. I wonder if it'll catch on.

This time the reactions come more quickly. I mean, it's not exactly a tsunami but you can tell there are a few people who've been waiting to see what I'll post next. I've gone from three followers to twenty-eight. It's impossible not to feel powerful.

There are questions, questions, questions.

Who are you?

Where is this?

Is this recent?

Are you their neighbour?

WTAF????

I bask in the glory for a while. Google Maddy's name to see if any rumours are rumbling. Nothing so far. I wonder if I should start a thread somewhere. There are forums where influencers are hung out to dry, apparently. Threads of pure vitriol. Fay loves reading them – but I decide waiting is better. Once I've posted the last of my videos tomorrow I'll see whether I need to help the rumours along. I hope not. Not just because I don't particularly like the version of myself who would do that, but because I wouldn't really have a clue how.

I need to go just far enough and not a step further. I don't want to set in motion anything I then can't look at myself in the mirror for. I unpack my weekend bag, then sit back on the bed with the notebook and pen.

What do I want? I write at the top of a new page. I need to clarify my thoughts, make clear in my own head what my motives are. Automatically, as if it has a mind of its own, my hand forms the words *A baby*. I scribble them out.

To pay Maddy back for what she did to me.

To expose her as a fraud.

To never have to think about her again.

A better life, I add.

A flat with no lodger.

To be happy.

I stop and wipe a tear away before it drips on to the page.

Suddenly feeling guilty, I pat the underneath of my eyes and then venture out of my room to find Carol. She's still where I left her, sprawled on the sofa, one of the eight million soaps she has on series link playing in front of her.

'I'm sorry I had a go at you,' I say to the back of her head. I wonder for a moment if she's fallen asleep. Then she pauses the TV and I brace myself.

'Oh god, don't worry,' she says, and the relief is almost overwhelming. 'I threw a hissy fit and chucked a box of garlic bread in the bin, so we both overreacted.' She laughs and I find myself laughing with her.

'You could at least have given it to me. I'm starving.'

She snorts. 'It's probably still only half thawed out. Help yourself.'

'I'm glad we're OK,' I say.

''Course we are. I'll curb my frozen food buying urges for a couple of weeks. Promise.'

I turn to go. 'OK. Well, see you later then.'

'Fancy joining me for a drink?' she says, brandishing her glass. 'I can turn this shit off.'

I panic. 'Oh. Um. I promised my mum I'd call her in a minute. Another time, though.'

'Of course,' she says. 'Another time.'

By the next morning, my followers have doubled (fifty-six, woo hoo) and there's a lot of activity on the hashtags. Not just that, but I have a private message from Lara K.

I have so many questions! How did you get this stuff? Do you actually know them??? Who are you??? Omg this could totally blow up her perfect goody goody image! Props, gurl!

I feel like a super hero: polite kitchen designer during the week and avenging villain at the weekends. I agonise over how to respond. I don't want to give too much away, but I want to keep her locked in.

Hi, Lara. It was just luck! I write back. *But once I realised what a fraud she is I had to try to get evidence. She's a complete fake, but you know that already! I have one more video coming. Get ready!*

I'm dying!!! she sends back.

The forums are suddenly alive with the sound of gossip. My videos are the talk of the anti-Maddy brigade. I spend most of the day in the back office looking at my phone, watching the hysteria and my follower count rise. I'm planning to post the final video tonight at six, get people's attention on their way home from work. I'm meeting Cally for a quick drink at half past, a regular Monday night catch-up we do if we haven't seen each other all weekend. Except that she texts at twenty past five to tell me she can't make it. *Frankie is being really grizzly*, she writes. *I just don't feel I can go out and leave him.*

It's fine! I write back. *Hope he's OK xx*

It's the fourth out of the last five Mondays that Cally has had to cancel. Not that I'm counting. I understand. I do. I just worry I'm going to be the eternal hanger-on. A charity case she and Fay have to find time for every now and then while their real lives take up most of their energy. Forever Auntie Rissa the add-on. I know I'm being ridiculous. Parents don't stop having friends just because they're now parents. But maybe for a few years at least it's easier to spend time with other people who are in the same boat as you. Who know first-hand what the sleepless nights and cracked nipples and hours of baby talk do to your psyche. Unless you're Steve, of course. In that case, you just carry on as usual.

God, I need to stop feeling sorry for myself.

Lara is still my most invested ally, so I send her a DM at ten to six: *Coming up on the hour!* Almost immediately she replies. *Literally hovering over my phone!!!* I lock the shop up at five to and sit in the back office to concentrate. I can't imagine there'll be a last-minute rush on waste disposals but it's tough luck if there is. I check three times that I've tagged everyone I need to tag and included every hashtag, and then, bang on six, I press Post. *How the mighty have fallen!!! Lee Fulford's new home!*

I watch it back. Lee trudging from his car, up the metal stairs to his flat and sticking the key in the door. It's pretty sad, if I'm being honest. But needs must.

By the time I get home armed with a mini food shop, I've got another message from Lara: *Holy shit! Honestly, you are my new hero! I've been trying to take down that smug b*tch for years!* And then: *Read my blog!* There's a link. I click on it excitedly. It's called 'No Filter' and it seems to be dedicated to taking apart influencers she believes are fake. Fay would love this, I think, and then I realise I can show it to her, I don't need to mention my own involvement. Today's entry is entitled *Is the fun over for Maddy and Lee Fulford?* I decide to prolong the anticipation. It feels like Christmas Eve. I'm desperate to get to the main event but I don't want the exquisite torture of the build-up to end either. Carol isn't home yet, so I make myself fresh tortellini (three minutes on the hob, I decide I can risk it), pile some parmesan on top and pour myself a bottle of Peroni. I take it all to my room and settle on the bed to savour the moment.

This weekend some, let's say, surprising videos surfaced on Instagram, courtesy of the Truth Teller account, it begins.

That's me, I think, my heart fluttering. I'm Truth Teller.

Videos showing that super mum and know-all wife Maddy Fulford — soon to be releasing her first book Making Family Fun — might have been faking it all this time. Who would have thought it? (me, that's who!!). Let's look at the evidence, and kudos once again to Truth Teller for filming these videos . . .

She then goes through each of my films to which she's added subtitles, and analyses what's being said. I skim-read this part. I'll come back to it later.

I think we can all agree that the evidence is pretty damning. Even if their split is recent, Maddy has a duty to be honest with the legions of fans who hang on her every word. How can she lecture us all about how to have the perfect marriage if hers is on the rocks?

Big questions, fellow sceptics. Tell me what you think . . .

Then there's an update from half an hour ago.

If you need any more proof of what a charlatan she is check out this new video on her Insta, posted just five minutes ago! We're on to you Maddy.

Did she? The notification must have come and gone while I was picking up my phone and putting it down again to tuck into my pasta. As I'm staring at my screen trying to work it out, it suddenly appears. *Fun with the Fulfords has posted a new video*. I suppose it isn't instantaneous. I have no idea how these things work. I click on it. It must be one of the two they were planning on filming yesterday. This one has the three of them – Maddy and the twins – all wearing big glasses and leafing through books. The song is 'Paperback Writer' by The Beatles. All three nod their heads from side to side along with the music as they stare at the pages glumly. They're lined up on one side of the kitchen table, all wearing shirts and ties, hair in high bunches. Partway through, Lee arrives, same big glasses, hair standing on end like a mad professor. He holds three copies of Maddy's book in his hands and, one by one, he takes away the volumes they're reading – all covered in brown paper and with *War and Peace* written on them in black Sharpie, I see now – and hands them each a copy of *Making Family Fun*. The mood changes. They're ecstatic. They flip the pages over, big smiles on their faces. Maddy looks at the camera. 'Family time is the most precious time there is. These little ones will grow up so quickly, and what's more important than making happy memories with them now that they can take with them their whole lives? In my new book I'll tell you how to get the most out of every second you spend with your loved ones . . .' She places an arm round each of them and gazes up at Lee adoringly. He puts his hands lovingly on her shoulders. '. . . because nothing is better than being with your tribe.' A big heart fills the screen, and then the words '*Making Family Fun* by Maddy Fulford. In all good bookshops June 22nd.'

Pretty damning under the circumstances, I would say.

I send the link to Fay along with one to No Filter. *Get a load of this!!*

By the time I decide to call it a night, having watched the comments rack up underneath Lara's blog all evening like it's the ticker tape at the Stock Exchange on the eve of the crash, there are two further articles floating around the internet: *Is Maddy Fulford really a fraud?* by a blogger called Maliciously Ella on a page named Too Much Information, and another entitled *The Fake Family Life of Maddy and Lee Fulford* on an anonymous page called Airbrushed. They're both rehashes of Lara K's piece, neither with an acknowledgement to her, although I get a mention in both.

It's happening, I think.

I've done it.

13.

Fay and I are walking in Richmond Park, Kieran in the buggy. It's a beautiful evening, still only just summer with rumours of a mini heatwave on the way. Kieran wears a bucket hat like a little nineties Oasis fan. It's idyllic, except that Fay is crying and trying not to let her son notice. I have never seen Fay cry. Not if you don't count those drunken hysterical late nights we all had in our twenties when it was impossible to even remember what had started us off in the first place. She hates showing any weakness, she always says so, even though both Cally and I have told her we would never see it as that. She's watched both of us break down enough times to know we think it's both normal and acceptable. I've even tried to encourage her before, worried that the way she bottles everything up isn't healthy, but she's steadfast in her stoicness. So now I'm staring at her wondering what to do. It's like she's been taken over by aliens. I reach out a hand and put it on her arm. She shakes her head at me as if to say she'll lose it completely if I show her any sympathy.

'He's going on another stag weekend,' she says. We all breathed a sigh of relief a few years ago when the last of Steve's close mates got married and his days of coming home after a couple of days away – once even a week – sweating booze, smelling of strange perfume and protecting his phone for a few weeks as if it contained government secrets were hopefully over. Fay had always been remarkably forgiving in a kind of 'boys will be boys' way, which infuriated me and made Jim – who has only ever been to stag dos of the 'eating nice food and doing something like go-karting if they're really crazy' variety – almost explode with the disservice she was doing to all decent men out there. For all her front, I knew it ate away at her. She would snap at me or Cally if we tried to suggest that Steve was out of order, which is always the way I know Fay is deeply upset by something. I think she just decided to wait it out. That eventually there would be no more mates left who hadn't settled down. Or maybe Steve would grow up. Stranger things have happened.

'Whose?'

She shrugs. 'Some bloke he works with. I think he's been out for a drink with him like twice. He barely knows him. They're going to Riga. Three nights. Twelve of them.'

'Fuckssake, Fay,' I say in a loud whisper in the hope that that won't end up being Kieran's first word. 'You know it's not OK, right? What would happen if you just asked him not to?'

She shakes her head. 'He'd guilt-trip me. Tell me all blokes do it and it's just a bit of fun and all that crap. Make me feel like a jealous saddo.'

'You do know that's not true, don't you? All blokes do not go off to shag random sex workers while their wives stay home and look after the baby.' I'm slightly taken aback that I've said this. None of us have ever acknowledged out loud that this is actually what Steve is doing in the guise of 'partying'. Not in front of Fay, anyway.

'That's not . . .' she says, but then she runs out of steam because she knows that's exactly what he's doing. 'Shit.'

I look down at Kieran's little feet, his legs flapping excitedly as he watches a squirrel.

'You can't spend the rest of your life like this,' I say gently. 'He is never going to change. Is that what you want for Kieran? For him to think it's OK for a man to treat his partner like this?'

'He'd still be his dad.'

'But you wouldn't be condoning how he behaves. Big difference.'

'Don't . . .' she says. 'I don't want to talk about it.'

I know I've said enough for now. If I push her, she'll push back. Come over all Tiger Mum protecting her family. It's a fine line between being there for your friend and looking as if you're criticising her choices. 'Well, you know where I am if you ever do.'

'Thanks,' she says, and the shutters are back up. She leans down over Kieran. 'Shall we go and find the deer?'

'So, what the fuck with Maddy Fulford?' she says when we've walked on a bit in silence and automatically joined the little queue at the ice cream van. 'Do you think it's true? That's it for her, surely? You can't pitch yourself as the world's greatest expert on happy marriages when yours is falling apart round your ears and you've been lying about it to your followers for god knows how long.'

I grin at her. 'I know, right?' I'm desperate to tell her. Desperate.

'Well, if it means you won't have to put up with seeing her pop up on *This Morning* left, right and centre then I'm glad. You can forget about her again.'

'Yeah, me too. Not that I ever watch *This Morning* because some of us are at work.'

She groans. 'See what my life has become? I'm one of those people who watches daytime TV.'

I laugh. 'It's not like you've retired. You're on maternity leave.'

'I need to get back to work,' she says. 'My brain is atrophying.' Fay is a teacher. Secondary school, not primary. *I couldn't stand all the screaming and shouting*, she'd said when she made the decision, clearly not factoring in that teenagers screamed and shouted too, only in a slightly scarier way. She coaxes the entitled offspring of celebrities and music moguls through their history GCSE at a smart private school near where she lives in Wimbledon. She'd worked out exactly when she needed to get pregnant so that the end of her maternity leave would roll into the summer holidays, giving her a few more precious weeks, and it worked. Just like that, she conceived exactly when she wanted to. Maybe even first time. Of course Steve's sperm would turn out to be alpha just like the rest of him. I should have been jealous – and I admit that there was a pang of it, deep down, a nagging question of 'Why her and not me?' I challenge anyone not to feel envy when someone else achieves your dream, however much you love and want the best for them – but because she was one of the people I value most in my life, I buried it. I swamped it with my conflicting feelings of joy for her, and joy won out. Isn't that how you know you really love someone? That you can feel genuine happiness when something you wish had happened to you happens to them? Tom and I never found out why it was taking us so long, by the way. We didn't get that far. He didn't want to. He said it would feel like apportioning blame, but really I think he was worried about feeling like less of a man if the problem turned out to be with him. We would have had to have some tests eventually, but now it strikes me that I might never know if I ever could have conceived or not. It also strikes me that Tom might have nurseries full of babies now. Four years is a long time.

I order two bottles of water and an ice cream for Kieran. 'Do you think it's bad that I'm happy about Maddy Fulford being exposed as a fraud?' I ask as we head for a bench in the shade.

'God, no,' Fay says emphatically. 'But, you know, don't get caught up in it . . .'

I almost tell her then. Later, I'm thankful that I don't.

14.

There's a tiny story in the *Mail* online. *Bad Influence*? the headline says. And underneath: *Has the fun gone out of mumfluencer Maddy Fulford's marriage?* God, Maddy really should have planned for every eventuality when she named her channel. It's a gift for sarcastic journalists.

> Self-appointed family expert and Instagram influencer Maddy Fulford, who has amassed a following of almost three quarters of a million with her wholesome videos featuring her adorable twin three-year-old daughters, and handsome husband Lee, and her wealth of tips for a happy marriage, has been the victim of an anonymous smear campaign this week, claiming that she's living a lie. Videos appearing to show that the couple are living apart surfaced on the Truth Teller Instagram account and have been widely shared. Mrs Fulford, whose first book *Making Family Fun* is published next month, was unavailable for comment.

Shit. That's me again. Truth Teller. I open Instagram half expecting to see I've somehow been unmasked, only to find I now have twelve hundred followers and scores of comments mostly of the *This is amazing. I knew it! Who are you?* variety. I feel like some kind of folk hero. The Robin Hood of betrayed women. I want to stand up and take a bow. Run and hide. Delete the account and pretend it never happened.

But, god, it's a rush.

I distract myself by calling Cally, but when she answers and I start to tell her about Steve's latest little act of cruelty and Fay's tears, she interrupts with a breezy 'I'm at baby yoga with Fay' which is basically code for 'I can't talk about her now.' Fay's voice suddenly comes on the phone. 'Baby fucking yoga. Can you imagine?' I laugh, picturing Kieran rolling around like a wrecking ball. 'I wish I could be there. Google Maddy Fulford when you get out. There's a bit in the *Mail*. She's toast, I think.'

'Wow. Karma. Oh, wait, we're starting, I think. Talk later.' I feel deflated. I want to celebrate my victory with someone. To take the credit I secretly feel I deserve. I open my messages intending to ask Lara if she's seen the article, needing to share this with the one person who'll really understand what it means, but a familiar icon jumps out.

Fun with the Fulfords.

Maddy has sent me a message. I feel momentarily light-headed, but then I tell myself it's only to be expected. She now knows that Truth Teller is the person who's been leaking stuff about her. I close my eyes for a second, afraid of what I might see. Remind myself that she has no idea who's behind the account. I open them again. The message is so short I don't even need to click on it to see the whole thing.

Iris, is that you?

PART TWO

15.

Maddy

Maddy has always tried to be positive. You get back what you project into the world, she believes. She's always been good at that. She used to tell her clients to send out only positivity and light. *It will be reflected back at you twofold.* She wishes she could have faith in her own words.

Eyes and teeth, her old dance teacher Miss Grenville used to say, standing in front of the line of leotard-clad little girls and smiling like a Cheshire cat as they pranced around. *Smile girls, smile!* Maddy was always her favourite. She was already an expert in smiling when she didn't mean it by the age of five.

But this is different. She doesn't know what to do. There's a tornado happening around her and she's powerless to stop it. Her whole life has been flung up in the air and she has no idea where it's going to land or how much of it will be intact when it does.

She's scared.

She needs Lee. She's always been the one with the drive, but Lee has kept her grounded. Safe. But Lee would just say *I told you so.* And he'd probably be right. Still, she's going to have to let him know what's going on. It affects him too. They need to find a way to get through this together or they'll have lost everything.

Her phone rings. Hattie, her agent. She can't. She

shoves it under a cushion hoping it will go away. She has never not answered a call from Hattie before, even if it's just to say *I'm bathing the twins, I'll call you back in half an hour*. She can clearly remember the first time Hattie got in touch with her. The excitement. All the possibilities that suddenly opened up in her head. 'You should be monetising this,' Hattie had said and then laid out how that might work. And Maddy had felt the weight of Lee's unhappiness with his job in sales lift off her shoulders. The stress that seemed to weigh him down when he finally got home at half seven every evening and sat comatose in front of the TV, one sleeping twin on each knee. 'I hardly ever get to see them awake,' he'd said to her once. 'And I'm just so fucking knackered all the time.' She could barely keep her eyes open at this point herself. Her days were a blur of pacifying one baby only for the other to start up. It was like they were involved in some kind of relay race. Tag grizzling. She had known twins would be difficult, but she'd never really grasped the extent of how much one plus one didn't make two but about six. There was never a break, except for a few hours at bedtime when they both obligingly dozed on their father's lap. She loved them with a fierce passion. She would do anything for them. Literally anything, she thought. But she had never felt this tired. Not ever.

She had persuaded Lee into making the little family videos at first as a bit of fun but then, when she saw how much people had started to respond to her, she had dared to wonder if this might be the beginning of something. If there might be a way she could use it to make their life better. Lee hated his job. Hated it. The banal banter he had to engage in to get his figures up. Trying to persuade people who didn't want a new photocopier that what they wanted more than anything was a new photocopier. The soul-destroying waiting to find out how much commission he'd earnt on top of his paltry salary every month. It was never enough. 'I wasn't expecting to have twins to support,' he'd said once when he'd been in a particularly foul mood, and then he'd taken it back and apologised over and over again and told Maddy that he loved her, Ruby and Rose more than he could ever imagine loving anyone, it's just that it was a LOT. He felt backed into a corner.

She'd been as surprised as him when she'd found out she was pregnant so soon after they started seeing each other. They'd been in that first flush of infatuation, when all the things that later started to grate on each other's nerves had seemed like delightful quirks: his habit of singing along to any piece of music he heard. Jingles, adverts, anything. If he didn't know the words, he improvised. Her tendency to see anything and every-thing that happened to her as an opportunity to be grasped. A lesson to be learnt. Everything about the other was still charming, endearing. They'd stayed up all night after she'd showed him the two lines on the test she'd taken that morning, getting caught up in the excite-ment of it, wondering what if? By daylight they'd made up their minds. They were going to be parents. At some point around four in the morning, Lee had proposed and she had tearfully accepted. 'I have twins in my family,' she'd said, laughing, and he'd laughed with her. What were the chances?

She had always intended to go back to work as soon as she could possibly manage it. She loved her job as a life coach. She had the opportunity – not to mention the ability – to change people's lives, to help them. But once she found out there wasn't going to be one baby, but two, she knew it wasn't going to happen anytime soon. She could hardly arrive at a conference with two little ones in tow and no support. And support cost money they didn't have. It made no sense.

Thank goodness Ruby and Rose are at nursery, she thinks now. She has to protect them from all this. That's the most important thing. Not that they'd understand (one blessing: they're not older), but they've never seen her upset like this. They've never even seen her cry. Not sad tears. Not even when their father moved out. She made sure of that.

That first time Hattie had called her and told her what she could hope to earn if she started to treat her hobby as an occupation and added a layer of professionalism, she'd actually gasped out loud. At first free stuff – nappies and clothing and formula, all the things they were struggling to afford – and then, as her engagement grew (it was all about engagement, Hattie had told her, and hers, even though her follower count was still relatively small, was good), actual money to promote stuff. She'd done her research just in case Hattie was a charlatan and trying to scam her in some way and discovered that everything she'd said was true. It would be hard work, Hattie told her. The videos would need to be slicker and scheduled to come out regularly. She had to decide what her message was, find her niche. It was all about deciding what your brand was and sticking to it. 'Making family fun,' Maddy had said without hesitation. She was meeting Hattie for the first time in a café in the Strand. 'I love it,' Hattie had said. And Maddy, whose family had been anything but fun growing up, had felt as if she was finally going to get her happy ending.

Now someone has been hanging round outside their house. It didn't bear thinking about. Even scarier that she has never seen them. She feels sick to her stomach when she thinks what might have happened to the girls. There are weirdos out there, and when you put your life up for scrutiny, on social media, you attract quite a few of them. People think they know you. Own you in a way. She knew it was a pitfall of the job when she started – Hattie had warned her to be a bit more discreet in what she said – but she'd thought she and Lee would always be able to keep their family safe. Now she's not so sure. There have been three videos so far, all from last Saturday. She knows because of what the twins are wearing. The little mirror matching outfits she'd bought for them last week in the new shop on the High Street. She has no idea if there are more to come. She has no idea who's doing this. She didn't even know about the Truth Teller account until after she'd posted the 'Paperback Writer' video. She can hardly take it down now, but she knows it'll be hard to explain if she's ever confronted with the facts.

She walks over to the window and peers out again. How could she not have noticed someone hanging round watching them? Was it even the first time? What was the point of the street WhatsApp group if no one kept an eye out for each other?

Not even the neighbours know that she and Lee have split up. At least, they didn't. They've been careful. And it's not as if they're famous among the general population, only to her followers. Maddy's Army, as they like to call themselves. Those lovely, loyal people who have taken them, the Fulfords, into their hearts. Of course, that could all be about to change. She's poised to enter the mainstream. Or at least that was the plan. First the book, then maybe a TV series. All her hard work finally paying off. She's made a career out of nothing, and a lucrative one at that, and it's all about to be taken away from her.

Well, not if she can help it. She's steelier than she looks. Attack her family and she will come after you.

She picks up the phone to call Lee. Even though things are strained between them, he always answers in case it's about the girls. He's a good dad. It's one of the things she's always loved most about him.

'Yep,' he says. The way he always does. Maddy tearfully tells him about the videos. The third film shows him going home to his rented flat. The one he chose because it's tucked away out of sight and so hardly anyone would ever see him coming and going. Whoever it was must have followed him from here, it occurs to her. She leans over and pulls down the blinds on the front window. She waits while Lee watches all three clips. She can hear him swearing under his breath and, for once, she doesn't berate him for it.

'Who the hell has done this?' he says eventually.

'I don't know. Did you see anyone?'

'Of course not. What are we going to do? Should we just ignore it and hope it goes away, do you think?' Maddy is always the decision maker. Lee prevaricates and defers to her. He always has. She used to like it, being the one who was in control, but now she feels as if she needs him to step up. She needs someone to tell her what happens next for once.

'I think you need to move home for a bit. Just in case they're still watching.' She wonders for a second if he might think this is all a ruse in order for her to get him back. 'I don't mean give up the flat. Just, you know, until it all calms down a bit. Please.'

He sighs. 'OK. Don't look.'

Don't look is what they've always said about the haters. She knew there would be some when they first started, but the volume and the ferocity knocked her sideways. How could what she was doing anger people so much? For a while she checked the negative hashtags obsessively. She'd wait for Lee to go out and then immerse herself like a secret porn addict. Every comment stung more than the one before. They tore apart her looks, her voice, her personality, her family. All these people who didn't know her. Then one day Lee came home unexpectedly early and found her in tears. They made a pact. They would pretend the comments didn't exist. Both of them had to agree not to read them, and they had to stick to it. One of them couldn't be worrying that the other had seen something upsetting and was trying not to let on. Internalising all the bad vibes to protect the other. And it worked, for the most part. Of course, occasionally Maddy would stumble across one or two mean jibes when she was replying to the fans, but she'd learnt not to dig any deeper. Although sometimes she did lie awake at night worrying about what she'd let her family in for by choosing this career. Was it fair on the girls? Would they resent her when they got older and discovered that hundreds of thousands of people had an opinion on them and it wasn't always a positive one? Would it mean their lives were handicapped before they really started? She was doing this for them, she always reminded herself. For their future.

'It'll blow over,' Lee says now. He's always been calm. Unflappable.

'What if it doesn't?'

'I don't know, Mads, do I?' he says with more than a note of irritation in his voice. 'You should have thought of that.'

'Should have thought of what? That maybe one day you'd choose to walk out on us?' She can't help but be angry with him. She walks back towards the rear of the house, paranoid that someone might be listening outside. Breathes in for a count of four, out for eight.

He sighs. 'That if you go around lecturing people about how perfect you are, they're going to be queuing up to expose you when you're not.'

'You were happy enough to take the money,' she snaps. She never loses her temper. She prides herself on it. The girls need stability and security, not to be tiptoeing around on eggshells in case they upset Mummy or Daddy. She allows herself to let rip so rarely it feels liberating now. She can imagine losing it completely, screaming and throwing things. She's wondered sometimes if it's all in there inside her somewhere. All the bitterness and bile she witnessed as a child. All the shouting and swearing and violence she tried so hard to blinker herself to. A volcano waiting to erupt.

Lee clearly knows how to push all her buttons. His role has always been to play the 'I'm so embarrassed by what we're doing, but if you insist I suppose I'll have to go along with it' role, while at the same time making absolutely no effort to find an alternative way for them to earn a living. She rarely allows herself to think like this, but he's shocked her lately. She had never imagined he might leave them. That's not the Lee she knows.

When she'd first told him about her new venture, he'd been all for it. If it took off he'd be able to find a job that took up less of his time, that didn't eat away at his soul. They could do up the house – they were living in his parents' old home, signed over to him when his mum followed his dad into a care home, but with a hefty re-mortgage taken out to pay the extortionate fees. It was starting to fall down around their ears, but they tried to ignore that by painting it cheerful colours and pasting up vibrant, happy wallpaper. Eventually they'd not only done it up but extended up and out. And Lee, who'd quit his job in a flurry of bravado one day, had never quite got around to finding a less arduous one. And she hadn't cared. It wasn't as if he sat round the house all day expecting her to wait on him. They'd been a team. And to be fair, he did still do occasional bits of work here and there. He was good with his hands, so he'd set himself up as a kind of odd job man locally and, if it suited him, he'd say yes to a bit of painting and decorating or low-level carpentry. It was all word of mouth, though. He'd never even tried to make it into a business because, he'd told her, he didn't want the hassle and he wanted to be around to help out with the girls. And he definitely did his share, that was one way she couldn't fault him.

God, she missed him. She'd always felt so secure around him. Cocooned. She refused to give up hope that they'd sort things out. That he'd come round. Come home.

'Just don't let anyone see you bringing your stuff back,' she says now. They have to try and fight this fire, and she doesn't care what it takes.

16.

Maddy

She always looks.

And so she sees the piece in the *Mail Online* soon after it appears. She sits down at the kitchen table, her heart pounding in her ears. Her phone tells her that Hattie has called eight times. There's no way she can ignore what's happening any more. She presses a button to phone her back just as call number nine comes through.

'Is it true?' Hattie barks. Maddy, who had been expecting concern and comforting words, bursts into tears.

'I . . .' she says, and then she can't say it out loud. 'I don't . . .'

'You have to tell me all the facts, that's the only way we can work together on this. I won't say a word to anyone else that we haven't agreed on.'

And so Maddy tells her how a few weeks ago Lee decided that they needed a break. How he told her he felt used and manipulated, a puppet in her life. A shadow of a man. How he was embarrassed that some of his mates' wives had seen the videos and he was now the subject of a torrent of barbs that passed themselves off as banter.

Maddy had been so blindsided that she'd snapped back at him. 'Get a proper job then,' she'd said, not really meaning it. Hitting him where she knew it would hurt.

He hadn't even answered because there was nothing he could really say to that.

He didn't want to be in the videos any more, she tells Hattie now. That was the root cause of their big, final argument. 'I feel like a twat,' he'd said, and then added, 'and I don't think it's good for Ruby and Rose. Not now they're getting old enough to know what's going on. They're going to look back one day and hate us for this.' That one stung, because she knew in her heart of hearts there was a grain of truth in it. In the middle of an occasional sleepless night, she too had started to wonder if what they were doing was fair on the twins, but she had buried that thought as quickly as it appeared.

'The book's about to come out,' she'd said in a hissed whisper. The girls were asleep upstairs. 'What do you want me to do? Give the advance back?'

She heard Hattie gasp when she tells her that part. Of course, all she was really worrying about was her percentage. Of course, all anyone cared about was themselves. To be fair, Hattie had done battle with the publishers armed with pages of stats and negotiated the advance up to almost double what they had been offering at first. Maddy had already received the first three payments of twenty-five per cent each and they had paid off the last chunk of the mortgage completely, and a state-of-the-art kitchen was on order.

'We need to come up with something. We can't have them pull their whole marketing budget at this stage.'

Maddy gulps. 'Shouldn't we just tell them the truth? Ask for their help?'

'No!' Hattie barks. 'You need to play it off as gossip. Put on a united front with Lee and come up with a plausible reason why either of you said what you said to each other in those videos.'

'He's already agreed to keep doing the song and dance routines till after we see what opportunities come up once the book's out.' She realises as she says it that there may not be any opportunities now. Her book may slip out unnoticed. None of the TV or radio shows are going to want to have her on if she's been exposed as a charlatan. 'And now he's moving back in for a bit.'

'OK. Good. That's good. Let me put a call in with Sorrel now before she gets to you. I'll tell her it's all made up nonsense and then you can back it up.'

Sorrel is Maddy's editor. She's always been kind and supportive and boosted Maddy's fragile ego in her insecure moments. She hates the idea of lying to her. But she can't lose everything. Not now. Not when she has no back-up plan. 'OK,' she says quietly.

'And don't speak to anyone else. Laugh it off if anyone brings it up.'

'OK. Who's doing this to me?' She wipes away a fat tear.

'No idea. Have you pissed anyone off? Or it could just be a random opportunistic thing. Someone wants to make a few quid. Except that they're anonymous, so that doesn't really make sense. All the paper had was the stuff they'd put on their Insta so it's not as if they've got some kind of exclusive. Beats me . . .'

Maddy has stopped listening. She hadn't even thought

it might be someone she knows. That is, she knew it must be someone who had a grudge against her, but she'd assumed a jealous fan or even another mummy influencer (she can't bring herself to say mumfluencer. It sounds, to her, like a character in a children's cartoon. A big lumbering monster. Watch out kids, here comes the mumfluencer! Run!). But maybe Hattie has hit the nail on the head. It's someone she's upset. Someone who actually hates her.

She opens her laptop – Hattie still talking theories in the background – and finds the account that posted all the videos. Truth Teller, no clue there. But she doesn't need one. There's only one person in the world that Maddy thinks it could be. Someone she thought she'd never have to get involved with again. Has she been here? Outside their house? For all she knows, Maddy might have passed her on the street. Maybe even with the twins in tow. It doesn't bear thinking about.

She types a message: *Iris, is that you?*

She let her win once. That's not going to happen again.

17.

Iris

Shit.

Fuck.

So this is what it feels like when people say 'I thought my heart was going to explode.' I can feel mine in my ears, my toes, the tips of my fingers. I have to sit down where I am. Straight down on the floor of the back office. Maddy knows. She's worked it out, or I've somehow given myself away. I scour my phone screen yet again for any giveaway clues on my account, but there's nothing. Does one of her neighbours have CCTV and they've spent hours searching through it for suspicious strangers creeping around in the bushes? Done some kind of reverse image search to find out who the culprit is? Am I going to get arrested? Shamed in the papers? All these thoughts flood through my brain at once, a series of ever more humiliating outcomes flashing before my eyes like an episode of Jeremy Kyle. I should delete the Instagram account, I think, although I don't really know what difference that will make. I'm pretty sure there are forensic internet sleuths who could still find crumbs that led back to me even if I removed all obvious traces.

I can hear Zak talking to a customer, that wheedling tone that hints he might have hooked a fish. I do it myself, even though I try and stop myself, embarrassed by the desperation that seeps through my attempts at conversation. It's all I can do these days to stop myself cutting across whatever inane question they're asking with 'Just sign the contract for fuckssake. I need the commission.' I lie back, my head on the hearth of the blocked-up fireplace, and try to calm myself down. She's fishing, I try to tell myself. She doesn't know anything for definite. If I don't respond, there's nothing she can do.

I drag myself up, shake some dust out of my hair and sit at the desk. I just need to keep my head down and the rest will take care of itself.

An hour or so later (which I've more or less lost to reading all the new mentions of Maddy that have sprung up all over the internet – mostly straight rehashes of the *Mail Online* story, but the odd one has put its own spin on the situation, or speculated who Truth Teller might be: an envious rival, a vitriolic blogger, a Maddy wannabe), just as I'm starting to think about going home, Cally calls me. I almost don't answer, but I decide the distraction is just what I need.

'Fucking Steve,' she says as soon as I answer.

'I know,' I say. 'How is she?'

'Miserable, obviously. Trying to pretend she's not. The usual.'

'I just don't get it . . .' I say. Cally and I have had a version of this conversation countless times before. We never come up with any solutions. If Fay won't leave Steve then what can we do?

'Me neither. I've persuaded her to come to Center Parcs with us while he's away. See if that'll take her mind off it a bit.'

'Oh,' I say. 'That'll be nice.'

'I mean, you're welcome to come too, obviously. But it'll be a bit . . . you know . . . kiddie . . .'

I would have said yes. Would have spent the whole weekend offering to babysit the kids so Fay, Cally and Jim could have a break, for that matter. I would have relished the chance to get away from my other life – the life where Maddy has just pointed an accusatory finger at me. But I feel as if her invitation is half-hearted, an afterthought. I had never figured in their plans. 'No, it's fine. Way too outdoorsy for me. Listen . . . I'm about to go down into the tube . . .' I press my phone to my ear so she won't notice the lack of street noise.

'OK. I'll see you at the weekend, yes? Are you still coming over?'

'Definitely,' I say. 'Sure.'

'We have to take the kids swimming in the afternoon. Fay's bringing Kieran, can you imagine? Half two, I think. But we can still have a quick lunch before.'

'Right. Great.'

Fun with the Fulfords has posted a new video. I'm in the bath. Candles lit. The sound of Carol pacing huffily in the corridor outside. Everything has been quiet on the Maddy front for the past couple of days. The forums are still speculating, but there's been no new intel. I'd pretty much convinced myself nothing had happened, and I felt as relieved as I did disappointed. I almost drop the phone into the water in my eagerness to see what's new. Maddy and Lee sit together in their kitchen. There's no sign of Ruby and Rose. They're both beaming at the camera in a slightly maniacal way. No silly costumes. No props. Holding hands. I can see shadows under Maddy's eyes that her make-up has failed to completely hide.

'Hi everyone!' she trills. 'We have a bit of a special message this evening. You may or may not have seen some nasty rumours going around about us . . .' She gazes up at Lee and he squeezes her hand. 'We were going to just ignore them, but we felt we owed it to you guys to be completely honest, so here we are.' Dramatic pause. 'No, Lee and I are not having problems. No, we are most definitely not splitting up.' At this Lee rolls his eyes and pulls a big 'Have you ever heard anything so ridiculous?' face. 'But, just like any couple, just like all of you, we sometimes have a little disagreement. And, if we're tired – because raising two little munchkins can be tiring even though it's the best job in the world – we can sometimes snap at each other too. We wouldn't be human if we didn't. So, to be totally transparent – because you know that I'm always honest with you guys – Lee has a little flat that we rent out on Airbnb. An investment that he bought before we met. And the other day, we had a bit of a tetchy moment about whose turn it was to clean up after the last guests. We're human, guys! We're flawed. Fallible. Just like all of you. Only someone was filming us! Secretly! Can you imagine?' Lee gives a big sad shake of his head. 'And they put it online to try and make it look as if we had been lying to you all and we were secretly living in two separate places! How sad is that? But let's not waste time thinking bad thoughts about that person. I feel sorry for them. There's obviously something missing in their lives, and they're so envious of mine . . .' Another loving gaze at Lee. '. . . that I should just pity them. Even though I'm hurt that anyone could do that to us. All we ever want to do is spread a little bit of happiness and positivity. But, you know, some people are just unhappy. Life hasn't turned out how they wanted and they feel the need to lash out like a wounded animal.' I baulk at this. Is that me? Am I lashing out because I'm damaged? Bitter? No, I tell myself. My anger is justified. On the screen, Maddy smiles a weak smile. 'Anyway, we're still here, we're still very much in love, we're happy, and we're having as much fun as ever. And . . . what's more, we made a new video for you . . .'

I watch transfixed, the water cooling around me. She's so convincing, the big green eyes blinking away tears, a look of righteous hurt on her face. I'd fall for it. 'Agadoo' bursts in. What is going on? They're faking it, obviously. I know what I saw. I know they're living separately, whatever she says. But how long can she lie to people and not get caught out?

'Iris, are you going to be long?' Carol's voice booms through the bathroom door. 'Only I'm desperate for a wee.'

'Five minutes,' I call, even though I could be out in

143

three if I put my mind to it. Not for the first time, I think I shouldn't be living like this.

And then before I can stop myself I call the Premier Inn in Marlow and book myself in for the weekend again.

18.

Maddy

Tom was the love of her life. There, she's admitted it. Only to herself, obviously. She's never said those words out loud to anybody. Not that she doesn't love Lee. Didn't. She's not sure any more. The man who is prepared to sabotage everything they have is not the man she married. But she and Tom had had something special. A magnetic pull that had made her feel powerless.

They'd met at a conference. She spent a lot of time at conferences. IT companies, insurers, accountants, personal trainers. She had made a name for herself on the slightly incestuous public speaking circuit so she was milking it for all it was worth, because the fee wasn't as good as people might imagine. Large firms liked to be seen to be offering their employees personal support and enrichment, but they didn't really want to shell out lots of cash in the process. She enjoyed them, though, and she would sometimes pick up private clients who would come to her for follow-up sessions in her little flat in Marylebone. Tom had been one of those. They'd chatted a little after her talk had ended – she always liked to wait around for a while in case anyone wanted to speak further – and he'd told her he'd found it interesting. Given that often what she was met with was indifference at best, reluctant employees sitting through her presentations because they'd been told they had to or to curry favour with the boss, she was always happy to indulge in a bit of positive feedback. It meant something to her to touch people, that was why she did what she did. Wasn't that what life was meant to be about after all, making connections? He had phoned and booked himself in for a private consultation a couple of weeks after the conference had ended. She hadn't recognised him when he first walked in, but after the first few minutes she'd remembered the conversation they'd had. How he'd told her he sometimes struggled to see the upsides. Not that he was depressed, he'd said – it never failed to amaze her how quickly conversations could cut to the chase and get intimate after she'd given one of her talks – but he felt trapped by life. Locked in a situation he couldn't see a way out of. She remembered giving him a card, telling him that some coaching might help.

His life was a bit of a mess, he had told her in their first one-on-one session, he needed to find a way to move on. The nature of her work meant that she inevitably became part unqualified therapist during private consultations. It was a fine line between the two disciplines – she focused on the future rather than the past, on forward-thinking solutions rather than unravelling what went wrong before as an analyst might – and that line often blurred. If a client wanted to talk about their history she indulged them, believing that it would help unclog their pathways, giving her a clean slate to work with. A blank canvas, as it were.

Tom had been one of those. She had wondered at the

time if his request for a private consultation had been more about him wanting to see her again than anything else. She sometimes got that. Men (and women too, on a couple of occasions) away from home and feeling flirtatious. Misinterpreting signals. She never minded. A client was a client, although most of the would-be suitors dropped out after the first session where she laid out the boundaries. Tom, though, had genuinely wanted to talk. At one point she'd even suggested that therapy might be more appropriate, but he'd told her no, he wanted to build a future without looking back.

After a couple of sessions, she knew that she liked him. She noticed the way his nose crinkled upwards just before he smiled, his habit of massaging the base of his thumb with the long fingers of the other hand when he was thinking. His shockingly pale blue eyes. But she'd also known that it was inappropriate. It was important to keep her work and home life separate.

Maddy's love life before had been a series of heartbreaks. She was a romantic. She threw herself into every romance with her whole heart and soul, desperate for her love to be reciprocated. She knew that she'd sometimes frightened men away with her intensity. She also knew that it all stemmed back to her childhood and the neglect that she'd tried to hide from the world. Her mum couldn't help it, she just didn't have the emotional capacity to be a mother. Maddy had long since forgiven her – she was a firm believer in the power of forgiveness; holding on to resentments only weighed you down – but she no longer thought of her as a parent, more a wayward sibling. And who knew where her father was. Life had at least been a little better when he'd finally walked out for good soon after Maddy's tenth birthday. At least the shouting had stopped.

When Maddy was little, she used to spend hours shut away in her tiny bedroom daydreaming about what her life would be like one day. As the dreams evolved over the years they still all contained one crucial element: security and a loving home. But she had no idea how to achieve those aims. She'd never been given a blueprint. She was in awe of the families of her friends who laughed together and had fun, with parents who showed up for school plays and dance recitals and who made a big fuss on birthdays and at Christmas. It was all she wanted, and she knew she showed that vulnerability to the world too readily. It brought out the worst in people. Made them want to exploit it. So, it was inevitable that she'd gone through one love story after another, each time convinced that this was it. And every time she'd been let down.

She had left home as soon as she could, taking up a place at the University of Westminster, to study sociology. She wanted to find out what made people tick. She thought that if she understood people better, she might be able to figure out a way to slot herself into the world, to create a loving unit around herself, somehow. She'd thought she might go on to be a social worker. She wanted to help people who needed it. Her father had been a lost cause, but she believed maybe her mother might have been different if she'd had some support, someone to teach her the right way to be an adult.

Ultimately, though, she wasn't sure she'd be able to keep her temper with the parents who neglected their children, parents like her own who should have known better, who should have grown up and taken responsibility for the tiny life they'd created, whether they regretted it or not. She dutifully went home to visit her mother in the holidays – cringing whenever her mum spouted a version of the *We've always been more like best friends than mother and daughter, haven't we!* fable that she now used to justify her shortcomings to herself – relishing her new independence that felt so different to the enforced independence she'd grown up with. Now when she cooked for herself it was because she wanted to, when she cleaned it was because she had pride in her home (even the grotty bedsit in Finsbury Park that was her refuge for her three college years). She was looking after herself because she was an adult and that's what adults did, not because she was a child and there was no one else who cared enough to do it for her.

She had stumbled into life coaching almost by accident, when she discovered in a conversation with her personal tutor that the techniques she'd used all her life to try to manifest a better future for herself had a lot in common with the coping strategies many practitioners espoused. She liked the idea of it. Of helping people look towards the future.

Maddy's way of dealing with her past had always been to close the door on it, but that didn't mean the insecurities weren't still there. Tom wasn't the only one who really needed therapy.

During their second session Tom had told her that he'd left his wife. It had been a long time coming, he'd said. He'd stuck in there as long as he could, but he realised now that that was mainly out of duty. Guilt. They had been trying for a baby. Looking into IVF. He'd realised it was now or never. He couldn't let his wife – Iris – get her hopes up, watch her drag herself through disappointment after disappointment as he'd seen happen to friends of his who'd gone that route, if he knew deep down it wasn't working. And, if he were being completely honest, he'd said, he was terrified that the IVF would be successful and that then he'd be trapped forever. He would never leave her to bring the baby up on her own. This was the situation he'd alluded to at the conference. He'd suddenly realised he didn't want to have children with her any more. Didn't even want to be married to her any more. He couldn't put his finger on what had gone wrong – and Maddy didn't pry – but something had, and he'd realised there was no way back. So, he'd let her down. Broken her heart. He'd cried as he told Maddy this and her own heart had gone out to him.

After his sixth and final appointment, Tom had asked if he could take her for a drink. She could see no reason to say no. She wasn't bound by a code of ethics like some other professions. His separation was a bit new, a bit raw, but she wasn't expecting that their innocent farewell drink would lead to a relationship. Maddy liked to trust her instincts. He seemed like a nice man and nice men didn't come along all the time. She'd asked him to wait five minutes while she freshened up.

That night they'd mostly talked about her. 'You've listened to me enough,' he'd said, nursing a pint of IPA as they sat in a dark wooden booth in the pub near the park, although she'd felt she really didn't know that much about him outside of the basics. She'd found herself opening up about her miserable childhood, her tendency to throw herself into relationships with unsuitable men. To give him credit he hadn't run a mile; he'd touched the end of one of her fingers with his and told her she was probably too special for most men. Then he'd laughed. 'God, that sounded creepy. You know what I mean.'

'No, I like it,' she'd said, laughing along with him. 'I'll take special.'

They'd ended up going back to hers and just talking. He'd insisted on sleeping on the sofa, and in the morning they'd gone to a local café for avocado on toast, something it turned out was on both their lists of favourite foods.

'Aren't you late for work?' she'd asked. It was a Thursday morning and she'd almost forgotten she had a client at eleven. He'd shrugged. 'It won't hurt just this once.' By the time he left – and she'd had to run back to her flat so as not to be late – she knew that she wanted to see him again, that this might be the start of something. 'Would you like to have dinner one night?' she'd surprised herself by saying as they'd said goodbye. 'I was just going to ask you the same question,' he'd said with a smile that had lit up the dull day.

He'd told her more about his marriage break-up the next time they met, two days later. 'Nothing happened,' he said. They were in the little Italian restaurant on the corner of her road eating huge bowls of pasta and drinking red wine. 'I mean, no one did anything wrong . . . I just knew I couldn't do it any more. I thought it would be fairer to her to get out sooner rather than string her along for longer.' She could see he was eaten up with guilt. 'It's the baby thing,' he said, swirling the wine round in the oversized glass. 'I think she can't get past that.'

Maddy should have heard the warning bells then, but the wine, the candles, the way he looked at her had left her helpless. She'd turned her hand palm up and slipped it under his.

19.

Maddy

She hears the doorbell ring as she's trying to distract herself by making the girls' favourite lasagne. Ruby likes the white sauce, Rose the red. Actually she thinks they both like both, but they're going through a phase of always having to state the contradictory opinion to the other. She smiles when she thinks of them, as she always does. She'll need to go and pick them up from their playdate in about half an hour. Face the world.

She doesn't know why he's ringing the doorbell. He still has his key. Usually he does it so they don't have to spend time together, seething over the twins' little strawberry-blonde heads. Maybe that was what did it for them. One of their neighbours casually walking past at the wrong moment, and that's how the rumours started, although how that could have got back to Iris she doesn't know. Maybe she's jumped to conclusions too quickly, she thinks, as she wipes her hands on a tea towel and heads for the hall. Maybe someone else in the world hates her enough to do this. Maybe there's now an army of haters united in their desire to bring her down.

Why is Lee being so stupid as to risk being seen again? He needs to burst through the door shouting 'Honey, I'm home!' just in case anyone's watching. Has he not grasped how important this situation is? He exasperates her sometimes.

When she'd suggested Lee move back in, she'd told herself she had to bury all her hurt for the duration, for the sake of the girls. It was already going to be confusing for them but, she was hoping, they'd just be so delighted that Daddy was home that they wouldn't overthink it. And not forgetting they couldn't risk being caught again snapping at each other on the doorstep. So she plasters a big smile on her face and flings open the door. She can chastise him later.

There's a young woman standing there. Maddy knows immediately that she's some kind of reporter; in fact, she thinks she recognises her.

'Maddy, hi!' She pushes her glasses up her nose. 'I don't know if you remember me? Sian Peters from the *Bucks Free Press*? I interviewed you once about that charity bake-off?' Everything, it seems, is a question with Sian. Her voice rises higher and higher at the end of each sentence. Maddy does remember her: young, keen, disarmingly open. And she knows exactly why she's here now. Act as if everything is normal, she tells herself. How would I have greeted her if she'd turned up at my front door a few weeks ago?

'Sian! Of course. How nice to see you. I'd invite you in but I'm literally about to go out to pick up the girls from their friends'.'

'Have you seen the *Mail* . . .' Sian starts to say but Maddy is distracted by the sight of Lee's silver car pulling up in front of the house. Not now, she thinks. Please not now.

'I have. What on earth? Obviously it's complete nonsense . . .'

Over Sian's shoulder she sees Lee get out. She knows his boot will be stuffed with his things. His big grey suitcase, his brown leather holdall.

'So, what were those videos all about?' Sian is so focused that she hasn't even noticed what's happening behind her. She has her phone in her hand, Maddy realises, recording.

Maddy tries and fails to catch Lee's eye. 'I can't even remember, to be honest. I think we had a little fight about a flat that Lee owns that we let out for Airbnb. Whose turn it was to clean it or something. Just a little domestic . . .'

'Hello, hello.' Lee bounds up the drive with a huge smile on his face. He's got the memo. He's read the room. Maddy almost faints from relief. 'Sorry I'm late, I got chatting. Hi . . .' He turns his beam on to Sian while at the same time grabbing Maddy up into a hug and planting a kiss on her head.

'Sian's from the *Bucks Free Press*,' Maddy says, imbuing as much meaning as she can into those three words. 'She's here about those silly videos.' They'd agreed on their story on the phone. It took them a while, but they concocted the best explanation they could that vaguely fit the dialogue.

'Never do Airbnb,' Lee says, turning on the charm.

'Or if you do, hire a cleaner.' Sian laughs. No, not even laughs, Maddy thinks, giggles like a teenager. What Lee lacks in conventional good looks he more than makes up for in attractiveness, that nebulous animal magnetism that overrides his pinched features. 'Storm in a teacup,' he says now, his arm squeezing Maddy's shoulders. 'The real story is who is the saddo that was hiding outside our house. I've talked to the police about it already . . .' He's going off script. They need to play the whole thing down, not create another story about a crazed stalker.

'I know, right?' Sian says, eyes wide. She's buying it, at least, but she's still recording so they need to be careful. 'Do you think someone has it in for you?'

'Gosh, no,' Maddy says with a smile, pinching Lee's back hard. She feels him flinch. 'They agreed with us that it was just a one-off opportunistic thing. Some poor person thought they could make a bit of cash. It's sad, right? The lengths people will go to. And it's mean on the girls for people to speculate like that.'

Sian nods enthusiastically. 'So, what would you say to your fans?'

'Business as usual,' Lee says enthusiastically. Maddy nods emphatically. 'We're only human,' she says. 'We have the odd little tiff now and again, who doesn't? But all the rest of it is nonsense.'

'We're still having fun,' Lee jumps in. The perfect soundbite.

'Always,' Maddy says, leaning into him and looking up into his face like an adoring puppy. *Eyes and teeth. Smile, girls, smile.*

'Well, I'm sure I can help you put this to bed,' Sian says. They've done it. They've convinced her. She puts her phone in her pocket. 'You should get CCTV, though. Just in case . . .'

'Lovely to see you again, Sian,' Maddy says. 'We really do need to go and pick up the girls now . . .'

'Of course. I'm done. Thanks for your time, guys. And . . . well, I'm actually really happy that everything's OK . . .'

Sian, Maddy thinks, will never make it as a big-shot reporter. She doesn't have the killer instinct. They wave her off and keep their megawatt smiles pasted on their faces until the front door is firmly shut.

'No stalkers,' she snaps as they stand in the hall, each trying to calm their breathing. 'No drama, we agreed.'

'I know,' he says sullenly. 'I was a bit caught on the back foot.'

She nods. 'Me too. We did well. Both of us.'

'We did,' he agrees.

They go and collect the twins together, holding hands awkwardly as they walk up the long, gravelled drive to their friends Gary and Lacey's large former farmhouse. Maddy shudders with relief that she didn't confide her family problems in anyone, not even Lacey, her nearest thing to a best friend. She'd known instinctively that it would be reckless, that even the most well-intentioned gossip could bring everything crashing down. And Lee had never been one to share anything personal. That was one of the reasons he'd grown to resent what they did: the over-sharing. He hated people knowing their business. She can tell that Ruby and Rose are ecstatic to see them arrive together. Maddy tries to work out if either Gary or Lacey have picked up on anything – the *Mail* piece, a stray word from one of the twins about Daddy never being home – but with four kids under the age of six she thinks they can't really have the space in their heads for rumours and gossip, and neither of them alludes to anything untoward.

'Your turn next,' Gary says and he hands her Ruby's backpack. 'Have them for a week if you like. A month. Me and Lacey'll go on a no-kids-allowed cruise.'

When they get back, Lee reverses into the drive as close to the house as he can get so he can offload his luggage later without being seen. Maddy still intends to scour the street for spies before he does so. She's taking no more chances. Ever.

'I think I might know who it is,' she says once the twins are in bed. Lee has bathed them and read them a story and the pair of them are hyper from happiness. Maddy feels a bitter sting. He's been denying them this, the happy, stable upbringing that was all she ever wanted for them. He was a great dad and then suddenly he wasn't there most of the time any more. How do you explain that to a pair of three-year-olds?

'What do you mean? Who?' He pours himself a lager, still in the fridge from before he left weeks ago. Even though Maddy doesn't drink – hasn't since she first found out she was pregnant – she hadn't had the heart to stash the cans away at the back of a cupboard and free up valuable space. They're sitting in the kitchen, the big, beautiful space at the back of the house. They haven't even discussed the renovation. Whether they're just going to cancel and lose their deposit. Whether their separation is temporary or permanent.

She has never told him about Iris. Never even really talked to him about Tom. She'd worried their break-up was so recent that Lee would think she couldn't possibly be over it and ready to embark on another commitment. Lee himself had been in a long relationship with a woman called Sue into his mid-thirties, but more or less single ever since. He had no obvious baggage. For a man of his age – forty-one when she met him, forty-five now – he was surprisingly naïve. He'd effectively never left home, except for the years he'd lived with Sue round the corner. He had the same friends he'd had since primary school. He'd had dalliances – his easy charm had always made him popular – but nothing more serious. Maddy envied him the simplicity of his life.

She tells him the potted version now. 'She's the only person I know who hates me enough,' she says.

'You don't know that,' he says, clearly not realising that that is hardly a comforting thought. She bats it away.

'And you really didn't see anyone when you were coming and going last weekend?'

He shakes his head. 'I mean, I wasn't looking . . .'

'Sian's right, we should get CCTV. Just in case.'

He looks at the floor. 'Mads, I'm not staying. Just till all this blows over and the book's out, like we agreed.'

'Of course.' She gulps back tears. The truth is that she can pretend to herself all she likes that she's angry with

Lee, but actually all she is is devastated. She just wants him to come home for good. 'I just meant for now . . .'

'Right. I'll order one of those Ring things.'

Maddy sighs. 'Hattie says we need to do a video addressing it. Showing a united front.' She knows he'll agree because he doesn't want them to lose their income any more than she does. Not when they don't have an alternative in place. 'We can put the "Agadoo" one out straight after.' They still have the second dance routine they recorded last Sunday in reserve. Pushing pineapples, shaking trees, all dressed in bright yellow T-shirts and homemade hula skirts. Lee with a Carmen Miranda- style hat on his head, painstakingly put together from papier-mâché by Maddy. He had been in a foul mood the whole afternoon, muttering 'I feel like a fuck-ing prick' under his breath when the girls were out of earshot. She wonders where this embarrassment has come from, why he's suddenly so concerned about how he looks. She knows he's not playing around. For all his cheesy flirtatiousness, she has never not trusted him. He's all talk. It can only be that he doesn't care about making her happy any more; he doesn't care about them, his family. That he's started to find her embarrassing rather than cute.

When she'd first been offered her book deal – a year ago now – Lee had picked her up and twirled her round and called her 'his little genius'. She'd felt so proud in that moment. Everything she'd been working so hard for had paid off. They were very comfortably off already thanks to all the ads and the endorsements, but this would take them to another level. And, maybe even better, they'd be celebrated as a perfect couple, an enviable example of how happy a family could be. Everything she had ever wanted. Until Lee had blown it all up, of course. The only reason she could think of that would make him do that was that he didn't love her any more.

'Sure,' he says now. 'I'm going to bring my stuff in.'

There's definitely no one on the street, they both check. No unfamiliar cars. It suddenly occurs to her that it really could be one of her neighbours. There's been no response to the message she sent accusing Iris and maybe they're the most obvious candidates to have noticed Lee's coming and going. Random jealousy rather than a targeted attack by Iris. Are they laughing at her now because they think they've got away with it? She scours the houses opposite for any sign of twitching curtains. She knows them all, though. Old Mrs Bailey at number 2 with her grown-up children who hardly ever visit, and her dodgy hip. Maddy has often taken her to hospital appointments when her son can't. Or won't. The Watsons at number 3 with their huge, soppy Bernedoodle that Maddy has babysat on occasion for free. The Simpson-Martins at number 4 with their three primary school-aged kids who Ruby and Rose look up to as if they were living gods. Maddy gets on well with them all. It's a small road. They look out for each other. Still, they sneak from the car to the front door now with Lee's bags like a pair of cat burglars. He hasn't brought much, she thinks sadly, noticing how light the holdall is. He's not planning on staying long.

20.

Iris

So far, there have been no more accusatory messages to my Truth Teller account. I dare to allow myself to relax. Just a little. And obviously, I've refrained from responding to Maddy's message. If I say nothing she can never confirm that Truth Teller is me. For all I know she may have sent the same few words, with just a change of name, to twenty different people hoping for a response. And then I realise, no, she sent it to the account that was calling her out, the anonymous account. Accusing only me. That's a pretty big statement. If nothing else, it confirms that she knows how badly she treated me. How justified I would be to bear a grudge. Strangely that makes me feel better.

I haven't spoken to Daisy since she dropped her bombshell. I thought she might phone me and apologise for her insensitivity, but that's not really Daisy's style. She probably didn't even realise that what she said to me might have been hurtful. I'm worried about her, though. I've spent my whole life worrying about her and it's a habit that I'm not going to break any time soon. Even when we were children and she was the older sister, I always felt I had to look out for her. Her otherworldliness made her a target for the other kids, even at primary school. I've tried calling her a couple of times, but the calls have gone straight to voicemail. There's no point leaving a message because I know she never listens to them. I know she hasn't told Mum her news because I would have been the first person Mum called, so my guess is she still doesn't know what she's going to do. Either that or she's no longer pregnant for one reason or another and she's not got round to telling me. As ever, when I think about my sister, I'm flooded with both protectiveness and irritation in equal measure.

I phone Mum and she informs me that the village tricentennial fever has reached critical mass with half of her street no longer speaking to the other half. 'It's better than *EastEnders*,' she tells me with a throaty chuckle. 'Honestly, there's never been so much entertainment.'

'Have you heard from Dais?' I ask after she's filled me in.

'Not for a few days. Isn't it the mindfulness course this week?'

My seesaw clunks down firmly on the side of irritation. 'Oh yes, I forgot. Sardinia, isn't it?' Daisy's self-improvement courses that Mum subsidises are never in Croydon or Luton. They're in Bali or Egypt or some beautiful bit of the Med. She always comes back with a suntan and precious little else (well, and a baby that one time, let's not forget that).

'I'll come down in a couple of weeks,' I say.

'Come for the street party,' Mum laughs. 'They've said residents only, no extra guests, so that would really put some noses out of joint.'

'Well, that sounds ideal,' I say, laughing along with her. I love my mum's rebellious spirit. I wish I'd inherited a bit more of it. 'I'll see what I can sort out.'

The receptionist at the Premier Inn greets me like an old friend. 'Usual room,' he says conspiratorially as he hands me the key card. I get that warm fuzzy feeling we all get when we're recognised somewhere as a regular. We're part of a club. If he knew why I was really here I'm sure he wouldn't be so friendly. Although, to be fair, I'm not actually sure why I'm here myself this time. Maddy and Lee are not going to slip up again so soon. They're going to be on their best behaviour. No more arguments on the doorstep. I think maybe I'm just here because it's nicer than spending the weekend in my flat. This is definitely not a cost-effective way to live.

I go straight out for a walk through the now-familiar park and out along the river. Despite everything, I feel my shoulders relax. After a while I turn back and head up the High Street, looking for somewhere to have a pre-dinner drink outside. It's a beautiful evening so I might as well enjoy it. I find the little courtyard off the main road with cafés with tables outside and order myself a glass of rosé. I find a sliver of sunshine and lean into it. I could happily just sit here all evening watching people walk by if it wasn't for the fact that they start to pack away the chairs and tables before I've finished my drink. The waitress waves a hand, 'No rush,' as she tidies up around me, but the moment's gone. I decide to potter around and find a restaurant that's not too expensive and has a space outside. 'I'm on holiday,' I tell myself. 'I'm just here to relax.'

I'm walking past a pub that has seating on the pavement, although most of the drinkers are standing, when I think I spot a familiar face. Is that Lee nursing a pint? I slow down. There's a couple sitting opposite each other at the far end of the benches, but the space across from Lee — because it definitely is him — is empty and, more importantly, clear of any evidence of anyone else's presence. I can't, can I? I shouldn't. All pretence of being here for any other purpose than to spy on Maddy's family goes flying out of the metaphorical window. Thankful that I've at least had one drink to give me courage, I stride over.

'Is anyone sitting here?'

He barely glances up. 'Go ahead.'

'Would you mind holding it for me while I just get myself a drink? I mean, if that's OK . . .'

'Sure,' he says, going back to his phone.

I shove my way to the front of the bar, not caring who I push in front of. I need to get back before he calls it a night and leaves, although I imagine he'll feel obliged to stay and hold my seat for at least a while. I order another glass of wine because it's quick. Flap my card at the reader. When I get back outside, Lee is still there, still looking at his phone.

'Thanks,' I say, swinging my leg over the bench. He nods briefly. Then I notice him frown.

'Don't I know you?'

Shit. No. Calm down, Iris, I tell myself. He doesn't mean what you're scared he might mean. 'I don't think so.' I look directly at him so I don't seem shady. Style it out.

'The Cats Protection woman,' he says and then he turns his attention back to his phone, pleased with his recall skills. I need to capitalise on the tiny connection we've made, but I can see he's not the slightest bit interested in talking to me. I pick up my own mobile, find video, press record and lay it face down on the table so it's capturing the deep darkness of the wood and – hopefully – our voices. I rack my brain. For something to say. This is the best I can come up with:

'Do you have a cat?'

'No. I like them though.'

Now what?

'I don't have one either, which is mad, considering. But my flatmate's allergic.' This isn't true, but what's the difference?

'Right.'

'Do you have a dog?' Jesus, I really am coming across as aggressively boring now. Boring and desperate.

Lee lets out a little laugh. 'No. No animals, sadly.'

'Me neither.'

We're in danger of sinking back into silence again when, god love him, he says, 'Oh, I donated by the way. On the website.'

I give him a big smile. 'That's really kind. They need all the money they can get.'

He takes a long swig of his beer and appraises me

properly. I sit up a bit straighter, hook my hair behind my ear. 'Do you work for them? Cats Protection?'

I'm ready for this. 'No. I just volunteer. They rely on volunteers a lot.'

'Well then, you're the kind one. Donating time is much harder than donating money.'

'Lucky old you,' I say, and I'm gratified to see he laughs. I wasn't sure if he actually had a sense of humour.

'That came out all wrong. I just meant that if you have any money to spare, however small an amount, it's easier to just hit a button on your phone to donate it than to give up valuable hours. I wasn't trying to . . .'

I put him out of his misery. 'I know. I was kidding.'

'So, who do you work for when you're not volunteering? If that's not too nosy.'

'Oh. I'm a kitchen designer. Marlborough Kitchens.' Sticking to the truth on this one is definitely the sensible thing to do. There are only so many lies I can juggle.

'I know it. West Street.' He waves an arm in the direction of the top of the High Street. Is there a branch there? I have no idea. My wanderings have always taken me in the other direction, towards his flat.

'No, that would be way too convenient. In London. Well, Kingston. I commute. I only just moved down here so, you know, I'm hoping they might transfer me . . .' I can't say I both live and work miles away, because why would I have been banging on his door for a charity donation? This is why I rarely lie. It's a minefield.

He visibly shudders. 'I used to commute. Couldn't

hack it. Absolutely miserable way to live.' Here's my chance to ask him what he does in return, but he's still talking. 'Why did you move out here? If it's miles from where you work, I mean.'

I shrug. 'On a whim, I think. I came down here for a random weekend and I liked it so much I stayed.' A stray thought shoots into my brain. I could do that if I wanted, move somewhere. Reinvent myself. I have no ties. Mum is in Dorset. Daisy is so far across London that it takes literal hours to get there from where I live anyway. Not that I visit her often. The area where she shares a house with four other equally directionless freeloaders consists of miles of run-down terraced houses interspersed with seventies housing complexes. The odd corner shop dripping with heavy metal shutters and graffiti. Groups of disaffected youth who should be in school watching menacingly from the shadows. I think about the baby calling that place home and I feel physically sick.

And Fay and Cally, well, I feel as if our lives are evolving separately anyway. Slowly but inevitably. We could see each other just as often. Shit, I think. I forgot to let Cally know that I can't do our lunch tomorrow.

'So, you've asked for a transfer?' I wonder for a second what he means and then I realise he's talking about Marlborough Kitchens. 'I have,' I say. 'I imagine I might have to wait a while before something comes up.'

'There's a branch in Wycombe too,' he says. 'I think. Or maybe it's Maidenhead. Anything's got to be better than travelling all the way up to London every day.'

I nod. I need to get him back on the subject of him.

'What do you do?' I wonder if he expects me to recognise him, but I can't imagine many people ever do. He's an afterthought in Maddy's films. A prop.

He gives a little self-effacing laugh. 'It's a bit hard to explain. I'm kind of an influencer, I suppose.'

I feign surprise. 'Aren't you meant to be a twenty-year-old girl off *Love Island* who now tells people how to contour their face?'

He laughs again, more robustly this time. 'We come in all shapes and sizes. Mine's family stuff. It's my wife, really, she's the real face of it. And our twin girls.'

'You have twins!' I say disingenuously. 'How old?'

There's no doubting that his face lights up now he's been given the chance to talk about his girls. 'Three. Ruby and Rose. They're a handful.'

'Three's a great age.' I smile at him. I know what question he's going to ask me next. I'm ready for it.

'Do you have any? Kids?'

'Sadly not. The timing was never right, you know . . .'

And then he says what everyone always says when confronted by my obvious disappointment. 'There's still time.'

'Sure,' I force myself to say. One of these days I'm going to answer that cliché with the stats. That the million or so eggs I was born with are now reduced to fewer than five thousand, that my chance of getting pregnant in any given month is now less than five per cent. And that's assuming there are no other underlying problems. 'So, what do you actually do, the four of you? I'm intrigued.'

He downs the last of his beer. 'I'm going to get another drink. Would you like one? I mean, if that's not too weird a question given we've only just met?'

'I would. I'd love a glass of Chardonnay. Thank you.'

He holds out a hand for me to shake. 'Lee,' he says, and I take it and say, 'Rissa. Nice to meet you, Lee.'

While he's gone I pick up my mobile and play back a bit of what I've recorded already, holding the phone to my ear to check you can hear what we're saying. It's surprisingly clear. I go to rattle off a quick WhatsApp to Cally and see she has already sent me one. *Bit worried we'll end up late for swimming. Let's reschedule!* Then I press record again and place it back on the table before Lee comes back.

I'm feeling more than a little tipsy by the time I buy the next round, so I switch to Diet Coke. Lee has explained their whole process and I'm not going to lie, it's fascinating. I think I always assumed that influencers posted content randomly and hoped for the best, but there are schedules to adhere to and commitments to fulfil. Of course, companies expect professionalism for their money. The Fulfords have deals with a kid-friendly holiday company, a kitchen appliance brand (hence all the baking videos), various food manufacturers and a well-known chain of clothing stores. And they all want value for money.

'So, what?' I ask. 'They send you stuff?'

Lee shakes his head. 'I mean they do, but they pay us. It's no different from advertising on the TV or whatever.'

'Right. So, they think their customers will relate to you, is that the point? You're like the meerkats, only for food mixers or whatever.'

He nods emphatically. 'Exactly. Well, something like that.'

'Nice work if you can get it.'

He gazes at the table, suddenly morose. 'I'm not sure how long the kids should keep doing it for, though. I mean, it's not exactly their choice.'

Interesting. I wonder if this is the fissure at the heart of Lee and Maddy's marriage. 'They enjoy it, though?'

'Mostly. But they don't really understand what they're doing. It was better when they were a bit younger because we could just make it a game, but now they get fed up with all the do-overs. They're starting to understand that it's not just about us having fun with them. And Maddy's a perfectionist . . .'

I edge my phone slightly closer to him. This is good stuff.

'So, would you want to stop? I mean, that would be hard, wouldn't it? If this is your livelihood.'

Luckily for me he's more than a little drunk by this point. Not slurring but his tongue has loosened.

'I think we should. At least until the twins are old enough to know what they're agreeing to. Otherwise we're exploiting them, aren't we? But, apparently, it's not that simple. Not yet at least.' There's an interesting hint of bitterness in his voice.

'Because you'd need to find alternative careers,' I say,

nodding, and he shakes his head. 'Well, that too. Mainly because we have a book coming out and that might take things to a whole other level . . .'

'You don't want to miss that opportunity. That's understandable.'

'When will it end, though,' he says. 'I've tried to tell her . . . Shit, I've drunk too much. I need to go home.'

I want to push it, but I know I can't. There'll be another chance. We know each other now.

'Me too,' I say, hoping he doesn't ask where I live.

He downs the last of his drink. 'Nice chatting to you,' he says, pushing down on the table as he stands. 'Night.'

I watch as he walks off down the street in the direction of the family home rather than the flat. Interesting. Has he moved back in? If so, he doesn't seem very happy about it. Or maybe he's just bored of our conversation and off to find another pub to drink in alone. He's swaying slightly. I'm tempted to follow, to see where he ends up, but it's not worth the risk. I feel a bit guilty – he actually seems like he might be a nice bloke and he's right, what they're doing isn't healthy for the kids, not as they get older – but not enough that I'm not excited about what I'll get to post on Instagram tomorrow. OK, so he didn't admit that he and Maddy have split up, but he basically owned up to not being happy, to wanting out. There will be telling soundbites I can cherry-pick from the audio I've taken. I scoop up my phone, excited to see what I've got. We've been chatting for nearly an hour. I go to stab the button to turn the recording off, and as I do I realise it's not on. In my saved photos there's a tiny snippet of film of my knees, the pavement, where I must have accidentally hit the spot twice, on/off, in quick succession. I stare at the screen for a moment as if willing it to change. It doesn't, of course. I've fucked up. This whole evening has been for nothing.

21.

Iris

The Little Hadham tricentennial decorations are restrained to say the least. The John Lewis bunting snakes elegantly from tree to tree in inoffensive arcs. Trestle tables rim the green, with white paper cloths and blue and red napkins laid out beside white china crockery. There are no garish flags or paper streamers because the committee has respectfully asked that residents refrain from putting up tacky homemade decorations. As the taxi approaches I see that my mum's house is a riot of tricolour glory, the sea of tat a metaphorical two fingers up at the committee. 'That one,' I say to the driver with a big smile.

Mum flings open the door before I've even got out of the car. She's wearing a tall stovepipe hat covered with Union Jacks and waving a triangular flag on a stick. I burst out laughing. Actually, it's so good to see her that I almost burst into tears.

'They're all furious with me,' she says conspiratorially into my ear as we hug. 'I'm really enjoying myself.'

I can see why she still lives here. The village is picture postcard pretty. Especially on a day like today, when the sun is shining and the late spring flowers are all ablaze. But, even though she insists she enjoys the petty victories she scores against the Little Hadham Preservation

Society and their increasingly draconian pronouncements, I worry constantly that she must be lonely. All her friends, bar one, have left.

'How's Cath?' I say as we drink tea in her sunny garden. The street party doesn't begin till five.

'Missing her grandchildren.' Mum's friend Cath's daughter has recently upped and moved to Dubai with her family. Unlike Mum who was a latecomer, only moving here after Daisy and I had left home, Cath brought her kids up here.

'That must be tough,' I say.

Mum squeezes my hand. 'At least you're only in London.'

I feel instantly bad for not making the trip down to visit her more often. 'It's so lovely to see you,' I say.

There's no space for me on the table allocated to Mum's street because, of course, I'm a gatecrasher. I'm tempted to hide it out in her house, but she's insistent we bring our own chair from her kitchen and squeeze it in. She orders everyone to budge up loudly – 'It's for my daughter. Of course she's welcome!' – while I cringe on the sidelines and wait for the ground to swallow me up. Linda bristles angrily, but she's too polite to say much in front of me. I can see that quite a few of the other revellers are amused by Mum's stance and give her furtive smiles. So, she does have some friends still, but they're young couples with little kids mostly, so I don't think they'll be inviting her into their social lives any time soon. It makes me feel better that she has a bit of back-up though, in case it all kicks off one of these days. Cath barrels over from a nearby table and half squeezes the life out of me. 'You need to eat more,' she says, poking me in the ribs.

'I'm about to,' I say, eyeing up the piles of sandwiches and fat Victoria sponges.

There's no point arguing with her. Cath's default position is that everyone would be happier if they ate more cake. And, who knows, she's probably right.

Mum has brought flags on sticks for all the kids. Egged on by her, our table is definitely the most badly behaved but also the one having the most fun. I settle for getting mildly pissed on Cava and watching the proceedings unfurl.

'Is it just you, Iris, or do you have siblings?' one half of a couple in, I'd guess, their early thirties, asks me as I pass him the water jug.

'I've got a sister. Daisy. She's away at the moment.'

'Any little ones?' Here we go again. For some reason everyone feels it's absolutely fine to ask a stranger this, the most intrusive of questions. Especially when they have children themselves. Because for them, I suppose, it seems so natural, so easy. You want them, you have them. Job done.

'Stop being so bloody nosy, Jake,' Mum says, but she says it with a twinkle so no one takes offence. 'Not everyone's churning them out like you two.' Jake and his young wife, Shar, have three kids who are all running round the green in a sugar rush-induced frenzy. Jake gives me a conspiratorial 'Isn't your mum a character?'

eye roll and I smile. I know he was only trying to make conversation, to make a guest feel included.

Our table all sticks it out till half past nine, just for the principle of breaking the curfew, and Mum and I half stagger back to the cottage, holding hands in the cool evening air. 'They're nice,' I say. The smell of honeysuckle is almost overwhelming.

'Yes, that little lot are. But they never stay long, the young ones. Not now the nearest primary school is more than five miles away. The practicalities get to be too much. Especially these days when all the kids are doing after-school clubs and sports and god knows what. The village is dying, that's the truth. I dread that some developer will come along one day and bulldoze the whole thing for a housing estate. It'll just be me and Linda glaring at each other over the embers, no one else will care.'

'I'm worried about Daisy,' she says later as we enjoy a chamomile tea in her front room. I panic for a moment that my sister has told her her latest news, but I know if she had, Mum wouldn't have been able to keep it to herself all afternoon. I need to speak to Daisy, to plead with her not to say anything to Mum until she has made up her mind what she's going to do, not to put the burden of a decision on to Mum's shoulders.

'She's fine,' I say. 'You know what she's like.'

'I just wish she'd find the thing that makes her happy and stick to it.'

The adolescent part of me that always surfaces when

I visit my mother wants to say 'What do you think I have in my life that makes me happy? Kitchens? Carol?' but, of course, I don't. I'm an adult. I understand that life can't always be exactly the way we want it to be.

I wonder for a second if that thing could be the baby. Maybe being a mother would give Daisy the fulfilment she needs. Maybe she'd be good at it. 'She could if she wanted to. You have to stop worrying about her.'

Mum raises her eyebrows at me. She's recently stopped dyeing her hair and embraced the silver. It suits her, but her eyebrows, pale against her tanned skin, give her a vulnerable look. 'I worry about both of you. It's my job.'

I lean over and squeeze her arm. 'Well, you don't have to. It's my turn to worry about you now.'

She pats my hand with hers. 'I'm absolutely fine,' she says. 'Just like you.'

Touché.

We go for a few long walks and drive to a local beauty spot with a picnic lunch. It's all very pretty, but I can't help thinking this is not the place for Mum to grow old. There is literally nothing here. Once she can't drive any more – which hopefully is a long way off, but that day will come eventually – she'll be cut off. Isolated. I add it to my list of worries.

Because the Wi-Fi and phone reception are patchy at best, I'm forced into having a mini digital detox, which means that after a day I forget all about Maddy and Lee. Since my visit last weekend there has been new content – a video and two posts – all business as usual, no more mention of the rumours that were swilling around but have died down again without any new fuel being added. On Tuesday I got a DM from Lara that just said *What a freakin coverup!* and I breathed a long sigh of relief that she still believed me at least. I'm tempted to tell her about my drink with Lee, but I can't face explaining how I messed up and didn't record anything useful. She'll think I'm an idiot. There have been no new mentions in the press, the rumours being consigned to just that. A blip in the road. For all my efforts I've achieved nothing (except a series of hotel bills, money I can't afford to throw away).

I'm out of ideas.

22.

Iris

I've finally heard from Daisy. Not with any news, that would be too much to hope for. I get a text when I'm at work on the Wednesday morning after my visit to Mum's asking if I want lunch.

Yes! I reply. I'm desperate to see her, to find out what she's going to do. *Can you meet me at the shop about 12.30?*

Can't you come here? comes the response. *Or the West End somewhere?*

I only get an hour! She knows this. And, of course, she has the whole day with no commitments, she could easily come to me. *Hour and a half tops. I don't have time to go into the West End. Let alone come to you. By the time I got there I'd already be late back!!!*

I wait for what seems like an age.

OK.

I can hear the sigh in the word. I tell Zak I'm going to take a long lunch, trying to frame it as if I'm owed for some nebulous extra time I worked once. Not that he cares, but I don't want him to start thinking it's OK to skive off whenever he feels like it. By ten to one Daisy still isn't here and I'm pacing around irritably. Zak chomps on an enormous ham and tomato panini and tries to make conversation, but I'm not having it. I'm too wound up about my sister's unreliability, the most reliable thing about her.

'My brother's the high achiever of the family', he's saying when the bell over the door dings and Daisy breezes in.

'Did you come via Northampton?' I say grumpily.

'Oh, am I late?' She looks completely unflustered as only those who have literally no responsibilities can.

'Take as long as you want,' Zak says. 'It's dead today anyway.'

'Ring me if you get a sudden rush. We'll only be up the road.'

'I thought we could go to one of those places on the river,' Daisy says. She has her hair in plaits like she's eight years old.

'We don't have time to walk all that way,' I say tersely, and then tell myself to lighten up. I want her to be honest with me, she's not going to do that if I snipe at her. 'Let's go to that nice Spanish café round the corner. It's got a garden.'

'Lovely,' she says. 'Whatever.'

We walk out into the sunshine and she digs a pair of bright pink sunglasses out of her bag. 'How was Sardinia?' I say, trying not to sound as if I'm being judgemental.

'Bliss,' she says, and then she launches into a long description of her course, which seems to have been some kind of self-awareness horseshit. Oh, the irony. The more courses she goes on in search of personal growth the more self-obsessed and less self-aware she becomes. And the vaguer the curriculum seems to be.

This one was just entitled 'Being', which feels like something she could have managed on her own. Still, I feign interest.

I wait until we've found a table in a shady corner of the café garden and ordered plates of cheese and patatas bravas and huge white beans with equally giant chunks of garlic before I broach the subject I'm really interested in. I've tried having a surreptitious look at her stomach even though I know it would be a bit too soon for her to be showing and, unsurprisingly, her skinny frame is as skinny as ever. Years of dedication to yoga means that her abs are as tight as the tightest Spanx. I imagine Daisy could be one of those people who sail through a pregnancy completely oblivious and then deliver a surprise baby on a trip to the loo one day.

'Have you ... um ... have you thought about what you're going to do?'

She looks at me as if she has no idea what I'm talking about, a chunk of Manchego between her tanned fingers. 'Oh. That. No.'

'You need to make a decision, Dais. You can't just ignore it.'

She yawns loudly, stretching her hands above her head. The silver bracelets that snake up her arms jangle. I try to suppress my irritation. 'I'm not,' she says. 'I'm just waiting for clarity.'

'Can't you pay someone to give you that like you usually do?' I snap. 'I'm sure there's some shyster guru out there somewhere who'd offer up an opinion in return for Mum's cash.'

'Unnecessary,' she says.

'This is a baby we're talking about.'

'I know that, Iris. And I have time to make sure I'm doing the right thing. Don't pressure me.'

'I know you do,' I say more softly. 'And I'm not. I don't mean to . . . I just . . . I'm here if you want to talk about it.'

'You'd be an auntie,' she says, poking me jovially with a long finger, and I swallow back a gulp. I've been thinking about this, of course I have. A baby in the family, a niece or nephew I could spoil. For a brief second I imagine us sitting round a Christmas table, Mum, me, Daisy and an enchanting, laughing, toddler, and then I pull myself up. When was the last time Daisy and I visited Mum at the same time? She's always AWOL at Christmas because she wants the sunshine, and some acquaintance or other is going on a trip to Morocco or Turkey that she can tag along with if she persuades Mum to give her cash for Christmas. Of course, she also knows that Mum always feels bad about handing over something so impersonal for a gift, so she'll have bought something too. It's win, win. I always worry about Daisy when she heads off on these trips with random half-friends. I'm waiting for the day she gets arrested at Gatwick with a bit of tourist tat stuffed full of class A drugs she didn't know were there. Even worse, that they pick her up at the other end before she even boards a plane. I've seen *Midnight Express*. I can't imagine how alarming it would be if she was dragging along the baby too.

'Just promise me you'll think through all the pros and

cons. You know I'll support you whatever you decide, but you need to know you can give this baby the best life possible if you have it. Stability, all that.'

Daisy laughs. 'Isn't it funny that you're not the older sister. I always think you should be. You're so ... sensible.'

I give up.

I haven't spoken to Fay or Cally for over a week. Not since they all went to Center Parcs. Not since the street party. That is, we've exchanged messages – a photo of Kieran in a straw sun hat, a snap of the five of them (Steve, I assume, was down the pub with his mates) at Cally's neighbourhood kiddies' barbecue, the support act for a more adult evening do. *We were too knackered to go in the end*, Fay says with a picture of Kieran asleep on Cally and Jim's green sofa. We have a long-standing date for this evening. Jim is on baby duty. Just the three of us at a Thai restaurant in Hammersmith. I can't wait to see them. It seems pointless to traipse all the way home only to turn round and leave again, so I stay at work a bit late, get to the restaurant a bit early. I nab a free table in the patio garden at the back. It's a bit too near the bins and the toilets, but it's such a lovely day it feels wrong to coop ourselves up inside. I order a bottle of ice-cold lager and some sparkling water and browse Maddy's social media. There's a new post extolling the virtues of a certain brand of ice cream maker. The twins appear covered in some kind of purple sorbet. No sign of Lee, but there usually isn't in these kinds of videos. He saves himself for the big production numbers, one of which Maddy promises for tomorrow. 'Two weeks on Thursday till the book comes out,' she sing-songs, waving a copy around. 'And I've just found out I might be going on *Steph's Packed Lunch*! Can you imagine?' I turn my phone off, feeling sick, and then worry that either Cally or Fay might be trying to get in touch to say they're late, so I turn it on again but put it face down on the table.

They arrive together and we all throw ourselves at each other in a group hug. They look tired, my friends, but still gorgeous. 'Did you bump into each other outside?' I say, peeling one of Fay's long hairs off my T-shirt.

'We've been at Water Babies. We just dropped them off at Cal's and came straight on.' Come to think of it, there is a faint smell of chlorine in the air. 'I've got photos, look.' I coo over Kieran and Frankie looking adorable in their little trunks. Frankie floats in a rubber ring while Kieran proudly sports red armbands.

'I'd love to come and watch one day.'

'Oh god,' Cally says affectionately. 'You really wouldn't. It's carnage.'

We order drinks from a lurking waiter and catch up, all talking over each other. I tell them about my weekend with my mum – both of them love her. Cally's mother has always been a bit emotionally distant, obsessed with doing the socially correct thing in any circumstances, while Fay's is a bit of a car wreck, preferring nights out with a succession of ever younger boyfriends to spending time with her daughter and grandson.

'She's my role model,' Fay says when I tell them about Mum's rule-breaking.

'You need to get her out of there,' Cally says ominously. 'Isolation is like the worst thing for old people.'

'I know, but I can't just pick her up and plonk her somewhere new where she doesn't know anyone at all. Even if she'd let me.'

We all sit there in silence for a moment, mulling it over. I'm so grateful for my friends. For the bonds that go back far enough that we know each other's family histories inside out. I'm just wondering whether to tell them about Daisy – I'm not sure if it would be too much of a breach of her confidence – when they start chatting about the requirements for the nursery Fay is trying to get Kieran into. 'We have to start going to church!' she says, topping up her and my wine. Cally puts a hand over her glass.

'That can't be right in this day and age,' I say.

Cally nods sagely. 'If you want them to go to a church school they expect it.'

'And do you?' I say to Fay. First I've heard of it.

'Not in the slightest. But it's the only one that's even halfway decent.'

'And they check up?'

'Too right they do. They use the vicar like a spy. I mean, I can stop as soon as he gets his place, but it's fucking boring.'

'And what does Steve think?'

Cally rolls her eyes at me. 'He'd probably want him to

go to one where the kids learn to fight in a bear pit every day. He's obsessed with toughening him up.'

'He's the toughest eleven-month-old I know,' I say, and Fay snorts with laughter.

'He is! He's like a little pitbull.'

'But don't you both have to go? I mean, if they care that much.'

Fay shrugs. 'I'm going to tell them I'm a widow. Fuck it.'

Cally nudges her arm. 'Tell her.'

I wait. The air feels loaded.

Fay inhales. 'I've left him.'

'Oh my god, Fay. When?' I want to say *that's brilliant* but I'm not sure that's appropriate. It depends how raw her wounds are.

'When he got back from Croatia. Center Parcs decided me. Kieran just seemed so much more relaxed without him around. I realised he must take in a lot more than I give him credit for.'

'Wow. So, what? A week ago? Tell me everything.'

'I need another drink,' she says, indicating to the waiter for a second bottle.

'How did he take it?'

'He was too hungover to really grasp what I was saying at first. And he stunk of booze and fags and about four different rank perfumes, so that made it a lot easier.'

'I have so many questions,' I say. 'Has he moved out?'

She nods. 'Back with his mum. He's been round every

evening to try and get me to change my mind, but I've had it.'

'He's never . . . I mean . . .' Cally and I have occasionally debated whether we think Steve could get violent. He certainly has done from time to time with lads that look at him the wrong way. We've always come down on the side of no, but it's there as a spectre of a thought all the time.

'I would literally fucking kill the man if he ever laid a hand on me,' she says. I believe her.

'So, you're keeping the flat? I guess he has to agree that, right, for Kieran's sake.'

Cally and Fay share a look. 'There's no point. It's rented anyway. I've found a place near Cally and Jim . . .'

'Oh.' It seems pathetic given what is happening in Fay's life that I'm upset about the fact she has made all these huge life decisions without once chatting to me about it, but I am. I'm hurt. 'Already?'

She nods. 'I'm moving this Saturday.'

'To Queen's Park? That's where the nursery is?' At the moment Fay lives in Wimbledon, which is not exactly close to me, but it's not a million miles away either.

'Well, it's more Kilburn . . .'

Kilburn, on the other hand, might as well be.

'That's great, Fay. I'm really happy for you. If you need a hand with the move let me know. I'm not doing anything this weekend.'

'Jim's got it all sorted,' Cally says apologetically. 'He's hired a van.'

When we were all in our early twenties there was a

period when Fay and I were going out with two good mates, AJ and Dean, who we'd met on the same night in a pub near to where the three of us were sharing a flat. They were both sweet-natured, uncomplicated and up for a good time. We started to go out together as a four-some most evenings – AJ and Dean were practically joined at the hip. AJ worked for an events company and he used to get free tickets to random shows that weren't selling out. Always four. Cally was single at the time and I remember how easy it was to get caught up in the moment and exclude her without even really realising we were doing it. In retrospect – once the first flush had faded and I realised AJ was a bit nice-but-dim and def-initely not long-term material – it struck me that she must have been hurt. Lonely. It didn't even occur to Fay or me to insist that we wanted her to tag along, or to arrange nights out without the boys. We both just went with the flow. So, I get it. I get that circumstances shift in even the most long-term friendship groups, even if it's only temporary. It's not that I resent Fay and Cally for their common ground. I get that parenting puts them in a subset from which I am excluded. I just wish things were different, that's all. The plan always was that we would have our kids at the same time, that they would grow up to be besties, and I reneged on my side of the deal.

'Come over as soon as we're in,' Fay says now.

'Definitely. I need a Kieran fix anyway.'

She looks at Cally. 'We're taking the kids to Legoland on Sunday but next weekend . . .'

'Love to,' I say. I lift up my glass. 'Cheers to the future. You've done the right thing.'

'I hope so,' she says.

Neither of them brings up Maddy and her near miss with social media death, and so I don't either. My obsession feels trivial compared to Fay's real world problems. Petty.

Sad.

Insignificant.

A bit like myself.

23.

Maddy

Maddy has never done an interview with a national newspaper before, let alone a photoshoot, but here they are, the four of them, dressed in vibrant jewel-coloured outfits provided by the stylist, and with their faces professionally made up, being told to jump and smile and hug each other by a serious-faced woman in skinny jeans and a Patti Smith T-shirt who is so effortlessly cool it's making Maddy feel intimidated.

Having the four of them in the pictures was a deal-breaker for the paper. Lee, of course, was not only reluctant but furious and she can feel it oozing off him as they clown about awkwardly now. When the make-up woman suggested a little bit of blusher on the twins' cheeks to give them a rosy glow, he'd practically swiped the brush out of her hand. 'Not too much make-up on the kids,' he'd said. 'If you don't mind.' She couldn't really see the problem herself. She would have made it all a big game, joked with Ruby and Rose about how silly it was, what a hoot. They're hardly going to be scarred for life by a bit of Charlotte Tilbury. But she needs to keep her husband sweet. They can't let any cracks show because the journalist is here, watching their every interaction like a hungry hawk.

Jas, the publicity woman from the publishers, has

impressed on them what a big deal this is. She had to jump through hoops to secure the slot in the first place. The paper owed her a favour because she'd secured them an exclusive with a TV chef who has a cookbook coming out. It's going to be in the family section, their perfect target market, a whole page hopefully. But for that the paper needs to know they're going to get something special. Jas had warned them they were going to have to talk about the rumours – 'You're not in a position to start refusing to answer questions' – and she'd advised that the best way to go was to talk about how devastated they felt that someone would want to hurt their family like that. To play the sympathy card and then just deny, deny, deny. 'Cry if you can,' she'd said. 'Although not too much. Keep bringing it back to how precious your family is. How much you love each other.' Maddy hadn't told Lee any of this, she'd just instructed him to let her handle it if anything came up. She was dreading the interview, if she was being honest. She had always dreamt of a day like this and now it had come, she felt nothing but fear that the walls of her life were paper-thin and could tear at any moment.

'Look at us,' she wants to say to Lee. 'Look how far we've come.' But it doesn't ring true any more. All she can hope for now is that the book sells well, that she gets a little bit of a profile, and then she'll have to come clean with the world and see what happens from there. She'll adjust the timeline a bit, of course. She can't admit that she's been lying, that they've been separated all along. And besides, she's still hoping it might be temporary.

She's been thinking about it and she's sure she can carry on making videos, advising people on happy families without having to involve either Lee or the girls. Maybe the promise of that would be enough to persuade him to come home. It'll take a bit of working out, but she'll manage. She's a fighter.

'Swing the little girls round,' the photographer calls and Maddy and Lee pick up a twin each and twirl with them. The twins are getting hyper, a sugar rush of attention. It can only be so long until they start to cry instead of laugh.

Thankfully things had been quiet since she'd made her accusation. Maddy still wasn't sure what to think. Was it because the Truth Teller really was Iris and she was afraid she'd been rumbled, or because it was someone else who didn't care enough to keep the vendetta going? They were already on to the next victim.

She had thought that maybe she could find Iris, confront her in real life. She'd googled her with Tom's surname – Smith – but had got nowhere. A mention of her at an interiors shop in Camden where, presumably, she used to work ten years ago, but nothing else. Maddy had tried to call it in case any of the other staff had kept in touch, but the shop no longer even existed and the number was dead. Presumably Iris had reverted to her maiden name these days, and Maddy had no idea what that was. She'd even thought about tracking Tom down to ask him, but she wasn't sure being in touch with Tom was a sensible thing to do. She wasn't sure how it would make her feel. She'd worked so hard to put all that behind her.

'OK, I think I've got it,' the photographer says, calling time on the shoot, already packing down a huge reflective umbrella. Maddy smiles and thanks her, and gets a curt nod in return.

Jas has offered to keep Ruby and Rose entertained while Maddy and Lee do the interview. Maddy digs out two lunchboxes from her bag, and two cartons of juice. The lunchboxes are decorated with each of the girls' names in pretty, swirly letters, to avoid the major catastrophe of Ruby being given Rose's raspberry-flavoured flapjack or Rose ending up with cucumber in her sandwich. Their preferences change almost every day, it's hard to keep up. Lee has a theory that they are trying to mark themselves out as individuals, not half of a double act called The Twins, and Maddy thinks he's probably right. It's hard being an identical twin, she can see that.

'Shall we find a quiet spot?' the journalist says with a smile. 'Those photos are going to be gorgeous.' Maddy allows herself to relax a little. Not too much, she knows she needs to stay alert to trip wires, but enough to imagine that maybe it's all going to be OK. She takes Lee's hand – they need to keep reinforcing the idea that they're a happy couple – and he grimaces at her as if he's in pain. He's never been a great actor.

Thankfully the interview is benign. The journalist only touches briefly on the 'silly rumours' in the context of a question about how they keep the children away from 'online negativity'. His wife loves them, he tells them, she watches all their videos with their four-year-old, and Maddy knows that it – this one interview – is going to be OK. She should be enjoying this. Everything she has worked for over the past three years has finally come together and all the dreams that she's occasionally allowed herself to indulge in are coming true. But she's living in a house made of straw.

Back at home she puts the girls down for a nap. They're fractious. Overstimulated. She's about to ask Lee if he'd like a cup of tea – she's going to sit in the garden and plan their next video – when she hears him shout 'See you later,' and the front door slams shut. Despite the fact that he's sleeping here, that they're putting on a united front for the world, he spends as little time here as he can, particularly if the twins are absent. He's kept on the dingy little flat because, she thinks, he wants to make the point that his return is only temporary, and she wonders if that's where he goes. Anywhere so as not to have to spend time with her.

She takes her drink out into the garden, leaving the back door wide open so she can hear if Ruby or Rose wake up and need her, pulls a wicker chair into the shade – she's terrified of the ageing effects of the sun on her pale skin – and indulges herself in a little cry.

24.

Iris

I send Fay a WhatsApp on Saturday morning: *Hope it all goes well today. Can't wait to see your new place!* – and she sends back a photo of Kieran sitting in a packing crate, head tipped back, laughing. *I'm terrified Trunky's going to get lost in the move*, it says underneath. *Not letting him out of my sight!* Trunky is Kieran's stuffed elephant, a present from me when he was born. It's his favourite thing in the world and just the sight of it is guaranteed to bring on a fit of arm-flapping giggles. *I've put an air tag on him. Trunky not Kieran! Xxx*. I spend way too long looking at Kieran's little face, just the sight of him warming my heart. I realise I have no plans. Verity is in Athens with a friend, Fay and Cally are, of course, occupied. I'm looking at another long, empty weekend. I hear the radio go on – way too loudly – in the kitchen and make a snap decision. I grab some clothes and tiptoe down the hall to the bathroom, ignoring Carol's shout of 'I was just about to . . .' Her MO in the mornings at weekends is to make a coffee and take it into the bathroom to drink while she soaks. Tough luck. If she'd already started to run the bath she would have officially staked her claim, but she's made a rookie mistake.

The drive doesn't even faze me now. I'm almost on auto-pilot heading for the M4. I have no agenda this weekend,

I just want to relax, to allow myself a pretence that I still have a life. I thought about going to Bath or Brighton or somewhere new, but I'm drawn to the now-familiar town by the river. I head straight for the Premier Inn but they have no rooms available. ('You should have warned me, I'd have saved you one!' the friendly receptionist says and then he sneakily hands me a card for a B&B run by someone he knows. 'Nice people,' he whispers. 'Clean.') I find myself in a neat little seventies semi on an estate of neat little seventies semis just a few minutes' walk from the High Street, with Jean and her husband Trevor. 'We've been doing it for thirty years,' Trevor tells me as he shows me to a spotless room with an en suite. 'You meet so many interesting people.' They still run it like an old-fashioned enterprise, with a full breakfast on offer in the morning. ('Most of them do that Airbnb these days,' Jean says, insisting I have a cup of tea. 'But we're too old to try and get to grips with that now.') I tell them I'm visiting friends just so I can get away without looking rude, and I go for a walk into town.

I pass Lee's flat on the way but there's nothing to see. I try to ignore the fact that I know Maddy and the girls will be leaving their dance class soon, that she'll probably take them to the park, maybe even with Lee this week in a show of solidarity. I'm not here for that. I'm here for a break. So, I walk straight across the top of the High Street and down an unfamiliar road, past the local branch of Marlborough Kitchens with the bestselling steely grey Manhattan range in the window. When I realise that I'm heading out of town, I turn back and weave down a long alley that I know, even if I'm not admitting it to myself, must bring me out near Maddy and Lee's house. I recognise the park ahead of me, the little hall where the classes are held to my left, the entrance to Hanwood Lane to my right. I force myself to cross straight over to the park and head for the café. It's a dull day but it's just warm enough to sit outside with a coffee. Right beside the playground. Who am I kidding? Of course I'm hoping to catch a glimpse of them. It's an itch I can't stop scratching.

My phone pings with a notification of a message on my Instagram Truth Teller account. I know it'll be Maddy-related because I only follow the anti-Maddy squad and the woman herself. I try to ignore it but then I suddenly panic that maybe it's her again with some actual proof the account is run by me, or saying *I can see you sitting there in the café, I'm coming to get you.* I scour the park anxiously. I brace myself and look at my messages. Breathe a sigh of relief when I see it's Lara. *Are you OK???* she says. *I can't believe they've managed to shut this whole thing down! They're actually going to get away with it!!!*

I know! I send back. *I'm all out of ideas.*

She replies immediately. *You were my last hope haha!* Followed by a smiley face. *We really can't let them off ffs! I mean, there must be something else you can get on them???*

I feel a bit guilty that I've let her down. I'm not going to lie, I was enjoying being the hero of the hour even though no one knew the real me. I can see why Spiderman gets such a kick out of it. And – slightly pathetically, I realise – I don't want to lose the little connection we have. The feeling of being in it together, on a mission to bring Maddy to justice. I send her a sad face in return.

Eleven o'clock comes and goes. I nurse my latte, trying to make it last. A few minutes later a stream of little girls with their parents leave the hall and parade past, some still in their leotards and tutu skirts. I keep my head down but there's no sign of Ruby and Rose. I can't imagine Maddy's the kind of parent who would just miss dance class one weekend because she couldn't be bothered, so there has to be another reason. They're unwell or they've gone away for the weekend. Rather than be disappointed, I actually feel a weight lift off my shoulders. If there's no possibility of seeing them I really can just relax. It's a freeing thought.

I'm not quite sure what to do with myself now I have no mission to accomplish. I watch as a couple of women about my age meet up on a bench across the way. One of them has a little border terrier who greets the other woman like she's its best friend. I don't want to go back and sit in the B&B, so I wander up to the High Street again and potter around aimlessly. A short walk from the town centre I pass a brand-new block of 'apartments for the over 60s'. It looks welcoming, with a green space out the front and a board noting all the amenities such as a communal lounge for those who want to socialise. Maybe Mum should move into somewhere like this, but could I even broach the idea with her that she take up residence in a retirement block? (What does that even mean? Lots of Stannah Stairlifts in the hallways? Or is it just to deter noisy young people from moving in? I need to google it.) Even though she retired from her job as an English and drama teacher over fifteen years ago, she would balk at the suggestion she be lumped in with other OAPs. I'd need to think carefully about what I was going to say to her.

I walk round to the side and peer through the window of a flat that looks empty, wondering what you might get for your money. It's boxy, but fairly spacious.

'Hi, Cat Woman,' a voice behind me says, and I jump, banging my head against the window. 'Shit, sorry, are you OK?'

I turn and see Lee, a look of concern on his face. I want to say, 'I thought you were away this weekend.' But, instead, I settle for 'Yes. Ow.' Of course, this is very close to his secret bachelor pad. I wonder if he's been hiding out there.

He laughs. 'Do you make a habit of peering through people's windows?'

I rub at my head. 'I was . . . never mind.'

'Planning a robbery?'

'Yes,' I say. 'Exactly that. It was going well till you came along.'

'Oh, it's for sale,' he says, noticing the sign. 'Are you going to have a look?'

'Yes, because a retirement flat is precisely what I need right now. How about you? What are your plans for the weekend? Family time? How old are your girls? Four?' As if I don't know. I'm babbling. My questions feel far too intrusive, but thankfully Lee doesn't seem to notice.

'Three. And their mum's taken them to the seaside for a couple of days.'

'You not invited?' I say, keeping the tone light.

'I'm painting their bedroom.' I wonder if that's true. Are they getting it ready to sell or back to playing happy families? There are no specks of paint on his clothes, his hands.

'Nice. Don't you actually need to be in the house to paint it?'

'Ha! Just taking a break. I suppose I should . . .' He waves a hand in the general direction of their house. 'Nice to see you. Maybe I'll bump into you later.' He raises his eyebrows meaningfully. Is he flirting with me? 'You should make an appointment to look at the flat. Nothing like planning ahead.'

I wave a hand as he walks off, and then I have to wait for him to disappear round a corner before I move off in the same direction, back to my B&B.

I try to sneak into Jean and Trevor's with the key they gave me and creep up to my room for a nap without bumping into them, but they're lurking in the kitchen doing something with pastry, so I feel I have to call out a hello.

'Would you like a tea or a coffee?' Trevor calls, and I say no, I'm just back for a little rest before I have to go out again. 'Shall I bring one up in an hour or so?' Jean pops her head round the door. 'That would be lovely,' I say. 'Thank you.' I must remember to leave them a rave review on their website when I leave.

Revived, later, and having eaten all the home-made

biscuits that Jean left on the tray outside my bedroom door, along with a pot of tea (and a tiny tap, tap, tap and call of 'Wakey, wakey'), I spend an age in the little en suite, probably using up all of Jean and Trevor's hot water. I've been playing the moment over and over in my head – the jaunty eyebrow raise when he said he might see me later. Lee was definitely flirting with me. He's on his own for the weekend and he wanted me to know it. I can't believe he won't be out and about tonight.

I just have to find him.

25.

Iris

The only thing I know about Lee's solo adventures is that he once sat outside the Chequers pub on the High Street for a couple of beers, so it makes sense that I head there first. I have no idea how many pubs there are in this town but I've seen a fair few, so my task could be like finding a needle in a haystack – except that I definitely believe Lee was giving me a message, an invitation and, if that was the case, he's going to be heading to the only place he'd expect me to look.

Two of the long tables are occupied, and not by Lee. I have to decide what to do. I could trail around randomly hoping to bump into him, or I could trust in my gut, get a drink and wait here. I opt for the second, talking myself into sticking to lime and soda rather than the big glass of wine I really want. It's still early. Earlier than I bumped into him here last time. I slide on to a bench and try to occupy myself with Wordle.

'Cat Woman! I thought I might find you here.' I look up and see him walking towards me. So, this *is* a date of sorts, I wasn't imagining it.

'Of all the bars in all the world,' I say, and he looks at me blankly.

'Can I join you?'

'Sure.'

'Drink?'

'Got one,' I hold up my glass.

'Save me a seat,' he smiles, heading inside. I turn on my phone camera and flip the picture so I can see myself. I fish a lip gloss out of my pocket and apply a thin coat. I don't bother to turn on the video, to try again to record our conversation. I have much bigger plans than that tonight.

'How's the painting going?' I say when he slides in opposite me, pint in hand. I have to remember that as far as he knows I think he's a happily married man, so no flirting unless he does.

He shrugs. 'Getting there.' I can see that he does now have a few paint flecks on his hands in those hard-to-get-to bits around his fingernails. It looks like a chalky buttercup yellow. The same colour from the 'Walking on Sunshine' video.

'Did they choose the colour?'

He looks down at his hand. 'Oh. Yes. This is Rose's side. Ruby's is orange.'

'Cute,' I say.

'They are. Monsters but, you know, cute monsters.'

I laugh. It's obvious how much he dotes on his daughters. It's going to take a while for him to get drunk enough for my purposes. I settle in for a couple of hours of chat. It might be enlightening.

'Will your wife be OK with you having a drink with me?' I ask as I offer to buy a second round. 'I mean, I know we're just chatting, but I wouldn't want . . .'

Still-sober Lee sticks to the script. 'Of course. She's never been the type to get jealous about nothing.'

'God, lucky you. My ex was,' I say, doing Tom a major disservice. 'That's good then, just checking. Solidarity and all that. Pint?'

'I think I'll switch to wine,' he says, and I nod. 'Me too. Red or white?'

'Surprise me,' he says. 'Whatever you're having.'

I get white so that I can top up my small glass with water to match the huge one I buy him. I need to keep my wits about me.

He's pretty easy to chat to, to be fair. We talk about our families – he's an only child – and he tells me how the house he and Maddy live in was his parents' old home. I explain about Mum and how I'm thinking a move might be the answer.

'Ah, the retirement flat,' he says, and I tell him how I think she'll dig her heels in if I ever say those words.

'I never thought my mum would agree to go into care,' he says. 'But she's happy there now.'

I dig at a loose splinter of wood on the table. 'It's so hard to know what the right thing to do is. I'd never want to upset her.'

'I bet you're a great daughter,' he says. 'I can tell how much you care about her.'

I find myself talking to him about Daisy. How I feel I have to balance out the worries she causes our mother by overcompensating about how settled and happy I am.

'And you're not?' he says.

'Not particularly. I mean, I'm fine. It's all first world problems.'

He gazes across the road. 'I hope Ruby and Rose get on when they're older. I can't imagine them not.'

'Twins are different,' I say, although I don't really know what I'm talking about. It sounds like something that might be true, though.

'Let's hope so. Do you think if you and Daisy had been twins it might be easier?'

'God, no. She'd still be a massive flake who drove me crazy, I'd just never be able to get away from her. I love her though, don't get me wrong.'

'She's probably envious. Or is she as pretty as you?'

'Oh puh-lease,' I say with a jokey eye roll.

'What?' he laughs. 'I'm paying you a compliment.'

It's actually a pleasant evening. There's nothing predatory about his flirting. It's part jokey, part hopeful and it would be easy to write it off as mere friendliness. A bit of harmless back and forth that neither of us would misinterpret.

By about half past ten, though, he's steaming. I've made sure that pretty much every other drink for me – the ones I bought myself – was a soft one and so, even though I'm a bit tipsy, I'm definitely not drunk. Now I've got him where I want him, I'm not sure what to do with him. Lee, though, makes the decision for me.

'I'll walk you home,' he says, as we finally decide to call it a night.

I obviously can't be inviting him back to Jean and Trevor's, so I have to think on my feet. He's so wasted that

I don't have to worry about subtleties. 'I actually have my aunt and uncle staying at the moment, so I don't want to disturb them.'

Thankfully he doesn't question why I haven't mentioned this before, he just picks up on the implied suggestion that if they weren't there I would have invited him in. He actually blushes. 'Well, you could come back to mine for a nightcap if you wanted.' (What he actually says is 'Wellyoucouldcomebacktomineforanightcapif-youwanted' in one long drunken slur, but I manage to pick the words out of it.)

Does he mean the house? Maddy's house? Would he really be that reckless?

'OK. Great. Is it close by?'

I can see the cogs turning. We're still standing outside the pub and he's a little unsteady on his feet. I wait to see which direction he'll lead me in. Left to the house or right to the flat. He moves to the right and I follow. The flat it is then. I'm a bit disappointed at not getting the chance to poke through Maddy's things but I can't exactly argue. He half staggers along the street, stopping to look in various shop windows. ('Look at that. Absolute shit,' he says of an artwork on display in a gallery. And 'Ooh, rabbits!' outside the toy shop.) We finally arrive at the entrance to the little close where, to be honest, I would probably think I was being lured to my death by a serial killer if I didn't know any better. At night it looks even more run-down and dismal.

I follow him up the steps to Flat 2. When he opens the door there's an overwhelming smell of unwashed clothes and old rubbish. He obviously wasn't planning on inviting me back here. He wasn't intending on getting this drunk. I feel a flicker of guilt. 'Sorry,' he says, going round throwing open the windows. 'I'm not here very often at the moment.'

He opens the fridge door, pops the caps off two beers and hands me one. I follow him through to the tiny living room where there's a two-seater sofa and an armchair in front of a big TV, and nothing else. He sits on the sofa and pats the empty space next to him with what I imagine he thinks is a sexy smile. I suddenly feel a bit nervous. What am I doing? No one knows where I am. I think about sending Lara a message: *With Lee in his flat! If you don't hear from me again by tomorrow call the police!* but she probably wouldn't even see it till tomorrow and if she even took it seriously it'd be too late. All my spidey senses tell me he's harmless. Said every woman who ever encountered Ted Bundy.

I sit where he indicates, but with my back against the arm and my feet on the seat between us – a sort of barrier that, I hope, gives off the vibe that I'm not up for anything just yet. He doesn't even notice when I pull my phone out of my pocket and start recording. I'm hoping for bigger and better things, but the odd confession wouldn't hurt.

'Where's the room you've been painting?' I ask. I want to see how much he'll tell me.

'Oh. No. That's . . . this isn't home . . .' he says, vaguely.

'So what's this place?'

'Airbnb,' he says without hesitation.

'Really? Do you get many takers?'

He must notice my sceptical expression, because he looks round at the state of the place and laughs. 'OK, you got me. That's what we're telling people. The official line,' he adds, doing exaggerated finger quote marks. I wait for him to say more.

'I live here. Well, I did, and I will again at some point probably . . .' He looks at me as if to say, 'Now do you understand?' which, if I didn't know exactly what was going on, I wouldn't. Luckily he's so pissed I can fill in the gaps without him noticing.

'Are you separated? You and your wife?'

He nods emphatically. 'Separated but pretending we're not.'

'Why? For the girls?'

His face drops and I wish I hadn't brought them up. 'No. Because of the book, you know . . .'

I decide I might as well spell it out, he's too wasted to realise. 'So, you and Maddy have split up but you're pretending you haven't because she's got a book coming out?'

He points a finger at me. 'Bingo.'

'And you've moved back home temporarily . . .'

'. . . because of the journalists,' he says, finishing the sentence for me. 'Fuckers.'

'Wow,' I say. 'How long do you think you can keep that up for? I mean . . . isn't it . . . ?'

He nods emphatically. 'Not good. Not good.'

'Poor you. What a mess.'

He looks me straight in the eye, or as straight as he

can with all the booze filling up his veins. 'You're a nice person, Rissa. Easy to talk to.'

I'm not done. 'So, once the book is out, you'll move out again?'

He takes a long swig of beer. I flick my eyes to my mobile on the seat beside me to check the red recording light is on. 'Yep. It's not right, is it? Making the kids perform like seals.'

'Is that why . . . ?'

He pushes his hair back from his forehead. 'Shouldn't be telling you this.'

'Why does it matter, though? If you're not together, I mean. Why pretend?'

'Because she peddles all that family shit. The whole thing is based on us being this happy family. But she cares more about being famous than what's right for the twins.'

I almost feel bad for Maddy. This is surely the final nail in the coffin.

I can see that Lee is falling asleep, the alcohol finally catching up with him. There's just one more thing I need.

'Go to bed,' I say. 'You don't want to wake up here.'

'Want to come?' he says wolfishly.

It's a half-hearted proposition, but it is a proposition nonetheless. I smile at him. 'Not this time.' I help him up to his feet and lead him through to the bedroom. 'I'll get you a glass of water.' He's pulling his T-shirt off as I leave the room. When I come back in, he's sprawled on top of the covers in his underwear. I snap a photo while he has his eyes closed – nothing graphic, just his top half. Then I place a hand on his chest – I painted my nails specially this afternoon using the Rimmel deep red that I found in Jean and Trevor's bathroom, something I can usually never be bothered to do – and photograph that too. It's clearly Lee. It's clearly a woman's hand. Surely that's enough. For good measure I film a quick pan around the sad, half-empty room, capturing him and my arm draped across him in the mirror. I'll triple check tomorrow that there's nothing of me that's identifiable. I shove my phone in my pocket and stand up, hoping I can just sneak out without him noticing. No such luck. He opens his eyes, screws up his face and blinks up at me as if he has no idea what I'm doing there, even though it's only been two minutes. 'You going?'

'I should,' I say. 'You need to get some sleep.'

He rolls over and snuggles down like a toddler. I feel the urge to pull the covers over him, smooth his forehead, make sure he's comfortable.

'Don't . . . I mean, I shouldn't have said anything.'

'It's OK.' I back towards the door, but I freeze as he lets out a sob. Is he crying? I hold the phone up. He doesn't even notice.

'Shit. We didn't . . . ?' he says half into the pillow. 'Did we?'

I leave him hanging.

'I love Maddy, that's the thing. I just want it all to be OK. I want us to go back to who we were before our lives turned into some big fucking *Truman Show*. That's all. I don't want to live here. I want my family back, but things need to change. I shouldn't have . . . shit, we didn't do anything, did we? Because that's not me . . . I've never cheated on her . . .'

'We had a nice evening. That's all,' I say. 'Night, Lee.' I leave before he can say anything else that ruins my resolve.

26.

Maddy

A couple of days away is exactly what she needs. The Kent coast, nothing too glamorous, but it's quiet and peaceful in the run-up to the school holidays. And the weather is beautiful. Clear and warm, the blue skies lasting long into the evening as she sits on the balcony of their little room while the twins sleep. The toll of the past few weeks was catching up with her. She needed to lower her stress levels and today she's really felt as if she's achieved just that. She's given the girls her full attention, no phone, no distractions, and she could see in their faces how thrilled they were. She'd sat and watched for hours as they constructed a castle out of the stony sand – in reality it was more of a formless heap, but the thought was there. As if on cue they had turned at the same time and smiled at her, and her heart had melted.

She tries to imagine what it would feel like to be so famous that journalists followed you on holiday, paparazzi lurked in the bushes hoping for a glimpse of cellulite or a roll of tummy fat as you relaxed on the beach. A rogue nipple. Waiting for the one fleeting second when your smile drops, and they can pitch an article about how unhappy you secretly are. Other bathers taking sneaky pictures they can pick over with their friends. Look at those stretch marks! Look at the way she scowls at her husband here! Or, god forbid, look at how tubby/skinny/neglected/entitled her daughters are. The thought makes her shudder. She's never really considered the downside of the success she craves until now. She'd only ever thought about the positives: affirmation, stability, respect. Of course that only works while the life you let people into is perfect, and who can truly say that with their hand on their heart? Maybe Lee is right, maybe it's not fair to drag Ruby and Rose into a spotlight they'll never be able to shake off.

She pulls herself up. It's not as if she's about to become a superstar. At best she'll be someone who pops up on TV occasionally, maybe fronts a show that runs for one or two series, has a couple of books out that are *the* gift for parents that Christmas, and that'll be it. She knows the shelf life for Instagrammers who break through the noise is generally short. It's all about cashing in while you can and then hoping for bigger and better sponsorship deals in the wake. She'll have made enough of a splash to secure their futures and that's what matters. She just has to get through these next few months.

She wonders how Lee is getting on with the painting. A tiny part of her is clutching on to the memory that he asked the twins for their choice of colours, and he wouldn't have done that if he was going to try and advocate they sold the family home, would he? He'd have insisted on a neutral, something that would have mass appeal. She wishes she could speak to him – she had called briefly earlier so that the twins could say goodnight, and he'd been on his way out to the pub. He'd have been hoping to bump into someone he knew, he always did. He knows a lot of people in the town, though he's not particularly close to any of them. The legacy of still living in the place where he grew up. A couple of pints and then home, it's always the same. She smiles at the thought.

Back in the hotel room, she can finally relax. Going to the beach as a single parent is hard work. She'd been terrified to lie down all day in case she'd dropped off and one of the girls had wandered away or worse. She and Lee had always been a team. Yes, he'd started to have issues with what they were doing, but he'd still always been there pulling his weight with the kids, telling her to take a break. He would have spent the day entertaining them, keeping watch while she slept, and then she'd have taken her turn. Tag teamed. She wonders if they'll ever all go on holiday together again.

Tom might have been the love of her life, but Lee is her rock. Her other half. Their relationship might never have had the passion, but passion burns out and it's what's left that's important. They have always been in it together, building a future for their girls. He has always been happy for her to be front and centre. 'I'm the warm air keeping you afloat,' he'd joked once. 'I'm the manically pedalling duck feet under your smoothly gliding swan-like body.'

'I don't think swans have duck feet,' she'd laughed. 'But apart from that, that's a good analogy.'

She can't imagine a life without the security net he provides.

Now she tries to use the time to plan their next video. She's deliberately picked a resort with notoriously poor Wi-Fi, otherwise she'd probably be spending all her free time on social media picking all the hateful comments out of the sea of lovely ones and blowing them up in her head out of all proportion. That was the thing when you grow up with low self-esteem; it doesn't take much to knock it back down again, to be back to being that clumsy five-year-old, the awkward eight-year-old. The truth is she's not really any more comfortable than Lee is in front of the camera, she's pretty sure she doesn't feel any less ridiculous, but she loves the message they're putting out there. Her little family is everything to her. And she's found a way to support them and give them all her attention at the same time. She should be proud of herself. She *is* proud of herself.

They should do a beach theme, she thinks. She could buy some bin bags in the morning and she and the girls can have fun filling them up with sand to take back. She tries to think of an appropriate song choice. 'Itsy Bitsy Teeny Weeny, Yellow Polka Dot Bikini'? Is that a bit creepy? She's not sure she wants to put them in swimwear. You can't be too careful these days. You don't know who's watching and she definitely doesn't want them to be the object of some old perv's attentions. Lee has always been paranoid about that. No, not paranoid. Understandably concerned. Maybe she can rustle up some old-fashioned costumes out of their ballet leotards and some leggings. Couple of rubber rings and arm bands. Thankfully her followers seem to like the fact that their videos have a homespun quality, that they're not too slick and over-produced. 'I Do Like to Be Beside the Seaside', that's the song. Lee has some cycling leggings from the brief period when he took up dressing in head-to-toe Lycra and going out on his bike on a Sunday morning; he can wear those under swimming trunks. She'll rustle him up a vest from somewhere. She can cobble together a goofy outfit for herself. They have a paddling pool at home, there's a shop on the front that sells big blow-up palm trees. She just has to work out the routine and a way to incorporate the book into it. It suddenly all seems like a lot of work and she leans her head back and closes her eyes. Remember why you're doing it, she tells herself. Remember the prize. They just have to keep it together. All of them.

She checks on Ruby and Rose and then goes back out to the balcony. Hits Lee's number again. There's still no reply. It's late. She doesn't leave a message.

27.

Lee

Lee wakes up with his face stuck to the pillow, a pungent puddle of drool next to his open mouth. There's a moment when he feels as if he might have got away with it, but then his head reels with a sharp, blinding pain that knocks him sideways. He reaches out a hand looking for something, anything, to drink. He's sure he left a half finished can of Diet Coke on the bedside table yesterday. His fingers make contact with a glass. He half sits up tentatively and sniffs the contents. Water. He can't have been in too bad a state if he brought water to bed with him. The liquid makes his stomach heave and he lies back on the pillow. It'll help, he just needs to keep it down. He's in the flat, he knows that much. He's not sure why he didn't go back to the house. He's supposed to be living there again now, putting on a show.

He turns on to his back, groaning. Maddy would be soothing his forehead if she were here. Bringing him Alka-Seltzer and a homemade juice that would miraculously settle his stomach. She'd smile indulgently and tell him she'd take the twins to the park to give him some peace and quiet. Instead he's in this shitty little hovel with nothing to show for his forty-five years on this earth. Except for Ruby and Rose, his greatest achievement.

He misses Maddy. He misses what they had when the job – because he most definitely thinks of it as a job – was still fun. When they were making it up as they went along and oohing with excitement when they got rewarded with a free box of nappies or a carton of bottles of baby lotion. Now there are rules. It's a chore. Yes, it's their living, but he's become plagued with doubts. It's not just that he's started to feel like a twat – emasculated, Maddy would say – because of the fact he's effectively living off her. It's the twins. Ruby and Rose. They've started to throw tantrums sometimes. To make a fuss when they're asked to dress up and perform when they just want to play. He remembers a story he read once about how, in order to make Shirley Temple give an authentically sad performance, a Hollywood director had waited until just before the cameras rolled and told her her mother was dead. He knows that bribing Ruby and Rose with sweets or promises of trips to the park is hardly on the same level, but he's worried about where it will end. He doesn't want his girls seeing that MaryNewman22 thinks they're a bit chubby or PaulaTheBrawler thinks they need braces on their teeth. He doesn't want random strangers hiding behind a username and avatar commenting on whether his babies are pretty enough or not. They're perfect. It's not up for discussion. And if he and Maddy can't agree on that then he doesn't think they can have a future.

The thought of that breaks his heart.

He staggers to the bathroom and pisses out something that resembles apple juice. There's a worry eating at the back of his brain, more than just the usual free-form hangover guilt. More than his constant anxiety about his family. He swallows down two paracetamol. He can't think about it now, he needs to sleep. He pulls the covers over his head.

He bolts awake, he doesn't know how much later. He was with someone. Last night. It all comes flooding back to him at once. Cat Woman. What was her actual name? Rita? Rissa? They'd had a few drinks together. Christ, had he invited her back? He pulls back the covers in a panic, inspects the bed. He leans over and sniffs the (grubby) sheets on the other side. Nothing except the musty fust of the too-long unwashed. He drags himself up and half runs into the living room, looking for clues. Everything seems as he left it yesterday. Maybe they got very drunk outside the pub and he staggered home alone. He might have made a bit of an idiot of himself. He can get a bit flirtatious when he's had a few but it was just banter. He can live with that. He's always hidden behind jokes and teasing. A jovial, laddy personality. It makes it easy to skim through life, getting on with everyone, never having to dip beneath the surface. Maddy is the first person he's ever really felt himself with. Not afraid to show that there are darker waters underneath. It was a relief not to always have to be 'on' with her, to be able to be pissed off if he felt pissed off, sad if he felt sad. She actively encouraged it, told him the only way he could truly be happy was to be authentic. To stop trying to hide behind a mask that said everything was fine. He could imagine her at work, making her clients' lives better, fixing them, sending them out into the future a better version of themselves.

When they met – she'd found his number on a local Facebook page that recommended tradespeople and she'd hired him to put up a few shelves in her new consulting room – she'd only recently moved to the town looking for a fresh start. He was keeping his hand in, working at the job that he hated all week, selling office equipment, and then doing odd bits of DIY on the weekends. Even with the re-mortgage the cost of his parents' care was debilitating so he needed to try to bring in as much as he could. His father was mentally out of reach by this point, off in his own world of vivid childhood memories that were more real to him than the people around him, the people who loved him. But he could see worry etched on his mother's face whenever he visited. *How was he coping? How could he afford to pay for the care home while he was still trying to get his own life in order? When would the money run out?* He spent sleepless nights himself worrying about it, but he would never have let her know that.

He'd been single for a few years at that point. He'd had casual flings, but he really hadn't been in the market for anything more. Maddy was not long out of a break-up and, even though she tried to pretend otherwise, licking her wounds. They'd got talking when she brought him some kind of god-awful herbal tea and a homemade biscuit that tasted like hay. He'd taken a chance and said that to her, and she'd laughed loudly, her whole face lighting up. Her perfect little white teeth showing. He smiles at the memory. God, he loves her. His previous relationship had been an exercise in point scoring: *you went out with your mates last night so I'm going out tonight; we saw your parents last week so now we have to see mine; I put the bins out so it's your turn to do the recycling.* Everything was a negotiation, a debit/credit balancing of the books, and he was always being told he came up short. He went along with it for an easy life, but it wore him down. His idea of a relationship was one where you were a team, where your main job was to make the other person happy. He'd learnt that from his parents. *Never go to bed on an argument,* his dad had said to him once. *Nothing is that bad it can't be sorted by talking it over. Have a bit of give and take. Compromise, that's the name of the game.* Sue had turned every decision into a battle. If he tried to talk to her about it she would blow up at him and then – almost worse – she would sulk. She could ignore him for days, simmering with righteous indignation. At first he would make attempts to cajole her out of her mood. He tried jokes and sweet gestures, bringing her flowers or packets of her favourite crisps, but she'd remain immovable. He couldn't bear the heavy silences. Their flat felt oppressive, weighed down by the toxic atmosphere. Eventually something would make her give and they would grudgingly make up, but the undertones were still there for days in her sighs and muttered comments. In the end he had given up trying. Sue was who she was and he either had to put up with that for the rest of his life or not. In the end he'd chosen not. Sue had seemed more angry than upset. She'd wasted half her life on him. She'd put up with his annoying habits and his stupid jokes. Who did he think he was that he could just walk out? *Why do you even care if we break up if you dislike me so much?* he'd said, and she hadn't really had an answer for that.

After that he'd shied away from commitment. He was fine with one-night stands and his own company. Until he wasn't. Until he realised that he was lonely right around the time he met a woman with a kind face, who made him smile and fed him a biscuit that tasted like hay.

Maddy had always filled their home with light and laughter. If they had a disagreement, one of them would apologise and that would be it. The air would be as clear as if it had never happened. Clearer, even.

When she'd told him she was pregnant he hadn't even questioned whether it was what he wanted, whether it was too soon. He'd just felt almost drunk with relief that this amazing woman had chosen him.

He should have tried harder to support her ambitions. After all, he'd been happy enough to take the money, to give up working and enjoy the spoils. Even when he felt stupid and humiliated dancing around in some kind of homemade tutu, he should have laughed instead of snapped. He didn't know where that side of them had gone, the Maddy and Lee who had fun. They'd lost it and it was all his fault.

Please god say nothing happened last night, he thinks now. He and Rissa flirted a bit and then they both went their separate ways. He's never been one for prayers, even though if you asked him he'd probably say that he

223

was a believer in a low-key, when it suits him, way. He'd said a quick one over his dad's grave a couple of times, when he'd gone there to talk to him and it felt as if he should. Now seems like as good a time as any to start. He closes his eyes briefly. Please let him not have fucked everything up. Please let it all be OK. He allows himself to think that it might. But there's some kind of shadow. Something tapping at his brain to get in. And then he sees them. Two empty beer bottles. Nothing unusual in that, except that they are at either end of the coffee table as if put there by different people.

Fuck.

He slaps the side of his head and then regrets it. He needs to get his brain in gear. Did he sleep with her? Rissa? Shit. He has no idea. He's still wearing his boxers – would he be if they'd had sex? He feels slightly turned on by the idea and then disgusted with himself for thinking it would be anything other than a disaster. A betrayal. Maddy is the best thing that ever happened to him. Whatever he's allowed her to think, he was never intending to move out forever. He'd just wanted to force her hand, to make her agree that they should pack it in after the book comes out, at least as far as involving the kids was concerned. And him too, he didn't want to do it any more. He's happy to be a full-time house husband while Maddy capitalises in whatever way she can. Or he'll get a proper job. Whatever. Fuck. He knew what he was doing. He'd found Rissa's attentions flattering and he'd definitely dropped a big hint about hoping to see her at the pub. But he'd never intended to take it this far. He'd just wanted that frisson of excitement, knowing that someone was interested in him, that he was more than the saddo who dressed up in stupid outfits and pratted about on camera for a living, feeling about as sexy as a CBeebies presenter. That there were possibilities out there if he ever decided he wanted to look for them. All the while knowing that he never, ever would.

He flops down on to the sofa and puts his head in his hands. What has he done?

And then, as if that wasn't bad enough, it hits him. What did he tell her?

28.

Iris

I don't know where I am when I wake up with the light streaming through the flimsy yellow curtains. I can hear a radio playing something classical and someone whistling along quietly. It's only when I stare at a framed print of an insipid mountainous landscape opposite the bed that I remember I'm in Jean and Trevor's spare room. I scrabble around for my phone and go into photos. They're there: my hand on Lee's chest, his sad bachelor pad. A long video of the ceiling that captured our conversation. I email them to myself for safekeeping. I'm never going through that again.

I can smell toast and bacon and I suddenly feel ravenous. Jean and Trevor are very proud of their full English and they've insisted I have one before I leave. I assume this is them making their own, though, so I take my time having a shower and getting dressed. I'm not sure I can face sitting and making conversation with them at this time of the morning. I'm leaving as soon as I finish — I'm not going to risk bumping into Lee today. I have no idea how much he'll remember.

The temptation to send the pictures to Fay telling her what I've done is almost overwhelming. To confess. But also because deep down I think she'd be impressed by my ingenuity. Although I think she'd then lecture me about moving on and leaving well alone, too. Plus, I wouldn't trust her not to tell Cally, the way they are these days, and I know Cally would be horrified. Neither of them has ever understood my inability to let sleeping dogs lie. I have form, so to speak. But the need to show someone is eating me up. So, I send a private message to Lara attaching one of the pictures: my manicured hand on Lee's bare chest, his expression up for interpretation, somewhere between comatose and post coital: *I've really netted a big one!!! This will be it!* As ever she replies immediately. *Shut. The Fuck. Up! Is that you?? This is insane!!! You didn't actually have actual sex with him, did you?* I don't know what to say to that. I don't want to deny it because maybe what I really did – setting up a drunk, unknowing man – would be a step too far even for her. Maybe she'd be disgusted that I'm trying to bring them down with an out-and-out lie. But I don't want to admit to it either, because even in my fantasy anonymous life, I have no desire to be that woman. So I fudge it. *What do you take me for??* With a load of laughing emojis.

Legend! Lara sends back. I smile. And then I pack up my bag and head downstairs for breakfast.

I'll be honest, I don't really want to go back to my flat. Carol will be in residence. Because I've been away every weekend for weeks, she's become even more at home and her belongings have spread out like duckweed across my kitchen. An air fryer she never uses, a rice cooker she never uses, a bread maker she never uses. I'm behind on everything though: cleaning, washing, ironing. My routine weekend tasks piling up behind me like a distant mountain range in the rear-view mirror. I need a bit of time to organise my life. And I need to put a bit of distance between myself and Lee.

An image flashes into my brain. Him letting out a sob. *We didn't, did we?* I push it away. I can't allow myself to get sidetracked now.

29.

Maddy

She'd been able to ignore the phone calls. Those had been worse for Tom than her, his mobile ringing incessantly whenever he turned it on. Ever-changing numbers so that when he blocked one, another – unknown – would appear. In the end he'd changed his own, but that was when, for Maddy, things started to get really bad. At first it had been the comments on her website. *Don't let this woman treat your husband if you want your marriage to survive*, and then *Madeleine Cartwright offers so much more than life coaching. She'll sleep with your husband too.* She'd known who it was, of course. There surely couldn't be more than one person in the world who would level these very specific accusations against her. She'd deleted the comments section (annoying, because usually the feedback she got was gushingly positive and definitely helped persuade new life-coaching-curious clients to take the final leap) and tried to move on. But then the Event Manager at Osaka Systems, the company Tom worked for and one of her best and most loyal customers, had got in touch. They'd had a complaint . . .

She'd watched as her life had started to fall apart around her, barely understanding what was going on. Surely Iris's problem was with Tom, not her. Tom had been the one who'd pulled the plug on their relationship before Maddy was even on the scene. When she'd first gone to his place he'd been living in a little rented flat in Holborn. A nice modern block, but the soulless space of a recently separated man who knew his life was in flux. She'd felt sorry for him. It had taken courage, she thought, for him to walk away – especially when he told her about Iris's desperation to have a baby, the conversations they'd started having about IVF.

He'd cried, later. From the guilt, he'd said. He knew he was taking Iris's dream away from her. He'd tried to still be there to support her, to remain a friend, but it was giving her false hope.

'I didn't mean to meet you so quickly,' he'd said as they lay in bed. 'The plan was never to fall in love with someone else this soon.'

'When you know, you know,' she'd said, stroking his face. 'We can take it slowly, but there's no point trying to fight it.'

After they'd been seeing each other for six weeks or so, he'd invited Iris to lunch to break the news. In retrospect it probably would have been better if it hadn't been her birthday. Iris had clearly read something into that, had thought that maybe he was taking her out to discuss how they might get their relationship back on track. Tom had thought that she might appreciate the gesture, that it might hint at setting up a new tradition whereby they met as friends on significant occasions. Iris would know she would still have him in her life, just not in the same capacity. He hadn't factored in her state of denial that he'd left for good in the first place. They were on completely different pages – her still hoping for a reconciliation, him ready to refile her permanently under 'Friends'. Maddy knew none of this. Tom had told her that Iris was coming to terms with the split, that he would be able to smooth things over, to pave the way for their future. She'd only realised how deluded he was when she'd looked at her website.

And then her doorbell had started ringing. Sometimes in the night, sometimes in the middle of a coaching session. She worked from home so, of course, her details were easy enough to find. There was never anyone there when she answered, but she knew.

They had tried to build a wall around themselves then, she and Tom, to protect what they had. They'd given up their flats and moved to the outskirts of London to get away. They'd set up home together way sooner than they ordinarily would have, their relationship put on to fast track because of their common enemy. Never healthy, she would have advised any client who'd asked. Tom had changed jobs. She had given her practice a new name, taken any personal details off her website and relied on old contacts and word of mouth, although most of them couldn't be bothered to travel all the way out to Rickmansworth, and who could blame them? She'd had to start building her practice up again from scratch. But however strong they made their defences, she had known Iris was out there somewhere, hating her, wishing them bad things. The thought of it made her ill. All she wanted was to make people happy, to love and feel loved.

The bottom line was that Iris had succeeded in

driving a wedge between her and Tom. It was almost as if she'd put a hex on their relationship. Cursed it. She hadn't tracked them down – Maddy didn't even know if she'd tried, although she felt it wouldn't really have been that difficult if she had. But it seemed she'd finally given up, got the message, come to her senses and backed away. The ghost of her was always there though, haunting them. Reminding them that their happiness had come at a cost.

It was enough.

And, in the end, Tom hadn't been able to take it any more. He couldn't watch her suffer, he'd said. He couldn't bear to see the shadow of herself Maddy had become and all because of him. She'd begged, pleaded, cried – they'd both cried – but in the end, she'd known he was right. What they had had been sullied forever.

It had been too much, too soon, for him, she could see that. If it hadn't been for Iris they could have taken their time, allowed their relationship to evolve. But her actions had pushed them together, united against a common enemy, fighting for their lives. Maddy had thought he'd owed her – it was his ex-wife, after all, who'd taken a hammer blow to her career. She had done nothing wrong. She should have kept quiet about it, calmly built herself back up without piling more guilt on to him, but she still thinks he handled it badly. Tom leaving her let Iris win whether she knew it or not. Maddy has often wondered if he got in touch with her, told her she was the victor, maybe even found himself back together with her – the brave thing to do would have been to stick it out, to prove to both Iris and the world that his and Maddy's relationship was worth fighting for.

He'd told her they needed a clean break and even though it had broken her, she'd respected that. They had left the house they'd only just moved into. Tom had been happy for her to stay there, but she couldn't have afforded the rent on her own. And besides, she didn't want to. The memories were too painful. She'd thought about moving back to Marylebone, but even after such a short time the Central London prices had spiralled out of her reach, and half of her clients had moved on. More. She had a cousin she liked in Buckinghamshire who'd offered to put her up while she got back on her feet and she'd grabbed the chance of a fresh start. She'd rented a little office space above a shop on the High Street and ordered a brass sign for the door: Madeleine Cartwright: Life Coaching Services.

She'd had a lotus flower – a symbol of strength and resilience – tattooed at the base of her thumb, so that she would always remember.

She had cried herself to sleep every night.

In less than six months it was all over. Her big romance. Her fairy tale that had turned sour. She'd let Tom go without a fight because she could see he needed to.

She'd let Iris win.

30.

Iris

I almost need to go back to bed after breakfast, I'm so stuffed full of eggs and beans and bacon. It's actually really lovely being cooked for, even if Jean and Trevor do stand and watch me eat like a pair of proud parents seeing their baby handle solid food for the first time. I write a glowing report in their guest book, give them both a quick hug and get on my way.

Carol is clearly not expecting me. I know this because she's wearing my favourite pale grey hoody when I walk in and bump into her in the hall on her way out.

'You're back early,' she says, trying to style it out. 'Did you have a nice time?'

'Lovely, thanks. Did you buy a new top?'

She flusters. 'Oh. I'm just popping to the shops and it seemed like it had got a bit chilly suddenly, so . . .'

I wait. 'So . . . ?'

'I just grabbed the first thing that came to hand. I didn't even realise.' She whips it off over her head. 'Here. Sorry about that.'

'Easy mistake,' I say, taking it from her. 'Are you going to the supermarket? Could you get some loo rolls?'

'Sure,' she says, making a dash for the front door.

'Aren't you going to be cold?' I call after her, and she

waves a hand as if to say I'm fine as she rounds the hall to the stairs.

When I first put my spare room up for rent, I spent a whole weekend agonising about what to do about the little household essentials. The bills we would split, that was agreed, but whose responsibility would it be to replace the milk and tea bags? Fay, Cally and I had spent a hilarious night in the pub crying with laughter as we imagined the various scenarios that could arise from co-habiting with a stranger. I must call them, I think. I miss my girls. Maybe one of them will be free tonight. In the end I had decided that the idea of asking my lodger to contribute to a kitty was just too petty. We were adults. We could be trusted to work it out fairly as we went along. In the brief time that Joanne was actually in residence, it had worked beautifully. So much so that I almost forgot all about it. It was as if we both instinctively knew when it was our turn to stock up. But I hadn't reckoned on Carol. It's not that she doesn't buy her share, it's that she always needs reminding. Several times. Never once has a jar of coffee miraculously appeared just in time, without me hinting that it's her turn. We once had a standoff over the last squirt of washing-up liquid that lasted three days, each eking out a tiny blob more so as not to be the one who discovered it empty. This is not how I thought I would spend my forties.

Fay answers straightaway. I can hear the radio on in the background, and I picture her singing along tune-lessly to make Kieran laugh. He always gets the joke.

Either that or he just laughs at anything given the excuse, which is equally endearing.

'I just came home and caught Carol wearing my clothes,' I say before she even has the chance to say hello.

'No fucking way! Tell me everything.'

'No, you first. How's the flat? Are you all settled in?'

'Just about. I mean, it's tiny but it'll be OK. Steve came round.'

'And?'

'I think he gets it. I mean, he's still talking about us trying again, but it's not going to happen. He can see Kieran though, as much as he wants. I'm not going to start trying to mess with that.'

'Good for you. You need to set boundaries, though. He can't just turn up.'

'I know, I know. Anyway, Carol, what the actual fuck?'

'You're not around tonight, are you?'

'No babysitter. Cally and Jim are at his mum's. Wait. Come over! If you want to, I mean. We can get Deliveroo.'

'Love to,' I say, feeling suddenly as if a weight has lifted off my shoulders. 'I can get there about half six.'

'Oh, and I can't really drink much, obviously,' she says as we say goodbye. 'Solo parenting. I'll be very boring company.'

'You're always boring company,' I say, laughing. 'I won't even notice the difference.'

Buoyed up, I spend the afternoon racing through my chores like a whirlwind. I do two loads of washing and use up all the space on the airer in the kitchen (Carol always does her washing on a Sunday evening – I can already hear the disgruntled huffing when she gets home and discovers she has nowhere to hang it), clean my room, give the kitchen and bathroom a wipe-down. I even iron a couple of shirts and a skirt ready for work. Carol has still not returned by the time I finish, so she's either lost in Tesco or she's skulking out of my way somewhere. It almost feels like the flat is my own. I plan my route to Fay's. It's about an hour-twenty by bus involving more than one change, plus a ten-minute walk at this end and again at the other. Jesus, London is so big. What's the point of a city where you can be further away from someone than if they lived halfway across the country? I decide to drive, even though the idea of nego-tiating the roads of Central London scares the shit out of me. We're not drinking anyway, and I think I'll be grateful just to throw myself into my car at the end of the night. It's still going to take me an hour at least. And I need to factor in getting-lost time. Fay won't care if I'm late, but I don't want to miss Kieran's bedtime.

Her flat is the ground floor of a scruffy two-storey red brick Victorian terrace. There are three green hire bikes lying on their side in the front garden. Later Fay tells me that her upstairs neighbour likes to use them to get home from, but not go to, work. Every now and then a van arrives and takes them away, but he always replaces them within a few days. I drive round for about five minutes looking for a spot to park that isn't so far away I'll fear for my life if I leave in the dark.

Fay and Kieran are at the bay window when I finally get there. I see her point to me and his face splits in half with a smile. I pull a crazy expression and his legs and arms flap like a fledgling about to attempt his first flight.

'Oh my freaking god, it's so good to see you,' she says as she opens the front door. There's a small communal hallway with two doors off it. One, I assume, to the upstairs flat. The pile of random mail that always inhabits a multi-flat shared space sits on the floor. Other than that and Kieran's buggy, there's nothing in there. I hug them both and she hands Kieran to me like a pass the parcel. He grabs my nose with one of his chubby hands and squeals.

She points at an open door. 'I'm in here.'

I follow her in. The flat is a bit sad compared to her and Steve's neat box. There's a faint smell of damp. The landlord clearly found a job lot of magnolia paint because it's everywhere. Bizarrely, the woodwork is painted brown. But Fay has made it cosy with colourful prints and throws. The beige carpet has the indents of a hundred previous tenants' bits and pieces.

'I bet there's a wooden floor under there,' I say, sitting on the green sofa and placing Kieran on my lap. She pulls a face. 'They won't let me take it up. Hopefully this place is only temporary, anyway. No point doing too much.'

'Are you still going back to work in September?'

'Of course.'

I bounce Kieran up and down on my knee. 'In Wimbledon? From here?'

'I don't know. I didn't think. I just wanted to get away, and Cally and Jim are up the road . . .'

I can't help myself. 'You'll be travelling, like, three hours a day . . .'

'I know!' she snaps. 'But I have to, don't I? Or don't I have to pay some of my maternity back?' It's so unlike Fay that I'm stunned into silence. 'I'm sorry,' she says, and I see a tear snake down her cheek. I turn Kieran towards the window to distract him.

'I can help you sort things out,' I say quietly. 'I'm sure they have exceptions.'

She nods and I smile at her. 'Shall I do bedtime and then we can have a proper chat?'

'I should have stuck it out,' she says once I've bathed Kieran, read him a story and tucked him up. He's completely adorable lying there in his bear-patterned onesie, hugging Trunky as if his life depends on it, eyelids drooping.

'No, Fay,' I say firmly.

'He misses his dad.'

'He can see his dad.'

She sighs. 'Is it worth it? To end up here?'

'It's warm, he's fed, you're here. He'll be fine. We just have to work out the job situation. Where's Kieran going while you're working?'

'A crèche right by the school. The staff all put their kids in there. It's good.'

'OK, well, that's something. We need to find out how

long you have to stay before you can change jobs and meanwhile you can look for something up here.'

'Yep,' her voice is flat.

'You can stay at mine, both of you, as often as you like. I mean, you'd have to share my bed or sleep on the sofa, but I'm fine with that if you are. If the journey starts to get to be too much, you know . . .'

'What about Carol?'

'Part of me is offering just to piss Carol off,' I say with a smile and she laughs for the first time. 'It would be fine. If you need to, at any point, you know . . .'

She leans over and gives me a hug. 'Thank you. Let's talk about other things. What's going on with you? Where do you keep disappearing off to every weekend?'

'I've just been getting out of London for something to do . . .' I don't want to get drawn into talking about what I've really been doing. 'Anyway, I have news. Daisy is pregnant.'

'Jesus. What? Tell me everything.'

I feel as if it's a bit of a betrayal of my sister, but it's just the distraction Fay needs. She's known Daisy for twenty-five years, she knows exactly what she's like. She almost laughs herself sick when I tell her the father's name. 'You just know Crazy Daisy would never get knocked up by someone called Kevin,' she shrieks.

'Oh god, don't call her that,' I say. 'I mean, she is, but we shouldn't . . .' I look at Fay and she snorts and then so do I. We laugh like a couple of fourteen-year-olds smoking mixed dried herbs that someone has told them is weed.

By the time I leave, Fay's mood has completely lifted, and mine too. 'I love you,' she says, hugging me. 'Sorry I haven't been around much lately.'

'God, no. Me too. I'll come over more often.'

'We can meet in the middle,' she says. 'Where even is the middle?'

I shrug. 'Acton?'

'Well, that'll be nice,' she laughs. 'Text me that you're home safe.'

31

Maddy

She can't even bring herself to read the article, the headline is so shocking. She'd woken up excited, knowing that today was the day. It was still nearly two weeks till the book came out, but Jas had told her it would drive up the number of pre-orders, essential for a big impact. This interview was the first big piece of publicity, and the hope was that it would spark more once other publications saw that Maddy was a good interviewee, that the kids were photogenic. She'd slept like the dead last night, exhausted from the sea air and the long day on the beach. The twins were still flat out, their pale red hair spread over the pillows of the little single bed they're sharing. She'd woken up feeling optimistic. She had asked the hotel receptionist if she could have a copy of the paper left outside her room, had almost said why although now she's glad she didn't.

I feel so guilty I've subjected my kids to online abuse and ridicule! the shoutline screams above a picture of the four of them looking serious. *Let's just do a couple not smiling,* the photographer had said. *Just in case.* And out of the hundreds of pictures of them having fun, laughing, playing, this was the one the paper had chosen to give the most prominence to. OK, so the others they've used are better, at least they're looking relaxed, happy, but, once you've read that headline they all start to look a bit sinister, it seems to her.

Influencer regrets exposing 3-year-old twins to harassment, the sub headline says. Maddy puts the paper down. She feels sick.

It's too early to phone Lee. He didn't call her back last night, so she deduced he made a night of it and got home too late. Either that or he thought there was no point calling after the twins would be asleep. That he had no desire to speak to just her. She almost doesn't want him to remember that today is the day the interview comes out anyway. She can feel the 'I told you so's' coming her way. She dares to look again. The piece itself is nice. Kind. The journalist has documented their answers faithfully, although he's given a bit more prominence to that one question than it merited. There is no hint that there's anything wrong in their marriage. She thinks she heard somewhere that reporters don't write their own headlines, that it's someone else's job to sensationalise with an eye-catching soundbite. She hopes that's true. It would make her feel the tiniest bit better that she hadn't been duped, that she wasn't that bad a judge of character.

She had been intending to make a big splash on Instagram showing the article off, but she doesn't feel she can do that now. She doesn't want anyone to see it.

She's glad the Wi-Fi is so patchy. She couldn't bear to see the comments below the online page. The vitriol from people who don't know her, who choose to believe anything they read so long as it's negative. She doesn't need to read them, she can imagine what they say: she's a bad mother, what she's doing is child abuse, she shouldn't be allowed to get away with it, her children should be taken away. And then a slew attacking her face, her thighs, her very existence. Lee would get off much more lightly. The real hate was always reserved for women.

She tries photographing the page in a way that cuts off the headline, but it just looks weird, as if she's trying to hide something. Which she is. She gives up and lies back down on the bed.

Her mobile beeps. *Great piece!* Jas says. Of course she thinks that. It's publicity, it's column inches; it doesn't matter if it eats away at Maddy's soul, if it makes her feel worthless. She doesn't reply.

32.

Iris

The fucking *Sunday Mirror*.

I only see it because I google Maddy's name while I'm drinking tea and eating toast in bed before I get dressed for work on Monday morning. I don't even think about it, I just do it on autopilot, like I look at the weather and my email. I'm always disappointed if there's nothing new, but then furious if there is and that means she's getting more attention. This is a big one. A full-on interview with both her and Lee – he kept that quiet – complete with photos. I grudgingly have to admit to myself that the pictures are gorgeous. If I didn't know better I'd think this was a perfect little family having, as they like to proclaim, fun.

I study each of them separately. Maddy first, of course. She looks, frankly, stunning. I already knew that the camera loves her, but with a bit of professional help it flat out adores her. It's easy to imagine her on TV outshining everyone else around her.

Lee – only because I know him – looks a little awkward. Not quite so happy to be there. But he's giving it his all, and when he's interacting with the kids he almost looks relaxed. He's clearly in Maddy's shadow. There's no doubt who the star is here. I wonder when they shot these photos. Were they already living a lie by then? Faking it?

The two little girls, of course, look adorable. But there's an element of forced smiles. A bit of pageantry. Their hair is curled and they have – is that lipstick? It's all a bit *What Ever Happened to Baby Jane?* I can see why it bothers Lee.

I can't even imagine how smug Maddy is feeling this morning, knowing that this huge piece of publicity for her book is out there. Knowing that god knows how many people might have ordered it already because of this. It makes me feel sick.

I check my phone. Look at the bombshell I have hidden on there. I go into my laptop and download the photos and videos that I emailed to myself, just in case I leave my mobile in a cab somewhere. It wouldn't be the first time.

There's a message from Lara, with a screenshot. *Look at my comment!!* it says with five crying laughing emojis. I open up the picture. It's from the section below the article online, where people have their say. *Such a fraud!* Lara K exclaims. *She and her husband can't stand each other. They just fake it for the photos. I have it on VERY good authority!*

I send her back a smile. I think about adding something of my own, telling people that Maddy is a husband stealer, but I know something would go wrong and my real name would end up on there for everyone to see, so I content myself by opening up the comments section and reading the bitchy remarks others have posted, imagining Maddy seeing them.

I hear Carol moving about in the bathroom. I've lost track of time. Shit. Now I'm going to have to go to work without having a shower, cross my legs on the bus and wait till I get there to use the loo. I dig out my spare wash bag with its emergency toothbrush and drag myself to the kitchen to brush my teeth in the sink.

I feel bad for Lee. He's a nice bloke. But ultimately, if it means Maddy's brand is tarnished, that she has to rethink what she's doing, it'll be better for the twins, won't it? They can retreat into the background and live a normal life. And for him, too. He won't have to be at Maddy's beck and call any more.

Obviously, once I make my pictures public I won't be spending any more weekends down by the river. Lee will one hundred per cent know it was me. Unless he's taking a different woman back to the flat every night, hoping he might get lucky one of these days. It's a price I'll have to pay. It'll be worth it.

I just have to pick my moment.

33.

Lee

He's panicking. What was he thinking? What did he do? He waited all day yesterday, nursing his hangover with Alka-Seltzer and bacon sandwiches, for his headache to recede in the hope it would all become clearer, but it's still a blur. Waves of guilt wash over him like the tide. He has to face Maddy today. She's due back about lunchtime and she's expecting him to be here when the twins see their new bedroom. The bedroom he was supposed to finish painting yesterday only he couldn't face going out, couldn't crawl further than the kitchen without feeling sick. So, this morning he's been round here since five finishing off, getting it all ready. He opens the windows now to take away some of the new paint smell and clears away the dust sheet and brushes back into the garage. He puts new duvet covers on the little beds, one orange, one yellow. His heart aches when he thinks about his girls. The way they adore him. The way they laugh at his stupid jokes. Their sleepy faces at bedtime, like a pair of tired puppies fighting to stay awake. His relationship with them is the only pure and honest thing in his life. And now he's fucked everything up. If Maddy finds out what he's done, there's no going back.

And he can't even think about the other way he's let her down – telling a virtual stranger that their life is a fraud. He can remember that much. Snapshots of conversation keep sneaking back into his brain. He cringes at his bravado, his desperate attempts to impress an attractive woman by telling tales on his family. He's pathetic. But he knew that already.

He's a man who's lost his identity, who lets his wife do all the hard work and support them all and then moans about how emasculating what she's asking him to do is. He's a joke.

He needs to talk to Rissa. He has to find out exactly what happened, however hard it is to hear. At the very least he needs to take back the things he said, to tell her he was exaggerating, making up stories to impress. He needs to make sure that the heat for what he's done stays on him and doesn't burn the rest of the family.

He scrubs down the kitchen and bathrooms while he waits for the paint to dry. Then he leans each of the twins' favourite toys along the walls beside their beds. For Ruby her bear, Bruno, her stuffed penguin, Fishy, and her baby doll, Jules. For Rose her identical bear, Grizzly, her toy cat, Kitty, and her plush cow, Cookie. He knows exactly what's closest to their hearts out of their hundreds of possessions. He could name their favourite songs, TV shows, colours, animals, everything. It's imprinted on his heart. He puts away everything else in their big wardrobe-cum-toy-cupboard, except for the doll's house they share and the huge farm they like to add to whenever they are allowed to go to the toy shop. On Ruby's side roam exotic animals – lions and tigers and rhinos; on Rose's it's pretty much all cows. Rose loves cows. He remembers the time he accidentally made Rose cry by joking that Ruby's tiger would probably eat all the cows one of these days. It had broken his heart to think that he'd been responsible for introducing her to the harsh realities of life. He sits down on her bed and hangs his head in his hands, wiping away tears.

Later, he walks up to the High Street to get some air and buys two bunches of cheerful sunflowers and puts one in the girls' room and one on the kitchen table. He unpacks a couple of sticky cream cakes he's picked up as a treat for the twins, and some fat salmon fillets – Maddy's favourite – into the fridge. He needs to grow up. His family are everything to him and he needs to stop acting like a petulant child and be there for them.

Maddy was floored by the interview in the paper. That fucking journalist. Lee knew he was too good to be true. All that stuff about his wife being a fan. Maddy needs him. At least, he thanks god, it wasn't him who said the wrong thing, who gave them that headline. When he spoke to her yesterday afternoon she didn't seem to have read the comments underneath the piece. He had. Pure vitriol. *Don't look*, he'd said to her. *What is it they say? It's tomorrow's chip paper.*

They need to have a proper adult conversation when she gets back. Maybe, he thinks hopefully, some good can come out of this. She'll see how things can turn on a headline. She'll surely agree with him now that the kids shouldn't have to participate any more, that they can't be subjecting them to this. He'll promise to up his game. They can still do the stupid song and dance routines, just the two of them. He's happy to bite that bullet. They can make it work. And he'll find a way to contribute more, he can build up his odd-job business into something that actually earns money. Whatever it takes.

He has no idea how to contact Rissa. They've only ever bumped into each other wandering around town or outside the pub; they've never even exchanged numbers. This makes him feel both better and horrified. He obviously wasn't really that interested in her if he hadn't asked for her number, but on the flip side had he slept with a woman about whom he knew nothing except her first name? When he was in his twenties, sure. It was a regular occurrence. But he's a forty-five-year-old married man. He has no idea where she lives. He knows that she works for Marlborough Kitchens. Didn't they have a conversation about her commuting once? He's in the shower washing the last of the paint and grime off him when he remembers. Kingston. He remembers her saying that at least the shop was on the right side of London for her to travel up from here.

He wraps a towel around himself and googles Marlborough Kitchens, Kingston, London. There are two branches. It's definitely not ideal to have this conversation over the phone, or while she's at work, but he needs to get the facts straight before Maddy gets home. He needs to know exactly how bad his crime was. And he needs to ask her to please never repeat any of the things he said.

He's about to punch in the first number when he hears a key in the front door. His girls squeal with happiness at finding him there. They both gabble at the same time and he scoops them up, one in each arm, and plants a kiss on each of their heads. They smell of the sea and fresh air. He catches Maddy's eye over their heads and smiles. She looks drawn. Stressed. He promises himself he'll make it better.

Later when the twins are having a nap he pulls her into him, kisses her closed eyelids. 'It's all going to be OK,' he says. 'Forget about the article. No one will remember it. And as long as we're all right, that's all that matters, isn't it?'

She looks up at him with watery eyes. He's always loved how much taller than her he is, how protective it makes him feel. He's been an idiot. He'll make amends. 'And are we?' The hope in her voice almost breaks him.

He pushes her hair away from her forehead. 'We are. We just need to be able to talk about things. The future . . .'

He stops as he sees the fear on her face. He's made her feel like this. He's such a fucking fool. 'I don't mean us. I mean the business. The girls . . .'

She nods. 'You were right. Once the book is out, we'll change everything up. No one can be angry at us for trying to protect our children, can they?'

'Exactly. New start. I'm sorry I've been such a dick.'

She nestles her head into his chest. He dares to allow himself to think for a second that it really is all going to work out. That it's that simple.

34.

Iris

I know that if I post the photos or the videos then I've crossed a bridge I can never uncross. I check the date of publication of Maddy's book for the hundredth time. It's a week on Thursday. Ten or so days away. Any minute now, she's going to pop up on the sofa talking to Holly and Phil. I need to get it out there, give it time to filter through the noise. But something's holding me back. Lee's face. His utter horror when he thought he'd done something that could never be undone. I wish there was a way I could target Maddy without him being part of the fallout. Collateral damage. But I can't start getting sentimental now, or what has it all been for?

Work always drags on a Monday, especially when the shop is quiet. Without Zak to chat to I'm left alone with my own thoughts for far too long. I try calling Fay and Cally but they're both busy. I leave messages: *let's meet up, I miss you both*. To Fay I say *stay strong*. I ring Mum who's fed up and sounding very unlike herself.

'Cath's moving,' she says.

'Oh, no. Where to?'

'To be nearer her son. Bristol. Well, the outskirts.'

'Oh, Mum,' I say. 'Maybe you should come and live closer to me.' I almost add *Or Daisy* but then I think better of it. At least if Mum was in Kingston I wouldn't have to worry that she was going to get mugged putting her bins out. 'Somewhere on the river. Richmond or Teddington.'

'No one moves into London when they get older,' she says. 'It's against all the rules of the universe.'

'I would have thought that would make you want to do it, if that's true,' I say fondly, and she laughs.

'I'm happy here,' she says.

'Even with Cath going?'

Mum deflects, as she always does when the focus is on her. 'More importantly, how are you?'

'Great,' I say. 'Really good.' We're so alike. Neither of us ever wants to burden the other with our worries, so we tell white lies with a smile on our faces, and we both pretend to believe the other. I have no idea how Daisy somehow missed that memo, although maybe her way is healthier. Offload every one of your feelings without a care for how much they might alarm the person you're talking to, then run away.

I decide to leave it for now. If I push she'll retreat. But somewhere in the depths of my brain a plan is forming.

Next, because the shop is still empty and because Mum still seems clueless, I call Daisy. Her ringtone sounds different, like she's abroad, and when she answers with a breezy 'Hola!' I assume I'm right.

'Where are you?'

'Fuerteventura. It's glorious.'

'Doing what, Dais?'

'I'm on a Breath course. It's fabulous. Actually, we're really not supposed to have our phones on.'

'Wait!' I say sharply. 'Have you made a decision yet?'

'About . . . ? Oh, the baby! No. But I'm showing, it's so weird. I have this little tummy . . .'

'I hope you're being careful.'

'God, Ris, you're such a moaner. Childbirth is *the* most natural process. Do you think cavemen sat around doing nothing for months when they were pregnant?'

'No, but I assume they also knew how to breathe without going on a course to learn.'

She sighs theatrically. 'Why are you in such a mood?'

'Grow up, Daisy,' I say and I end the call without saying goodbye.

I feel down. Cut adrift. I write a message to Lara. *How are you doing?* She's probably at work herself – I have no idea what she does for a living. *I'm bored rigid*, I write. I wait a few moments for a response, but there's nothing. She probably has better things to do than being on Instagram at two o'clock on a weekday afternoon.

I find myself googling prices of houses near Mum's in Little Hadham, curious to know what hers would be worth if she sold up. It's hard to tell because they're so few and far between, and the prices vary enormously depending on what facilities the village has left (none in her case), but she could probably afford to downsize to one of those retirement flats in Marlow with change to live on. She'd only be an hour away from me, I could visit every weekend if I wanted.

Who am I kidding? I won't be able to show my face

there soon. Once I post the latest video, Lee will one hundred per cent be able to put a face to the Truth Teller account. Mine. I can't ever go back. My phone beeps. *Fun with the Fulfords has posted a new video*. I look around guiltily as if someone was reading the thoughts in my head.

Maddy and Lee are sitting against a bright orange wall. *Look what this man did!* she says. *I took Ruby and Rose to the seaside for a couple of days' fun on the beach, and when I got back he'd decorated their bedroom as a surprise!*

Not a surprise, I think. You all decided on the colours before he started. I pause the video on a shot of Lee. He looks exhausted. Stressed. His always-plastered-on smile looks as if it's hurting. Not with the hint of irritation and embarrassment he usually can barely conceal, but with something like sadness. Fear even. My first thought is that I feel sorry for him. I press play. Maddy pans the camera around the room oohing and aahing over every detail. *Look how he's done half orange for Ruby and half yellow for Rose. She's out of her pink phase. It's all about the yellow now. And the duvet covers! It must have taken so much secret planning!* We pass a row of stuffed toys, a doll's house. *Isn't he the best dad? By the way, it's only about ten days till my book comes out* . . . She produces a copy from somewhere. *There are so many ideas in here for making all your family time quality time. Because it's all about appreciating the blessings you have and making memories. Something as simple as this – a couple of cans of paint and a bit of hard work – can make your kids' day. You can order it here* . . . A link pops up on the screen. Lee reaches over and squeezes her hand. He looks at her with such hopeful adoration that I feel momentarily nauseous. It's apparent to everyone how much he really loves her.

I snap my phone off, angry at myself that the main emotion I'm feeling is pity for him.

I can't do it. However much I hate Maddy, I can't punish Lee like this.

35.

Lee

He waits until Maddy takes the kids to the park on Tuesday morning, claiming he wants to clear up the mess he's left in the garage, and then he dials the first number for Marlborough Kitchens, keeping watch out of the front window in case they return unexpectedly. He almost bottles out when someone answers.

'Hi, I wonder if you can help me. Is this the branch where Rissa works?' he puts on his best posh voice. He doesn't want to sound like a weirdo.

'Who, sorry?' the woman on the other end says.

He almost loses his nerve then. 'Rissa. I don't know her surname. I met her at the weekend and she left her purse behind. I just want to return it.'

'No one of that name here. Sorry.'

He can't get off the phone fast enough. 'Thank you. Sorry to trouble you.' He checks the other Kingston number. If this is a no-go he's got nothing. He's screwed.

A man answers. Lee coughs and then asks the question again. He waves at his neighbour Shirley as she walks her huge, curly-haired dog past the house towards the park.

'Oh. Do you mean Iris, maybe?'

'Rissa,' he says again, but an alarm bell is suddenly ringing in his head.

'Yeah, I think you want Iris. That's what her friends call her. She's nipped out. Can I take a message?'

Lee can't think straight. There's something about that name. Iris. Where has he heard it before? He needs to get off the phone. He does his best to sound jocular. 'No, thanks, I'll try again later.'

He ends the call, picks at a bit of hard skin around his thumbnail. Pulls on it too hard and makes it bleed. A memory comes flooding back.

Iris.

The woman Maddy told him was the only person she could think of who had a grudge against her.

The woman she believes is trying to ruin their lives.

Rissa, the woman he may or may not have had sex with, who he certainly told secrets about the cracks in his and Maddy's perfect façade, is Iris.

He doesn't understand. It's a coincidence, surely? There is more than one Iris in the world. But for one to come into his life just at the point when his family started getting targeted? It's like one of those nightmares where different worlds collide and nothing makes sense.

He feels a sudden wave of nausea and runs for the downstairs toilet. He only just makes it in time, heaving over the bowl. What has he done?

What the fuck has he done?

36.

Iris

I hadn't realised how much darkness I was carrying around. The relief that I feel when I decide enough is enough. I suppose that's what happens when you plot bad things. They start to define you, to change your idea of who you are, what you're capable of. I got caught up in the thrill of it, the power. I can do that sometimes, get a bit obsessed. I think we all do. In our heads, we're avengers. In reality though it's a lot more messy. A lot more unsavoury. A lot less attractive.

I look back over my photos and videos, finger hovering over the delete button. I know I should erase them, that then my slate would be wiped clean, but I can't quite make myself. Surely, so long as I never show them to anyone, then I can pretend they're not there, that I'm not the sort of person who would ever do such a thing. I hesitate. No. I have to do this properly. I have to be able to look at myself in the mirror. I hold my breath and hit delete, delete, delete. It feels good.

I message Lara. I know she's going to be disappointed in me, but I remind myself I don't even know her. Yes, she's a woman with a grudge against Maddy, but she doesn't even have a personal reason like I do, so far as I know. If I can let it go then surely so can she. *Do me a favour and delete that photo I sent you*, I say and she comes back immediately. *No way! Why???*

I set him up, I say. *It's not fair.*

I wait for her to object, to tell me that we can't give up now, that all's fair in love and war, but instead she sends back: *Fuck. OK. Oh well. Done!* A weight lifts off my shoulders. I feel as if I've grown weirdly close to her. That a lot of what I've done has been fuelled by her encouragement, how impressed she's been, how I don't want to puncture her image of me. And, I'm not going to lie, it's felt good knowing there was someone out there who hated Maddy as much as I do. I've even wondered if we'd be friends if we met in real life.

What I need to do is make plans for the future. Forget Maddy. Whatever happens with her, it doesn't impact on me. My worth is not contingent on someone else's failure. I dig out my journal and write that down, proud of how it sounds. It doesn't mean I can make myself believe it, but I can try. It's something I've always struggled with, not comparing myself to others. Even though I know it's unhealthy, I struggle to keep the destructive thoughts out of my head. I'm not as good, as successful, as attractive, as happy. I'm less than. Lacking.

I know I need to be proactive, take steps to change the things in my life that are weighing me down. An idea forms in my head. I phone Mum and ask her what she's doing at the weekend.

'Are you coming down?' she says hopefully.

'No, you're coming up. Or, at least, not to London. Are you still OK driving?'

Mum sounds affronted. 'Of course I am.'

'OK, well, it's about two hours' drive. I'm going to check if I can book rooms for us, though. I'll call you again in a minute.'

'Ooh, you're back,' the receptionist at the Premier Inn says when I give my name to secure the two rooms.

'With my mum in tow this time.'

'Love it,' he says.

I phone Mum again and give her the details. 'Just to see if you like it as much as I do,' I say when I've come clean about my mission. There's no point trying to fool her, she'd see through me in a second and put her guard up. 'And, if you don't, you don't. No pressure. There are other places. We'll still have a lovely couple of days.'

She's sceptical, obviously. But I think she's just relieved I'm not still trying to sell her the big city, so she agrees. 'Only because it'll be lovely to see you,' she says as we say goodbye.

I ask for Friday off. Mum will arrive around lunchtime so I decide to book us into somewhere nice to eat in the evening and go from there. For the first time in weeks I start to feel as if things are under control.

I'm going to concentrate on the future. The past is done. I'm over it.

37.

Lee

He can't tell Maddy. He can't warn her that her nemesis is real, that she's much closer than Maddy thinks. How would he explain how he found out? He should have tried to find out Rissa's – Iris's – surname, he thinks, although he couldn't exactly have asked her colleague without it all looking a bit sus. He tries googling *Iris, Marlborough Kitchens* and *Kingston* but they don't seem to list their staff anywhere. He doesn't know how else he can track her down. But leaving it to bumping into her in the High Street randomly one day is hardly a plan. And what if it happens when he's with Maddy?

He trawls through as many of their conversations as he can remember, hoping for a clue as to where she lives, but all he can recall is her vaguely waving a hand in a direction that covered a third of the town, when he asked her once. Had the whole thing been a set-up? Had he been stupid enough to believe she might actually fancy him? Fuck. He's never going to flirt with anyone ever again. He's learnt his lesson.

Maddy is upping the content in the run-up to the publication of the book. She wants to post a new song and dance routine every day for five days, but with all the distractions and their near split they haven't done any of the usual prep, so he's been sent to Smiths to buy crepe paper while she works her magic on the sewing machine. *Don't go too slick*, Jas, the publicity woman, had advised, but there was precious little chance of that to be honest.

He walks up and down the High Street twice, eyes peeled in case he spots Iris's long brown hair. Even though he knows she'll be at work he peers into every shop he passes. He thinks about going into Marlborough Kitchens on West Street and asking if they have some kind of staff directory, but he doesn't want to do anything to alert her to what he's discovered, and who knows if she's friends with the staff there, or if there's some policy in place for reporting potential stalkers. He doesn't have a clue what he can do with the information now he knows who she really is, what she's been doing to them, but he knows he doesn't want to blow the element of surprise just yet.

He can't be too long; he has to go home and turn the back garden into a beach scene with the sand Maddy hauled back from Kent in three stuffed bin bags. Despite everything, he finds himself smiling at her ingenuity, her commitment. They're doing 'Oh, I Do Like to Be Beside the Seaside' tomorrow and then 'Puff the Magic Dragon' while the sand is still in place (because Puff lived by the sea, obviously), and then 'Boom Bang-a-Bang' the day after (he's been tasked with painting cardboard bombs, flames burning their wicks) and he can't remember what comes after that. He has no idea where Maddy finds these songs, he hasn't heard of half of them. He just knows it's going to be a few days of chaos, of all hands on deck, and he wants to be there doing his bit. The first video needs to be ready to post on Saturday.

He can't even think about the humiliation of Iris watching them all, laughing at his family – at him being a crab with big cardboard pincers that they're planning on making this afternoon, and then a dragon breathing cardboard fire. But the days of being embarrassed about what they do are over. He needs to support his wife. He needs to get through the next week and a half without fucking anything else up.

He has no idea what Iris is planning. He can't bear to think about it, but fear keeps crashing into his brain and knocking everything else sideways. Because if it was all some kind of set-up and she didn't try and seduce him for the hell of it – and definitely not because she found him irresistible – then she did it for a reason.

And that scares the shit out of him.

38.

Iris

This is definitely the kind of place Mum should move to. Somewhere with a bit of life and community. She'd make friends soon enough. Daisy might even make it this far for a visit. I check into my room and then, fired up, I get myself a coffee at the café next door to the hotel and walk up the High Street. I'm nervous about bumping into Lee. Hopefully he has no memory of what happened back at his flat, and I can reassure him that we didn't get up to anything untoward. Maybe he won't remember me being there at all – he was pretty slaughtered – and I can let him believe we said good night at the pub. I'll feel better once I've been able to smooth things over. He never needs to find out who I really am. I can forget about him – and Maddy – and get on with my own life. Let her be successful. Let her get rich. Who cares? I'm just going to focus on myself.

I stop at the first estate agents I see and browse the window. The first thing I think is how beautiful so many of the properties are. The second is how expensive. Not London prices – nothing like – but certainly not country prices either. But Mum would be downsizing. Her house in Little Hadham is way too big for her. I think when she bought it she was imagining me and Daisy filling it with husbands and hordes of grandchildren some day, and we all know that's never happened. At least, not yet. I push Daisy out of my mind. Really what Mum needs is a flat – one with a bit of outside space, admittedly. But she only needs two bedrooms, one living room. All the properties in the window are huge, detached houses, most with acres of land or riverside views. They must have more normal homes on their books, they just don't display them in the window. I'm too intimidated to go in and ask, so I keep walking and stop at the next one I come to. It's the same deal: dreamy piles and gigantic price tags. Maybe this is a stupid idea. I should have done more research. There must be other little towns and villages around that are less obviously desirable. Cheaper. I decide to go somewhere where I can sit and browse PrimeLocation. I'm just trying to decide where – I still have the coffee on the go – when a woman about my age in a pretty summer dress and holding a GAIL's bag appears at my shoulder.

'See anything that catches your eye?'

I jump and my coffee sloshes out of the little hole in the lid.

'Just window shopping.'

'We have plenty more inside,' she says. Ah, she works here.

'Nothing I can afford, by the looks of it. Or my mum, I should say.'

'What's she looking for?'

Oh god. I hate it when anyone tries to give me the hard sell. It's guaranteed to make me run a mile. 'She's

267

not. I mean, she hasn't decided yet. But a flat. With a patio. Or a balcony.'

The woman flicks her shiny caramel ponytail to one side. 'How many beds?'

'Two, I suppose. I'm really just browsing . . .'

'Well, we have a few of those,' she says smiling. 'Tell you what, wait here a sec and I'll grab you some details, then you can take them away and look through them without me breathing down your neck. How does that sound?'

'Sure. I . . .' I look at my phone. 'I mean, I need to . . .' I flap a hand that I hope conveys I'm in a hurry.

'I'll be quick,' she says, heading inside. I feel as if it would be rude to just leave, so I stand there sipping my coffee and staring at the photos of houses I would never in my wildest dreams be able to afford.

She's good to her word. She's out again in a couple of minutes clutching a sheaf of papers. 'Here's a few to be going along with. I wasn't sure what price, so I just grabbed whatever there was that wasn't in the luxury range. There are a couple of little houses in there too. Just in case.'

I take them from her. 'And here's my card,' she says, handing it to me. 'There, that was painless, I hope.'

I laugh. 'It was, thanks.' I wave goodbye and wander back down the High Street, ditching my half-finished coffee in a bin and looking for somewhere to sit and peruse the details. There's a table free outside a little Italian café, so I take a seat and order a tomato and cheddar toasted sandwich and a sparkling water. I skipped breakfast and it's catching up with me. I'm disappointed as soon as I look at the first property. Seven hundred and fifty thousand pounds is definitely not my idea of a bargain. To my reckoning Mum would get about four for her house. Four fifty at a push. The pile is arranged in no particular order, so I sift through, pulling out anything that's that price or lower. I spot a gorgeous little two-bed terraced house with a patio garden that's more than Mum can afford, but it's considerably less than my London flat is worth. Without thinking, I add it to the heap of possibles. There are seven flats in Mum's price range. Three are in the same retirement development that I looked at before. Of the four others, three have two beds and a garden or balcony. I discard the one that has no outside space. A plan is forming in my head. At least I know what I'm going to be doing this morning now.

I take my time, savouring my sandwich, enjoying watching the people go by, and then I put the first couple of addresses into Maps and stroll in the direction of the closest. I only look from the outside, of course, just to see that the streets are nice, the front gardens well kept. I sling out one of the flats because there's a pane of glass broken in the communal front door and the piece of cardboard covering it looks as if it's been there through several rainstorms with no one bothering to repair it. I wander past the second. It's a smart block, well kept. I turn down a corner on the page of details. The same with the next. I don't bother to visit the retirement block again; I know it's a possibility if I can just get Mum to look past the word.

I find myself planning my route back so I have to pass the house that caught my eye. It's on one of the busier roads out of town. And it's tiny. The door is barely higher than my head. There's a single front window and I peer in. It's lovely. A doll's house. I can see through the little living room with the original fireplace to a light-filled kitchen at the back that must be a more recent addition. A dark wood staircase rises upstairs between the two. The whole two storeys are probably only the same square footage as my flat, but it's a world away. I pull myself away, I need to stay focused on my task. Mum will be arriving in an hour or so.

I need to play this carefully. I don't want to ambush her with a fully formed plan because she'll feel cornered. She hates people making decisions for her. I need to show her the delights of the town first, let her start to imagine herself living here, and then swoop in with all the potential new homes I've found.

Back in my room, I lie on the bed, my head buzzing with an overload of information. Could I really persuade Mum to move down here? *Imagine living in that little house*, a voice in my head says out of nowhere. *Imagine not having to share it with anyone*. I push that thought away. Why would I uproot myself from my whole life and move somewhere where I don't know anybody? *Because you don't know anybody in Kingston either*, the traitorous voice in my brain says. *Except Carol and you spend your whole life trying to get away from her.*

I could start a whole new life. I have no ties, no responsibilities. I can do whatever I like.

But my job is in London.

And let's not forget that Maddy lives here.

Not to mention Lee.

39.
Iris

Mum appears in reception looking dishevelled. It's eighty degrees out and her usually neat bob is sliding limply across her face in tendrils.

'You got here!' I squeak pointlessly. I grab her up for a hug.

'Well, isn't this lovely?'

'It is. Did you park OK?'

I take her overnight bag from her and lead her towards the reception desk.

'Right outside.'

The nice receptionist – Pasha, I now know his name is – gives us a big smile. 'You must be Ms Wilson's mother. Welcome! I've put you in the room next to hers.'

'How nice,' Mum says. I can tell she's assessing him as a future son-in-law. She would love to see me coupled up again. I don't have the heart to tell her I've seen the photos of his beautiful wife and their new baby that he was showing to anyone who stood still for long enough last time I was here.

'Do you want to have a shower or anything before we go out?' I ask as I lead the way up the stairs. 'You must be knackered.'

'Just a five-minute sit down. What's the plan?'

'Mainly eating based,' I say, opening the door to her

room. 'There are lots of gorgeous cafés where we can have lunch, and I've booked a table at The Ivy this evening. Shall we go and find a coffee once you've had a moment?'

'Yes, please. Ooh, and the loo. I've been desperate since Reading.' She rummages in her bag, comes up with a smaller one and heads into the bathroom and I sit on the bed and wait. I hear a blast from the hairdryer and a few minutes later she's back looking cooler and more collected. 'Sit down for a minute,' I say.

'No, I have a second wind now, let's go and explore.'

We catch up as we leave the hotel and cross over to the park. Mum is in uber people-pleasing mode, something she does when she's overcompensating for feeling a bit anxious, and she oohs and aahs over every little thing we pass. I lead her down towards the river, the town's USP. She's as captivated by the boats as I am, and we sit on a bench and take it all in. She's probably wondering if I'm going to try and push her into a decision she's not ready to make and, at the same time, wanting to seem open to it. I need to give her time to relax. I lean back and close my eyes, the sun on my face, and when I open them a second later I see that she's done the same. I could sit here all day except that I forgot to put any factor fifty on and I'll look like a beetroot by lunchtime. I reach out a hand and place it over hers.

'Lovely,' she says.

'You don't have to like it just because you think I want you to,' I say. 'Or, you can like it but not think you want to live here. No pressure. Really.'

She nods, eyes still closed. We sit there like that for about five minutes. I'm almost asleep when she taps my hand and says, 'Shall we go and get that coffee?'

'Mmm. Inside or out?'

'Oh, out, I think. It's glorious. We can find some shade.'

We haul each other up and wander back through the park towards the High Street. Mum tells me that Cath has accepted an offer on her house. 'I keep trying to help her pack up, but we get so distracted we never do anything. We spent the whole of yesterday looking through photo albums.'

'Who's buying it? Do you know?'

Mum nods. 'A young couple.' We pass the Resolute, a few people sitting outside nursing drinks and chatting. I fix my eyes on the gate to the street and keep walking. I'm all too aware that the café is right beside the playground where Maddy and Lee's twins often play. While I need to speak to him, I can't do it while I'm with my mum, and definitely not while he's with Maddy.

'Oh, how about here? This is nice.' Mum veers off towards it like a homing pigeon. I follow reluctantly.

'Don't you want to see the High Street?'

'We can walk up after,' she says. 'This looks perfect. I'll get them. Skinny latte?'

'Thanks,' I say. I know there's no persuading her to go somewhere else now. I find a table while she goes inside and sit with my back firmly to the playground and the park. I'll let Mum have the views. I'm lying low.

40.

Maddy

She's exhausted. More tired than she can ever remember being. She keeps finding glitter in her hair and sand in her shoes and her fingers are rainbow coloured with spray paint, but they did it. Five videos in three days, and they didn't argue once. OK, Ruby and Rose got a little fractious at times, but they also got carried away by the excitement of it all. There were moments when it felt like old times, when they all just threw themselves into it headfirst, and even when things went wrong they laughed. A lot.

She could tell that Lee was faking it for the most part, but that only made her appreciate him more. She knows he hates performing, but the fact that he tried so hard, that he put on a – mostly – convincing show of loving every minute of it filled her heart with love. He was doing it for her. For them. It's all going to be OK. *They're* going to be OK.

They've shovelled as much sand as they can back into bin bags, and Lee has taken them, and the twins, to the tip along with the huge cardboard crab claws and dragon fire and the alligator tail they made for Lee to wear in 'Croco-dile Rock'. The girls love the tip. It's up there with Legoland as one of their favourite places to go. Rose has already declared a desire to work there when she's old enough.

She gets back to her editing, skilfully cutting different shots together, making it work with the music. She adds the all-important link to buy the book. An alert pings on her computer and she feels a little flutter of excitement. She's set up a notification to let her know whenever the book is mentioned in news. She's been hoping there might be reviews for a few days, but this is the first alert she's had.

Maddy Fulford is the marmite of influencers, it says. *You either love her wholesome squeaky clean (and squeaky voiced!) videos with their cheesy dance routines and off-key singing, or you'd rather be covered in honey and slowly eaten by a group of hungry bears than watch. I'm of the love, love, love camp!*

Maddy breathes a sigh of relief. OK, so it's not exactly the kind of glowing, unequivocal praise she was hoping for, but at least this blogger – Jax Loves Boox – is on her side. Because she's realised that's what her life is now. Sides. People who love her and people who hate her. She doesn't know what she's done to provoke such extremes. She tells herself to just enjoy Jax's words, to see the positive.

Maddy, cute husband Lee and their adorable twin girls bring a kind of naive down-home simplicity to a world that is anything but these days. The book is actually filled with great practical ideas for getting the best out of your family time, and, as the mum of a boisterous four-year-old myself, I really found the plethora of suggestions extremely helpful.
Four stars!!!

Maddy screenshots it and sends the picture to Lee. *You know how much I love marmite!* he sends back. She smiles.

41.

Iris

I take Mum to one of the cafés in the little courtyard off the High Street for lunch, and we sit under an oversized umbrella, out of the glare of the sun, eating bowls of pasta and bean salad. I can see that she loves this place already. That she's picturing herself sitting here on her own or with new friends. How do you make friends when you're seventy-six? Same way you always do, I suppose (although I can't quite imagine her sitting outside the Chequers getting drunk with a stranger). You find people with common interests even if that's just that you share the same front door.

'There's a lot going on here,' I say, picking a bit of tomato out of my salad and eating it with my fingers.

'It looks like it,' Mum says. I can tell she's still anxiously waiting for my big sales pitch. I totally understand because I'd be the same. One hint that someone wants me to do something for their own reasons and not mine, and I'm out. A move here would be a huge step, and I don't want her worrying that I'm suggesting it so that I can tick her off my list of responsibilities and leave her to get on with it.

'There is. And it's literally an hour door to door for me. Less, even, sometimes.'

She nods. 'I don't want to be a bother to anyone.'

'Oh, Mum. You're not. I just want you to be happy and to be able to see you more. But you don't have to go anywhere if you don't want to. And you certainly don't have to decide after one morning.'

'Cath sold her house quite easily. I was surprised.'

'Do you know how much she got?'

She tells me. Cath's house is quite a similar size to Mum's, in not quite as nice a road. Mum could easily afford to buy one of the flats I've been checking out. I don't say that though. She needs to come to that decision herself.

'It certainly is a lively town,' she says with a smile.

'Like I said, it doesn't have to be here . . .'

'No,' she says. 'I like it. And it's really only an hour to you?'

I try to swallow my excitement that she's even considering it. 'It is. And, you know, I've been thinking I might not stay in London forever. Maybe I need a change, too.'

She looks at me. 'Here?'

I think about it. Now that I've deleted the videos, who knows? Perhaps I really could live here too if I wanted. Lee and Maddy have no idea who I actually am. Why not? 'Maybe. If I could sort work out.'

She gives me one of her Mum smiles that makes me feel as if I'm eight again, and she's just reassured me that the world is a safe place. 'I wonder what you get for your money.'

'Well,' I say, reaching into my bag, 'funny you should say that.' I pull out the sheaf of papers the estate agent gave me this morning. 'These are just to give you an idea . . .'

'You have been busy,' she says, but she says it with an amused look on her face.

'Flats, obviously,' I say, handing her the top one. 'But all with a bit of outside space . . .'

'I'm that age, aren't I? When people are going to start worrying about me going up a flight of stairs.'

'I'm just thinking long term, Mum.'

'I know. I was teasing.' She studies the details and I pass her the next in the pile, watching her expression. It's hard to tell what she's thinking, but she's not throwing them back in my face shouting *How dare you insult me like this!*, so I'm hopeful. She holds out her hand for the next.

'Obviously these are just from one estate agent so there'll be more. It's just to give you a sense of what you could get, really . . .'

'This looks nice. Big rooms,' she says, holding one of them up. I decide to chance my luck. 'Maybe we could . . .' I'm stopped in my tracks by the sound of her phone ringing. She looks at the screen. Smiles. 'It's Daisy.'

I wave a hand, go ahead. Lean back in my chair. Typical Daisy to steal the moment.

'Hello, sweetheart. How are you?' Mum says. I watch as her face falls from happiness to worry. 'Take your time, love . . .' She shoots me a look and I have to stop myself from rolling my eyes. 'Slow down . . . where are you?' Daisy, of course, does not ask her where she is in return. 'Oh, love,' Mum says. 'It's not the end of the world. How long, do you know?'

My ears prick up. Is Daisy telling her she's pregnant?

In – I assume – floods of tears as if she's only just found out. Over the phone, without even checking if Mum's OK and in a fit state to deal with the news. I can't listen. I stand up and mouth the word 'loo' and set off into the café to find one. I'm fuming.

I take as long as I can. When I come out I can see she's still talking so I order us more tea and wait while it's brewed.

'Don't worry,' Mum is saying as I carry out a tray with a teapot, milk and two fresh mugs. The day feels ruined. Daisy and her giant bombshell have devastated it. But I'm glad that at least Mum isn't on her own to absorb this news, even though Daisy doesn't know that. I take the dirty cups back inside the café and put them on the counter. 'You know you can call me any time,' she's saying when I come out again. 'You always have me. Love you, sweetheart.'

'So?' I say once she's ended the call. I can hardly look at her, so I pour the tea.

She sighs. She suddenly looks years older and I can clearly see the vulnerability under the surface that she usually hides so well.

'Daisy's pregnant,' she says, and I have to stop myself saying *I know. I've known for weeks. Why is she calling you in a state as if she's only just found out?*

'Right,' I say.

'Unexpectedly, obviously.' She rubs at her fingers with the other hand.

'And she's upset about it, clearly. I mean, judging from what you were saying . . .'

'It's a shock, I suppose. I should go and see her . . .'

'No, Mum. Let her come and see you. She's pregnant, not ill.'

'You don't seem very surprised,' she says. 'I mean . . . oh, I'm so sorry, Iris, this must be really hard for you. I'm not thinking straight.'

I put a hand over hers. 'It's fine. It's just nothing would surprise me with Daisy any more. But she's a big girl. She can handle this.'

'She sounded in a terrible state . . .'

'She always sounds in a terrible state. It's what she does,' I snap and then wish I hadn't when I see Mum's face. 'I don't mean to be horrible. I just wish she wouldn't offload it all on you.'

'Who else has she got?'

'I'll call her. Has she decided what she's going to do?'

She nods her head. 'Oh, I don't think there's a question that she's keeping it. It's all a bit fresh, I think, so she's upset. But she wants to have the baby. Gosh, it's a lot to take in.'

Everything goes fuzzy. I feel as if I've been hit on the head. Maybe I should be celebrating the fact that I'm going to have a niece or nephew, but instead I feel sick. Why her? Why not me? Why not the one who has wanted a baby all her adult life?

'Wow,' I say quietly. 'You're going to be a granny.'

Mum dabs a tear away from the corner of her eye. For all her worries about Daisy, I know that this must be a big moment for her. A bittersweet big moment.

I wish I could have given her this. Without all the residual drama.

Fuckssake.

I wait for her to go inside to use the bathroom and then I text Daisy.

You're keeping it?

Oh, have you spoken to Mum? she replies.

I'm with her now. What the fuck are you doing telling her like that? She's really upset.

I just made up my mind and I thought she deserved to know. I felt bad that I've been keeping it from her for weeks.

Of course she deserves to know, but why didn't you talk to her like an adult? What's with all the tears and hysterics?

It was a difficult decision, Iris.

I know it was! But you could have talked to me, not her. Or at the very least gone down to see her and told her face to face. She's just going to worry now.

I thought she might like to hear she's going to be a grandma! What's wrong with that?

I actually gasp.

You are fucking unbelievable. Grow up.

I turn my phone off.

Mum is preoccupied for the rest of the day. She tries to act as if she's enjoying herself, but I can see right through her. She goes off to her room for a sleep after lunch while I pace round the park fuming, and then we walk up to The Ivy for an early dinner – me forcing myself not to look across the street at the pub opposite in case Lee is outside his favourite watering hole – but our conversation is strained. Not for the first time, I'm furious at my sister. I know how much Mum would love a grandchild, but not like this. Not one she'll have to worry about its whole life in case Daisy accidentally leaves it behind on a bus or in an ashram in Bangalore. I once read something that said a mother can only ever be as happy as her least happy child, and I realised I've seen that with Mum all my life.

'I should offer to go and stay with her. Daisy. Once the baby's born, I mean,' she says as we walk home from the restaurant, showing exactly what's been on her mind all night while we've been struggling to make conversation like two polite strangers.

'Don't let her take advantage of you.'

'It's important she knows I'll be there if she needs me,' she says.

'Trust me, Mum. She knows that. It's what she's counting on.'

'I know how difficult this must be for you,' she says as we hug goodnight. 'But try to be happy for her too. Maybe this can bring you closer. It might be the making of her.'

'Sure,' I manage to say. But I don't believe it for a second.

42.

Iris

The shadow of Daisy hangs over the rest of the weekend. There's no point pushing the idea of going to check out some of the flats, so on Saturday I drive us both to Cliveden House and we walk round the gardens and have lunch in the smart restaurant looking out over the magnificent grounds. I can tell that Mum's mind is on other things – one other thing – even though she does her damnedest to pretend otherwise. Of course it is – her forty-five-year-old daughter is accidentally pregnant for the first time with a man she doesn't know anything about and with no means, practical or otherwise, of caring for the child. I suddenly panic that she might just dump the baby on Mum and expect her to bring it up.

And then a lightning bolt hits me. A solution that could work for us all. I don't say anything to Mum, I don't want to give her any more to fret over. But when we're back in our rooms after having agreed to meet again at five, I phone my sister.

'I could bring the baby up,' I say before she even has a chance to speak. 'I could adopt it. That way you could still see it, but I'd be its mum. I mean, it could know that you were its biological parent, I would never lie to it about that . . .' I stop gabbling and wait. My heart is pounding in my ears. 'Dais?'

'What the fuck?' she says.

'Think about it. You could keep doing what you do. You wouldn't be tied down . . .'

'You're calling me to tell me you want to steal my child?'

'Don't be so overdramatic. You've never wanted kids.'

'Well, maybe I do now. I thought you didn't want to be a single parent.'

'Well, maybe I do now,' I say superciliously.

Silence.

I need to back down. Move much more slowly. If you push Daisy into an entrenched position she just digs in further.

'That came out all wrong. What I mean is, that if you regret your decision at any point, or you feel you can't cope, then I'm here. I could help.'

'Fine. You can babysit.'

I shut my eyes. 'OK. It was a stupid idea. I'm sorry.'

There's a heavy silence. I should just say goodbye, but I hate leaving things on such a bad note. I should have kept my mouth shut, dropped a few – well-spaced – subtle hints and left it to fate. Not blundered in all guns blazing.

'You want to know the truth?' she says, and I can tell from her tone that she's not accepting my apology just yet. 'I was too late. I'm further along than I thought . . .'

I let that sink in. 'But what about Leaf? I thought you knew exactly when . . .'

'Well, I didn't. OK, Iris? So, now you can really feel superior.'

'I don't . . .' I say. 'I'm not judging.'

'Of course you're judging,' she snaps. 'You're always fucking judging. Just because you've got your life together and I'm a massive flake . . .'

Is that how she sees me? 'I really haven't got my life together. My life is a mess.'

'Yeah, right,' she scoffs. 'Perfect Miss Iris. The one Mum and Dad could always be proud of. With the job and the flat and the fairy-tale wedding.'

I can't believe I'm hearing this. 'With the run-of-the-mill job, the flat that I can hardly stand to be in because of my godawful lodger and, in case you hadn't noticed, the fairy-tale wedding led to him cheating on me and a divorce? I mean, really? You think I look down my nose at you?'

'You've always looked down your nose at me. *Crazy Daisy fucks up again.*' The Crazy Daisy thing started at school. Some of my friends coined the phrase and I went along with it willingly, enjoying poking fun at my sister. She was older, so it never occurred to me that it might be hurtful – or that she even knew.

And, to be fair, I do judge her. I always have. No wonder she always offloads on Mum instead of me.

'I'm sorry,' I say quietly. 'I didn't know that you felt like that.'

'Well now you do,' she says, but the edge has gone.

I have so many questions. *If Leaf's not the father, then who is? Will they help? How will you cope?* But now is not the

286

time. Now I need to step up for my sister. I need to stop fixating on other people's families and concentrate on my own.

'Call me any time. I mean it. If you're worried, or you need anything . . .'

'Thanks. I'm a bit scared if I'm being honest.'

'It'll be all right. Talk to me, OK?'

I hear her sigh. 'I will. Love you.'

'You too,' I say.

I wave Mum off on Sunday morning, both of us in a much better mood. After I spoke to Daisy yesterday, I had decided to put as positive a spin on her news as I could muster to try to dissipate Mum's anxieties and, by the time our main courses came (we were in a smart Italian restaurant in what seemed to be a crooked old barn), we were speculating about what names my sister might think appealing. Or, at least, I was, and Mum was trying to pretend she wasn't laughing.

'Mozzarella,' I said, having gone through Cloud, Meadow, Serenity, Savasana and Nectarine to a reception of varying degrees of eye rolling.

'Don't.'

'Amaretto. Fusilli. Breadstick.'

Mum tried to stifle a smile. 'Stop being mean.'

'I'm teasing.'

I'd almost managed to convince myself that the day wasn't a disaster. Almost.

I'd also managed to claw back some of Mum's enthusiasm for the town and all it had to offer. 'You'd still

287

be miles away from Daisy, but a lot fewer miles away. And she could easily bring the baby down to stay. The Elizabeth Line goes all the way from Stratford to Maidenhead.'

'I'll come down again in a few weeks,' she says as she leaves. 'Maybe we could look at some flats?'

Once she's gone, I decide to go for a walk before I tackle the drive. I can't face a long Sunday in my flat anyway. I find myself strolling up the High Street and turning right, past the little cottage with the For Sale sign. I've googled it now and seen pictures of the two small bedrooms with the beams in the ceiling, the compact kitchen and bathroom and the little paved patio garden. The large window is right on the street and I find myself peering in again, waving at a small spaniel who is eyeing me suspiciously from his bed on the floor. The front door opens directly on to the living room – just enough space for a two-seater sofa and one armchair in front of the fire. I'm peering through to the kitchen out the back, hands cupped round my face to cut out the reflections, when the front door opens.

'Can I help you?' A woman a few years older than me stands there. I have no idea how I didn't see her coming. She must have been sitting in the chair and somehow nipped to the door while I was admiring the dark wooden stairs that separate the front from the back room.

'Oh. God. Sorry. I have your particulars . . .' I say, rummaging through my bag, as if that's all the credentials I need to prove I'm not a would-be burglar casing the joint.

'Do you want to have a look round?' she says. I wasn't expecting that. I want to tell her she shouldn't let any old stranger like me in, but I suppose she has the dog (though he's gone back to sleep) and maybe a bodybuilder husband hidden away upstairs for all I know.

'Really? I wouldn't want to waste your time. I haven't even put my flat on the market yet.' As I say this, I realise that that's what I'm going to do. I'm going to sell the flat that's never made me happy (and Carol with it, if they'll have her) and find somewhere that does.

'You might as well now you're here. It's not like it'll take more than five minutes.'

I have to admit I'm curious. But I'm also sure I shouldn't be taking up a stranger's offer to step inside their home without anyone else in the world knowing where I am, however nice they seem. 'OK. Thanks,' I say, before I can stop myself.

'Gina,' she says as she moves aside to let me enter.

'Rissa.' I hold out a hand and she swerves it and bumps her fist against mine. 'This is lovely.' The dog springs to life again and throws itself at me, tail wagging, and I make a fuss of it. 'Where are you moving to?'

She pulls a face. 'Somewhere bigger. We need more space. The estate agent told me not to say that to anyone, but trust me, if there're more than two of you this is not the house for you.'

'Just me,' I say, and it hits me how lovely that would be. Just me. I could even go back to using my own living room.

'Well, we've loved living here. But now our son is

bigger we're all tripping over each other. This is the kitchen. Excuse the mess.'

I follow her through. It's tired and a bit worn but the space – a small extension – is pretty. There's a glass door on to the patio. 'Needs doing,' Gina says.

'Don't ever get a job in property sales, will you?' I say and thankfully she laughs. 'Luckily I work for a kitchen company so, you know, I have strings I can pull.'

'Oh god, will you come and do our new place? It's a disaster.'

'I could certainly draw you up a plan, but the branch I work for is in London, so . . .'

'Are you going to commute?' She heads off up the stairs shouting, 'Clothes on, everyone! We have a visitor.'

'That's the bit I haven't thought through yet. They have a few branches round here, but I haven't even made enquiries. That's why I don't want to waste your time. It's early days.'

The bathroom is on the half-landing above the kitchen extension. 'You don't have any contacts at a bathroom company too, by any chance?' she says as I peer in. It's basic but functional. Overrun with clutter.

Upstairs there are two doors, both closed. She raps on one and opens it without waiting. 'Teenage boy's room. Stinks.' It's the smaller of the two bedrooms, and probably half the size of my room at home. There's an original fireplace and wooden beams on the ceiling. There's also a lump under the covers that I think might be the actual teenage boy. As we back out into the hall, a man comes crashing through the other door. He must be six foot five and has to almost bend in half to fit through.

'Morning,' he says loudly. 'I'll take Rex for a quick walk, Geen, get out of your way.' We all shuffle round each other on the landing. The main bedroom is sunny and bright. There's a double bed, a heavy wardrobe and a chest of drawers all jostling for space.

'I absolutely love it,' I say to Gina. 'I'm probably not supposed to say that, either.'

'I want to sell it to someone who wants to live here,' she says. 'Not someone who's going to let it out and not give a damn. I know that's stupid, but there you go.'

'I wish I was in a better position . . .'

'Well. If it's still on the market when you are, come back. We're actually not in a massive hurry. The new place is like a bombsite.'

She gives me her number and tells me to call her if I ever want another look. Hugs me like we're old friends.

I spend the whole drive home making plans. I can't force Mum to move here, I can't force Daisy to hand over her baby, but I can make my own life better.

43.

Iris

By lunchtime on Monday I have lined up two estate agents to come and value my flat. I text Carol: *Someone coming to look round 7 today!*

I broke the news to her yesterday that I was selling up. I expected – well, I don't know what I expected. Tears? Annoyance? Even a proprietorial *But it's my flat too. Where am I going to put all my garlic bread?* What I actually got was an encouraging *Good for you* and *How exciting* when I told her my plan to quit London altogether. I had swooped as soon as I got home, fired up on a cocktail of optimism and excitement. I could picture myself living in that house, making the town my home, making new friends. Gina being one of them. Could I really live somewhere where I might bump into Maddy any time I left the house? The monster who had haunted my dreams, both sleeping and waking, for the past four years? She would never know it was me, but I would always know it was her. It already felt less potentially provoking than it previously had. Maybe it was like aversion therapy. I'd reached the stage where they brought in a toy tarantula and made you stroke it. The more familiar it became, the less terrifying. Next step, the real thing. I had been resisting looking at any of Maddy's social channels. It was an addiction I needed to wean myself off. I could do it. Whatever happened to Maddy did not affect me. I chanted my new mantra in my head all the way home (having had to look up what I'd written, because I'd forgotten the wording). *My worth is not contingent on someone else's failure.* By the time I reached home I truly believed it.

'Show me the house you like . . .' Carol said. She was toasting cheese under the grill.

I went and dug out the details from my bag. 'Oh my god, it's like a little hobbit house. I love it,' she said. 'Look at the beams!' I waited for her to ask what was going to happen to her, or if I thought it was fair to just land this on her, but she was nothing but positive.

'I'll give you as much notice as I can,' I said, as she pulled a bubbling slice of cheese on toast from under the grill and replaced it with a second. She handed the first to me.

'Oh god, I'll be OK. You can hardly move for rentals round here. How exciting. So, tell me about the town. Why there?'

Of course, I felt awful. Nothing about Carol was bad or malicious or calculated. So, we didn't gel as flatmates. So what? I should have at least been nicer to her.

'We should clean,' she said once we'd eaten and I'd rinsed the plates in the sink. 'Because they never give you much notice when they want to show people round.'

So, we did. We put Taylor Swift on and blitzed the whole place, singing along loudly as we hoovered and scrubbed and dusted. We filled three bin bags with clutter and stuffed the rest in cupboards and drawers. It was fun. Cathartic. Symbolic, even, of my decision to make a fresh start. Once we'd finished, we opened a bottle of wine and sat back and admired our efforts.

On it! she texts back now, by which I'm guessing she means she'll have a quick whizz round with the hoover when she gets home from work.

The first of the two agents is punctual and earnestly pompous. He lectures Carol and me at length about the local area and the housing market and the financial crisis the country is heading into, and then he quotes a market price that's way higher than I even imagined.

'It'll never sell for that,' I say to Carol as he heads down the stairs, just in time for number two to arrive. 'He's dreaming.'

'He just wants to lure you in and then in a couple of weeks he'll suggest a price drop, you watch.'

'Exactly. Waste of time.'

The second agent is ten minutes late, distracted and dishevelled, but I like her. She had a family emergency, she tells us, so she had to go and pick her kid up from football and deliver him to his friend's house before she came. She's straight and to the point. 'I just sold a flat in here a couple of weeks ago,' she says as she whizzes in and out of each room. 'Same size. Bathroom slightly better, kitchen slightly worse. Got the asking price in three weeks.'

'How much?' I ask. She quotes an amount that sounds infinitely more reasonable than the previous bloke, but still would enable me to make all my dreams come true.

'Done,' I say.

'We need to arrange floor plans, photos, energy certificates,' she says as she rushes out the door. 'I'll email you a list of everything and our contract tomorrow.'

'Great,' I say to her retreating back. 'Thank you.'

I can't quite believe that just happened.

The next morning passes in a blur. The shop is quiet, but my brain is a frenzy of lists and plans and potential pitfalls. I call our regional manager and enquire about a possible transfer if anything comes up, and he's fine with the idea in principle, even though there are no vacancies at the moment. 'I can commute up in the meantime,' I tell him. I don't allow myself to stop and think in case I talk myself out of what I'm doing. I don't even call Fay or Cally and tell them in case one of them tries to talk me out of what I'm doing. I think about phoning Gina and telling her I might be a potential buyer after all. I'm terrified that the house will be sold out from under me. I have spent all night picturing myself there, where my furniture might go, the little dog or cat I might rescue to live there with me. But I decide that that would just be messing her around. I'll wait till I have an offer on my place. There will be other houses if the timing isn't right.

Zak gets wind of what's happening and pulls sad faces and says he'll miss me if I leave, so I distract him by showing him photos of the house and we spend the rest of the morning discussing décor and paint colours.

By lunchtime I feel drunk on excitement. I've never felt a high like it. Well, maybe in the run-up to my wedding and we all know how that turned out. I don't know why I didn't do this years ago.

I finally sit down in the back office, thankful I grabbed a sandwich on the way in this morning because I wouldn't have any energy left to leave the building now. I lean back in the chair and close my eyes.

I hear a cough. Zak is standing in the doorway.

'Um,' he says, his eyebrows raised so high they almost disappear into his hairline. 'There's someone here to see you.'

'Really?' I say, pulling a face. I never get unexpected visitors at work, so I'm assuming it's a customer popped in wanting to tweak something on their order. I heave myself up reluctantly.

'It's . . .' Zak stage whispers as I get close to him, but I don't need him to tell me, I can see over his shoulder.

There's a man standing in the shop, bending over to admire a Silestone worktop. I actually gasp. Tall, skinny, angular. Lee.

He looks over and I see a slight blush as he spots me. I almost hear an explosion as my two worlds collide.

'Iris,' he says.

44.
Iris

Zak is standing with his mouth open as if it's Beyoncé who's walked in, not an all-singing all-dancing F-lister from Instagram. 'Do you want to go to lunch?' I say to him. I can't even think about talking to Lee with an audience. How did he find me here?

'I'll just pop to Pret.'

'Take the full hour,' I say, emphasizing the last two words. He's not the only one who could take eyebrow raising to Olympic level.

I wait until he shuts the front door after him. I have no idea how to play this, so I try giving Lee a smile and saying, 'What on earth are you doing here?'

'You're Iris?' he says, and for a moment I wonder if he's lost it, but then I realise he's calling me by my full name. I don't say anything because I don't know what to say. I have no idea how we got here. 'You have some kind of weird history with my wife?' He says it as a question although he clearly already knows the answer or he wouldn't be here.

I screw up my face. 'Why are you here, Lee? How did you find out where I work?'

'You told me,' he says. 'You just didn't tell me your real name.'

'Rissa *is* my real name. It's just an abbreviation my

friends call me. I was hardly trying to hide anything from you.'

'Right. Except the fact that you've been waging some kind of hate campaign against Maddy.'

Someone peers through the window at the display cabinets. I walk over and flick the lock to closed. I can't look at him.

'All those things I told you. About me and her. What was that all about?'

Maybe I should be apologising to him. Maybe absolution is what I need to truly move on. But he's glaring at me aggressively. I realise I have no idea what he's capable of. He doesn't seem like the kind of person who has a dangerous side, but who knows how people act if you threaten their family. I'm proof of that. I wonder if I should text Zak and ask him to come back. A million thoughts run through my head. For a split second, the overwhelming emotion I have is shame. That he would know what I was capable of. My darkest hour.

'You're the only one who can answer that. I didn't exactly force you to tell me anything,' I say defiantly. I've never been good with people hurling accusations at me, even if they're right.

He slumps against a counter. 'So, you're not the one who's been posting the videos?'

'What videos?' I say. I hate lying to him, but what choice do I have? Whatever happens I can't admit to that. To being a troll, the lowest of the low. And it's not as if he can have any actual proof.

'Don't fuck about, Rissa. You know what I mean.'

'I really don't. And I don't appreciate you barging in here, where I work . . .'

'I thought we were friends,' he says more quietly.

'We are. I don't understand what's going on here.'

He rubs a hand over his face. He suddenly looks exhausted. Broken.

'Whatever happened between us the other night . . . whatever I told you . . . please don't use it against her. She's hanging on by a thread as it is.'

'She's selling all those people a lie,' I say. I can't help myself.

'So, it *was* you?'

I don't say anything. Fuck. I have no idea how to handle this. I just know I've ruined everything. My shiny bright new future.

'She told me about all those other things you did – her website, spreading rumours about her . . .'

I look at the floor. I should just take responsibility, come clean about everything, put him out of his misery. But I'm feeling cornered, attacked.

So instead I say, 'Does she know about you and me?'

45.

Maddy

Maddy tries to relax as she leans her head back in the chair while the therapist threads her eyebrows. Next, she is having shellac painted on to her fingernails – she's already chosen the colour, a bright, happy green that she's been promised should last at least two weeks – and then later this afternoon she's having a conditioning treatment on her hair. The girls are over in a corner being entertained by the salon owner and her small blond dog. When she'd booked all the appointments she'd assumed Lee would be on twin duty, but this morning he suddenly announced that he'd had a message from his mum's home asking him if he could collect her and take her to the hospital for a scan on her hip because they'd made the appointment when she'd had a minor fall the other day, but now they were too short-staffed to get her there.

'I don't think I should take the girls,' he'd said apologetically, when he'd told her. 'We'll probably be hanging round for hours.'

'I can cancel it all and come with you,' she'd said. She'd always had a slightly tricky relationship with her mother-in-law, whose default mode was to be suspicious of any woman who her son showed an interest in. It all stemmed from Sue, Lee had told her. From the miserable near-decade he'd endured. His mother was only being protective. Maddy had understood at first, but after four happy years and two babies together she'd thought maybe she'd earnt a bit of a break. She was thankful – when she dared admit it to herself and only herself – that her mother-in-law was in a care home and not able to pop round whenever she liked. She took the twins in to see her every three weeks or so, and smiled happily as her parenting skills were criticised, along with most of her life choices and her job – which Pauline didn't understand in the slightest, but had very strong opinions on for someone so clueless. When she was young Maddy had often fantasised about the new mother she would find for herself when she married. Someone she could turn to, lean on, have bonding days out with. Have the conversations her own mother had never been capable of having. Sadly, Pauline was not that woman. So she was hoping Lee would say no, but if he needed her she'd be there, she'd just suck all the negative stuff up as usual. *Smile*.

'God, no,' he'd said. 'I wouldn't expect you to do that. Can't have you on *Steph's Packed Lunch* with raggedy eyebrows, can we?' He waggled his own and she laughed. 'Can you take the girls with you, though? Or we could see if Gary and Lacey could have them?'

'It's OK. I'll just take them along.'

He'd hugged her then and told her that he loved her. 'Funnily enough I love you too,' she'd said.

He was still trying to make amends for having walked out on them, she could see that. The guilt was eating him up. He'd told her yesterday that he was giving notice on his little flat and moving back in permanently. 'If you'll have me,' he'd said, his voice wavering. It had only ever been meant as a gesture, he'd explained. An expression of how seriously he took all their futures. But he'd taken it too far. 'It was never going to be forever,' he'd told her. 'But it was still a dick move. I'll understand if you don't want me to come back.' She'd flung her arms round him as an answer.

Now she pictures herself on the TV show. The outfit she's picked out to wear – red wide-leg trousers and a short-sleeved green top. Jas has told her she needs to scream fun – bright, vibrant colours – and she's taken her at her word. There will be hair and make-up on the day (go for natural, Jas had said. Don't look too stiff or unapproachable). She runs through some stock phrases in her head that she has ready to parrot out if asked. *Our families are our whole world, so we need to make that world somewhere we want to live. Making happy memories is one of the most important things you can do as a parent. Even when times are hard you can make things fun for your children.* She has a phone call this afternoon with one of the researchers from the show to run through what exactly they might talk about, and then she, Lee and the girls are getting the train up to Leeds tomorrow morning for the filming. They have compromised on her doing the chat alone, but with Lee, Ruby and Rose ready to do a wave to camera on cue. She's allowing herself to get excited now. This is the culmination of everything she's been working towards. The Truth Teller seems to have given up their hate campaign – they probably ran out of fingers to point once Lee moved back in. She's still convinced it might be Iris, but she's decided to consign it to history. File it under near misses. Look to their – happy – future without looking back.

46.

Iris

All the colour drains from his face.

'Why are you doing this?' he says. 'What have I ever done to you?'

'Not you,' I say. 'Her.'

'She told me all about it,' he says. 'You think she went off with your husband, but he was single when she met him. You'd already split up.'

'That's blatantly not true,' I say. 'She's just telling you what you want to hear so you don't judge her.'

He rubs a hand over his eyes. 'Say, for a moment, that what you're saying is the truth. Are you really going to ruin her life – my life, *the girls' lives* – four years on?'

'We were trying for a baby,' I say.

I don't know why I tell him. He won't understand. I wait for him to give me the platitudes everyone else does: *There's still time, it's not too late, you can still meet someone else and try again,* but instead he says, 'Shit, I'm sorry. That's rough. But it's not Maddy's fault.'

'We would have got there,' I say, a tear leaking out on to my cheek. 'We were going to try anything. Everything. Whatever it took.'

He reaches out a hand and rubs my arm. 'Please don't cry.'

Of course, those words have the opposite effect. I

almost can't bear the sympathy. I let out a loud sob and then cover my mouth, trying to keep it together. Lee steps forward and wraps me up in a hug and I cry loudly into his chest. I'm crying for the babies I never got to have but also for the mess I've made of my life, the person I've become who was willing to destroy this man who's been nothing but kind, writing him off as collateral damage. I've spent years fuelled by hatred even when I thought I'd buried it. I have never been able to move on because I'm stuck in the quicksand of the past. The what might have been.

Lee pats me on the back gently, like he's soothing a toddler. How can he even think about being nice to me after everything I've done to him? He'd have every right to hate me. He should be railing against me for everything I've done – following him and his family, spreading secrets – but instead he's comforting me.

I gulp audibly as I try to get myself under control. I pull away from Lee, wiping my face on my hand. He produces a tissue from somewhere and I blow my nose and dab at my face. I can't stop crying. It's like I've turned on a tap that's been stuck for years and now I can't turn it off again.

'Nothing happened between us,' I say. Lee just looks confused. 'Us,' I repeat, pointing at him and then myself. 'We didn't . . . you just fell asleep and I went home.'

He looks as if he might pass out. He grabs at the counter behind him. 'Fuck. Thank god.'

'And you did tell me some stuff, but I won't . . . I haven't . . . It stops now.'

He exhales loudly. 'Thank you.'

'I'm sorry, Lee. Really I am. I've fucked everything up.'

'It's forgotten,' he says, being way more generous than I think I ever could be. 'Are you going to be OK?'

I nod. 'I'll get there. Are you?'

'Yep.' He reaches out and rubs my arm.

'Will you tell her? Maddy? Who I am?' I could never go back to Marlow if he did. Never show my face.

He thinks about this for a second. 'I don't want to lie to her any more. But, no. I don't think it benefits anyone. If it's definitely all over I think we should just all get on with our lives.'

I close my eyes. 'Thank you. And it is. Over, I mean. One hundred per cent.'

'Good. I'll see you around, OK?'

I manage a watery smile. 'OK.'

He turns towards the door. 'Take care, Iris.'

'Rissa,' I say. I don't want to be Iris any more. I'm done with that person.

47.

Iris

'I'm going home. I'm not well,' I say as soon as Zak turns the key in the lock. His eyes are like saucers looking at my red face and swollen lids. I don't even try and explain why I've locked myself in or pretend that nothing is wrong.

'That was who I thought it was, wasn't it?' he says.

'I'll see you tomorrow, OK? You can take the afternoon off. Or the morning if you want. Come in late.' I can see that he's desperate for me to fill him in, but I'm done with telling tales on the Fulfords.

'Are you and Lee Fulford having a . . . thing?'

'No,' I bark. 'Absolutely not. He just had some bad news for me about a mutual friend, OK?'

'OK. No need to bite my head off. Do you want me to find you a cab?'

'No, I'll be OK. Sorry, Zak. I didn't mean to be such a bitch.'

He shrugs. 'I'm calling you an Uber now. Take a couple of paracetamol and go to bed.'

'Who put you in charge?' I say, attempting a joke.

'One day,' he says, waving an arm round theatrically, 'all this will be mine.'

I do take to my bed when I get back to the flat. Surprisingly I sleep for I don't know how long, but I wake up feeling like a different person. I can see why the Catholics are so big on confession. Honesty is definitely good for the soul. I reach for my phone and go on to Instagram. I delete all the content on the Truth Teller account. I feel bad about Lara. If she'd suddenly disappeared on me one day, wouldn't I have felt let down? Anxious? She has no idea who I am, so she'll have no way of checking I haven't fallen off a cliff. Or been pushed. I send her a quick message: *Having a sm break for a while. I need to sort my life out. Didn't want you to worry about me!*

No probs comes the reply. *See you on the other side.* I think about sending her my phone number so that we can keep in touch, but I'm not sure what the etiquette is. I can always seek her out on Instagram again if I want to, one day.

I turn off all notifications for Fun with the Fulfords. I know Maddy has been putting up videos every day this week, and I've been steadfastly trying to ignore them. I can see there's a new one from this morning. I'm not getting sucked back in. If I knew how, I'd close the account altogether, but all I can find is *Temporarily deactivate my account*, so I do that. I have no idea how long 'temporarily' is, but at least I've neutered it for now.

My phone rings as I'm making myself a coffee. It's Jennifer, the estate agent, asking if she can bring someone round this evening.

'God, you don't waste time,' I say groggily. 'But yes, sure.' I have no idea if my plans are going to go ahead now. Am I really going to move to a place where practically the only person I'm on first-name terms with knows the absolute worst of me? Should I start exploring other towns, or put the whole thing on hold? Weirdly, though, I trust Lee. I think he'd probably let me forget the entire sordid episode so long as I behaved from here on in. And I'm selling my flat and moving out of London whatever, I decide.

The prospective buyer is being shown round at half past six, the agent tells me, so I reluctantly agree to meet Carol in the pub round the corner to wait it out. She's sitting there with a bottle of red on the table in front of her and two glasses, and my heart sinks. I do not want to make a night of this. I'm tempted to tell her I'm doing Dry June and that she'll have to drink it on her own. She's the kind of person who one hundred per cent would know there's no such thing, though, and she wouldn't be afraid to call me out on it.

'Well, this is nice,' she says, pouring me out a glass.

I check the time on my phone. 'She's going to text me when they're finished.'

'Who knows, you might get an offer tonight,' Carol says. 'I can never get over how fast things sell in London.'

'Let's not get over-optimistic,' I say, settling down in the chair opposite her. 'Shit. I meant to ask you to put the rubbish out when you got home.'

'Done. And I ran round with the Pledge too.'

'Fab. Thanks.'

We sit there for a few minutes not saying anything. I realise I know almost nothing about her outside of her job, her desire to get back at her ex and her bathing habits. 'Do you have any family?'

She shrugs. 'Not so as you'd notice. Not any more. Mum died more than twenty years ago. Never knew my dad. One brother who left home at seventeen and we never really heard from him again.'

'God. That's tough. Do you have any idea where he is?'

She shakes her head. 'Someone I know bumped into him on the street in Manchester once. A few years after he left. Said he was off his head. I did think about going up there to look for him, but . . .'

I wait. 'But?' I say gently. Daisy might be a nightmare, but I can't imagine losing all sight of her.

'Mum was ill by then, and I blamed him. She was never the same after he left. I don't know. I thought even if I found him he'd be a mess and he'd only break her heart all over again. I told her he was alive, though. Said my friend told me he'd got his act together and he'd asked her to tell my mum he sent his love. All bollocks, obviously. What he actually did was nick her phone out of her hand when she went to talk to him, and run. God, this is a heavy conversation when we're less than a glass down.' She tops up our wine, even though I've hardly touched mine.

'Shit.'

'How about you?'

I feel a bit bad telling her about my relatively functional family, the solutions to our problems firmly within reach if we wanted to find them. I tell her about

Daisy, but it all sounds a bit lame compared to her situation.

'There are all sorts of terrible mums out there who seem to have everything to offer on paper. It's definitely not an exact science. Who knows?'

'She's never wanted kids, though. I mean, really never.'

Carol nods. 'People change their minds.'

'Yeah. I know. I need to give her a break. It just doesn't seem fair.' I look at my glass. It's suddenly empty, even after Carol topped it up. I should slow down. I check my phone. No text from the estate agent yet.

'Did you want them yourself?' Carol asks, draining the dregs of the bottle into our glasses.

I exhale, puffing my cheeks out. 'Yes. Yes, I did.'

Before I know what's happening our empty bottle is substituted for a full one, and Carol is flapping her card at the reader in the hand of the barman. I think about protesting and then I think fuck it. We don't have to drink it all. My phone beeps. *All done. He liked it, I think.* I show Carol the screen.

'Might as well drink this now we've got it,' she says, pouring again. 'I did, too. Want kids. But Danny was adamant he didn't. It was a deal breaker. To be fair, he told me right from the off. I knew what I was getting into. I chose the relationship. That worked out fucking well.' She cackles.

I find myself not knowing what to say. In fact, I want to throw out all the words of comfort people offer up to me that drive me so crazy: *It might still happen, you could meet someone else tomorrow and bam! Look at Daisy, she's older than you* . . . It's actually almost impossible to keep my mouth shut. It's so natural to want to try to make someone feel better when it's obvious they're hurting. I shouldn't be so quick to jump to the conclusion that people are insensitive or tactless.

'That sucks,' is all I say in the end.

'And, of course, his new girlfriend is now pregnant, so . . .'

'Fuck. I'm sorry, Carol.' I feel awful for her. I can't imagine how much that hurts.

She exhales. 'It is what it is.' I can see she has tears in her eyes. I blink away my own.

'So, what was your story?' she asks.

I tell her about Tom, and Maddy. Their affair, not my subsequent behaviour. I try to lighten the mood by describing Maddy's online output. The cringy videos. 'Oh my god, let me see her,' she says, picking up her phone. I show her the account and then I stand up. 'I'm trying to go cold turkey. Not look at them any more. I'll go to the loo.'

I'm slightly unsteady on my feet. I'm not used to drinking so fast. When I come back, Carol looks at me wide-eyed. 'Fuck me. I mean . . . really though, fuck me. She's like Bonnie Langford on crack.'

I slump back in my chair. 'She has a book coming out this week. She's some kind of big deal now.'

'Who cares?'

'I do. But I'm trying not to.'

'He looks like he's being held at gunpoint.'

I laugh. 'He's nice, actually.'

'You know him?'

I share the last of bottle number two between our glasses. 'Kind of.'

She raises an eyebrow. 'That's not your ex?'

'Jesus. No. It's a long story.'

She leans back in her chair with a smile. 'And . . . ?'

I have no idea why (except for the wine, of course), but I tell her the whole humiliating tale over bottle number three. The videos, the staged photos. I leave out nothing. No detail too unsavoury. There's a freedom in not caring if she judges me or not. If I sell my flat and move away I'm pretty sure I'll never see her again. There's no reason for us to keep in touch. I remember crying at one point and Carol saying, 'Maybe we shouldn't drink the rest of this,' and us holding each other up as we staggered home. At various moments I remember her looking horrified, impressed, sympathetic, disgusted, as she forced some toast into me at the kitchen table.

My only hope when I wake up – somehow in my pyjamas and in bed – is that her memory of the evening is as hazy as mine. I feel embarrassed and ashamed. But most of all, sick. Very, very sick. I shuffle over and look at the alarm clock. It's gone ten. I was due at work twelve minutes ago. I try to summon up the energy to get up and find my phone to call Zak. I notice a piece of A4 folded over with my name on in black Sharpie, leaning against a bottle of water. I reach out a weak arm and grab it.

Stay in bed! it says. *I called your work and left a message saying you have food poisoning.* I almost cry with gratitude when I read that sentence. *Eat more toast (maybe my garlic bread ha ha!), drink water and sleep it off. And don't feel bad. We all do things we're not proud of. It's how you handle them after that counts. We can talk later, or not, I'll leave it up to you. Call me at work* . . . here the writing starts to go up the side of the page as if she's run out of space – *if you need anything. Cx*

I realise I'm crying again. I lie back against the pillows and just let it happen.

I wake up an hour or so later feeling marginally more human and suddenly ravenous. I drag myself to the kitchen and shove bread into the toaster while I try and negotiate with my stomach about whether or not I could keep a coffee down. I don't want to get straight back into bed, so I take my spoils into the living room I rarely venture into these days, and slump on the sofa.

My phone beeps with a message from Carol: *Turn on Channel 4!!!!*

I turn the TV on with the remote just as Steph McGovern announces that her next guest is influencer Maddy Fulford who has a book out tomorrow full of ideas to help you make the most of family time.

Maddy looks nervous. I can see it in the slight twitch of her lip as she smiles. I wait for the visceral reaction I always get whenever I see her. The sudden swoop of anger and hurt. But I realise I feel nothing. Maybe it's the hangover talking. It's blunted my senses. Perhaps I need to live the rest of my life in a state of morning-after nausea. I try to poke at the sleeping bear inside me: this woman stole Tom from you, she stole your chance of babies. Nothing. I try to imagine what I would feel if I was watching the show with no idea who she was. I'd think she seemed pleasant enough, marginally interesting. I would forget her the minute I switched over. Perhaps I'd have a vague recollection if I ever saw her again, but that would be it. She would not have eclipsed Kim Kardashian in my brain as the world's new mega influencer.

I watch as the picture cuts to a shot of Lee and the twins watching from the wings. And then I turn it off and go back to bed.

'Have you thought about counselling?' Carol spoons fusilli on to the dish in front of me and pours a tomatoey garlicky sauce on top. I've already eaten three pieces of the infamous garlic bread and it's just about the best thing I've ever tasted, ever. Somehow Carol, home from work, seems to be completely hangover free.

'God, don't hold back,' I say, managing a laugh. There's something about Carol's approach to my problems that I'm finding refreshing. She's a judgement-free zone.

'I mean, I'm a fine one to talk, but you clearly haven't dealt with everything . . .'

'We could get a two for one deal.'

Carol guffaws. 'Can you imagine? You wouldn't get a word in edgeways once I got going, I'm telling you.'

'Have you ever done it?' I ask, scattering parmesan on to my food.

She shakes her head. 'No. But I should have. I've let him take up far too much space in my head for years. I gave up all my mates for him. They all thought he was a bell-end and I wouldn't have it. Do you want more garlic bread?'

'Definitely. Carol, I'm sorry I've been such a bitch of a landlord . . .'

'Oh god, don't start this again,' she says, laughing. 'Half an hour of this we had last night.'

I have no memory. 'Shit, did we?'

'It was after you insisted we open the bottle of Baileys that's been in the cupboard since before I moved in.'

My stomach heaves. 'Oh, god.'

'And, like I told you last night, it's fine. All forgotten. I know I can be a bit full on . . .'

'No! It was all me . . .'

She holds up a hand. 'Iris. No disrespect but I cannot live through this conversation again . . .'

I start laughing, and then I can't stop. Carol joins in, and we sit there setting each other off like a pair of Furbys.

We eventually run out of steam and then I say, 'Just don't use my candle again,' and that starts us both off one more time.

'I feel sick,' I groan, clutching my stomach. 'How are you not hungover?'

She shrugs. 'I am. Just not as badly as you. It's all a question of degrees. Here's to a new start,' she says, holding up her water.

I clink her glass with mine. 'Definitely. New start.'

By the following afternoon there are two offers on my flat. Two! It's only been a few days and two people are vying to pay less than the asking price, but still an awful lot of money, to take it off my hands. One of them, Jennifer tells me – who thankfully came to look round this morning while Carol and I were both out at work – already owns a few properties locally and rents them out, and will probably not mess me around.

I wander round the shop, straightening things that don't need straightening. The idea of uprooting my whole life feels overwhelming, but I can still picture myself living in that little cottage. Even the thought of commuting up and down to work doesn't tarnish the vision. I decide to text Gina: *Hi! It's Rissa. I've had an offer on my flat! Did you sell yet?*

Absolutely not!! she replies almost immediately. *How exciting!*

Let me get my act together, I send back. Shit. Am I really going to do this?

48.

Maddy

It's gone well, she thinks. The reaction to *Steph's Packed Lunch* was reassuringly positive, with hundreds upon hundreds of comments from her followers telling her they were going out to buy the book at the weekend. She'd scoured the messages for her detractors and there they'd been, maybe one in every thirty or forty comments standing out like they'd been highlighted. She heard Lee's voice in her head: *Don't look*. She'd dragged her eyes away from someone telling her she was a narcissist, and hooked on to a gushing compliment instead. She knew that believing the OTT complimentary messages was probably as damaging as believing those that were jaw-droppingly vile, but at least those ones made her happy. On Thursday morning she'd lain in bed imagining her book finally out in the world, telling herself that this was it, she was an author. It still hadn't sunk in.

A handful of local radio stations have been in touch with Jas, asking if Maddy would like to appear, and so today she's going up to London, into a studio at Broadcasting House – Broadcasting House! – to chat 'remotely' with people in Cumbria, Cornwall and Berkshire.

They're over the worst, she thinks. Lee is back home, they're over their hiccup. The Truth Teller account seems to have disappeared, at least for now. The danger looming on the horizon has receded.

Maddy feels almost relaxed for the first time in weeks. She pees on the white stick she picked up in Superdrug yesterday. She had thought her period was late because of stress. She's hardly been eating, after all. Or maybe the perimenopause. She'd heard of women whose cycle started to become erratic in their early forties, years before the actual headline act began. But there was a nagging feeling inside her that made her wonder if it was something else. Something miraculous.

She waits. Lee has taken Ruby and Rose to feed the ducks, each clutching a little bag of the floating eco-friendly food Maddy purchased online. She writes an Instagram post with a photo of her smiling up at the camera, detailing the radio appearances she'll be making and the times. Thanks her fans for their support. She has an hour till she needs to drive to Maidenhead and get on the Elizabeth Line. She's going up early, of course, in case of delays. She can have lunch in a café somewhere if she has time before she has to meet Jas outside the iconic building, potter around the shops if not. She allows herself to feel excited, to leave everything else behind.

She checks the time. Turns over the white stick.

Two lines.

Her face cracks into a huge smile. She can't quite believe it. She's having another baby.

49.

Iris

My day is a whirlwind of admin. I've brought my laptop in with me and I sit in the shop calculating and recalculating, organising a meeting with the mortgage adviser at the bank (tomorrow, in working hours, Zak will have to suck it up), finding a solicitor, booking a survey on the cottage. I drove down on Saturday and Gina showed me round again, unfazed by the fact that I have, as yet, no finance in place. *It's meant to be* she said as we drank coffee in the bright kitchen. *You have to come round and see our new place as soon as you move in.* Somehow I seem to have made a new friend in my chosen town already. I told her I'd make an official offer as soon as I had all my ducks in the road, as Fay once said to our tutor who had asked her why she hadn't delivered an assignment. She'd done it to make me laugh and, when I did, she'd said *Sorry, I've been up to my thighs*, and I'd snorted into my bottle of water and then succumbed to a coughing fit. The tutor had looked from one of us to the other, but Fay's wide-eyed innocent expression had won him over as it always did, and he'd given her an extra two days.

'Row,' I said quickly. 'I meant row. Sorry, I'm overexcited.' That's the trouble with spending too much time with Fay. You lose your grasp of the English language.

Thankfully Gina was too caught up in the moment to really notice.

Pasha was able to squeeze me in to a room on the second floor and showed me the latest photos of his ridiculously cute daughter as he handed me the key. For once I managed not to blub at the sight of someone else's adorable piece of good fortune. I was too happy, too excited at the prospect of what was to come. Fay was wrong, after all. Happy endings do exist, you just have to look for them.

50.

Maddy

She hands Jas a turquoise Tupperware box filled with homemade biscuits that she baked this morning, high on her good news. Needing to do something with her hands to calm her racing mind. A new baby. Maybe even a new set of twins. She feels both alarmed and exhilarated by that thought. 'Treats,' she says. Jas who, unknown to Maddy, is attempting to achieve ketosis and is sent into a panic at the mere sight of an unscheduled carb, looks at them as if they're a bomb she's been asked to defuse. 'Thank you.' She shoves them deep down into her bag so she doesn't even have to look at them. 'I'll eat them later.'

Maddy flies through the first interview holding her secret close to her heart, feeling as if she's lit up inside by the power of its glow. She has to keep her news to herself till tonight. She can't blurt it out to Jas, or heaven forbid to the audience of the Stevie Jefferies show. Lee has to be the first to know. She knows it's a cliché at best and a complete fallacy at worst when people think that having a baby will help repair a fractured relationship, but she and Lee are almost healed already. This news will smooth away any scars. They'll be like new. Somewhere in the back of her mind the thought crystallises that she could shift the focus of Fun with the Fulfords to the pleasures of life with a newborn. Lee could hardly object. His problem with the twins was that he worried they weren't enjoying the process any more. He had never had any concerns when they were babies. They would have three or so more years before they had to worry about the same thing happening again. She could use that time to gradually redefine her USP. She chastises herself. She shouldn't be thinking of her baby as possible content.

She's never been on the radio before, but she loves it. The unrehearsed pace of it. The way she has to think on her feet to keep up with Stevie's rapid about-turns and asides. It's a fun, frothy show. No danger of any tricky questions or tripwires. It's all over in a flash.

'You're a natural,' Jas says as they sit in a corridor, sipping coffee and waiting for the next. And Maddy beams. She is, she can feel it.

They have the best part of an hour to kill, so after a while they run out of conversation and Jas starts scrolling through her phone. Maddy checks her messages. She had hoped Lee might have found a way to listen, might have sent a text telling her she'd done well or maybe with a photo of whatever the twins were up to, but there was nothing. He was probably run ragged, playing horses or building a fort out of cushions. She digs a book out of her bag – she's endeavouring not to look at social media except when she's in work mode, and she doesn't want anything (a negative comment, a catty aside) to distract her from the next interview. She reads a passage about manifestation. Closes her eyes and imagines herself and a beautiful smiley baby sitting on the *One Show* sofa. *Family expert, Maddy Fulford*, Alex Jones says, *is here with her gorgeous little boy, Jonas* – no, Aiden, Maddy thinks. Or Rhys. Ruby, Rose and Rhys. Alex corrects herself in Maddy's head – *Rhys, to give all you new mums out there some tips on how to keep your baby – and, of course, yourself – healthy and happy* . . .

She hears a barely stifled gasp from Jas. Opens her eyes and looks over. Jas is staring at her phone, finger scrolling up and down as if she's trying to take in what she's seeing.

'Is everything all right?' Maddy says. She hopes Jas hasn't had bad news. Maddy has always found other people's unhappiness almost unbearable to deal with. Her natural instinct is to try to help, to make it better for them.

Jas puts her phone face down in her lap. Gives her a forced smile.

'Yep. Everything's fine.'

51.

Iris

My to-do list is getting longer. It's almost overwhelming what I have to achieve without anyone else to help me, but I keep hold of the dream in my head and tell myself I'll get through it. People do this every day. It'll be a few weeks of mayhem, sleepless nights, my stress levels rising, and then suddenly one day it'll all be over. Sorted. It's all happened so quickly I haven't even told anyone other than Carol, so I take advantage of the shop being empty and call my mum.

'I'll come up when you first move in, if you want.' She's excited for me, I can tell. 'Help you get it all straight.'

'Yes, please.'

'You've inspired me. I'm going to arrange to have my house valued.'

'Yay, Mum! That's brilliant news.'

Neither of us mentions Daisy. I assume that my sister has shared her disgust at our last conversation and that Mum is being diplomatic as ever. I should call her too, I think. Smooth things over. I think I can do it now, be a good aunt, a supportive sibling. Daisy and the baby can come and stay, I can help out.

Cally is bemused by my news, and I realise I have never even mentioned a desire to leave London to her, let alone that that notion might have crystallised into an actual life plan. I haven't spoken to her in more than a week, or to Fay either, although we've all left each other voice notes. *I miss you. Let's catch up.* Already there's a gulf in our knowledge about each other's day-to-day lives so big that I don't even know where to start to fill her in.

'But you won't know anyone there,' she says.

'I'll get to know them. I'm practically best mates with the woman who owns the house I'm buying already.'

'God, Riss, I mean . . . I'll miss you.'

'It's honestly no further to get there than it is from mine to yours now. Not really.' I stop myself from saying that we hardly see each other these days anyway, so Cally probably won't even notice the difference. I've made a decision to stop being so judgemental, to let shit go. Everyone is dealing with their own problems, trying to do their best. All you can do is be there if they need you.

Fay is next. I decide to start with the most shocking news. 'So, I like Carol now.'

'Fuck right off!' she says. And then: 'Shit, sorry Kieran. Don't say that word. OK, tell me everything. Leave no stoat unturned.'

'Well, first of all, I'm moving . . .'

'A whole house? Jesus, Rissa. That's incredible,' she enthuses once I fill her in. Kieran bounces up and down on her lap singing to himself. He hasn't quite grasped the concept yet that the person on the tiny FaceTime screen is his favourite auntie.

'It's smaller than my flat. Well, maybe the same size. I'll send you a picture.'

'And . . . what? Wow. I'm speechless.'

'This has literally never happened before. I'm honoured. You can come for weekends. You and Kieran.'

'You're on.'

Her school are looking into a transfer for her to their equally posh North London sister school, she tells me once I've bored her to death with details of the house. 'They've been brilliant, I have to say.'

'Well, that would be fricking amazing,' I say, suddenly remembering my offer of her and Kieran staying at mine and the small fact that I won't be there any more.

'Shit,' she says. 'I have to go. We're taking the kids to the park. Cally'll be here any second. Can we meet up? Soon?'

'Definitely.' I hear a noise from the back office. 'The shop phone is ringing. I have to go too.'

I realise I'd almost forgotten I was at work. I put down my overheating mobile and pick up the extension on the counter.

'Marlborough Kitchens, how can I help?'

It's a voice I recognise. 'Is that Rissa?'

'Yes. Hi. How are . . .'

'How could you?' he says, angrily. 'What the fuck have you done?'

52.

Iris

I have no idea what he's talking about. I grab on to the counter, shocked by the venom in his voice.

'Lee? What?'

'You fucking know what,' he hisses. It's so unlike the Lee I've got to know that I momentarily wonder if he's been putting on an act all along. 'You vindictive . . .'

I miss the last word because the bell over the shop door dings as a young couple walk in, eager faced, ready for a conversation. I can't do this now. I try to keep my voice steady. 'Lee. I have a customer.' I give them a fake smile and hold up a finger: *One second.* 'I can't . . . give me your number and I'll call you back the minute I can. I haven't done anything. I promise.'

'Fuckssake,' he says. 'You know exactly what I'm talking about.'

'Give me your number,' I say more firmly. 'I have to go.'

I'm shaking when I put down the phone. Something has happened. Something momentous. I plaster on my manic grin again. I want to scream. To cry. What is he accusing me of? I have to stop myself telling the punters I need to shut up shop because of a family emergency.

'Hi!' I say with way too much fake enthusiasm. I just

need to get through this as quickly as possible, put up the closed sign and find out what has happened.

Of course they want an in-depth discussion. Of course they do. They're moving in together, they tell me. The flat they're buying is perfect except for the outdated kitchen. They've done their research online, so they know the range they're interested in. Ordinarily my senses would be in overdrive by now, a sniffer dog with a mission. I'd be circling, moving slowly in for the kill. But I rush them. Talk over the end of their sentences in an effort to speed their departure. I can tell they think I'm offhand, bordering on rude, from the little looks they start to exchange. They've made a mistake coming here, they're thinking. If the service is this bad before they even commit to spending thousands, imagine how awful it might be once they've handed over their cash. I see the young woman tug her partner's T-shirt in a way she clearly hopes is subtle. He stops mid-sentence and looks at her.

'I think that's enough for today, don't you?' she says forcefully. 'You've given us a lot to think about, so we should go and process it all. Don't you think, hon?'

I watch as the penny drops. 'Exactly,' he says. 'We'll have a think and come back.'

I know I'll never see them again. I don't even care.

I lock the door behind them. Go into the back office so there are no distractions, and dial Lee's number. I take a sip of water from a plastic bottle as I wait for the call to connect, my mouth dry.

'Take it down,' he says when he answers. It's like a bad

thriller, one where I have absolutely no idea what is happening.

'What? What are you talking about? Lee, what the fuck is going on? Stop talking in riddles.'

'The photo,' he says. 'The picture of me and you.'

53.

Lee

He'd been having a good day. He and the girls had waved Maddy off on her big adventure and he'd decided it might be fun for the three of them to bake a cake for her return, until he'd discovered the still warm rack of biscuits cooling on the counter. So, he'd got out the paints and paper, covered the kitchen table in the wipe-clean cloth, and challenged Ruby and Rose to paint whatever they thought Mummy might be doing up in London. He flicked through the Fun with the Fulfords Instagram while he kept half an eye on them. The account had gained a few followers this week – a good sign, he hoped. Usually Maddy was the one who handled their socials – she had a far better grasp of what was needed than he did – but they'd agreed that this week he should be the one to keep it updated so that Maddy could stay focused on her publicity drive. So he had filmed her departure for her day of radio – shutting the front door, book in hand, waving from the car – and she was going to ask Jas to film the obligatory hopping about and pointing at stuff with two hands aiming like pistols that everyone seemed to do these days. Broadcasting House itself, probably a BBC sign, the studio. There would be a shot of Maddy, headphones on. Maybe one of her getting coffee from a machine. They would edit them together tonight and put some music over for a post tomorrow. It would look exactly the same as every other reel everyone else put up, and it was all a bit cringy if he were being honest, but it was content and that was all that seemed to matter. He decided to film bits and pieces of his day with the girls and edit them together to make a little video to show her when she got home. For her eyes only, not for the fans. She would love that. He looked over at them now, covered in paint already, earnestly working on their art. His heart swelled.

He remembered to check for any posts they were tagged in, before he embarked on his project. There were a few, as there always were these days. He reposted the first – a glowing comment with a picture of a copy of the book – to stories, the same with the second. The third he passed over because it clearly had only two stars stamped over the top of the photo so he was pretty sure it would be a negative review. He couldn't make out what was in the next image, and he was about to pass over it in favour of the next – no point reposting a picture that didn't immediately tell a story – when something made him look more closely.

It was a blur of flesh, red fingernails, a bed.

Fuck, no.

He'd started to shake uncontrollably. He'd dropped down into the nearest chair, suddenly unable to stand.

He read the post.

Know who this is? This is Lee Fulford, Maddy Fulford's devoted husband, and a woman who most definitely isn't his wife. Look

at her hand – no wedding ring. No lotus flower tattoo. Maddy is
all over the media boring on about how she has found the secret to
a happy family life, but it looks as if Lee didn't get the memo!
Remember the videos of them fighting, and him going off to his
own flat a few weeks ago? The ones they denied meant anything
except a little domestic about whose turn it was to clean their
Airbnb? Well, they were clearly lying. I mean, they have a book
to promote, right?

Ruby held up her painting to show him. He had no
idea what it depicted. 'Brilliant, darling,' he managed to
say. He had to hold it together for the girls. He looked
back at the screen. It was a new account – Burn Maddy
Fulford Burn – and this was their first post. Rissa's first
post, because the author was clearly her. There was no
one else he'd ever let himself get in that position with.
There was a slew of hashtags that made sure all of Maddy's fanbase were covered. He refreshed the screen and
suddenly the account with no followers had nearly a
thousand, and the comments were racking up. There
was no containing this now.

He felt overwhelmed both with anger and fear. He'd
ruined everything. His life was over. And then he remembered Maddy still had two radio interviews this afternoon.
He had to make sure she didn't see any of this. Not yet,
at least. There was no way of preventing her finding out
later. Probably when she was on the train on the way
home. Shit. He googled the number for Maddy's publishers and told them he needed to get in touch with Jas
the publicist urgently. Thankfully they let him have her

number without arguing. He couldn't call her, because she would almost certainly be with Maddy now. He sent a text.

Hi Jas, sorry for this message out of the blue. This is Lee Fulford. Can you make sure Maddy doesn't look at Instagram before her interviews are over? I know this sounds crazy but no time to explain. Thanks.

He waited anxiously for a response. His phone beeped. *Sure* the message said. *Let me know if it's anything you need help with.*

He didn't bother to reply. The best he could hope for was that Maddy got through the interviews none the wiser. That the radio hosts didn't see this and sideswipe her with it, anxious to get a scoop. That he hadn't fucked those up for her as well as everything else.

And then he checked that Ruby and Rose were still happily occupied and keyed in the number for Marlborough Kitchens in Kingston.

54.

Iris

'I don't know what you're talking about,' I tell him. 'I haven't done anything.' His tone of voice is scaring me. He's angry. Really angry. 'Lee, what?'

'So you're not Burn Maddy Fulford Burn?'

It takes me a second to realise what he's saying. I dig in my pocket for my mobile, prop the shop phone between my chin and my shoulder and navigate the screen with shaking fingers.

'No. Wait. Are you talking Insta?' I put the account name in wrongly first, my hands clumsy. When I get it right, I gasp. 'Fuck.'

My brain is whirring. Lee is saying something, but I can't take it in. There's only one person in the world who has seen this photo other than me. 'I know who this is.'

'What do you mean, you know who it is? It's you. It can only be you. I know you hate Maddy but this will ruin my life too. You know that, don't you? You just couldn't give a fuck.'

I rub a hand over my eyes. 'I do. I . . . I took that picture, yes. Obviously. But I sent it to one other person. I know I shouldn't have . . .'

He cuts me off. 'You took a photo of me half passed out and made it look as if there was something going on between us?'

'It was a shitty thing to do. No, much worse than that. But I didn't go through with it. I know that's no excuse . . .'

'Imagine if I'd done that to you. If you were lying there half-dressed and completely pissed and I'd put my hands on you and taken a picture.' He stays quiet to let that sink in for a moment. He's right, of course. 'You sent it to someone. Who? You need to get them to take it down. Now.'

'I don't . . .' Shit. 'I'm so sorry. This is so not what I'm like.'

'I don't care about you,' he says. 'You know Maddy's in the middle of doing interviews. If they start asking her about this . . . shit.' His voice cracks and I feel swamped with shame and guilt. I'm a grown fucking woman and I've been behaving like an adolescent. 'Who was it?'

'I don't know her full name. Lara K. She's . . . well, she's a troll basically, I think. It can only be her. Them. I don't even know if she's a she.' She could be an eighty-year-old man for all I know. It hits me how reckless I've been. 'Fuck, Lee. I don't know what to do. I can ask her, but she'll probably ignore me.' I scrabble around on my phone, taking an age to log back in and reactivate my Instagram, and message Lara. *Lara, take that photo down. Please! ASAP!*

'I've asked,' I say. 'I don't know what else to do.'

'You're literally going to ruin our lives,' he says. 'I hope you can live with that.'

55.

Maddy

She's buzzing when she finishes the final interview. She's good at this, she can tell. The conversations flowed easily, the presenters seemed pleased. Not that any of them had said anything. After they said goodbye on air she'd hung on, unsure whether it was rude to just take off her headphones and leave, but they'd all sailed seamlessly straight into another topic and the moment had gone. Jas had surprised her as they hung around between shows, suggesting photo opportunities and ideas for little video moments to add to her montage. She'd been much chattier than usual, regaling Maddy with stories about her overachieving family. The afternoon had flown by. Maddy says goodbye to Jas in the airy foyer and decides she'll treat herself to a cab back to Paddington. She wanders round to the rank she noticed earlier and beams at the driver of the taxi at the front of the queue.

'Someone's having a good day,' he says matily as she clambers in the back.

'Very,' she says.

She digs her phone out of her bag. The first thing she sees is a text from Lee. *You were absolutely brilliant,* it says. *All good, but can u call me as soon as you get out x*

She hits his number. If the friendly cabbie wonders why she's crying by the time he drops her off he's too embarrassed to ask.

56.

Iris

Haha! Lara replies. *I wondered if you'd seen it. It's OK, no one can trace it back to you!*

Jesus.

You have to take it down. The papers are going to pick it up.

I know! Have you seen how many comments there are now!

I'm panicking. I don't know what to do. Why on earth did I send it to her in the first place? Trying to impress someone I've never even met. A ghost.

I sent you that photo in confidence I say, desperately. I wait anxiously, pacing up and down the shop.

Yeah, but it's not like you were going to do anything with it . . .

There's no point. I could waste all day trying to persuade her to remove the picture, delete the Burn Maddy Fulford Burn account, but why would she listen to me? I've never even found out what her own grudge against Maddy is. Did Maddy steal her husband too? It seems unlikely. There are only so many hours in the day. But there must be something that fired up Lara's anger. Maybe I can get to the root cause of that, defuse the bomb that way.

Why do you hate her so much anyway?

I wait.

Because she's so smug and annoying! Why do you??

Shit. I've been so stupid. Lara's agenda is based on

nothing but a loathing for a random celebrity. She probably sends hate messages to half of the cast of *Love Island* regularly too.

I don't any more I send. *I'm over it.*

Shit, she writes back. *The bell's gone. Gotta go!*

I stare at the screen. The bell's gone. Either Lara works for the stock exchange or she's still at school. The first seems – to say the least – unlikely. So, she's a kid. An adolescent. Eighteen at best. I scroll back through her posts. Why have I never done this before? There are photos of influencers – some I recognise, some I don't, but the hashtags give their names away. Vitriolic comments underneath. Puerile stuff. *Look how ugly! What a loser! Fucking saddo!*

I put my mobile down on the counter and bury my head in my hands.

What have I done?

57.

Lee

Lee is waiting at Maidenhead station beside Maddy's four-by-four when the train pulls in. The twins have already eaten and been cajoled into their pyjamas, bribed with a trip to surprise Mummy if they were good. He stands, one in the crook of each arm – he forgot slippers so he daren't even put them down for a second such is the dirt and grime on the pavement – waiting for a glimpse of her red hair. They can come back and pick up her car tomorrow. He doesn't want her driving now.

Somehow he got through the rest of the afternoon, focusing on his daughters, blocking everything else out. He has checked countless times, but the picture is still there. The comments and likes racking up with each refresh.

'It's not what you think,' he says as soon as he sees her tear-stained face. Maddy had shut down his attempt to discuss it over the phone. 'I can explain everything.'

There's an agonising forty minutes while they try to pretend everything is fine in front of the twins. Maddy sings and smiles and his heart breaks for her. For himself.

When the girls are finally both asleep he tells her everything. The only detail he leaves out is the fact that his and Rissa's final meeting wasn't coincidental. That he had more or less invited her to join him. It's the thing he feels most ashamed of. The sober, calculated possibility of betrayal.

'Iris?' she says, the confusion written all over her face. 'You slept with Iris?'

'I didn't sleep with her. Nothing happened, not even a kiss, I swear. But she set me up.'

She can't seem to get her head around why he's ever even met Iris, let alone ended up in this compromising position with her. And who can blame her? It makes no sense to him either.

58.

Maddy

It's the most famous she's ever been, that's the irony. The little piece on the *Mail Online* stating that 'Family Expert' Maddy Fulford's husband was cheating on her so she clearly hadn't been listening to her own advice, and with a copy of the offending photo, marks her out as a minor celebrity who they think their readership might be interested in. Everything she's ever wanted. But not like this. *Don't look*, Lee had said, of course. But Lee had no say in what she did and didn't do any more.

She's been up all night. Refreshing and refreshing the Burn Maddy Fulford Burn account and deliberately hurting herself with the comments. It's a train wreck that can't be prevented now. There have been too many shares, the picture has taken on a life of its own. The red fingernails. Lee's half-conscious expression, open for any kind of interpretation.

Last night she ignored emails from Hattie her agent, from Sorrel her editor. She can't face anyone. Can't face the sympathy, or worse, the pity. What she really wants is to run away and hide from them all, from the world. But Maddy Fulford – the brand – is fearless. Her fans will be expecting her to come out fighting for her family. A wounded lioness. She doesn't know if she has the energy. And for what? Her marriage is clearly over this time.

Lee begged and pleaded. He told her a convoluted story about meeting a woman outside the pub one night and having a harmless conversation. Having no idea she was Iris, his wife's nemesis. She had wanted to say, *It doesn't matter who she was. Why were you with her? Why was she back at your flat?* He'd got steaming drunk, he told her. He'd passed out. Nothing, absolutely nothing had happened between them.

But this isn't nothing. This photograph. The truth doesn't actually matter any more – and strangely, Maddy does believe him. He's not a cheat. Never has been. What matters is that this picture is going to define the rest of her life. She can't let that happen.

She opens the door of the spare bedroom on her way down to the kitchen. Lee lies back on the pillows, phone in hand. He looks wretched, but this time she can't really find it in her heart to care. 'You need to go back to our room,' she says, curtly. He looks at her with an almost hopeful expression, and she scowls at him, 'Before the girls wake up. They can't find you in here.'

59.
Iris

Carol finds me hunched over the kitchen table, a glass of wine in one hand and my mobile in the other.

'You OK?' she says, shaking the rain off her coat. She's been at a yoga class locally, part of her new plan to get fit and get a life.

I've been sitting here for nearly two hours. More. I tried to phone Fay as soon as I got home, but she was at a tapas restaurant with Cally and Jim ('Jim's mum is babysitting the kids!') and she kept thinking I was making a joke about being upset. 'I really need to talk to you. One of you,' I'd said tearfully in the end and she'd promised to call me back asap. 'Oh, the food's coming,' she said. 'I'll ring you right after.'

'Don't worry,' I'd said. 'Have a good night.' I realised I wouldn't have known what to tell her anyway, where to start.

I knew I couldn't burden my mum with this. I would lose her at posting a mean comment about someone publicly. She simply wouldn't understand why I would ever have done that. And Daisy would probably either refuse to take my call or have a field day relishing the fact that I was the one to completely fuck up finally. There was no one else.

Carol's comment is a platitude. A rhetorical question.

I don't think she's expecting my answer. 'No. I'm not.' And that I would then proceed to tell her why.

'And you have no idea who this Lara person really is?' she asks after I get to the end. If she's shocked then she keeps it to herself.

I shake my head. 'She could be anyone. It's too late now, anyway. That picture has been copied thousands of times, probably.'

She exhales in a low whistle. 'It'll blow over eventually.'

'No,' I say emphatically. 'It won't this time. At least, it will, but Maddy will be finished by then. Oh god, I'm a horrible person.'

To give Carol credit, she doesn't just immediately agree with me. I wouldn't blame her if she did.

'Where are my friends?' I moan at one point. 'They can't even fucking phone me back.' Even though I didn't push it with Fay, I thought she might be curious to know what was upsetting me. Worried even. I might not want to tell her the truth, but it would have been nice to think she cared.

'They might be busy,' she says. 'I mean . . .'

'They couldn't give a fuck about me any more,' the miserable thirteen-year-old inside me wails. 'They just want to do mum things together. Not even that. They're out tonight without the kids and they didn't even think to invite me!'

'Maybe you should cut them some slack,' she says. 'They're probably both so knackered and they couldn't believe their luck that they got to have a night away from childcare it didn't occur to them you might want to go.

People fuck up. Most of them are just trying to do their best.'

'Who died and made you Yoda?' I snap.

She picks up an apple and takes a bite. 'OK. Well, we just have to think what you can do to put it right.'

My phone rings, and I jump. Fay. I turn it over, ignoring her call.

'It's too late,' I say again. Carol reaches out a hand and puts it over mine. 'Rissa, look at me. We can sort this out. OK? There's no point wallowing. We just need to be practical.'

I nod, wanting someone else to take over and tell me what happens next.

'The first thing we have to do is find a way to stop this in its tracks. You can't take that photo back now, but you can neutralise it.'

'OK,' I say quietly. 'Tell me how.'

Which is how I end up facing Carol's phone camera like it's a firing squad. Gulping back tears of shame and embarrassment.

'My name is Iris Wilson,' I say, and Carol smiles at me encouragingly. 'And I took the photo of Lee Fulford in bed . . .'

60.

Maddy

She knows she has to answer the growing list of emails – Sorrel asking if she's OK, Hattie trying to suggest solutions to contain the situation, Jas telling her about all the new press opportunities that have suddenly opened up – but she just wants to hide. The complete and utter humiliation is too much. She tells Lee to take the girls to the park – luckily it's a beautiful morning, the air already warm, the sky cloudless – and then she goes back to bed, pulling the covers over her head, shutting out the world.

She wakes, she doesn't know how much later, to Ruby and Rose clambering on to the bed. 'Sorry, I tried to tell them you weren't well,' Lee says softly from the door-way. She ignores him and opens up her arms to the twins. They snuggle in, both jabbering about the dogs and the ducks they saw, and she strokes their hair until they grow sleepy. It will send their day out of kilter to have a nap before lunch, but she doesn't care. Lee can entertain them when they're hyper this afternoon, for now she needs their comforting warmth.

Later she becomes aware of Lee peeling Ruby from her arms. He places a mug on the bedside table.

'Look at Truth Teller,' he says as he cajoles Rose to wake up.

Maddy scowls at him. 'Look,' he says again.

She waits for them to leave and picks up her mobile. There are eight text messages showing up on the home screen. She ignores them. She finds Instagram. Goes to the Truth Teller account. There is only one post. Everything else – the videos of her and Lee, the film of his flat – has been deleted. A woman looks at the camera. Is this her? Is this Iris? She exhales slowly to try to steady her racing heart and hits play.

My name is Iris Wilson. And I took the photo of Lee Fulford in bed. This is my account. I set it up purely to target Maddy Fulford . . .

Maddy screws her face up. This woman looks so . . . normal. Nice, even. Vaguely familiar, possibly. This is Tom's ex-wife. Lee's . . . well, god knows what she was to Lee. She knows that monsters come in all shapes and sizes, but Iris looks so . . . harmless.

. . . I'm not proud of myself. In fact, I'm ashamed. Really ashamed. I'm basically a troll, I suppose. Not that I've ever done this to anyone else. Or I'm ever going to do it again. Just Maddy. I want to say I had my reasons, but there's absolutely no justification. None.

She pauses then and looks at whoever is filming. Gives an almost imperceptible nod as if to say she's ready to carry on.

Anyway, the main reason I've come on here is to say that nothing happened between me and Lee Fulford. Absolutely nothing. I set him up, pure and simple. I contrived for that situation to happen and then I made it look as if something was going on between us. My intention was to post the photos on here, to coincide with Maddy's book coming out. To try to get some negative press for her, I suppose. But I thought better of it – I'm not trying to make an excuse, but it's true. I decided it was too mean. Too much. But I made the mistake of sending one of the pictures to someone else. Stupidly. I wanted a pat on the back, I think, I don't even know. I did ask them not to show anyone. I told them I'd changed my mind. But anyway. I should have known better. I'm not going to name them. To be honest, I don't even know if the name I know them by is real. Almost certainly not. To cut a long story short, they created the Burn Maddy Fulford Burn page and put up the picture. But it's still my fault. All of it.

I'm ashamed of myself. Really fucking ashamed. I've ruined people's lives. I got caught up . . . I don't know. The bottom line is it's all crap. Lee is not cheating on Maddy and never was. He adores her. They're happy together. The photo in the paper isn't real. The stories aren't real. It was all me. And I apologise from the bottom of my heart.

The video ends. Maddy realises there are tears streaming down her cheeks. She's angry, of course she is. Iris has tried – actually tried – to ruin her life. She should hate her. But what she feels is relief. There's a way out of this after all.

She gets out of bed and washes her face in the en suite. Takes a few slow breaths. She can hear Lee and the twins in the kitchen, crashing about doing something, the girls squealing with laughter. She knows how hard this must be for him, pretending everything is OK for their sake – she's had to do it herself often enough recently – and she feels bad that she didn't listen to him, didn't give him the benefit of the doubt. They have lost that blind faith they used to have in one another. Admittedly because his naïvety almost jeopardised everything and – if she's being absolutely fair – him taking a woman back to his flat for whatever reason, whatever state he was in, was disrespectful to say the least, even if his intentions were no more sinister than wanting someone to keep on drinking and chatting with. But she should have listened to him. Should have heard him out.

When she opens the kitchen door there's a cloud of flour in the air and her daughters are flicking something at each other from two mixing bowls. She blinks back tears. Puts her arms round Lee's waist and leans into his back. She feels him exhale as if he's been holding his breath waiting for her. He puts both his hands over hers and pulls her in closer to him.

61.

Iris

I have about thirty seconds to ask Carol to delete the post before someone looks at one of the many hashtags she's included and it's out there forever. My shame.

Carol, I have to say, has been a rock in the last couple of days. A beacon of sanity. I owe her. She jabs a finger on the mobile and comments start to appear. I don't need to read them. I know what they will say: *what a bitch, what a piece of shit*. I can't argue with them.

'Right,' she says, turning the phone off and handing it to me. 'We've done what we can.'

There are texts from Fay and Cally when I get up the next morning. *Riss, what is going on?? WTAF?? What were you thinking??* Clearly my confession has done the online rounds. I can sense their disappointment in me. Their embarrassment to be my friend. I've let them down. I've let everyone down. I barely slept, even though Carol made me take one of her sleeping pills and confiscated my phone. She's sitting at the kitchen table, her own phone in her hand. 'The shit's hit the fan,' she says when she sees me. 'But you knew it would. It'll blow over. You just need to wait it out.'

I nod. I feel numb. 'Did you sleep?'

'Not really.' She hands me my mobile. 'I'd just keep it off for the day if I were you.'

'I should get ready for work.'

'You're not going in?' she says. 'I don't think you should.'

I flick on the kettle. 'What am I going to do, hide for the rest of my life? Otherwise I'll just sit here and read people telling me how awful I am all day.'

'You're in the eye of the storm,' Carol says. 'Today is the worst it's going to feel and then people will start to forget, I promise. You did a good thing.'

I need to warn Mum, I think. Not that she would ever see it herself, but I'm sure some kind soul will show her. I can't face it, though. Not yet. I can't face her disappointment and confusion.

'I'll take the day off with you, if you want,' Carol says. 'You shouldn't be on your own.'

I manage a weak smile. I'm slightly blown away by her kindness. 'Thank you. But I'll go in. I'll be OK.'

Zak is unlocking the door when I arrive. He looks at me imperiously. He's obviously up to date. 'I wasn't expecting you.'

'Well, I'm here,' I say. 'And I don't want to talk about it. I just want to get on with work.'

'Fine by me,' he says.

We barely speak all day. Zak is young enough to be unequivocally unforgiving. The world is still black and white, cops and robbers, saints and sinners. There are no nuanced grey areas. I try to bury myself in a backlog of paperwork, anything to focus my mind. I left my phone at home, at Carol's suggestion, and I feel panicky without it, as if even more awful things than I'm imagining might be happening out there without my knowing – although I'm not sure what those things might be. I wonder if Lee or Maddy have seen my post. It's hard to imagine they haven't. If it's helped at least unite them against me.

Carol is going to call the estate agent for me to say I'm taking the flat off the market again. There's no point going through with it now. I have nowhere to move to. Marlow is obviously out of the question. And what would be the point? I wanted a new life. A new start. A new me. But I have a feeling this old one is going to haunt me for a while.

62.

Maddy

She feels strong enough now to return the emails to Hattie and then Sorrel. She needs to hold her head up high and let people know that none of this was her fault.

'Are you OK?' Hattie says, having called her seconds after the email was sent. 'That woman must be a basket case.'

'I'm fine,' Maddy tells her, although the truth is it will take a while. 'I just wanted to check in.'

'Well, the figures are good anyway . . .'

Maddy had forgotten it was Tuesday. The day – Hattie had explained to her early on – the official sales figures for the previous week were released.

'They only go up to Saturday night, so before all this . . . you know . . . madness . . . and you were only published on the Thursday, but it's at number twenty-seven in the Hardback Non-Fiction chart, so . . .'

'Is that good?' It sounds good. Anything with the word chart in it must be good, surely.

'Definitely a solid start. That'll be *Steph's Packed Lunch*. And obviously you did all that radio since then . . .'

What she doesn't say but Maddy hears in the silence is 'and became notorious overnight'.

'So, they're pleased? Sorrel?'

'Definitely. Solid start, like I said. Are you up for doing more press this week? Jas was asking.'

Maddy thinks about it. Does she really want to be out there airing all this dirty linen in public? She knows that's all they'll ask her about now. That for a while she'll be known as nothing but the woman whose family got targeted by a troll.

'I am,' she says. She needs to take ownership of what's happened to her. Turn it into a positive.

'Tell me everything,' she says to Lee later once the twins are asleep. 'I promise I'm not trying to start a fight, but I need to know all the details. We can't have secrets.' So, he catalogues the times he met Iris. Tells her nervously that he's worried that the night of the photos, even though nothing happened – nothing, he needs her to believe him on that – he might have been a bit flirty, bravado and his hurt at the way his and Maddy's marriage seemed to be imploding making him reckless.

'It's OK,' she tells him softly. And it is. It's fine. She strokes his hair and a tear rolls down his cheek.

'I'm so sorry I got us in this situation, Mads,' he says quietly.

'You didn't,' she says. 'Iris did.'

63.

Iris

It's one thing to know what you've done. It's a whole other to read it reported by people who have filled in the blanks with their own imagination. I'm a monster. A danger to decent society. Maddy is made out to be some kind of saint, and I know I deserve that. Carol watches helplessly as I catch up on every nasty comment, every mean-spirited blog, once I'm reunited with my phone. I can't face work on Wednesday. There's only so much of Zak's judgemental nostril flaring anyone could take. I leave a message on the voicemail when I know it's too early for him to be there.

I tell Carol I'm just going to stay in bed, but she insists on staying home too. I leave her to it, grateful for the occasional noise of life in the other room. She brings me cups of tea and runs a bath for me in the afternoon, which might just as well be a hint that I smell a bit as an act of altruism. I'm languishing in there, occasionally topping up the hot water, when I hear the doorbell. I can't make out who's there, but next thing I know the bathroom door opens and my sister walks in. Water sploshes on to the floor as I try to cover up.

'What the . . . ?'

'Are you OK? I went to the shop and that snippy boy told me you were off. You poor thing, come here . . .'

She leans over and grabs me up in a soggy hug. It's so unexpected that I'm stunned into silence.

'What are you doing here?'

'I read that thing online. I've been trying to call you.' I'd noticed that, obviously, but I assumed she wanted to tell me she was glad I was now the family fuck-up, or to borrow money while my mind was elsewhere. I've been checking my phone constantly for missed calls from Fay or Cally, or even Lee. Nothing.

Carol appears at the door with a mug of something that she hands to Daisy. Now there are two people looking at me sitting there naked. 'I should get out,' I say wiping mascara from under my eyes. Daisy holds up a towel and I clamber into it. She wraps it round me like Mum used to do when we were little.

'I need to call Mum.'

'I've spoken to her,' Daisy says. 'I didn't want to risk someone else telling her first. I gave her a kind of edited version and told her the whole thing was exaggerated, obviously, and it was just all a big misunderstanding. I'm not sure she really knew what I was on about, but I managed to convince her you were OK.'

'I . . .' I start to say, but I'm so surprised by Daisy taking charge and doing the grown-up thing that I don't know how to continue. 'Thank you.'

'Have you eaten today?' I shrug. I pull on clean pyjamas.

'Right. Carol, do you have any miso soup?' Daisy shouts.

'No, but I can run out and get some.'

'I'm OK . . .' I start to say.

'And some ginger, maybe some berries. Oh, and crappy white sliced bread for toast, she always liked that when she was sick.'

'I am here, you know.'

'On it,' Carol says, and seconds later I hear the front door slam. I decide to just give myself over to it. Let them do what they want with me. I don't have the strength to argue.

'Here, let me dry your hair,' Daisy says, and leads me into my bedroom and sits me down at the dressing table. I sit there passively as she combs her fingers through my tangles and runs the warm hairdryer over them. It's so comforting I start to cry quietly.

'Come here,' she says, and leans over my back to hug me. 'We all mess up. It'll pass.'

'It won't,' I say with a sob. 'I'm all over the fucking internet. Everyone thinks I'm a psycho.'

'They'll forget. And if they don't that's their problem.'

I look at her. 'Thanks for coming, Dais. Really.'

'You're my sister,' she says, as if it's obvious. 'I know we don't always get on, but . . .'

'How are *you?* Are you doing OK?'

'Sick as a pig,' she says, laughing. 'But me and little Willow are fine.'

'It's a girl?' I say, with a gulp. My niece.

'Yep. And I'm starting to show, look.' She takes my hand and runs it over the almost imperceptible bump. I've had a rounder stomach when I've eaten too much breakfast.

I follow her into the living room and we sit on the sofa waiting for Carol to return. It's still tidy from when we cleaned up for potential buyers. Carol's piles of magazines and bottles of nail varnish and random detritus have not yet reclaimed the space.

'Are you going to ante-natal classes, all that stuff?' I ask. I realise I know nothing about Daisy's pregnancy plans. I've been avoiding the whole subject.

'I'm doing it all by the book, I promise. I know you think I'm a flake, Riss, but I'm getting it together.'

'I don't . . .' I start to say, and then stop. I've told her I do often enough.

'You do. And I get it. We're just different.'

I nod. She was only in the year above me at school, something that felt a world apart when we were twelve and thirteen and she was christened Crazy Daisy, but really we should have been allies. Friends. I was confident at school. Brash. Worldly. Popular. Daisy was a bit of an oddball even then. A one-off. An outsider. She stood out. I should have been nicer to her. Just because she was older didn't mean that she was stronger.

'Do you want to be my birthing partner?'

I think I must have misheard. 'Wait. What?'

She shrugs. 'Why not? It's either you or my housemate, Gordon.'

'You have a housemate called Gordon?'

'He's a reiki healer.'

'Does Gordon just want a sneaky look at your vijay-jay?' I say, and she snorts with laughter. I always could make her laugh.

'Rissa! That's gross. He's into spiritual birthing. He's coaching me.'

'OK, I don't know what that is, but trust in the midwives. And drugs.'

'I mean it,' she says. 'I'd love you to. You could be the first person she meets.'

My throat catches. I'm powerless to stop the tsunami of tears that start to course down my cheeks. I rub at my face and my nose starts to run. I try to say something, to apologise to Daisy, but no words will come out. Daisy jumps up and runs out of the room, returning with the loo roll, and I grab a handful and try to clean myself up, but the tears won't stop coming.

I start telling her everything. Tom and Maddy. Everything I did. The whole shameful story. Me leaving Maddy bad reviews, trashing her on her website, making appointments and then cancelling them, ringing her doorbell day and night. The time I went to see her in Rickmansworth with my fake life problems. The words just tumble out and I can't stop them. Things I've never confessed to anyone. How Tom eventually called Fay and told her I needed help and she, Cally and Jim staged an intervention and holed up with me in Cally and Jim's flat until I felt strong enough to let it all go. How they gave up everything else they had going on for days and fed me, made sure I washed, distracted me with trips to the cinema and long walks. How I swore to them that I'd stopped, that I would leave Tom and Maddy alone. And I did. For four long years. I tell her about the way seeing Maddy again, on the verge of success, fame even, pulled the rug out from under my carefully constructed life. How I stumbled across a newly formed crack in her marriage and forced it open wider. Every dark, humiliating secret I've tried to keep hidden.

'So, you see, I'm the family fuck-up. I'm the crazy one.'

Daisy listens, her arms round me. 'It's OK,' she says when I eventually run out of steam. 'It'll all be OK.'

I wake up in the morning with Daisy's tanned feet in my face, a silver toe ring glinting in the sunlight. We've topped and toed in my bed the way we sometimes used to when we were little and I was scared of the dark. Last night she and Carol fed me what felt like a whole loaf of Warburtons, toasted slice by toasted slice, and made me miso soup and ginger tea by the bucketload.

I should get up and go back to work, but I still can't face it. I want to stay here, hidden in my room with my sister and flatmate keeping the wolves at bay. I'm dozing off again when I become aware of Carol putting a mug down on the bedside table.

'Builders,' she says. 'I figured you'd had enough herbal stuff to last a lifetime last night.'

'Thank you,' I say sleepily.

'Daisy,' I hear her say in a loud whisper. I feel her shake my sister's shoulder at the foot of my bed. Daisy is a heavy sleeper. This could go on a while.

'I've made you a tea in the kitchen,' Carol hisses. I only half wonder why she hasn't just brought Daisy hers in bed too.

Daisy moans. 'No . . . too early.'

'No, it's not. Come with me. You stay in bed,' she says to me. 'I'll call you in sick again.'

A while later – an hour? Two? – I get up to go to the loo and find them both sitting white-faced in the kitchen.

'What?' I say, my heart starting to flutter. 'What's happened?'

'Nothing terrible,' Carol says with a forced smile. 'You might want to read this, though. It's nothing to worry about. It's only online, not in the actual paper, I checked . . .' I notice then she's fully dressed and has clearly been out to the shop already. There's a folded tabloid on the table in front of her.

'What is it?' I feel sick. Daisy reaches out and takes my hand. 'Remember, even if people read it it'll all be forgotten about tomorrow.'

'Let me see.'

Carol turns her laptop round to face me. Filling the screen is a big picture of Maddy looking hurt and sad, and a smaller one of me – a still from my video. The headline screams at me: *Vicious troll tried to ruin my marriage*. My knees buckle under me and I sink into the nearest chair.

'I can't . . .' I say, pushing the computer away.

64.

Maddy

The newspaper had got in touch with her directly. Shouldn't she properly tell her side of the story now Iris had confessed? Her fans were surely concerned about her. She could clear up anything that she needed to clear up, get her version out there, and then forget the whole nasty episode forever and move on. They would pay. Maddy had passed the request over to Jas who had told her she, Maddy, had to decide for herself what she felt comfortable with, but that there was no doubt this would boost both her profile and sales dramatically. Maddy had seen it as justice too. A way to put Iris through a bit of what she went through herself. Show her what public humiliation really felt like. She felt almost possessed with the idea of getting her own back, swept up in a quest for justified revenge. It was such an un-Maddy like feeling that she had shocked herself at first. But then came the euphoria, the overwhelming sense of impending victory. And it had felt good.

She'd consulted Lee, of course. They were a team again. She had forgiven him for whatever inappropriateness had led him to be alone with Iris in the first place. She still wasn't quite sure she understood what had gone on there, what lines had been crossed. But she had to let it go if they were going to move ahead together. You couldn't live with someone while harbouring doubts about their loyalty, it just wouldn't work. She knew that he loved her absolutely, wholly. And she did him too. And that meant forgiveness, trust, a clean slate.

He was unsure about the interview, she could tell, even though he told her she should do exactly what she felt would give her closure and he would support her. She wondered if he was worried about how it might affect Iris, whether he somehow didn't want her to have to face the inevitable ire of Maddy's Army, her loyal fans. Whether he felt it was too much. It made her want to do it more, if she were being honest. For the first time in her life she'd wanted to inflict pain.

So, she'd told Jas yes. She would do it. The money offered turned out to be a pittance, but that hadn't been the point. They'd sent a journalist and a photographer down that afternoon – yesterday afternoon – and she'd spilled the whole story from the very beginning. Meeting a man at a conference. His vengeful ex-wife trying – and then eventually succeeding – to ruin the relationship. 'He was single when we met,' she kept stressing. 'They were separated, she just couldn't accept it.' The way Iris had reappeared in her life four years later, seemingly on a mission to destroy everything. It felt cathartic getting it all out there, finally admitting that her world wasn't perfect but through no fault of her own. The photographer had snapped away as she chatted and she'd soon forgotten he was there. Then he'd taken a couple of pictures of her and Lee in the garden, her head leaning on his chest. They had insisted the twins be left out this time, that had been a condition of saying yes. Lee had taken them over to Gary and Lacey's to get them out of the way, just in case the photographer tried to persuade them on the day.

Afterwards she hadn't felt joyous as she'd expected to. She hadn't felt like celebrating. She'd felt empty.

Now, looking at the article, what she feels is numb.

The response is overwhelming, both in the comments and on her social media. Righteous indignation floods in. It's pantomime, she knows that, but still the vitriol against Iris shocks her. Why can't people just support her without wanting to tear someone else down at the same time? She's grateful for the kind words directed at herself, of course she is, but they're tainted somehow with the amount of hate that accompanies them. Whoever it's for.

'Just forget about it now,' Lee says, when she confides in him that she's feeling conflicted.

But she can't.

65.

Iris

I've heard people talk about rock bottom and this, I imagine, is what it feels like. When you can't sink any lower. Or you believe you can't. And then your phone rings. I recognise the number as that of my line manager, Eric. He sounds apologetic. But what he says is, 'Iris, you can't be bringing the name of Marlborough Kitchens into disrepute like this,' as if we're some kind of think tank on ethics and not a glorified builders' merchant.

'I'm fine, Eric, thanks for asking,' I say. 'My life is falling apart but your concern means everything.'

'I've been told to call you,' he says in a stage whisper. 'They're not happy.' By 'they' I assume he means head office and not MI5 or the Vatican. He means the people who make the most money from Marlborough Kitchens and who are now worried my behaviour might dent the profits.

'Neither am I,' I say.

I hear a door clank. 'Hold on, I'm shutting myself in my office. How are you doing really?'

'Shit,' I say. There's no other answer. 'Am I going to lose my job?'

'I don't think they can sack you for this. You'd have grounds to object. Don't expect a promotion any time soon, though.'

'So, the point of this call is . . . ?'

'Formal warning, I'm afraid. Oh, and to let you know Zak has asked for a transfer.'

That stings. 'Good for Zak. He can have the one I asked for because I don't need it any more.'

'OK, well, stay off sick for a bit. Till Monday at least. Get a doctor's note. Keep your head down. And keep in touch, I'm on your side.'

'Thanks,' I say. I should try to remember he's one of the good guys.

I go for a walk with Carol and Daisy, half expecting people to be throwing things – both insults and objects – at me in the street, but no one even glances my way. What feels like headline news to me is a throwaway story to be read with their morning coffee to most people. Another D-list drama. I finally get up the courage to call Mum while we sit outside a café on the river and the worry in her voice nearly floors me. I try to put her mind at rest, to explain that I haven't suddenly become a bad person. 'Daisy is looking after me,' I say and I hear the smile in her voice when she says, 'That makes me happy.' I have to explain that Marlow is now out of the question for me. Thankfully I don't think she computes that my interest in the town only began in the first place because of my obsession with Maddy; she's happy to believe it was all a huge coincidence. 'I'm sorry, Mum,' I say, sadly.

'I'm still putting my house on the market. I'm still going to look round that area even if you don't want to any more. I want to be closer to you both.'

'I'll help,' I say. 'I promise. Maybe we can find another town we both fall for.'

'That would be lovely,' she says, and I feel a weight lift off my heart.

The truth is, though, that I'm not sure I can be bothered to try to recreate my dream somewhere else. It all feels too much like hard work.

66.

Maddy

Jas has been inundated with offers for follow-up interviews, she tells Maddy excitedly. Radio, print, even TV. Everyone wants to talk to the Fulfords. 'You're on fire,' she says. Jas talks about cashing in and striking while the iron is hot. She makes it sound as if it's a thrilling opportunity and one that Maddy would be irresponsible to miss.

'I don't want to be defined as "that woman who was trolled" though,' Maddy says. She's said her piece, got it out of her system. It doesn't seem fair to keep on dragging Iris's name through the mud just to sell books. 'It's not very on-brand for me to be out there being nasty about someone,' she adds, hoping that Jas might see the business sense in protecting her image.

'This is your chance to break through,' Jas tells her. Maddy smiles at Ruby and hands her a plastic glass of juice. Rose and Lee are playing football in the garden. Ruby hates getting muddy so she's bathing Fishy her stuffed penguin in a bowl on the kitchen table. Maddy cuts off a couple of slices of cucumber and Ruby places them over his eyes. 'To really become a household name.'

'I don't know, Jas,' Maddy says. 'Let me talk to Lee.' She just wants to buy some time, to work out how she really feels. Who she wants to be. 'I don't think I want to do it,' she says to Lee. She's taken him out a cup of tea and Rose a juice. They're both red-faced with effort and the unrelenting heat.

'Then don't,' he says. 'Don't agree to anything you're uncomfortable with.'

'I want to find a way to wipe the slate clean,' she says. 'Will you help me?'

He leans over and kisses her forehead. 'Of course. Whatever, you know I will.'

She just has to decide what that is.

67.

Iris

I'm not sure why I've agreed to this. You know that bit in a horror film when a character says, 'I'm just going to go down to the cellar' and the whole audience shouts 'No!'? This might be that moment.

I make sure Carol knows where I'm going. She tries to insist on coming with me, but I persuade her it's better for me to turn up without reinforcements. Daisy returned to her own place a couple of days ago and I had returned to work, but we talk on the phone all the time. I've seen a new side to my sister. She's steely underneath all the chaos. Loyal. I still haven't heard from either Fay or Cally. They clearly don't want to go through this with me again. I get it. They've moved on. They've got their lives together. I'm the reoffender who has let everyone down, shattered their faith in me, thrown all the time and effort they put into trying to help me go straight back in their faces. I'm a lost cause. The gap that had been slowly opening up between us has split wide open. There's no way to bridge it.

Lee had brokered the deal. 'For you,' Zak said, holding the phone out balanced on two fingers as if he was afraid he might accidentally make contact with me. It was the first time he'd spoken to me all day. I didn't even bother to say thanks. Fuck him if he's not prepared to give me a second chance, if he chooses someone he's never met over someone he was supposed to be friends with. He needs to grow up.

'Hello,' I said, turning my back on Zak.

'It's Lee,' the familiar voice said. I felt all the blood plummet to my feet. 'I'm here with Maddy.'

'Right . . .' was all I could come up with.

'She'd like to meet you.'

What? This wasn't what I was expecting at all. 'Why?'

'To clear the air,' he said.

'I . . . um . . .' I had no idea what to say. Was this a trap? Had she arranged for the paparazzi to jump out and snap pictures of us together? The troll hounding her victim? That would probably fetch a bit from the tabloids. 'No, Lee. I already said how sorry I am. I've already had a thousand people telling me I'm the world's most evil bitch. I just want to try and put it behind me for good.'

'So does she. I think you owe her this. Both of us. I promise it won't be confrontational.'

'Shit. OK. Fuck.'

He named a pub in Beaconsfield where Maddy wanted to meet Saturday lunchtime. I wanted to say, *Can't we just do it tonight? Get it over with?*, but I meekly went along with his suggestion.

'I'll be there too,' he said. 'I promise it's not some kind of set-up if that's what you're worried about.'

So, here I am sitting in my car opposite the Royal Saracens Head, trying to recover from both the unfamiliar drive and the fear of what's to come. I check myself over in the rear-view mirror. My hands are shaking so much I can't open the lip gloss I was going to apply to give me courage, so I just give up. Who cares what I look like? I close my eyes for a second. Here goes.

In any other circumstances I might have appreciated the old beauty of the pub, but all I'm looking for is someone with red hair possibly coming at me with a meat cleaver. I spot her sitting in a corner. Lee standing by her side. My instinct is to turn and run, but he sees me and waves me over. I don't want to do this. I want to pass out.

I walk over slowly, prolonging the inevitable.

'Hi,' I say so quietly I'm not sure I've even said it aloud.

Maddy looks at me as if she's just spotted the last known dodo in the wild. I guess I'm her nightmare, the same as she was mine. And now I'm real. Actual flesh and blood. I wonder if she remembers the woman who came to her practice in Rickmansworth and told her about her under-achieving life or if she genuinely thinks this is the first time she's ever seen me.

'Sit down,' she says with – and I can't believe I'm saying this – a slight smile. 'I won't bite.'

And then she looks over my shoulder at someone behind me.

'Ah, there you are.'

I look round, confused. Standing there looking equally bemused – no, make that horrified – is my ex-husband, Maddy's ex-lover.

Tom.

68.

Iris

I can't quite take it in. Is this some kind of hidden camera stunt? Are Ant and Dec going to jump out from behind a pot plant?

'What's going on?' Tom says, the understatement of the year. He glares at me as he says it as if I might have set this whole thing up.

'Search me,' I say. I can hardly look at him. I haven't seen him for four years but I've thought about him every day.

'Sit down, Tom,' Lee says, taking charge. 'I'm Lee, by the way. You know Iris.'

'You didn't tell me she'd be here,' he says, meaning, I assume, me.

'I wasn't exactly party to this either,' I say huffily. He looks older than the Tom in my head. Of course he does. I wonder if he's assessing my crow's feet. I doubt he cares. He ceased having any interest in me years ago.

'Tom, sit down, please,' Maddy says softly. 'It's good to see you.' Lee pours some fizzy water into a glass from the large bottle on the table and places it in front of Tom. Tom sits heavily, edging his chair away from me as if he's worried people might think we're together.

'Care to tell me what's going on?'

'I thought . . .' Maddy starts and then she stops. Tom

and I hang on her words, waiting. 'This whole thing started because Iris and I couldn't agree on what the truth was. You're the only person that can clear that up. And then maybe we can all forget about each other and get on with our lives.'

Tom shuffles in his chair as if he's about to get up again and leave. 'I don't appreciate being duped like this.' I wonder how Maddy got him here. What was the pretext?

'And again, me too,' I say. 'Who would have thought we had so much in common.' I see Lee let a small smile slip. I'm glad he doesn't hate me.

'Please don't go,' Maddy says to him. I can see he still has feelings for her. He wants to storm off but he's powerless to ignore her. 'For my sake. I need this to be over. We all do.'

He grunts in acknowledgement.

'OK,' Maddy says. She's more assertive than I imagined she would be. 'Iris thinks we had an affair while you were still with her. You told me you were single. You're the only one who can definitively tell us which it was . . .'

Tom looks at the table. 'It was a long time ago,' he mutters.

'I think I'd remember whether I was screwing around on my wife or not,' I snap. Maddy raises a hand as if to say stop.

'See, this is why I can't talk to her,' Tom says petulantly.

'Tom, you can see why Iris might be upset,' she says. 'Let's just stick to the facts. You were living in your flat in Holborn when I first met you, right?'

I start. I look between her and him. 'What flat in Holborn?' Tom looks like he's going to be sick.

Maddy screws up her face. 'Theobalds Road.'

'He never lived in a flat in Holborn.' I turn to stare at Tom. 'When we split up I moved out of the house in Camden and he stayed there till it sold and you both moved to Rickmansworth.'

'I went there,' she says.

'When was this? We separated in February,' I tell her. 'February the fifth, to be precise. At least that's when he told me he wanted out. We clung on for a couple more weeks until he told me about you. He said he hadn't been able to stop thinking about you, that he wanted to be free to pursue you, but I knew it wasn't true.'

Maddy gulps. 'Early January, I think.'

I look at Tom. 'You had a secret flat?'

He stares at the table. 'When did you first get together?' I ask Maddy.

'Before Christmas,' she says quietly. 'Honestly, I . . .'

I cut her off. 'I knew you had someone else,' I hiss at Tom. 'You swore blind you didn't. You made me feel so stupid.' I want to cry for past me who begged and pleaded to be told the truth, who was told she was jealous, paranoid, a fantasist. I turn back to Maddy. 'How did you meet? At the conference?'

'Yes,' she says. 'In the October. Then he booked in to see me. He told me he'd split up with his wife in the second or third session. And then a few weeks later we went for a drink . . .'

'You disputing any of that?' I say to Tom. He ignores me and stands up.

'I don't have to do this. I thought this was going to be a civilised catch-up.'

'Oh, stop being so fucking pompous,' I snap.

Maddy fixes him with her green eyes. 'Tom, you owe this to us. Both of us. Let's just all be honest. We don't need to fight about it. We've all moved on.'

Good luck with that, I think. He sits back down.

'Yes,' he says belligerently. 'I was still married to you, Iris, when I started seeing you, Maddy. Yes, I told Maddy I wasn't. Yes, I rented a flat for a few months so that I could take her there and she would agree to sleep with me because I knew she wouldn't if she thought I was still with my wife. Happy now?'

I'm stunned into silence. Not by the scale of his deception because that comes as no surprise – although the existence of the love nest shocks even me, not just the planning but the money it must have cost – but because Maddy genuinely thought he was a free man. She didn't set out to steal my husband as I've believed for all these years. She met someone who told her he was single, who took her to his bachelor pad to prove it, and she fell in love. I've been so stupid. So blind. So monumentally wrong.

'You fucking bastard,' I say. 'You lied and lied and lied. You let me take it all out on Maddy and it never even occurred to you to tell me the truth.'

'It's not my fault you're unhinged,' he says. 'What sort of person carries out a campaign of harassment

377

like that, whatever they think the other person has done?'

'One who's devastated. One who has had her heart broken in a million ways and can't even get a straight answer about what happened,' I say, too loudly. People look round uncomfortably. 'One who has been fucking lied to so many times she has no idea what to believe any more. So, you were never working in Birmingham? All that was a smokescreen?'

He ignores the question. 'You're a basket case, Iris. I had a lucky escape. You're a joke.'

'Stop,' Maddy says. 'That's enough.'

I can't look at him. I hate him. He's not just a liar, he's a coward. He could have confessed everything to me, but he cared more about me believing he was this tortured, devastated man struggling with the choice he had to make and trying to do things in the honourable way than he did about protecting Maddy from my desire to punish her. He couldn't bear to be seen as the bad guy even as he shattered my world.

'All I ever wanted was the truth,' I say finally.

'Ha,' he says. 'You keep telling yourself that. You wanted revenge pure and simple.'

'Maybe I did,' I say. 'I'm not proud of that. But you could have made sure I left Maddy out of it.'

'You're pathetic,' he spits. 'And now the whole world knows it. You're a bitter old internet troll who gets her kicks from hurting people. The lowest of the low.'

Lee, who so far hasn't said a word through this whole thing, holds a hand up. 'I think it's time for you to go.'

'Happily,' Tom says. He stands up again, slamming his glass down on the table. 'Oh, you should congratulate me, Iris. My wife's pregnant with our second kid. Apparently I wasn't the one with the problem.'

I hear myself gasp. Blink back tears.

'Fuck off, mate,' Lee says with a definite note of threat in his voice. 'I mean it. Now.'

The three of us sit there in silence as Tom storms off through the bar and out into the road. 'What a cock,' Lee says as the door slams behind him.

I look at Maddy. She's looking back at me, big eyes watery. 'I'm so sorry,' I say. 'For everything. So, so sorry.'

'It's OK,' she says quietly. 'It's done.'

69.

Maddy

She had tracked him down easily – he still had the same mobile number from when they were together, the new one he'd got so that Iris couldn't call him again. He'd been surprised but – she thought – pleased to hear from her. He'd wanted to know if she was well, he'd cooed about the twins, told her he had a two-year-old son himself now. He was happily married to a woman called Rae. He had seen the piece in the paper. 'Fucking Iris,' he'd said. 'Are you OK?' She hadn't known how she would feel talking to him after all this time, but he just felt like an old acquaintance she had lost touch with. She was curious to know where life had led him but that was it. No more.

She'd told him she was calling because she'd been thinking about him, wondering how he was. She wanted him to know she was happy, she'd said. That everything had worked out. Maybe they could have a drink one day soon. She'd realised, she'd said, that she needed to make more of an effort to stay in touch with old friends. She and Lee were going to be in Beaconsfield at the weekend – wasn't that quite near Rickmansworth? If, indeed, he was still based there. It was, and he wasn't, he replied. But he was in Amersham, nearby. Of course, she had to assume that he would bring Rae along, and that had made her uneasy – she didn't want to drag another woman into his mess – but she'd lucked out when he said that his wife was taking Rafa, their little boy, to stay with her best friend in Cumbria for the weekend for a kiddies' birthday party, which, he said laughing, he'd managed to swerve by promising to take Rafa out for a whole day next weekend so that Rae could get a break.

'What a shame,' Maddy had said. 'I hope I get to meet her another time.'

She hadn't felt comfortable with the deception, leading Tom blindly into the mouth of the lion's den, but she reasoned that if what he'd always told her was the truth – that he was a single man when they got together – then he had nothing to be afraid of. They could clear the air and it would benefit all of them. And, despite the way he had bailed on their relationship so easily, Maddy had never had any reason to doubt him.

'Lunchtime on Saturday?' he'd asked.

'Let me just check with Lee,' she'd said, knowing that Lee would be fine, but she had yet to ask him to approach Iris. 'If not, can you do the evening? Or Sunday?'

'In all honesty I have no plans at all this weekend beyond mooching about wishing Rae and Rafa were at home. I'm all yours.'

She'd felt hopeful when she'd hung up. She hated feeling as if there was bad energy in her world. She knew enough to acknowledge it was a hangover from her childhood: the helplessness to diffuse the poisonous atmosphere in the house, the air heavy with silent resentments that, awful as they were, were marginally better than the noisy explosions that inevitably followed.

The guilt that she had felt assuming that she must some-how have been the cause of it.

She had wondered how she would feel seeing him after all this time. She had never really stopped loving him, even though he had let her down. Not in a romantic way – she was a one-man woman and Lee was her one man these days – but as a beautiful memory. Her love for him had shaken up her life as if she'd been caught up in a hurricane and, like a hurricane, it had left a trail of destruction in its wake. It had been the best and worst few months of her life. When he walked into the pub she had almost gasped. He looked exactly the same: the broad shoulders, the olive skin and the shock of those blue eyes. She'd put her hand over Lee's – she knew he was nervous about meeting the man who had left such a big hole in her heart, and she wanted to reassure him. Close up she could see that Tom had aged after all, just like they all had. It was only to be expected.

What she hadn't expected was this. For Tom to be forced to admit that her fairy tale had been just that. A fiction. It turned out she actually was the other woman after all. That all the time she was falling helplessly in love and barely believing she had found this good, kind, decent man, he had been lying to her – and worse, to his wife. The depth of his deception floored her. To have gone to the lengths of renting a flat (no wonder it was so sparsely furnished, she thought now). She had felt sorry for him. He'd told her he wanted to do the honourable thing and move out and he wasn't about to start stripping the family home of the things Iris loved. He would start again and that was fine. He only needed the basics. Looking back now she can see his words were like a bad script, but at the time they only served to reinforce her belief that he was one of the good guys. She had been so stupid, but how could she have known? Her own strict moral code was what had been her downfall, she supposed. Tom knew she would never have an affair with a married man and so he'd made sure she never knew he still was one.

And Iris. Iris who Tom had painted as a woman in denial, deluded, vengeful. Yes, to an extent she had been all those things, but now at least Maddy could understand why. Tom had been living a double life and she had had no idea. Of course she must have thought Maddy knew about her, that Maddy had blithely taken up with her – still very much present – husband. He had duped both of them.

She watches as he strides out of the pub, his needlessly cruel last words hanging in the air. And she finds she feels nothing for him. Nothing.

Iris looks shellshocked. Shattered.

'I'm sorry we blindsided you,' Maddy says. 'I didn't think you'd come if you knew. And I'm sorry I believed him for all those years.'

'I . . .' Iris starts to say, but then she shakes her head. 'I owe you a big apology,' she says finally. 'Another one. For back then . . .'

'He was the villain,' Maddy says gently. 'He's the one who should have apologised. To both of us.'

'Not Tom's style though, right?'

Maddy nods. 'Right.'

70.

Iris

'I'm sorry he said that shit to you at the end,' Lee says. 'That was uncalled for.'

'I should go,' I say, making to stand up. I need to be on my own, to process what just happened.

'Stay and have a drink,' Maddy says. 'You shouldn't be driving after a shock like that.' I look at her. She doesn't sound as if she has an agenda, but then she set this whole meeting up as a massive gotcha so who knows what she's capable of.

'Maddy's right,' Lee says. 'Let me get you something.'

I realise this is my only opportunity to ask questions, to finally fill in any of the gaps that have been tormenting me for four years. I have to take it, however scary it seems. 'Just a coffee, please.'

'Me too,' Maddy says. I almost say *I'll get them. Don't leave me on my own with her.* I don't know if I'm ready for this. If I ever will be.

'Will you tell me everything?' I say once Lee is at the bar. 'From when you first met. I have to assume his version is totally bullshit.'

She looks almost relieved, as if she's been wanting to get it all off her chest, to clear her name. 'Of course.'

*

So now I know it all. The whole truth and nothing but the truth. I know that Tom was the only villain. That all the hatred I directed towards Maddy was misplaced, that her Fun with the Fulfords persona isn't a cynical hypocrite trying to dupe her loyal followers, it's actually who she is. She loves Lee, she loves her twins. And she used to love Tom, same as I did, with no idea he was hiding the fact he still had a wife.

'I don't know what either of you saw in him,' Lee says, attempting a joke. 'He seems like an absolute knob.' Both Maddy and I let out a weak laugh.

'He is,' I say. 'He always was. I know that now.'

'I expect we'll bump into you,' Maddy says as I finally go to leave. She's been so much kinder than I deserve. I'm confused for a second.

'Oh. No. I don't . . . I actually still live in London. I was . . . Marlow was just to keep an eye on you. Although I was just about to move there for real but not now, obviously.'

She screws up her face. 'Why not?'

'Well, I mean . . . it's a bit . . . you don't want me on your doorstep.'

'It's over, Iris,' she says. 'I never hold grudges, life's too short. There's literally no bad feelings any more. They've gone.'

'Thank you,' I say. 'I can't believe you're being so nice about this.'

'It's what she does,' Lee says, looking at her proudly.

Back in the car I burst into noisy, messy tears. I fish

around in the central console for some tissues and end up wiping my face on my sleeve. Over the road I see Maddy and Lee leaving the pub hand in hand. I watch as they turn left and walk off down the road, presumably towards their car. She looks up at him and he pulls her in for a hug, burying his face in her hair.

It's almost an hour before I feel I can safely drive home. I feel wrung out. Empty. As if all the hate and resentment and bitterness that's been fuelling me for years has been cried out and left a void. One I can fill with good stuff. With friendships and positivity and looking forward rather than obsessively looking back. I feel like Scrooge on Christmas morning: it's not too late.

It's never too late.

71.

Iris

Five months later

She has my mouth. Willow. Everyone that sees her says the same: *Doesn't she look like you? You'd know she was your niece anywhere.* It feels like a miracle, this tiny human who has my genes. Some of them, anyway. Daisy, it turns out, is a born mother. Calm, nurturing, laid back. There's a distinct possibility she might go straight from flake to earth mother, bypassing the whole 'acquiring wisdom and maturing like a normal human being' phase. I thought she might take advantage of my besotted state and abuse my offer to babysit anytime, but annoyingly she seems happy to look after the baby herself. I find myself encouraging her to have a night out so I can get some quality cuddle time. There's still no father on the scene (*Maybe it was Wolf*, she said out of nowhere once. *I think we might have . . .*) but Willow is surrounded by love and people who want the best for her.

You'd think it would be easy to fit the contents of a flat into an actual house, but I've spent the last few weeks going backwards and forwards to the tip dumping everything that feels superfluous to my new life. It's been cathartic. Still, there's too much clutter for the tiny space.

On moving day we had to take my bed apart in the street because the front door was clearly built for a hobbit, and now my new bedroom is basically a bed with walls round it. I couldn't love it more. I'll change the bed for something smaller when I can find the energy to manoeuvre it down the stairs again. The sun wakes me up every morning (no curtains yet) and I lie back and look at the rickety old beams on the ceiling and I can't believe I'm really here.

I made the decision on the drive back from the pub that day. I was still going to pursue my dream of a new life. I called the estate agent from the car and asked her to find out if either of my potential buyers was still interested.

Somehow Carol has come with me. Not, thankfully, in my spare room. I told her I needed space. Time on my own. A freezer that was mine and mine alone. A bathroom that was free whenever I wanted. But, truthfully, I was happy when she asked me what I thought, whether it was too much, too weird for her to follow me out of town. She's a good person. A real friend. She has a new job, working in accounts for a freight-handling and logistics company on the edge of town, which she complains is mind-numbingly boring, but she has been on three dates with people she's met through work already so she's sticking it out for now.

She's no longer my lodger, but she is sharing a flat with my sister. The world has gone mad. It turns out they hit it off while they were spending time together trying to bring me back from the brink. Carol in her leopard-print Lycra leggings and Daisy in her handwoven hemp espadrilles that stink like wet dogs. God knows what common ground they found, but now that Carol has found a flat to rent (she stayed with me for a few weeks while she looked in her spare time, reinforcing my belief that I couldn't live with her again, fond as I am of her), she has moved Daisy and Willow into the second bedroom, Daisy having thankfully decided that there are better places to bring up her baby than where she was living before. The arrangement is supposed to be that Carol goes out to work and pays the bills while Daisy stays home with the baby and cooks and (occasionally) cleans and pays a token rent courtesy of the state. They're basically a 1950s couple without the sex. I'm not convinced the arrangement can last. Daisy will get itchy feet or she'll get complacent and take advantage. Or maybe not. Maybe she'll realise how good she has it. I hope so. I'm keeping out of it, but I'm enjoying having them both around, being able to be part of Willow's life.

To complete the picture, my mum has just taken possession of her own new home – a ground-floor flat with a sunny patio in a small block near the station. A reasonably sized two-bedroom that has everything she needs. She's already made friends with the neighbours – an eclectic bunch aged from twenty-something to eighty-something. I think she misses the countryside, but she can't believe her luck that she has both her daughters and her granddaughter on tap. Plus Carol. Carol loves my mum. She visits her every weekend. Like I said, the world has gone mad.

I have a new job at Harvey Jones. I needed to move on from Marlborough Kitchens, I knew the rumour mill would follow me. That my record was blemished. Eric gave me a glowing reference and told me they were sorry to see me go. Zak pulled a sickie on my last day, so we didn't even say goodbye. His loss, I try to tell myself, although it stings. Now my commute is a five-minute walk door to door. My first assignment: Gina's new kitchen. I've given her a hefty discount.

I hear from Fay and Cally every now and then. Like a pair of only vaguely interested aunts who feel obliged to check that their wayward niece is still functioning, but no more. It's fine. I wouldn't want someone who'd behaved like me around either. Who had taken all their good intentions and thrown them back in their faces. There's too much history. They've been through too much with me already and they don't trust me any more. Maybe we'll drift back together one day – I hope so – but I think I'll have to prove myself to them and I'm not quite sure yet how I can pull that off.

I bump into Lee or Maddy occasionally. For a while I avoided the park on Saturday mornings or walking past the Chequers pub in the early evening. I felt awkward, unsure of how they might feel if they saw me, or me them. I've seen her pop up on the TV from time to time. She seems to be doing well, although I always hit the remote whenever I see her just in case it sets off a negative reaction that I don't want to deal with. A wave of self-loathing – they're becoming fewer and further between but they're still there – waiting to floor me every now and then. But I was mooching around Sainsbury's one after-noon and suddenly there they were, all four of them, checking out the fresh vegetables right in front of me. I froze, a nervous smile on my face, prepared to look away if they didn't acknowledge me, almost hoping they wouldn't, but Maddy said hello in such an unforced, friendly manner that I was completely disarmed. They asked how I was settling in, introduced me to the (ador-able) twins.

And then I noticed that she was pregnant.

I managed to congratulate them. I waited to feel the pangs of jealousy, bitterness, resentment.

I felt none of them.

In fact, I realised I was pleased for her. For them. As if any residual guilt I was feeling had been absolved by their good fortune. As if it's all just checks and balances and this had levelled the scales.

Now we run into each other from time to time and we say hello, we exchange pleasantries, we're almost friends of a sort. I wish them nothing but the best and I honestly think they would say the same about me.

Tonight, I'm home from work in time to luxuriate in the bath (my own bath!) before I have to get ready and go out again to meet Gina in the pub along the street at seven. Carol is coming to join us. As is my mum. Daisy might walk Willow up and down past the window if she can't get her to go off to sleep, lifting her little hand and waving it at her granny and her aunties both real and honorary, through the glass. I shut my front door behind me and drop my keys on the side table. I'm still in that phase where coming home every day is a repeating series of joyful surprises. This is all mine! I have stairs! I have a garden! I flop down on the sofa for a moment and jump as something lands on top of me. Oh yes! I have a cat! Pudding is a bit old and a bit toothless and a bit scared of everything except me. Me he loves with a purring, dribbly passion. It's mutual. At the risk of sounding tragic, I have a lot of love to give and he's only too willing to take it all. I got him from the local Cats Protection. It seemed appropriate.

I allow myself to sit for a moment and take it all in.

I'm at home here. I've found the place I want to put down roots.

I'm happy. Finally.

I really am.

Acknowledgements

Huge thanks as ever to the army of people who make me look good. At Michael Joseph: My brilliant editor Maxine Hitchcock, the amazing Louise Moore, Gaby Young, Emma Plater, Steph Biddle, Bea McIntyre, Lee Motley, Alice Mottram, Christina Ellicott, Laura Garrod, Hannah Padgham, Sophie Marston, Kelly Mason, Anna Curvis, Akua Akyamaa-Akowuah, Colin Brush and Charlea Harrison.

At Curtis Brown: The fabulous Jonny Gellar, Viola Hayden, Ciara Finan, Sophie Storey, Rowan Jackson, Nadia Farah Mokdad, Kate Cooper, Sam Loader and everyone I've forgotten.

Thanks as ever to Charlotte Edwards for her eagle-eyed reading, and to Bex Parramint for answering my questions about influencers and their income. I've taken a few small liberties with the geography of the beautiful town of Marlow, so apologies for that.

Jane Fallon
THE MILLION-COPY BESTSELLER

WHICH BOOK WILL YOU READ NEXT?